Cardiff
www.cardif

Llyfrgelloedd Caerdydd
www.caerdydd.gov.uk/llyfrgelloedd

KT-364-817

DANCING JAX

ROBIN JARVIS

HarperCollins *Children's Books*

First published in hardback in Great Britain by
HarperCollins Children's Books February 2011

HarperCollins Children's Books is a division of HarperCollinsPublishers Ltd
77-85 Fulham Palace Road, Hammersmith, London W6 8JB

Visit us at www.harpercollins.co.uk

Text copyright © Robin Jarvis 2010
Illustration copyright © Robin Jarvis 2010

ISBN 978-0-00-734237-2

Robin Jarvis reserves the right to be identified as
the author and illustrator of the work.

Printed and bound in England by Clays Ltd, St Ives plc

Conditions of Sale
This book is sold subject to the condition that it shall not, by way of trade
or otherwise, be lent, re-sold, hired out or otherwise circulated without
the publisher's prior consent in any form, binding or cover other than
that in which it is published and without a similar condition including
this condition being imposed on the subsequent purchaser.

Mixed Sources
Product group from well-managed
forests and other controlled sources
www.fsc.org Cert no. SW-COC-001806
© 1996 Forest Stewardship Council

FSC is a non-profit international organisation established to promote the
responsible management of the world's forests. Products carrying the FSC
label are independently certified to assure consumers that they come
from forests that are managed to meet the social, economic and
ecological needs of present and future generations.

Find out more about HarperCollins and the environment at
www.harpercollins.co.uk/green

For my mother, who loved dancing.

Sticks and stones may break our bones, but words can do so much worse. I used to take words for granted. But words hold tremendous power. Arranged in the right order, they can make you cry with laughter or understand a stranger's pain. And yet it only takes one to hurt another human being. In some countries there are laws against the use of certain words, and that's a good thing. Those words are charged with hatred and need to be locked away until they and their power are forgotten.

The same is true of books, only more so.

Some books are harmful, even dangerous. They twist people's minds and feed the darkest recesses of the human soul. They should be banned or destroyed. This is a story about one of them, written by one of the most evil men ever to have lived. I hope there are enough of you left out there to read it and believe and resist – before it's too late.

Martin Baxter, yesterday

Welcome, sacred stranger. Enter the magickal Kingdom of the Dancing Jacks, with a brisk step and blessings upon you. Your place at Court is reserved and your presence long anticipated. Within these rousing pages, rewarding new friendships await. You are warmly invited to learn our ways and stories. Walk and play with us, repair by our fires and share our dreaming and restorative pleasures. Herein lie the understanding, acceptance and belonging you have so yearned to find. Join us, cherished reader, and escape the travails of those earthly measures that daily erode your humble spirit. Come to us – we shall coddle you, safe and close.

So mote it be.

Austerly Fellows, Imbolc 1936

Beyond the Silvering Sea, within thirteen green, girdling hills, lies the wondrous Kingdom of the Dawn Prince. Yet inside his White Castle, the throne stands empty. For many long years he has been lost in exile and thus the Ismus, his Holy Enchanter, reigns in his stead — till the day of his glorious returning and the restoration of his splendour evermore.

1

THE DOOR SHIVERED. One more powerful kick and the lock ripped from the rotting frame.

It burst inward with savage force. Splinters and crackled paint exploded into a large, deserted hall and decades of dust rose up in a dry cloud. For the first time in too long, fierce daylight bleached its way in and insects clattered their escape over bare and lifting floorboards.

A pair of greedy eyes darted round the empty house as the man leered across the threshold.

"Nice one."

Dragging the back of one grimy hand over his mouth, he stepped inside and the glittering dust whirled around him.

"Damp and the urination of rats."

He was describing the stale must of the house, but the description suited him just as well.

He was a wiry stoat of a man, dressed in scuffed jeans and a torn biker jacket that had known three different owners, in almost as many decades, before it had come to him. He liked that it had a history and often claimed that it owned him, rather than the other way round.

His face was always alert, never still – feral and filthy and hostile. The skin that clad it was white and clammy and poorly nourished. When other substances were available, food was spurned by Jezza.

Even now his nicotine fingers were trembling and twitching. It was half eleven in the morning. All he'd had was a can of Red Stripe and that was only because he'd finished the last of the stolen vodka the night before.

Behind him a female voice asked, "Was this worth our last spit of petrol then?"

Jezza's magpie eyes danced over the dingily patterned wallpaper that ran up the stairs to the landing. It was blotched here and there with black mould. The house was a big one and must have been impressive in its Victorian heyday, but now it was dark and damaged through years of neglect. Yet the man knew there were treasures to be harvested.

He was determined to gut the place and make a few quid. There

was a bloke in Southwold who paid cash without questions for this salvage junk. Original fireplaces were bloody good money. If they'd already been snatched, there were always copper pipes, taps and internal doors. Most of the windows were boarded over and those that weren't were smashed so there was nothing to be had there. Jezza's rancid gaze ran over the banister rails. Yes, even them.

The girl edged in behind. She was no more than twenty, but the knockabout life with Jezza and the others had leeched the bloom of youth from her face. The peroxide had long grown out of her dark hair and now only the spiky tips remained a lifeless yellow. A straggling streak of turquoise at one temple was the last effort she had made, but that too was faded.

"Told you it was a big old place," she said. "Keep us juicy for months this will."

Jezza shrugged his narrow shoulders.

"Depends what's left," he answered, swaggering down the spacious hall towards a blistered door. He paused to circle a covetous, dirty finger around the tarnished brass knob, sourly reflecting that it was exactly the same colour as her hair tips, except that the doorknob had retained some shine. He wrenched it around.

"Sod all come here," the girl muttered to his back. "I told you."

Behind her, two figures pushed through the entrance. The first was around six foot tall. The other had a much shorter, slighter build. The burly one was dressed in a shapeless camouflage jacket, with a long, ratty ponytail hanging down his back and an unkempt beard half covering his face.

"Hello, home, I'm honey!" he announced, throwing his arms wide.

The other gagged as he pushed him inside. "Have you blown off again?"

"I'm a fart starter – a twisted fart starter!" sang the laughing reply.

"Your backside makes my eyes bleed, man."

"Mmm… Bisto. You can dip your bread in that one, Tommo."

The man called Tommo dodged around him and fled deeper into the hall. He wore grubby denim and his brown hair was loose and curly. "There's got to be a rotting alien in your guts, Miller," he spluttered. "Them guffs aren't human."

"Grow up, for God's sake," the girl told them irritably. "We should've brought Howie and Dave instead."

"Howie and Dave don't have our power tools," Tommo answered, raising his hand and pressing an invisible trigger as he made a drill sound behind his teeth.

Miller lumbered further in and flexed his arms, sucking in his stomach at the same time. "And we is the muscle," he declared. "Jezza needs he-men to rip this place to bits."

"By the power of Greyskull!" Tommo called out, holding an imaginary sword aloft.

"The power of the Chuckle Brothers," she observed dryly.

Before the girl could stop them, he and Tommo seized her hands and started pulling her from side to side.

"To me, to you, to me, to you!" they chanted in unison.

"Get off!" she yelled, which only encouraged them to do it more.

"You lot!" Jezza's voice called out to them sharply. "In here – now."

The game stopped immediately. The girl threw them filthy looks. "Saddo losers," she snapped, but there was a smirk on her face when she turned her back and followed Jezza into the nearest room.

"She meant you," Miller told Tommo.

Tommo pressed his forefingers against the other man's temple and made the drill noise again.

The girl's grey eyes flicked about the spacious reception room. At first she could not see Jezza. The rags of light that poked through the imperfectly boarded windows contrasted with the deep wells of gloom around them. Apart from a card table and a red leather armchair, blackened with mildew, the room seemed empty. Then, as her vision adjusted, she found him. He was standing before a grand fireplace, leaning on the mantel as if he was already master of the house.

There was a sneer on his face.

"No one ever goes there, Jezza," he said, repeating her words of the previous night and nodding at the opposite wall.

The girl turned and looked at the rotten panelling. It was covered in painted scrawl.

"Only kids," she said with a shrug.

"Kids have sticky mitts," he spat in reply before returning his attention to the fireplace and running his hands over it.

"Marble," he announced, trailing his fingers through the mantel's grime. "You have to tease these out dead gentle. Should fetch in

15

plenty, and if there's more, we'll be laughing."

The young woman touched the graffiti-covered wall, quietly reading the peeling words.

"Marc Bolan, The Sweet, Remember you're a Womble, Mungo Jerry… this was a kid from a long time ago," she said with a faint smile. "They'd be old as my mum now."

"Young Wombles take your partners!" Miller sang as he and Tommo came waltzing in. "If you Minuetto Allegretto, you will live to be old."

"You two won't if you don't stop dicking about," Jezza warned them.

The men ceased and Tommo pointed to the mouldy chair.

"That's what your fetid innards look like," he muttered at Miller.

"You're obsessed by my bowels," the man answered with a bemused shake of the head.

"That's because I can't escape them! You keep making me breathe them in all the time!"

"You love it!"

Any further bickering was quelled by a fierce glance from Jezza. Then his eyes darted back to the girl. She was kneeling and rustling paper.

"What you got there?" he demanded.

"Kids' magazine," she answered, not looking up. "All yellow now and crinkly – look at those flares and the dodgy hair! There's some old cans and sweet wrappers here too, Fresca and Aztec bars. Been a long time since this break-in."

"Is it a girly mag?" Tommo asked brightly.

"For kids?" she snorted. "It looks like it's all about the telly, besides – you've got enough of them mags already, Tommo."

"He could open a library," Miller agreed.

The girl looked at the magazine's faded cover. Bold chunky type declared it was called *Look–in*, but there was also a name written on the corner in biro by a long retired newsagent:

Runecliffe.

She let the magazine fall to the floor.

Jezza stared about the room, his face twitching. "I don't get it," he said. "How come no one comes here? How come this place hasn't been knocked down or tarted up by some rich knob with three cars and a split-level wife and an illegal immigrant nanny for their spoilt Siobhans and Zacharys? Prime, this place is, prime and begging for the developers."

"The location, location, location's no good," Miller said, "We're in the middle of nowhere here, and it was a long drive down that track full of potholes. We wouldn't have guessed this place was here if we didn't know about it and were looking."

"Dirty big places like this don't vanish off maps or land registries," Jezza answered. "It don't make sense. It must belong to someone."

"If it does, they can't care about it," Tommo said. "Look at the state of it. Mr Muscle, where are you now?"

"We could squat in it," Miller announced. "Get everyone over and fix it up a bit. Be a palace this would."

"No!" the girl interrupted, rubbing her arms. "This is a sad house. It's sad and depressing and I don't like it."

"All the more reason to pull it to pieces," Jezza stated. "Nice, sellable, chopped-up pieces, and who's going to complain? Perfect job this one, couldn't be tastier!"

"I'll start unloading the van," Tommo said. "Come with me, Gasguts."

"There you go again!" Miller cried. "You're obsessed!"

"Wait!" Jezza barked suddenly. "Leave the tools for now."

He was looking at the girl. She had risen and was staring into space, the expression drained from her features.

"Shee," he said. "Shee!"

The girl started.

"How did you know about this place?" he asked.

The question nettled her and she moved towards the door.

"I just did," she answered evasively. "I need a smoke and my lighter's in the van."

She hurried from the room, through the hall and out into the bright sunlight. The large, forbidding bulk of the house reared high behind her and she shivered as she fled back to the shabby camper van, parked up the overgrown drive. It was a horrible house. She hated it. She couldn't wait to get out of it.

The VW's familiar orange and cream colours reassured her and she let out a great breath of relief as she leaned against the dented passenger door.

"Stupid beggar," she rebuked herself, pulling a cigarette out of

her pocket and letting it hang in her lips as she lifted her eyes to gaze back at the imposing building.

It was a drab, ugly edifice, built of dull, grey stone in the heavy-handed, Victorian Gothic style, with a corner tower and too many gables. Planks and boards obscured the ground-floor windows, but higher up they were mostly uncovered and shaped like they belonged in a church.

Shiela hissed through her teeth at it. "Don't you look at me like that," she whispered.

Tall, misshapen trees crowded around it; there was even a tree growing in the middle of the drive, which was why they had to park the van so far away.

A rook or a crow cawed somewhere above and the lonely, unpleasant croaking made her shiver.

"Like a graveyard," she murmured. "A graveyard for dead houses. There's no life in that place, no life and never no love."

Then a jangling rattle dragged her attention back to the front porch, where Jezza was standing, shaking the van keys.

"What freaked you out in there?" he asked as he sauntered over.

"I wasn't freaked out. The air was bad. Stuffy and stale."

"You put up with worse, with Miller in the back seat."

"OK, I just don't like that place. Give me them keys, I'm gasping."

He snatched his hand away from her, dangling them just out of reach.

"That's two questions you've avoided now," he said, beginning to

19

sound irritated. "Do you want me to force the answers out of you?"

"No, Jezza!" she said. "Just let me light up – for God's sake!"

He threw the keys at her and a minute later she was dragging on the cigarette. Her fingers were trembling.

"It's just a place I've heard about," she explained, blowing out a stream of pale blue smoke. "Every town has one – the deserted old house. A place other kids dare you to go to, knock on the door, break in and spend the night."

"What is this?" Jezza sounded annoyed. "Scooby sodding Doo? Don't give me that crap."

"It's bloody true!" Shiela swore. "If you were from round here, you'd know, you'd have heard about it. Only in this case it's not made up. That's a… I dunno – a sick place. Not even kids dare each other to come here any more."

"They're too busy stuck in front of their Xboxes or glued to the Net to do anything real these days," the man said.

"Good for them," she muttered.

"The Web's for rejects," he pronounced. "All them misfits hiding in their rooms yakking away to other people they'll never meet, using fake pictures and pretending to be someone else. No one knows who they are any more and those who do aren't satisfied with it. You never know who you're really talking to on there."

She understood it was no use arguing with him. Jezza liked to make sweeping, preaching statements and wouldn't listen to anyone who disagreed with him. He certainly hadn't listened to her for a long time now. As for "misfits", what else were they?

"It's good for finding out stuff," she said half-heartedly.

Jezza smirked sarcastically. "Yeah," he said. "All that information, branching out from here and there. It's the tree of knowledge of good and evil, Shee – and how mad is it that people are accessing it via their Apples! Ha – it's Genesis all over again and we're cocking it up a second time."

"I wouldn't call this Eden," Shiela said.

"And you're not Eve," he told her bluntly, before considering the house again. "And you're not blonde enough to be Yvette ruddy Fielding either. Got ghosts, has it?"

She shrugged and flicked some ash on the ground.

"No such thing," he stated. "Only real things matter in this life, and there's enough nasty realness to keep you worried and scared without inventing other mad stuff. The things to be frightened of in this world are just round the corner, hiding in your beans-on-toast existence. That's where true evil breeds best. Under your noses, in plain sight: it's the domestic abuse of the terrified wife three doors down and her neighbours who turn the telly up to drown out the noise; it's the nurse in the care home who hates herself and takes it out on the patients; it's the kids too scared to speak out; it's the man kicking his dog in the ribs because it doesn't bite back... it's everywhere around us. Society, that's the Petri dish where evil flourishes, not in empty old houses like this beauty."

Shiela looked at him, at the sharp features that she had once found attractive: the sly, crafty shape of his narrow eyes and the unhealthy pallor that had marked him out as different and interesting. Then, unexpectedly, he turned his crooked smile on her and she was surprised to find that she still fancied him. She was always surprised. Jezza possessed a mesmeric charm, a way of making her overlook his bullying ego and ruthless self-interest. He exerted it over the others in the group too. He was, without question, their leader, and gathered waifs and strays to him like some kind of street prophet, and in their own inept, confused way, they were his disciples.

Taking the cigarette, he leaned beside her and stared intently up at the great, unlovely house.

"We could live off this dump for a year or more," he said. "Must be all sorts in there. Might even be stuff left in the attics – or the cellars, and the odd stick of furniture too. You did good, Shee."

"Wish I'd never said anything about it," she said softly.

"I might just keep you around a while longer," he chuckled with a wink, but she knew he probably meant that veiled threat.

Suddenly, inside the house, a man's voice screamed.

Jezza sprang forward like a cat and rushed back to the porch. Shiela lit another cigarette and waited.

Bonded to the Ismus, though by no means his only dalliance, is the fair Labella, the High Priestess. She outranks the other damsels of the Court, yea — even the proud queens of the four Under Kings and see how their eyes flash at her when she parades by. Coeval with her are the Harlequin Priests — that silent pair arrayed so bright and yet so grim and grave of face. Let not they point to the dark colours of their motley — dance on and dance by quick, my sprightly love.

2

RICHARD MILLER WAS sitting on the stairs. He was sweating and shaken and seemed to have shrunken into his shabby camouflage jacket, like a tortoise in its shell. Tommo stood in front of him, looking completely bemused and wondering if he could risk laughing and not receive a thump or a kick in return.

"What's gone on?" demanded Jezza when he came rushing in.

Tommo put one hand over his heart. "Nothing to do with me!" he explained hurriedly. "Pongo here had a fit going up the stairs."

"Sounded like you'd fell through them!" Jezza said.

Miller lifted his face and looked warily over his shoulder. "There was something up there," he said in a hoarse whisper.

"What?" Jezza snapped.

"Dunno… just something."

"Like what?"

"Like nothing I ever felt before," the big man answered slowly.

"Where?"

It was Tommo who answered that one. "Just up on that little landing there," he said, with a definite chuckle in his voice. "Stopped dead in his tracks he did and then, wham – he bawls his head off and leaps about, like he had jump leads clamped to his bits."

Jezza looked up to where the staircase turned at a right angle to the wall before continuing to the first floor. There was nothing to see in the gloom, except a tall, boarded window and a particularly large patch of black mould that seemed to bleed down from the upper shadows.

"Go on then," Jezza said impatiently. "What was it, a floating face or a demonic monkey or something?"

"Nah," Tommo sniggered. "Evil monkeys live in closets."

"I'm sick of this ghost garbage, man," Jezza said. "First Shee, now you."

Miller wasn't listening. He was tentatively sniffing the back of one hand. Then he pushed his sleeve up to the elbow to inspect his heavily tattooed forearm.

"What you doing?" Tommo hooted. "You madpot!"

Miller looked up at them. "There was a terrible stink," he said.

"Always is with you!" Tommo agreed.

Miller shook his head. "A stink of damp!" he said. "Terrible stink of damp – like rotting leaves – or worse. Decayed and rotten and rank and death, cold death."

"Just normal damp and wet rot," Jezza told him. "What d'you expect in a rancid dump like this, Chanel No 5 potpourri?"

Miller wiped his hand on his clothes. "No," he breathed. "No, it wasn't normal. There was something else. When I touched…"

He jumped up, almost knocking Tommo over, and glared back at the staircase.

"That wall!" he cried. "When I put my hand on it. The bloody stuff moved! Ran over my bloody hand and up my arm! I had to shake it off!"

"What stuff?" asked Jezza sternly.

Miller turned a bewildered, fearful face to him. "The mould!" he said. "The black bloody mould! I felt it on my skin – it's alive!"

He gave the stairs one last look, then blundered towards the front door, only to find Shiela standing there.

"Jezza," she called. "Let's ditch this place. I want to go – right now."

The man looked at her and placed his hand on the banister. "Just cos Miller puts his great mitt in a web and feels a spider run over him?" he said. "Don't be a stupider cow than normal, Shee."

"It wasn't no spider!" Miller shouted.

"Roaches or woodlice then," Jezza said, not caring either way. "Get real. There's no way I'm leaving this gold mine. It belongs to me now. I'm going to strip it right down and flog even the bricks, if they're worth anything."

"Listen to Miller!" she told him.

Jezza ignored her and jumped nimbly on to the first stair.

"Jezza!" Shiela said urgently as he began to ascend. "Don't! It's a bad place."

"Don't go up there!" Miller joined in.

"Oh, Mr Ghostman…" Jezza sang out as he climbed slowly, step by step. "I'm so going to kick your see-through arse and evict you off my property. This is my gaff now, you hear me? And unless you can pay rent, in living cash, you aren't welcome."

"Ha!" Tommo laughed. "You tell him. Who we gonna call? Umm… just Jezza – he ain't afraid of no ghost!"

"Belief in the supernatural is cut from the same twisted psychology as the need for religion," Jezza began propounding. "It's a man-made hang-up, yet another method of controlling the gullible proletariat by the fat cats at the top to keep us down and scared and not dare to ask real questions of the real people. Instead they made us kneel and pray against the terrors in the night that they invented. It's always been about control; there is no evil substance to darkness – it's just an absence of light.

"Like I always say, you should only be afraid of realness. It's not some vampire that'll get you along the lonely midnight lane, but the paranoid schizophrenic who prefers junk to his meds and believes

26

his Ricicles are telling him to collect human livers in a blue bucket. Be scared of that poor sod, and the NHS trusts who turf him into the community expecting him to function without proper care because it's cheaper and they can afford some extra salmon on the buffet when the next bigwig comes round for the usual glad-handing and a mugshot in the local rag."

"Listen to me, for God's sake!" Shiela cried. "I know who that kid was, the one with the magazine. I know what happened to him. Jezza – stop. Come down!"

The man reached the small landing. He half turned to grin at them. That conceited little grin which always preceded some proud, pig-headed action. Then, turning away into the wedge of shadow, he reached out with both hands and placed them squarely in the centre of the mould on the wall.

"Stupid to the power of ten," Shiela uttered in disgust.

The three disciples waited. Staring up at the back of the man they knew only as Jezza, they watched and wondered. Jezza remained perfectly still. He made no sound. He just stayed with his hands against the wall and the moments dragged into minutes. Shiela dug her fingernails into her arms. The tension was unbearable.

"That's enough!" she said, unable to take it any longer. "This isn't funny!"

"Yeah," Miller called. "Joke over."

Jezza did not move.

Tommo smiled at the others. "Chill," he told them.

"Rich," the girl said to Miller. "Go get him. Bring him down."

The burly man hesitated.

"Bring him down!" she repeated forcefully, pushing him forward.

Miller moved towards the stairs. Passing a puzzled-looking Tommo, he began to climb, reluctantly.

"Come on," he called up. "Enough's enough. You're spooking Shiela."

"You two are so over-reacting," Tommo declared. "Jezza's winding you up. Whirrrrrrr – there you go."

Miller neared the small landing. His forehead began to sweat as he recalled the terror that had overwhelmed him before. He took a deep breath and smelled the same putrid reek of decay, and coughed as it caught the back of his throat.

He took a step closer to Jezza. The man's head was hidden in the gloom and when Miller leaned sideways to catch sight of his face, he could see nothing but a black profile.

"Jezza, mate," he said. "Stop this now."

In the corner of his eye something moved over the wall. He jumped back and stumbled down two steps.

"Jesus!" he cried.

And then Jezza stirred. He jerked his head back then turned slowly around. His narrow eyes danced over his followers as if viewing them properly for the first time and a smile spread across his face.

"Look at you," he laughed softly. "Doesn't take much to panic my little chickens, does it? Another minute and you'd be screaming – and all for the fear of nothing at all. Very instructive."

"You're bleeding hilarious you are," Shiela snapped.

"And you're terminally predictable," he answered coldly.

His eyes left her mutinous, wounded stare and fixed on Miller in front of him.

The big man was looking past him, at the wall. But there was nothing to see in the shadows there, just the staining mould.

"You're in my way," Jezza told him.

Miller shook himself. Whatever he had thought he had seen was no longer there. He lumbered about and stomped back down the stairs, glad to feel the floor beneath him once more. With far lighter, almost dancing steps, Jezza followed.

"I wasn't scared!" Tommo piped up. "Dunno what's wrong with these two today."

"Shut it, you tedious prat," Jezza instructed, without even looking at him.

Shiela grimaced. Sometimes he repulsed her. He could treat people like dirt, even those closest to him. She saw Tommo react as if he'd been slapped and she wanted to be far, far away from this life she had chosen for herself. Why did she and the rest of them put up with it? Why did they keep coming back and seeking this creature's approval? What did it ever get them?

"I'll be in the van," she declared, moving back into the sunlight that streamed through the door.

Before she even set foot on the porch, Jezza was behind her. He seized hold of her wrist and spun her around. Grabbing the back of her hair, he pulled her face to his and kissed her roughly on the mouth.

Shiela struggled and kicked him on the shin.

"Sod off!" she spat.

"Don't go yet," he said, releasing her. "Come on, there's more to see. Let's me and you explore on our own. Come on, girl."

She blinked at him in surprise. He hadn't kissed her like that for a long time.

"Tommo, Miller!" he ordered, "You two go look through the rest of these rooms down here."

The men glanced at each other uncertainly. Neither of them wanted to be there any more.

Jezza turned the full power of his stare on them. "Only this floor mind," he warned. "No one, but no one, is to go upstairs. Do you hear me?"

"I wouldn't if you paid me," Miller muttered.

"Be about it then, rabbits," Jezza said with a nod towards the other rooms.

With a cautious look at Shiela to make sure she was OK, they made for one of the other doors leading off the hall. If they had rechecked the first one, they would have seen that the red leather of the armchair was now no longer covered in mould.

"Just you and me, kid," Jezza said, smiling at Shiela.

The girl was wiping her mouth on her sleeve. "What have you been eating?" she asked, spitting on the floor. "Tastes like... soil or something. Have a mint!"

"I'm just an earthy guy," he said and there was that wink again. Then he surprised her a second time by taking hold of her hand, only

gently, far more gently and tenderly than he had ever been. "This way," he said, leading her further into the hall.

"I don't want to be in here," she protested. "I want to sit in the van. I'll wait there."

But he was so insistent, his voice so coaxing and persuasive, that, before she realised, they were standing before a door in the panelling beneath the stairs. With a flourish, Jezza yanked it open.

It was pitch-black inside and a waft of cold, dead air flowed across Shiela's face.

"What's in there?" she asked, backing away.

"Cellar," he replied.

"There's no chance in hell I'm going down there! Even if we'd brought torches I wouldn't."

Jezza reached into the darkness and caught hold of a Bakelite switch dangling on a corded flex from the sloping ceiling. An instant later a dim bulb illuminated a flight of steps leading downward.

"How did you know that was there?" she asked. "How come the power's still on?"

Jezza was already descending. There was a strange, barely contained excitement in him. It was as if he knew what was down there, as if he knew exactly what was waiting.

"It'll be swarming with rats!" she said. "I'm not coming with you."

He looked back at her – his eyes shining like an owl's in the light.

"There's no rats down here," he assured her with consummate confidence. "They're not allowed."

Shiela watched his figure bob further down the steps. "Come back!" she called. "Jezza!"

He disappeared round a corner and she wished she'd kicked him harder.

"Jezza…?" she shouted.

She was alone. "Tommo, Miller…" she said, but her voice faltered and wherever they were they did not hear her.

Shiela looked anxiously at the open front door. The sunlight had dimmed and the outside seemed grey. A wind was shaking the trees.

"Save me, save me," she whispered urgently. Everything appeared threatening. Shiela thought of the magazine and what had happened to the boy it had belonged to all those years ago. Suddenly a gust of wind banged the front door against the wall. It bounced back and slammed shut. The hall was plunged into darkness.

The girl yelled and flung herself down the stairs.

"Jezza!" she cried. "Jezza!"

She leaped down two steps at a time and whirled around breathlessly. The cellar was built of vaulted grey stone that formed small, dungeon-like chambers, each with a single light bulb suspended from the apex of the ceiling.

The first chamber was empty, but a draught was moving the hanging light and the shadows swung sickeningly around her.

"Jezza…" she called again. "Damn – what the hell am I doing down here? You need your brains testing, you crazy—"

She couldn't find a word dumb enough to describe herself. She

shivered, but noticed that although it was cold down here, it was the only place in that awful house that was not damp.

"Jezza!"

No answer. She moved warily across the chamber to the next archway. That too was empty, except for strange drawings chalked on the walls, but this was not childish graffiti like the scribbles above. Here were intricate geometric patterns, interlocking circles and squares, surrounded by florid lettering spelling out Latin words. Shiela stared at them and her skin crawled. She had seen Howie, another of Jezza's disciples, tattoo similar pentacles on the backs of many heavy-metal fans and wallowing emos.

"Beautiful, isn't it?" Jezza spoke in her ear.

The girl flinched and hit him. "Take me to the van right now!" she demanded.

"Wait till you see this," he said, leading her to the next chamber.

"I've seen enough!" she replied, tugging away from him.

"No, just this," he said firmly. "Come on, girl."

They passed into the third chamber. It was larger than the previous two. Three wide, concentric circles had been inscribed into the stone floor, in the centre of which were six large wooden crates.

"What's them?" she asked.

"The jackpot, girl. Only the ruddy jackpot."

"But what's inside?"

With a triumphant laugh, he leaped into the circles. A rusty crowbar was lying across the top of one crate and he grasped it with both hands.

"Let's open them and find out!" he yelled.

"No," Shiela objected. "Leave it. There could be anything in there. Jezza, leave it!"

The man took no notice and was busily prising off one of the lids. The old nails squeaked and the wood splintered. Shiela looked around and cursed herself for ever suggesting they come here.

"Bobby Runecliffe!" she blurted, edging away. "That was the name of the boy. He was famous, all over the news back then. My mum knew him. They were in the same class. Bobby disappeared one night when he was thirteen. He was missing for three days. They finally found him wandering out on the motorway, but he was different – mental. He couldn't speak. When they took him home, he killed all his pets, strangled them. Then he tried to do the same to his kid sister. He's been locked up ever since. Nobody knew where he'd been, but it must have been here. Oh, God, it was here and it drove him crazy. Jezza – don't open that! Please!"

He only laughed in answer as the final nail was torn free and he wrenched the lid clear.

Shiela was shaking. The adrenalin was coursing through her veins. She was ready to race away at the slightest thing.

"If something flies out of there," she said.

Above them, in the rest of the house, Miller's voice was bawling. "Guys! You will not believe this! Guys! This is seriously weird, man!"

Shiela spun around. "What?" she cried. "What did he say?"

Jezza dropped the crowbar and the noise of it clanging on the

stone floor made her scream.

"Don't do that!" she yelled.

"Calm down, baby," he muttered, gazing admiringly into the open crate. "Calm down."

"That was Miller," she said. "He might need help."

Jezza chuckled. "I think our flatulent friend has merely discovered my conservatory," he told her. "Nothing to worry about."

Shiela stared at him. "How do you...?"

He grinned up at her and beckoned with his cigarette-stained fingers. "Come look," he said. "Look what we found."

"I don't want to see," she told him. "I'm so out of here."

Jezza dipped his hand inside the crate.

"Don't be scared, my honey, my pet," he said.

In spite of herself, Shelia remained. Jezza was always bizarre and never behaved as society expected him to. That was part of the attraction. But this was different. She had not seen this side to him before.

Now he stood before her, holding something that caused his eyes to widen, and he drew in a marvelling breath.

"Look at this," he whispered reverently. "There's plenty more in the box. Each one is packed with them."

Shiela lowered her eyes to the thing in his hands and the surprise and relief almost made her laugh out loud.

"It's just a book!" she exclaimed. "Just a... kids' storybook!"

His grin grew wider as he gave it to her. In the stark glare of the bare bulb she could see it was old, but had never been read. The dust cover was in mint condition, with only a few foxed marks speckling it. The illustration was an outdated style, but it had a certain period charm and she read the title aloud.

"Dancing Jacks."

Jezza pressed his face against hers. "Yes," he said, breathing damp and decay upon her as he smiled. "It's just a book, my fair Shiela... bella."

And so: those rascally Knaves, who set the Court cavorting. How they do behave, it's really worth reporting. The Jill of Hearts, a hungry temptress, she'll steal a kiss from lad and lass. The Jack of Diamonds prefers shinier pleasures, gold and jools are his best treasures. The Jill of Spades is coldly cunning, a secret plot and you're done in. The Jack of Clubs, beasts and fowl adore him, all raise a shout and sing aloud – four Dancing Jacks have entered in!

3

"SIT DOWN AND settle down," Martin Baxter said in that practised tone that only experienced teachers ever seemed capable of. It was loud enough to be heard above the scuffle and din of thirty kids flooding into a classroom, yet it wasn't shouting and it required no great effort on his part.

"Coats off. Hurry up. Glen, do that tie up properly. Keeley, take your earphones out. If I see them again, your MP3 player is going in my little drawer till the end of term. Don't think I won't – it'll be company for the mobiles."

Surly young faces stared back at him and he beamed pleasantly in return. That always annoyed them. He hated this Year 10. Yes, actually hated them. They were just as bad when they were in Year 9. Actually, no, not all of them; some of the kids were OK. There were some genuinely nice, bright ones. But most of them, even the most naive and idealistic of the new staff had to admit, were hard work and there were one or two that he had long since classified as downright scum. Unfortunately that very scum were in his lesson right now.

In the far left corner, Keeley slid on to her seat in front of her two friends, Emma and Ashleigh. The three of them immediately began singing a Lady Gaga song and only stopped when they caught sight of Mr Baxter staring at them.

"Where do you three think you are?" he asked.

"In a boring maths lesson," the hard-faced Emma answered.

"We're going to enter the next X Factor, Sir," Ashleigh explained.

"Don't you need even a modicum of talent for that?" he inquired.

"Yeah, so we've got to practise," Keeley argued.

"We're going to blow that Cowell bloke away!" Ashleigh said. "We're going to be famous and be in all the mags."

Their teacher looked surprised. "Are there many specialist publications just for gobby imbeciles then?" he asked. "Actually that'd be most of them," he murmured under his breath.

"You're mean and sarky, Sir," Emma grumbled.

"Ain't that the truth," he retorted with a fixed grin. "You've got as much chance of being singers as three cats yowling in a dustbin."

The girls pouted and fell to whispering to one another.

"'When shall we three meet again?' probably," Mr Baxter muttered, although he knew he was slandering Macbeth's witches. Over the past few years he had come to realise that these three girls had no redeeming qualities and were getting worse. They had absolutely no regard for anyone except themselves and constantly showed their displeasure at having to attend school instead of being allowed to stay at home watching Jeremy Kyle.

"And who do you think you are?" Mr Baxter told one boy who came traipsing in with his trousers hanging down over his backside, displaying his underwear. "Pull them up!"

"You can't discriminate against me, Sir," came the rebellious reply. "It's my identity, innit. I'm doing it to support my brothers. I won't yank up my saggys."

Martin raised his eyebrows. "Your brother works in Halfords," he said with a weary sigh. "And I didn't realise bright purple pants with Thomas the Tank Engine on them were very hip hop."

"Yeah, well, my best ones is in the wash and I wouldn't wear them to this poxy school anyways."

"Be that as it may," Martin said, above the titters. "The fact remains, that's not how you're supposed to wear your uniform so pull them up or you'll be staying behind every night this week and every night after that until you do pull them up."

"You is well bullying me, Sir."

"Owen," Martin said with a weary sigh. "Why do you insist on speaking like that?"

"It's who I is, innit."

"No, it isn't. For one thing, you're ginger, for another – you're Welsh."

"I is ghetto."

"You're as ghetto as Angela Lansbury, only nowhere near as cool and I'm sure she doesn't reek of Clearasil and athlete's foot powder. Now save who you is till you get outside the school gates, then you can drop your trousers down past your bony knees for all I care."

Owen hitched his trousers up and sat down noisily, slinging his bag on the desk before him.

Martin Baxter groaned inwardly. He didn't mind what cultures the kids tapped into. It was normal and healthy to seek for an identity, but in recent years he'd become aware just how homogenised that identity had become. Was it any surprise though when just about every other television programme was fronted by presenters with forced mockney accents, as if working-class London was the centre of the cool universe and nowhere else mattered. It made him wince whenever he heard the kids here in Felixstowe trying to mimic the cod East End accents that grunted around Walford. Whatever happened to quirky individuality? Sadly he reflected that, like the coast here in Suffolk, it was being eroded.

The maths teacher felt it was going to be one of those days. Thank heavens it was Friday. He had no idea just how bad that day was going to become. No one did.

When the shuffling and unrest had subsided, he sat at his desk and pulled a sheaf of papers from his battered leather briefcase.

"Before we start," he said. "Let's have a look at last week's test."

One of the three huddled girls looked up in alarm.

"You're not going to read the marks out, Sir?" she asked in exaggerated dismay.

Martin beamed again. "Oh, you betcha!" he said brightly. "Let's all have a laugh and see who the thickies are – as if we needed reminding."

"That is so not fair," she said, covering her face.

"Shall I start with you then, Emma, and get it out of the way? Here we are, 23 per cent – that's a new record for you. You must have actually been awake during one lesson. Now Ashleigh and Keeley, 19 and 21 per cent respectively."

"No respect about that!" roared one of the boys, slapping his desk. "That is so shaming!"

Martin smiled at him next. "Kevin Stipe, a whopping 17 per cent! Who'd have thought chatting to your pals and larking about instead of listening to me would produce such lame results? There can't be a connection there, surely? Coincidence? Nah…"

Kevin Stipe sank into his chair while Emma and her cohorts shook their hands at him and jeered.

"Quiet!" Martin called. He read out a few more pitiful scores before looking across to the side of the class where a thin-faced, pretty girl, was hiding behind her hair.

"Sandra Dixon," he said, this time with a genuine smile.

"Ninety-four per cent. Well done, Sandra. Now who would have thought that paying attention and getting on with your work in class could produce that result? You know, I really do think there's something in that theory. Take note, the rest of you."

Emma and her cronies pulled faces at Sandra's back and Ashleigh scrunched up a scrap of paper to lob at her head.

"You just dare!" Martin growled at her. "You'll be in the Head's office so fast, your shoes will leave skid marks on the corridor floor."

"Skid marks!" Kevin guffawed.

Just then the door opened and a tall, fair-haired lad with a sports bag slung over his shoulder came ambling in. Without so much as a glance at Martin Baxter, he headed for his empty seat. Keeley and Ashleigh whistled through their teeth at him. They had recently decided his was the best bottom in the school.

"Conor!" Martin said. "Where've you been? Why are you drifting in here so late?"

The boy looked at him insolently. "I was helping Mr Hitchin, Sir," he said.

"Then you'll have a note from him for me to that effect."

"No, Sir."

"OK, you've just earned yourself some extra time here tonight."

"Can't do that, I've got football."

"Conor, you've been here long enough to know how this place works. If you come to my lesson late, without a valid reason, then it's automatic detention."

"But there's a match on!"

"If that was so important to you, you'd have made sure you were here on time and not get detention."

"That's not fair!"

"Excuse me, do I know you? Now sit down."

Conor slumped in his seat and mouthed an obscenity when Mr Baxter wasn't looking. Then he glanced round to see if any of his classmates had seen him do it. Sandra Dixon's disgusted eyes met his and he mimed a kiss at her. Sandra turned away.

Martin Baxter looked up just in time to catch that exchange. He felt sorry for students like Sandra, the ones who enjoyed their lessons and worked hard. Even the ones who weren't as capable but tried their best were a pleasure to teach, but the number of wasters and wilfully ignorant, disruptive kids was growing every year and the government's policy of inclusion meant that they dragged everyone else in the class down to their level and held them back. As teachers, they weren't even allowed to use the word "fail" any more; they were now instructed to adopt the phrase "deferred success". Martin had to laugh at that; some of these kids would be deferring success for the rest of their lives.

The profession was not the same as when he first started, over twenty years ago. Now he was also expected to be a policeman and a social worker, but he absolutely refused to be a clownish entertainer like some of his colleagues. They had lost the respect of their pupils and now had to perform every lesson in order to engage and keep their attention. Consequently very little proper teaching was done. As far as Martin was concerned, the kids were here to learn and, for him, that meant the old-fashioned way of drilling it into them. He didn't care if they found it repetitive; this method worked – or at least it did for those who listened and were prepared to apply themselves.

"OK, open your books!" he told them. "We're going to find the area of triangles today – you lucky lot."

He was deaf to the expected groans from the usual quarters.

"I haven't got a pen, Sir," Keeley drawled.

"I hear what you're saying," he answered, with his broadest smile yet, "and I'm filing it away under 'Not My Problem'."

The rest of the day passed uneventfully. Two periods with Years 8 and 7 went by smoothly. They were usually the best years – the bored cynicism and slouching indifference hadn't taken control yet – but even so, kids just weren't the same as they used to be. Teachers were constantly being told to be mindful of attention-deficit syndromes, a condition which Martin always relabelled 'bone-idle'. Those pupils with supposed limited attention spans were more than capable of spending hours on their PlayStations without any problem. They wouldn't have been able to get away with that excuse thirty years ago, but now they were aware of it and played up to it – though not in his classes.

After detention, Martin Baxter walked down the polished corridor to the staffroom to make a much-needed coffee before heading home. For the umpteenth time that day he wished he could change jobs and do something else entirely, but at the age of forty-three that really wasn't a viable option.

Entering the deserted staffroom, he deposited his briefcase on the

44

nearest chair and rinsed a mug in the sink. The view from the window showed the staff car park and the school gates. A few of the older kids were still lingering beyond them. He recognised Emma and the other two members of her coven leaning against the railings, no longer practising their tuneless singing. He knew they'd never stick at it. Like so many other people nowadays, they expected wealth and celebrity without having to do anything to earn it. They saw other people becoming famous for having no discernible talent or having to work hard, so why should they? Role models now were celebrated, even idolised, for their stupidity; no wonder it was such a fight to get some of the kids to understand why an education was important.

"Can I have a word, Martin?"

A broad, big-shouldered man with a paunch and a florid face had popped his head around the door. Martin Baxter always thought the Headteacher looked like an actor who only ever played snarling detective superintendents on television. Maybe that was why he was such an effective Head. Most of the kids held him in awe. The good ones respected him and the rest instinctively recognised his innate authority. Barry Milligan tolerated no nonsense from anyone and even intimidated some of his staff.

He didn't intimidate Martin. They'd both been at this school too long for that. They were the longest serving members of staff. Martin often reflected that if they'd committed murder instead of starting work here, their prison sentences wouldn't have lasted so long and they'd be free by now.

"What can I do for you?" the maths teacher asked. "I can offer you a very horrible coffee, but I'm afraid all the Hobnobs have been pinched."

Barry wandered over. He always looked like he was going to arrest you and yell, "You're nicked, you slaaag!" right in your face. Martin suppressed a smile.

"I've had Douggy Wynn griping about some lad you kept in detention instead of letting him play football," the Head explained.

"Conor Westlake?"

"That's the toerag. Our Mr Wynn isn't happy that his best striker didn't get to the match till half-time."

"Are you having a go?"

Barry patted his old friend on the back. "Douggy never sees the bigger picture," he said. "He only thinks about his own subject and winning trophies."

"Well, he hasn't won any in the two years he's been teaching here," Martin replied. "If that gymnasty has got a problem with me enforcing some kind of discipline on the mouthy Conors of this place then he can come say it to my face instead of moaning to you."

Barry raised his hands. "Only passing it on," he declared. "Mind you, if we played rugby at this school instead of football…"

"I wouldn't dare spoil your favourite game!" Martin laughed.

"Game?" Barry gasped, looking mortified. "Don't blaspheme, Martin! That's my religion you're talking about and I'll be worshipping at the blessed temple of my beloved Saxons again tomorrow."

Martin shook his head and chuckled. Barry's main love had always been rugby. He had even played for Felixstowe in his youth. In their early years at the school, he would often appear on Monday morning with a curious, curler-shaped bandage in his hair or a black eye or scabby, scraped forehead where a boot had trodden on him. That was another reason the kids respected him, that and the way he used to fling wooden-backed board rubbers at the heads of the lads who weren't paying attention in his classes. Yes, you could actually do that sort of thing back then and not be sacked or put on some sort of register – and so his legend had grown. Nowadays though, Barry Milligan was resembling the shape of the ball more and more.

Martin lifted the mug of steaming black coffee to his lips when he realised Barry was regarding him curiously. He mentally classified this expression as *Do yourself a favour, you lowlife – and tell us what we want to know.*

Then Barry said, "If the kids here ever found out about your religion, Martin, and what you were into, they'd make your life unbearable and eat you for breakfast."

Martin grinned. He knew Barry was right. He blew on his coffee and glanced out of the window.

"Hell!" he shouted, slamming the mug on the side and rushing for the door.

It only took an instant for Barry to clock what was happening before he too rushed from the staff-room.

Outside, Emma and her friends were kicking and punching Sandra Dixon.

The Jockey: that tittuping mischief-maker in caramel colours, he who rides all at Court and makes them chase in circles for his impish glee. Not even the Ismus escapes his naughty, wayward pranks. Though they beat him, flail him and lock him in the tower gaol, this toffee-toned trickster always springs back, ripe and ready for more games and wicked japes. Tiptoe by, lest he set his jaunty cap at you and sets your dance a-spinning for his fun.

4

SANDRA HAD STAYED late to do her homework in the library. It was easier there than at home, with her two younger brothers arguing all the time and cranking their music up to deafening levels to spite each other. Besides, she liked being surrounded by the books and the glow of computer screens that weren't displaying high-speed chases or shooting bullets at marauding zombies.

When Miss Hopwood, the librarian, turned the screens off and announced it was time to leave, Sandra and the other six members of

the after-school homework club packed their bags and filed outside.

She was an intelligent, quiet girl who didn't make friends easily. Throughout most of her school life her best friend had been Debbie Gaskill. They had gone everywhere together. They were both tall and willowy and had often been mistaken for sisters. They shared the same interests and had never quarrelled once. But last term Debbie's father had been promoted and the family had been compelled to move to Leicester. So now Sandra found herself alone. Of course, she stayed in touch with Debbie via Facebook and texting; they spoke once or twice a week and visits were planned – but it wasn't the same.

Sandra threw herself into her studies even more and ignored the jibes from some of the other pupils. She enjoyed maths and English and was good at French, so what? They enjoyed reading Heat and squealing at celebrities displaying cellulite or with spotty foreheads and wearing clothes that were a size too small.

As she passed through the school gates, she only became aware of Emma, Keeley and Ashleigh when they spoke to her.

"Miss 94 Per Cent!" Emma said in a taunting jeer.

"Miss Brown Nose!" added Keeley. "It's right up Baxter's behind."

Ashleigh made a slurping sound behind her teeth.

"Don't you get sick of sucking up all the time, you freak?" Emma asked, as the girls began to circle her.

Sandra tried to ignore them and walk on, but they weren't about to let that happen. They were just warming up.

"You keep them cow eyes off Conor Westlake," Keeley ordered. "You listening?"

"Yeah," Ashleigh chimed in. "He's not interested in a stuck-up drip like you so back off."

Sandra couldn't believe what she was hearing.

"Conor Westlake?" she laughed. "What are you on about?"

"Don't give me that!" Emma screamed in her face. "I saw you two today. You was throwing yourself at him, flirting with him in front of everyone. Getting him to blow kisses!"

"Slapper!" Ashleigh taunted in agreement.

"You got nothing he wants!" Emma continued, jabbing a finger in the girl's face. "So jog on, you skinny munter!"

"Minger!" Ashleigh contributed.

"There's no way anyone wants to bounce on a bag of antlers like you!"

Sandra stopped walking and, with a cool dignity that maddened the girls even more, said, "Conor Westlake has never read a book in his life that he hasn't coloured in. He's almost as retarded as the three of you, so why on earth would I…?"

Before she could finish the sentence, an incensed Emma had thumped her in the stomach and Sandra had crumpled to the ground. Then they laid into her.

Conor Westlake was brimming with resentment. At that moment he despised Mr Baxter with all his young heart. Because of that miserable old maths teacher he had missed the first half of the game,

by which time it was too late and their team couldn't hope to recover from the beating the other school was giving them. He had stormed off the field as soon as the whistle blew and grabbed his stuff from the changing room.

Still in his kit, the boy stomped towards the gates, the studs of his boots clacking over the tarmac path. When he heard the shrieks and squawks of Emma and her friends, he snapped out of his brooding resentment and stared at them for a moment, wondering why they were kicking a large coat on the floor. Then he realised that coat was really another girl and he raced forward.

"Hoy!" he bawled. "Get off her!"

Emma and the others looked up and glared at him, snarling like young lionesses over a carcass.

"Here's lover boy!" Keeley spat at him.

Emma would have lunged at him as well, but it was then that Mr Baxter and the Head came rushing from the school.

The girls screamed abuse and ran off, leaving Conor shaking his head at them and Sandra quailing on the ground, clutching her sides and stomach.

"You all right?" he asked, kneeling down.

Sandra turned an ashen, angry face on him and only then did he realise who he had saved. "Stay away from me!" she yelled. "Don't you touch me!"

"I didn't do nothing!" he exclaimed. "Ungrateful cow! I shouldn't have bothered."

"Get off me!" she cried.

The thunderous voice of Barry Milligan interrupted them. "Westlake!" he hollered furiously. "Outside my office, now!"

"But I didn't do…"

"I said now!" the Head shouted, his face turning purple.

Conor took a last, confused but angry look at Sandra and stormed back into the school.

"How bad is it?" Martin was asking the girl. "Can you move?"

Sandra nodded, but she was trembling.

"Get her inside," Barry said. "She's in shock."

"She needs an ambulance," Martin answered. "She shouldn't be moved till they've had a look at her."

The girl brushed his hands away and, with a grimace, raised herself off the ground. "I'm all right," she told them as she picked herself up. "It's nothing."

"It's a police matter," the Head corrected her.

And then a new sound made all three of them turn. Behind the main school building, on the football field, there were furious shrieks and shouts and wild screaming. A pitched battle between the two teams and their supporters was under way.

"It's a war zone, this place," Martin muttered. "These kids are out of control."

The next hour was a bit of a blur. Martin had helped Sandra into the staffroom and made her a cup of sweet tea, then called her parents to come and collect her. Meanwhile Barry had run to the field to see what was going on there.

Martin had been right. It really was a war zone. Douggy Wynn and the games teacher from the other school stood on the sidelines, powerless to stop the violence. They blew their whistles and tried to pull fighting groups apart, but it was no use. About forty kids were engaged in a fierce confrontation. Barry looked on in shock and disgust. This was pure animal savagery.

Here and there around the field, stunned parents were watching and at least one of them had already called the police because soon a siren could be heard racing down the main road.

Some of the kids scarpered at the sound, but others were locked in combat and were oblivious to the blaring wail that grew steadily louder and closer.

"What a bloody mess," Barry said.

Two police cars turned up at the gates and the caretaker had been on the ball enough to open the barrier so they drove straight on to the field. Seven boys were arrested, two of them in their torn kits. The others pelted away.

Barry was in a cold rage and, if there was any space not filled with anger, it was topped up with shame. When he spoke to the police officers, he could see they held him, as Head, partly responsible. It was no comfort to discover that only three of the arrested lads belonged to his school. Then both of those emotions turned to shock when a police officer showed him the four-inch knife she had found on one of the boys.

"We've never had anything like this before," he said.

"You do now, Sir," the stern young policewoman informed him.

"This could have been a lot worse than it was. There could have been a fatal stabbing here today. We're going to need you and everyone else to make witness statements about this incident."

Barry nodded then he remembered Sandra Dixon. "There was another incident, just before this," he said. "One of our girls was beaten up outside the gates by three other girls. I was just about to call you about that."

"Not a good day for this place, is it, Sir?" the policewoman said judgementally.

Barry Milligan had to agree with her.

Quarter to seven on a Friday night and Martin was still stuck in school. He'd called Carol, his partner, to warn her he was going to be late and give her a brief sketch of events, but she was incensed about something else. The bank had been on to her, or she had been on to the bank... either way she was livid. Martin was not in the mood to listen to her woes on top of everything else so he was relieved when Barry Milligan came into the staffroom and he could make his excuses and ring off.

"Tell me what else could go wrong today?" the Head barked, making a beeline for the kettle. "It's a bloody asylum this place! The governors are going to love this."

"Was anyone hurt on the field?" Martin asked.

"Busted noses and fat lips mostly. We was dead lucky it wasn't worse. A knife, for God's sake! A sodding knife!"

"It wasn't one of our lads though."

"Doesn't matter whose it was, I'm not having that kind of thing anywhere near my school. I knew it'd happen here one day, but not so soon. This isn't an inner city."

"We still have gangs and hoodies and joyriders round here though."

"Yes, well – just wait till Monday morning!"

"What do you mean?"

"Had a word with the police. They're going to set up a knife arch at the gate first thing. If any of our lot are bringing knives in, we'll know about it."

Martin shook his head. "I remember when the most dangerous thing you'd find in a kid's bag was a spud gun."

"God, I miss those days," the Head sighed. "It's the feminisation of education, that's what's brought this on. And too much government interference, trying out each new trendy idea instead of leaving us to do our jobs properly. Just look what we've ended up with – a bloody chaotic shambles and kids armed to the teeth, thinking they're gangsters."

Martin wasn't going to enter into that debate, even though he agreed with him.

"So how did it kick off?" he asked.

"More bloody oiling," Barry told him.

Martin understood. Oiling was the latest unpleasant method of attacking someone in Felixstowe. Martin knew several people who had been oiled, his partner's mother for one. It had been a terrifying and upsetting experience for her. Bottles of vegetable oil were cheaper than boxes of eggs and the oil itself was messier and smellier and more difficult to get out of clothes. A jumbo, 3-litre container was only a few quid and could be decanted into empty sports drink bottles, the type with the pull-up nozzle that could squirt several metres. Such small bottles could also be carried very discreetly in the large pockets of a fleece or a hoody. Gangs would steam through a crowded street and douse their selected victim with the stuff. It was disgusting. The situation had grown so bad that the police had advised local supermarkets not to sell vegetable oil to anyone under the age of eighteen.

"By the way," he said. "Sandra's mother came while you were with the police. She's taken her to casualty to be checked over, but said she'll be in touch."

"I bet she will," Barry grunted. "I don't blame her. Those three girls are going to get a visit tonight from the law. They already had a word with that Conor lad."

"Oh," Martin said. "Sandra told me he had nothing to do with it."

Barry shrugged. "Well, they've taken a statement anyway. This coffee really is foul muck, isn't it? You know what I need right now? About half a dozen pints. I'm going to swill this bloody awful day away – you joining me?"

Martin declined. Barry spent too many hours in The Half Moon in Walton. That and his devotion to rugby were what had driven his wife away two years ago. She had taken the Labrador with her too. Barry missed the dog far more than her.

At ten past seven, Martin Baxter finally sat in his car. As he drove

out of the school, he tried to close his mind to the traumas of the day. No one, especially him, suspected that much worse was yet to come. This weekend was going to be the turning point in the lives of everyone. At long last the world was going to learn about Dancing Jacks and it would never be the same again.

5

JIM HOWIE'S TATTOO and piercing parlour, INK-XS, was tucked away off the Port of Felixstowe Road. It was a small place, but not too seedy. It was split into two halves: the back part was where the inking was done, behind a shoulder-height partition, and the front was for customers to wait in and browse the designs pinned to the walls and in the three folders on a low table. There was also a knackered sofa, which came in very handy for the squeamish ones who fainted when they felt the needle or glimpsed the blood. At the rear of the building was a monotonous vista of huge sea containers. They were dwarfed by the massive cranes straddling the horizon, which always reminded Howie of steel dinosaurs. Appropriate enough for the stark tundra of the largest container port in the UK and one of the biggest in Europe.

Howie was a big-bellied man in his thirties, with a square-cut, gingery beard, shaved head and enough tattoos on his fleshy body to reupholster that old sofa. He sported two piercings in his lower lip, another through his septum and one more through his right eyebrow.

Looking around at his shop, he moaned as Tommo and Miller hauled another of those large wooden crates through the door.

"Hey, c'mon," he complained. "That's five of them now. How many of these things are there?"

"Just one more," Tommo told him. "If you'd give us a hand, you'd have seen that yourself. These aren't filled with fresh air, you know; we could do with the extra manpower."

Howie waved the suggestion aside. "I'm an artist, man," he declared. "I can't risk damaging these delicate instruments with a load of splinters."

Miller and Tommo shoved the fifth crate alongside the others they had fetched from the van and leaned on it to catch their breaths and rest their aching muscles. It had taken two long trips from the strange, ugly house to Howie's shop to bring all six crates over, to say nothing of the struggle hoisting them up from that cellar. Jezza had been insistent though.

"It's time for them to leave home," he had said, "and make their way in the world."

"I can barely squeeze by them!" Howie grouched. "Just for tonight, capiche? I can't have these blocking my shop. I've got a business to run – and don't tell me what's in them, I don't want to know, but how hot is it? We talking tepid or scalding? If the filth come sniffing around, you're not dropping me in it. You got that? I'll tell them exactly who it belongs to – or doesn't."

"Peace, brother," Jezza's voice interrupted as he came in. "This is… legit merchandise."

Howie raised his eyes heavenward. "Like the Blu-ray players you stashed here last month?" he asked. "Yeah, they was so bona fide they burned a hole in the lino!"

Jezza ran his hands along the edge of one of the crates. "I'm done with all that," he announced. "The old life is over, no more hooky gear. I've got a better, higher purpose now – and if you're a good little bunny, you can come with me. The door of destiny has just swung open and I'm inviting you to step through it."

"Hallelujah!" Howie mocked. "He done seen the light!"

Jezza's eyes glinted at him and he showed his crooked smile. "You couldn't be further from the truth, Mr Tattoo Man," he said.

Miller shifted uneasily and glanced at Tommo.

"Bring in the last box," Jezza told them. "I want Howie to see what he's storing for me."

"An' we want to see what we've been busting our guts over," Miller said.

"Less of the guts, please," Tommo pleaded. "Come on. Let's go get the last Alexander."

"The last what?"

"I'm wasted here," Tommo sighed.

The three of them returned to the yard where the VW was parked,

leaving a puzzled Howie scratching his beard. He'd never seen Jezza behave like this before.

"He's been like that since we went into that vile house," Shiela spoke from the doorway. "It's weird, like… oh, I dunno – like it's him, but it isn't."

Howie looked at her. "What happened in that place then?" he asked. "No one's said."

The girl frowned then shrugged it off. "Mad stuff," she finally answered. "I freaked out big style and so did Miller – but Jezza…"

"What?"

"I wish I knew – or maybe I don't."

"Are you all on something? Nobody's making sense."

"Wait till you see what else we found," she said. "What's still back there – in the manky conservatory."

"Mind your backs!" Tommo called, lumbering in, carrying the final crate with Miller. "There! That's the lot. Now my gaseous friend's innards here are rumbling like Krakatoa so we'd better get some food in him. Come on, Methane Maker, let's…"

Their exit was barred by Jezza. He was standing in the doorway, eyes gleaming.

"We haven't finished yet, boys," he said, removing the loose lid from the last crate and reaching inside. "This is only the beginning. You have no idea of the incredible honour you've been granted. You're here, right at the start of everything. We've each been chosen and should be on our knees in gratitude. Take a breath and look around you. Remember this momentous night. The whole world is

61

about to change and this is the last time you'll see it like it was."

A look of panic flashed over Howie's face. "Bloody hell!" he cried. "You've never got guns in them boxes?"

Jezza laughed as if it was the funniest thing he had ever heard.

"What then?" Howie demanded. "Bombs or something? You're out of your greasy mind and way out of your league! You're crazy!"

Jezza continued to laugh. It was a horrible, throat-rattling sound. Shiela clutched at the collar of her denim jacket. The voice she heard was not his.

Then he slammed his palm on the side of the crate and the laugh subsided to a dry chuckle.

"Guns and bombs have been tried," he said in a far-off kind of way. "Tried and failed, tried and failed, time and again. That's not how to do it. Wars are finite. They blaze for a few years and it's fantastic and showy and spectacularly loud and operatic. Then suddenly peace breaks out like a rash and you're back where you started and you have to foment it all over again. War doesn't work. It unites more than it destroys."

"What's the matter with him?" Howie demanded.

Before the others could answer, Jezza flashed his teeth in a wide grin and threw something at him.

Howie ducked and jumped out of the way, half expecting it to be a hand grenade. This was lunacy.

The thing landed at his feet and he peered down at it warily. When he saw what the thing actually was, he thought it even stranger than if it had been an explosive.

"A book?" he exclaimed incredulously.

"It's time for you all to have one," Jezza said solemnly, his voice recognisably him once again. "Take them, cherish them… coddle them."

He passed the copies around. Only Shiela had seen the book already, but she stared at it with the same fascination as the first time.

"Dancing Jacks," Howie read. "Where did you get a load of second-hand kids' books from? And what for?"

Jezza was relishing the looks on their faces as they turned the book over in their hands. They had no idea what they were holding.

Shiela flicked through the slightly musty pages, the occasional illustrations skimming before her eyes. There was a faint, almost inaudible sound as the leaves parted after being pressed together so long. It was like a soft, dry kiss between the ink and the paper.

"They're not second-hand," Jezza said. "Not one of them has ever been owned, not a single one has ever had eager eyes scan its pages. The moment they were printed and bound, they were packed away. They haven't seen daylight or felt a human touch for seventy-five years. They've never been read. They're fresh as virgins and just as ripe and anxious to be treasured and explored."

"First editions then," Howie said. "How much are they worth?"

"Everything," came the cryptic answer.

"Who's this Austerly Fellows?" Howie asked, reading out the author's name. "Never heard of him."

"Not many have… yet," Jezza replied with the hint of a smile. "But they will. His name will ring out at last. We promise."

"Is this all that's in them boxes?" Tommo grumbled in disbelief – hugely disappointed. "Is this what I've broke my back for all afternoon? The way you was talking, I thought it was the family silver or something. I thought we was going to be minted."

Jezza took out a book for himself and opened it at the first page. "This is worth far more than silver," he guaranteed, the cream-coloured paper reflecting up into his eyes and making them unusually bright. "All things will be as dross beside this. We've waited a long time, but now our words are ready to be heard, to seep into the mind and smite the heart."

"Riiiiiiight," Tommo said. "So aren't we going back to gut that house?"

"Not to gut it, no. Besides, we don't need to now."

"I was never one for reading," Miller said dismissively. He put the book down and took out his mobile to order a curry.

"Beyond the Silvering Sea," Jezza began, "within thirteen green, girdling hills, lies the wondrous Kingdom of the Dawn Prince…"

The others exchanged embarrassed glances as he read aloud. What was he doing? They each felt uncomfortable. It was a peculiar situation and Tommo almost giggled. It was so bizarre and silly – and so totally out of character for Jezza.

"And the Dawn Prince went into exile," he continued, "vowing to return to the Castle of Mooncaster only when he deemed his subjects worthy of his golden majesty."

Tommo found the matching page in his copy. Almost without realising, he began to follow the words as they were read out, his lips

moving with Jezza's as he spoke them.

"But who would rule in the Lord's stead?" Jezza uttered. "Who would keep the knights and nobles, the Jacks and jostling Under Kings in order?"

Howie lowered his eyes to the book in his hands. Jezza's voice seemed to be spinning slowly around him and the words were beating to the rhythm of his heart. There was reassurance here – a cosiness he had not felt since… he could not remember. It was an inviting, nostalgic sensation: back to when large hands scooped him up and held him close, when sweet lips kissed his grazed knee, when perfect comfort was a favourite blanket with a silken edge and a sucked corner. He felt warm and loved and safe. Within his rusty beard, his own lips began to move like Tommo's.

"So forward stepped the Holy Enchanter," Jezza read, his face alive and alight, "the one thereafter named the Ismus. Only he could command the quarrelling Court and bring order to the squabbling subjects whilst the Dawn Prince remained in exile. Yet first he must endure the Great Ordeal to prove himself…"

Shiela stared in mute disbelief at Howie and Tommo. Then she saw that Miller had retrieved his copy and was nodding in time to the tempo of the words.

"Stop it!" she cried suddenly, snapping her book shut. "Stop it!"

Jezza's reading ceased and he lifted his gaze to her. His eyes narrowed and a gleam went out in them.

"Call Dave," he instructed Miller, without releasing Shiela from his glance. "Say I want him here by eight tonight, no excuses. And get Tesco Charlie as well – tell him to bring his lorry. Don't fail me."

Miller and the others were blinking and rubbing their foreheads as if rousing from sleep. They closed their books reluctantly.

"Er… sure," Miller said, pulling out his Nokia once more. "How about Manda and Queenie?"

"Why not," Jezza replied. "Let's make a party of it. You can do that on the way, Big Man. We've got one more thing to collect from that house this evening."

"I'm not going back there," Shiela stated. "It'll be dark."

Jezza turned back to her, his face impassive. "I don't need you," he said. "I'm taking Howie and Miller this time."

"I'm not doing any heavy work," Howie refused.

"Don't worry, Leonardo, your lily-white handies won't come to any harm."

"What about me?" Tommo asked.

"You make yourself useful," Jezza told him. "Get some cans and anything else you can lift. Those girls are too tight to bring anything."

"But I'm skint!"

"Howie, give him cash."

"Why me?" the tattooist cried.

Jezza grinned at him. "Cos we're in your emporium," he said. "And you'll have had a busy day, raking in the readies from the witless drones who come in here wanting to copy whatever mass-market pap idol has been hyped to them this week, only to have them regret it once that particular scrap of ephemera has stopped flashing in the pan. Then there's the tribal squiggles or bands of

66

barbed wire smothering their pimply skin because they think it makes them look hard and macho or mysterious and more interesting than they really are. Why don't you simply scribe 'I'm a mindless sheep' on their foreheads while you're at it?"

"Pack that in," Howie warned. He didn't mind when Jezza pontificated, but not when he slagged off his clientele and, by extension, himself. Although… he suddenly recalled the nineteen-year-old upon whose back he had once inked, in the early days of his shop, a group portrait of the members of Hear'Say, only for her to return eight months later to ask if there was any chance he could go over it and make them look like the boys of Blue instead. At the time Howie had somehow managed to control himself and politely told her that, as Blue consisted of one person less than Hear'Say, it would be impossible. As soon as she had left in a dissatisfied strop, however, he had almost made himself sick with laughter.

The tattooist grudgingly opened his well-padded wallet. "Here's forty," he said, handing the notes over to Tommo. "But I want change!"

"Give him more," Jezza told him.

"That's plenty for beers and a cheap bottle of voddy!" Howie protested.

"It's not for the booze."

"Takeaways?" Miller suggested hopefully.

Jezza took Howie's wallet off him and handed it to Tommo. "I want about thirty big bags of charcoal," he said.

"Barbecue stuff?" Tommo asked.

"That's right, we're having a great big luau."

"On the beach? Cool."

"No, not on the beach, and it'll be anything but cool."

Howie grabbed the wallet back and removed all his plastic, except the Clubcard, then returned it. "Make sure you use that," he informed Tommo. "I want the points."

"Points?" Jezza scoffed. "You really think they're doing you some sort of favour and actually rewarding you for being loyal? Were you born half an hour ago? Wake up, brother. What they're doing is building up a detailed profile of everything you buy, every time you use that and every other card you've got. They know what you eat, what you wear, what you read, where you travel to every day and where you're likely to be at any given time. They know what music you listen to, what TV you watch, what websites you visit and what you download, what turns you on and what makes you laugh on YouTube. They know what your politics are – it's all on your file now and who's merrily filled it in for them? You have, like the good little lemming consumer you are."

Howie shrugged, "I still get money off," he said.

"Peanuts," Jezza snorted. "They're conning you into building up a comprehensive database about yourself and paying you in half-price spaghetti hoops to do it. There's a computer somewhere that can calculate how often you take a dump because it knows precisely how much aloe vera impregnated bog roll you buy and when you buy it. They know everything about you, my son. But you, and millions like you, aren't even slightly disturbed by that. You're

just happy to get your reduced Hovis and bargain garibaldis."

"Jammie Dodgers," Howie corrected.

"Are we going or what?" Miller interrupted.

Tommo laughed. "Don't talk about food when the gasworks here hasn't eaten for a whole four hours."

Jezza inclined his head – the sermon was over for now – and he herded them through the door.

"So where we having this barbie?" Tommo asked.

Jezza beckoned them round the side of the building and gathered everyone in the yard at the rear. Then he gestured to the alien landscape of the immense container port.

"In there," he announced.

No one said anything. They each gazed at the wide prospect of stacked metal containers in the distance.

"You really have lost it this time," Howie eventually said. "You're out of it! Totally out of it. Why in there?"

Jezza's eyes remained on the mountainous gantry cranes on the horizon. "Because the reception will be best," he said enigmatically. "And you'll be safer."

"It's a mad idea!" Tommo crowed. "And I love it! Let's go rock that place!"

Howie tore at his beard in exasperation. "You're both loonies!" he cried. "For one thing, you'd never get inside in a million years – the security is tight as an airport nowadays."

"Then isn't it lucky we know Tesco Charlie and his big shiny lorry?" Jezza answered. "He's in and out of there all the time."

The tattooist spluttered. "You're not serious!" he shouted. "Do you know the heavy crap you'll get into when you're caught? And you will be caught! They've got their own police unit in there. Those guys are all ex-military, there's no one under six foot five. They don't play nicey-nicey and accountable like the town regulars. They'll rough you up, crack your head open – and then throw you in the nick."

Jezza put a calming hand on his shoulder. "The port's pigs will be otherwise engaged tonight," he informed him. "A lovely diversion has been arranged and they, and the fire crews, are going to be so very busy to even notice li'l ol' us."

"What?" Howie cried. "Even if you could arrange to get rid of them for a while, which I don't believe, they've got top-of-the-range CCTV in there. Those cameras can zoom into bedroom windows across the water in Harwich!"

Jezza continued to stare at him. "Let this fear go, man," he said. "Come on, don't be so uptight. Live a little – or are you really going to miss out on this and stay trapped in your pinball boundaries with your loyalty cards and gas bills? It's a once in a lifetime offer, Jimmy Boy – come join me. Leave all that just for tonight and follow me… Beyond the Silvering Sea, within thirteen green, girdling hills, come – be a part of something amazing. I promise, tonight will blow your mind."

The tension in Howie's shoulders eased and he nodded slowly. "OK," he agreed. "But I must be even madder than you."

Tommo whooped and grabbed Miller's hands and the pair of

them danced back to the camper van.

Howie and Jezza followed, leaving Shiela standing alone in the yard, silhouetted against the distant lights that were already coming on over the container terminal. To her, the giant cranes looked like titanic sculptures of giraffes.

"And me?" she called out. "What'll I do?"

Jezza glanced over his shoulder and gave her an empty smile. "You got the most important job of all, doll," he declared. "You've got to guard the books till we get back."

"Here, on my own?"

"But you're not on your own," he answered in earnest. "The Dancing Jacks are with you."

It was growing dark when the camper van pulled up the overgrown drive for the third time that day.

"Creepy as hell!" Howie exclaimed, staring up at the louring building. "Who lived here then, the Munsters or the Addams Family?"

"You raaaaang?" Miller droned in his ear.

"If I see a hand running along the floor," Howie informed them, "I'm stamping on the bugger and breaking its bloody fingers."

He studied the large house critically. It must have been expensive even back in the day, but it could never have been a handsome building. From a design perspective, it was simply hideous. Still, he knew several goths who would happily spend their holidays here and read gloomy poetry by candlelight.

"Inside," Jezza said.

Slabs of shadow covered the large hall. Miller's skin prickled as he entered.

"Don't tell me," Howie said, "designed by Tim Burton."

"You've seen nothing yet," Miller whispered. "You should go out back. It'd turn Alan Titchmarsh's hair white."

Jezza crossed to the stairs. Howie moved to follow him, but Miller hesitated.

"Stay there, both of you," Jezza commanded. "Wait for me and don't go wandering. This old place can be … dangerous in the dark."

Miller shivered. He knew Jezza wasn't talking about rotten floorboards. He suddenly wished he had stayed behind with Shiela. Besides, he'd like to read more of that book…

Jezza's wiry figure disappeared up the stairs, into the impenetrable shadow of the first-floor landing.

In the spacious hall the two men waited.

Minutes ticked by.

"Who's up there with him?" Howie asked.

Miller did not answer. He too had heard a muffled voice speaking in one of the rooms above, but he preferred not to mention it. Neither of them could make out what was being said up there, the voice (or was it voices?) was too remote and the creeping darkness seemed to soak up the sound like a sponge.

"I thought this place was empty," Howie said.

Miller looked uneasy. "No one lives here," he muttered.

"So is he talking to himself up there?"

"That's not what I said."

"What's up with our fearless leader today? He's been acting weird since you turned up with them first three boxes."

"I think it's going to get a lot weirder," Miller predicted. He had never been more right in his life.

Suddenly there was a deafening crash. A tremendous, clanging weight had toppled to the floor over their heads.

Miller almost jumped out his skin and grabbed hold of Howie.

"What the hell?" the tattooist cried as plaster flaked from the ceiling and rained on top of them. "Did someone drop twenty pianos?"

"I'm gone!" Miller declared, heading for the front door.

Then a different sound commenced: a slow, scraping noise. Something unbelievably heavy was being dragged across the floor. Miller paused and lifted his face upwards. They could hear Jezza's grunts and shouts as he strained and pulled whatever it was on to the landing.

"OK," Howie murmured. "I'm officially freaked now – and this close to soiling myself."

"I think I already have," Miller breathed.

The scraping continued – down the length of the landing, to the top of the stairs. They heard Jezza struggling and swearing with exertion. Then there was a calamitous din that echoed through the house and shook the banisters.

Something large came smashing down the staircase, thudding and banging with a dull metal clash, like the chiming of a huge leaden bell. It slid like an avalanche of old bedsteads down to the small landing where Miller had experienced terror earlier that afternoon and thundered into the wall beneath the partially boarded window.

The two men stared, open-mouthed, and waited for the echoes, that were bouncing through every room and vibrating the broken glass in the window frames, to ebb away.

Then Jezza's sweating, ghostly-white face appeared over the banister above and he laughed softly.

"Dear God!" Howie gasped, pointing at the great shape that had crunched into the wood of the half-panelled wall. "What the hell is that?"

And when the Dawn Prince was in exile, he sent neither message nor sign back to his Kingdom. So, whilst the Ismus and his subjects waited, they filled their days with merrymaking and happy pleasures. But every party has to end when the revellers grow weary, yet still the throne remained empty and no word came to Mooncaster... O how they longed for tidings.

6

"I'VE HAD MY identity stolen!" Carol yelled at Martin Baxter as soon as he opened the front door.

"Who are you now then?" he asked.

"Some scumbag has been using my credit card details to get flights to Barcelona, a huge flat-screen TV, a tumble dryer and God knows what else in Comet — and a massive shopping spree in Homebase. The best part of four grand they've rinsed me for!"

"Hello to you too," he greeted her.

"I'm furious!" she seethed, brandishing a statement she'd printed out from her online banking.

"And I'm Martin. Shall I go out and come in again?"

The woman glared at him for a moment, then wilted and managed a smile. "Sorry," she said. "I'm covered anyway, so I've not really lost that money. It's so bloody annoying though. I was on the phone for over an hour trying to sort it out. Can you believe these people? How dare they?"

"There's a lot of scum in the world," he said. "It's mad, isn't it? You've got to shred every trace of who you are on every letter, bill and envelope before you throw them away, otherwise they'll have you. Destroying yourself before someone else does. You wouldn't believe my day, by the way. Where's Paul?"

She pointed upstairs.

"Daft question really," Martin said.

Carol went over to him and welcomed him home properly, with a hug and a kiss. "I've already heard a bit about your day," she said. "Got a call from my mum who'd heard all from some neighbour or other. Sounded bad."

"It was! Good job you picked Paul up today to take him to Gerald's. It was mental."

"I was just going to get changed. My shift starts at nine. We left you some lasagne. I'll nuke it for you."

"Thanks – I am starved."

He took his jacket off and hung it in the narrow hallway before following her into the kitchen. Carol Thornbury was a pretty woman, seven years his junior, with dark brown hair and a feisty personality. If there was one word to describe her, it would be

'capable'. But then, as a nurse, she'd have to be. Whatever life threw at her, she dealt with it in her usual efficient manner. She might have a bit of a rant to begin with, but she quickly applied her common sense to whatever the problem might be, without any unnecessary fuss or drama. When her husband had walked out on both her and their five-year-old son, she had been as organised at sorting out that mess as with everything else in her life. She had managed perfectly well without a man for several years until her path crossed Martin's. Sometimes he felt that she had even organised getting the two of them together. If she had, he was thankful.

"You got a parcel today," she said, waiting for the microwave to ping. "I think I see more of that postman than I do you. Wouldn't mind if he was remotely dishy, but he looks like Fungus the Bogeyman's uglier brother."

Martin's face lit up and he hurried into the lounge where a medium-sized parcel stood on the coffee table.

"Bless you, eBay!" he cried, snatching the package and dashing upstairs with it.

"What about the lasagne?" Carol called.

"In a bit!" he answered. "First things first."

Carol rolled her eyes. "We're going to need an extension at this rate," she told herself.

It was a three-bedroom semi, but only two of those were ever slept in. Whenever guests came to stay, they were compelled to sleep on the sofa downstairs. The third bedroom was Martin's own private sanctuary. Somewhere he could escape the grinding rigours of teaching at a modern High School and the Emma Taylors of this world. A place filled with things that his pupils would hang him out to dry for if they ever found out about them.

"Paul!" he shouted, knocking on the box-room door as he passed by. "It's here!"

The maths teacher took a shallow breath before entering his own 'inner sanctum'. Then strode inside.

The few visitors who were ever privileged to be ushered in here were always lost for words. There was too much to see, too much to take in straight away to be able to formulate any coherent sentence, so they always made the same sort of exclamations.

"Oh, wow!"

"Amazing!"

"Blimey!"

Only Carol's mother had ever been practically minded enough to come out with, "How do you dust it all?"

Martin Baxter, the cynical, down-to-earth maths teacher who took no nonsense from any of his students, was a monumental, dyed-in-the-wool, sci-fi and fantasy geek – with a capital G.

His special room was crammed from floor to ceiling with all manner of merchandise: DVDs, costumes, props, limited-edition prints, toys, action figures, models, replicas, books, comics, magazines and framed photographs of himself meeting the stars of his favourite films and television shows. There were busts of just about every character in the Lord of the Rings movies and daleks

of every dimension, from the tiny 'Rolykins' version up to life-size (a particularly extravagant, pre-Carol present to himself). Spaceships from diverse universes flew in formation from the ceiling – followed incongruously by Chitty Chitty Bang Bang. There were Star Fleet uniforms, complete with a selection of various comm badges and tricorders, and even a genuine phaser from the first season of the Next Generation (another expensive present to himself in his bachelor days).

A preposterously long, multicoloured scarf festooned a hatstand, an Alien egg with the face-hugger just crawling out of it, a bottle of Tru:Blood, a prop business card used in the 1957 movie Night of the Demon by the black magician Julian Karswell – with the silver warning written on it – the Clangers, together with the Soup Dragon, Iron Chicken and froglets, a lamp housed within the golden head of C-3PO, several magic wands in display cases, a chunk of Kryptonite that glowed in the dark, a top-of-the-range lightsaber which made movie-accurate sound effects and many more objects which had taken Martin years to accumulate. One of his most prized acquisitions, however, was also one of the smallest – an actual authentic Liberator teleport bracelet from Blake's Seven. Now that had been expensive!

Even with his mathematical skill, Martin had given up trying to calculate how much it had all cost him, but he knew it was far, far more than the sum Carol's identity thieves had stolen from her account.

He set the parcel on his crowded desk and began tearing off the packaging. A young face appeared around the door behind him.

"Let's see!" Paul cried.

Paul Thornbury was eleven. He had curly, fair hair and was small and slight for his age. He shared Martin's love of fantasy though and the two of them could spend hours together glued to a DVD or poring over comics or discussing the latest monster in Martin's all-time favourite show. Was it as good as the Zygons, or was it as dismal as the Myrka? During such conversations they spoke in a language that Carol, quite frankly, didn't understand. She had no use for science fiction and fantasy. She preferred real life, but was more than delighted to leave them to it, while she sat in front of Casualty or House with a glass of white wine. Martin could never understand why she watched those programmes. Didn't she have enough of that at work? Carol would always nod, but added that she enjoyed laughing at the mistakes.

Paul stood beside Martin and watched him pull the bubble wrap and newspaper out of the adapted cardboard box. He had found this for Martin. He had entered it as a special search in eBay and had been checking it for the past seven months, without success. Then, a few weeks ago, one had come up and now here it was.

Martin tore the last piece of packing from it and turned the glass object in his hands so that it caught the light. It was a fresnel lens. Quite hard to come by nowadays, but essential if Martin was going to build the full-size Police Box he had always wanted. It would be nothing without the lamp on top.

"Mum'll go spare," Paul chuckled.

This was their big conspiracy. They had been keeping it a secret from her for ages, ever since they discovered a website giving instructions on how to build one. When they had moved in, Carol had consigned all of Martin's 'toys' to the one room and not even the mugs or fridge magnets were allowed in the rest of the house. If so much as an X-Files coaster appeared anywhere, it was swiftly returned to the inner sanctum with a Post-it note attached, on which she'd drawn an exclamation mark.

"We'll just have to outvote her," Martin said. "How good will one of these be in the garden?"

"Most excellent!" Paul agreed.

Martin rubbed his hands together gleefully then hid the lens inside an accommodating R2-D2.

"She'll come round," he said hopefully. "We'll get it started one weekend when she's working and she won't be able to stop us."

"What happened after school?" Paul asked. "I heard Mum talking on the phone."

"Good job you had your piano lesson and weren't there," Martin told him. "Two very nasty fights. The Head is furious."

"Wish I'd seen it," the boy said, disappointed. Then he added, "She put too much salt in the lasagne again."

Martin returned downstairs and discovered that for himself. Back in his own room, Paul surveyed the beginnings of his own crazy collection. His shelves were already full of fantasy figures and graphic novels. He was glad his mum had found and teamed up with Martin.

An email alert sounded from his computer and Paul hardly heard Carol shouting goodnight to him as she left for work. It was going to be a very busy, traumatic night in the hospital.

Paul frowned at the email. He didn't recognise the sender. It was just a number, 7734, but it didn't appear to be an advert for Viagra or a phoney bank scam and there weren't any dodgy attachments.

"Tonight at Nine!" read the title.

He opened it.

☺☺☺☺☺☺☺☺☺☺☺☺☺☺☺☺☺☺☺☺

Flash mob at the Landguard – tonight at nine. It'll be a blast! Great sounds! Mystery A-list celeb! Bring your mates! Bring a bottle – or ten! Be a part of this awesome happening. It's gonna be on the news. We're going for a record!!!!!!!!!

☺☺☺☺☺☺☺☺☺☺☺☺☺☺☺☺☺☺☺☺

"Weird," Paul said. He had no idea who would send him anything like that. It wasn't any of his Facebook friends. Not even Anthony Maskel or Graeme Parker, his closest friends at school, would have sent him something like that. Usually they sent him links to daft things they'd found on YouTube.

He thought about the Landguard for a moment. It was the huge old fortress down on the peninsula, dating back hundreds of years. It always struck him as strange that such a historic building should be slap bang next to the modern, industrial container port.

Paul rushed downstairs to tell Martin. The man laughed. He wasn't the slightest bit interested in something like a flash mob and had looked forward to a quiet night of escapism in front of a DVD.

"But it'll be huge!" Paul said. "Cameras and famous people. The email said so!"

Martin sighed. "You know," he said. "The Internet is fantastic for stuff like eBay, but I think I preferred the world when it was simpler. When I was your age, the most new-fangled piece of kit we had was a pocket calculator and…"

"This isn't the breast thing, is it?"

"Have I said this before?"

"You and your friends," the boy recited wearily, "used to key in the number 5318008, then turn the calculator upside down and snigger."

Martin chuckled. "Happy days," he said.

"Ummm… whatever," Paul muttered with a baffled grimace. He liked Martin, but sometimes he really did say some daft things for a forty-three-year-old maths teacher.

"Oh, go get your coat on," the man told him. "I can watch the universe being saved again tomorrow night."

Paul was already in the hallway zipping up his fleece.

"There'll be no one else there, you know," Martin said. "We'll be stood there like two trainspotters without a station."

In Felixstowe that evening, every young person under the age of twenty received that very same email. Afterwards, when the tragedy was being investigated, nobody could ever trace where it had originated.

The first part of the harrowing diversion was being created.

Where are the Exiled Prince's sheep so rare,
their fleeces of finest gold?
Dead and dying from lack of care and frozen by the cold.
Shun the Bad Shepherd, drive him from your sight.
Where was he when the lambs did stumble and bleated in
their plight?

7

EMMA TAYLOR THREW her hair straighteners across her bedroom and yelled an angry stream of filth. She had only finished half of her hair when they had sparked and smoke started to pour out of them.

"What do I look like?" she screamed at her reflection. "Britney Spears in meltdown mode!"

Stuffing her unfinished hair under a baseball cap, she stormed out of the house, without a word to her parents, and strode furiously down the street towards Ashleigh's.

Taking out her mobile, she punched up her friend's number aggressively and waited for her to pick up.

"What you gawking at?" she snapped at a group of teenage lads on bicycles, giving them the finger as she clomped by.

In her ear Ashleigh's tinny voice answered. She was squealing with excitement.

"Ohhhh, myyyy God!" she cried. "You will not believe the email I just had!"

"I need to use your straighteners!" Emma demanded, ignoring her. "Life or death emergency. My crappy ones have exploded – thank you so much, Dad, you cheapskate. Nearly burned my eyebrows off! Seriously though – I was well terrified, no word of a lie."

"Shut up and listen!" Ashleigh retorted and she read her the email about the flash mob.

Several minutes later Emma was sitting on her friend's bed, frantically finishing off the other side of her hair while Ashleigh was trying to decide what jacket to wear. They had called Keeley, and discovered that she too had received the same email and arranged to meet her in fifteen minutes so they could go together.

"I bet the sly tart wasn't going to tell us," Emma said. "Bet she was going to go on her own."

"She'd push anyone out of the way to get what she wants," Ashleigh agreed, rifling through the wardrobe and pulling out possibles.

Emma grunted and peered around the room, making faces at what she considered to be minging tat.

"I love your room," she lied.

"Can you believe it?" her friend blurted. "Something finally

happening in this dead town! What if the celeb is a rock star or a footballer or someone off telly or films? What if we get papped? This could be the best night of my life! The start of something really big! Fame, Emma – proper fame!"

Emma looked at her own clothes. She hadn't dressed for something so potentially glitzy. All she had anticipated was a typical Friday night hanging round on the beach outside a bar, cadging Breezers off the lads. She watched as Ashleigh selected her best leather jacket, a cheap copy of something Beyonce had worn once, and then started to apply her Saturday-Night-in-Ipswich face so she could pass for seventeen or eighteen.

"I'm not going in this," Emma declared decisively. "I'm not gonna be the ugly one next to you and Keeley in your glad rags and prozzy paint that make you look better than you are. I'm going back home and changing."

"You look fine!" Ashleigh commented, hardly looking.

"I don't want to look 'fine'!" Emma screeched back at her. "'Fine' isn't going to get me in Hello, or a snog off a millionaire footballer so I can sell my story to the News of the bleedin' World, is it?"

"You don't have time to change. We've got to go if we're gonna be there on time."

"Then we'll have to be late! I am NOT going like this! I haven't even got my clubbing bra on!"

Ashleigh pouted her freshly glossed lips in the mirror. "I'm not waiting," she said flatly. "There's no way I'm missing a minute of this and Keeley won't neither. These celebs don't hang about. They do their appearance then jump back in their limos – it says so on Popbitch."

"Fine!" Emma shrieked, flinging the word back at her. "Some mate you are! You go with Keeley and I'll get a lift of my own. Selfish cow! And by the way, no amount of concealer is going to cover up those zits and you should've shaved your tache!"

She slammed the door and returned to her own house. The boys she had passed earlier jeered as they cycled by. They too had heard the news and were already heading to the Landguard Fort.

Emma sat in front of her small dressing table and worked quickly. She was about to phone around and beg a lift off someone when a text beeped in. It was an unknown and impossibly short number, but that fact was lost on her.

From: 7734
Get out of the house Emma!
The cops r coming 4 u!!!!!!

The girl swore, swept up her bag and coat and tore from the bedroom. Tottering down the road in her heels, she hurried as fast as she could and cut down the first turning to get off her street. She wondered if Ashleigh and Keeley had received similar texts. If this was about Sandra Dixon, the police would want to talk to them as well. She reached into her bag to call them. Then, remembering Ashleigh's attitude, spitefully decided to let the girl find out for

herself. It would be hilarious if a visit from the law caused Ashleigh to miss out on the biggest event to hit Felixstowe for years. Serve Keeley right as well.

Emma was so engrossed in relishing that thought that she didn't notice the car crawling along the road beside her.

"Oi! Oi!" called a voice as a hand reached out and flicked up her short skirt.

Emma swerved aside and yelled abuse as she fell into a hedge.

Kevin Stipe was leaning out of the passenger window of an old Fiesta, snorting like a delirious pig. Behind him, two more lads she recognised from school were hooting on the back seat.

"Morons!" she bawled.

"Where you going on your own?" Kevin asked. "Where's the rest of your posse?"

"Same place you're heading I expect!" she replied.

"Ha ha!" the boys laughed. "Get in, we'll give you a lift."

"No way, losers!" she refused.

"Take you forty minutes to walk there from here, Lemon Face," Kevin said. "You'll miss the best bits. Everyone's gonna be there."

Emma considered the offer quickly. She knew they were right, but she didn't want to be seen dead with any of them. They were spotty lads in hoodies and fleeces. But how else was she to get to the end of the peninsula, down the long View Point Road, on time? No chance in these heels. Besides, there was every likelihood the police would be out looking for her once they discovered she was not at home.

"Go on then," she said. "But I'm ditching you soon as we get there – understood? So don't get any ambitious ideas."

The rear door opened. "Get in, Sexy Legs."

"Err, in your dreams, mentals!" she snarled. "I'm not getting in the back of no car with you, Brian Eastland, and as for you, B.O. Humphries…"

"Shame!" they booed.

"Come on then," Kevin relented, getting out of the front seat and squeezing alongside the boys in the back. Emma didn't thank him, but clambered into his vacant place and slammed the door.

"What is that stink?" she complained, turning to the driver whose hood was pulled up over his head. "You lot drinking meths or something?"

"Here!" she cried in sudden recognition. "Danny Marlow! What you doing?"

"That's our Baz's overalls," he told her, meaning the smell. "He does decoratin'. I bunged them and the turps rags under the seat. Don't worry, you won't get paint on you."

"That's not what I meant!" she said. "What you doing in this motor?"

Behind her, Kevin tapped her on the head and leaned into the gap between them. "'S all right," he said. "It's his brother's car, innit. It's not nicked or nothing."

"But he's like, in our year – so that makes him the same age as us!"

Kevin guffawed. "See!" he laughed. "You are good at numbers – Sarky Baxter would be proud!"

Fifteen-year-old Danny revved the engine and, even as Emma hastily fastened her seat belt, the Fiesta roared away.

Conor Westlake had left the house as soon as he received the email from 7734. A mad night out would do him the world of good after today. The haunting image of Sandra Dixon's pale face glaring up at him was a memory he wanted to wash away, or at least dilute. The fridge at home was empty though so he hoped to bump into some of his mates down at the Landguard. None of them were answering their phones right now, but he was certain they'd be there.

A cold wind was blowing in from the North Sea and the darkening sky looked threatening. He pulled his hood up and continued walking. When he joined View Point Road, he saw that there were many other young people heading down the peninsula, like a great herd of thirsty beasts seeking a watering hole. Most were on foot, but there were also some cars driving past and groups of cyclists. Two figures were even weaving in and out on Rollerblades. The skateboarders who usually hung out near the cinema were here as well.

The road was long and, apart from a kink at the beginning and end, ran a tediously straight course. On the right, behind its high perimeter fence, was the container port. To the left, a caravan park that gave way to a stretch of sandhills and the sea.

Casting around, Connor guessed many of his fellow eager

pilgrims were older than him, but he saw a few who couldn't have been more than ten years old, dragging their older brothers or sisters forward. Here and there the odd parent stood out like a watchful pillar of negativity and disapproval and he hoped they would have the good taste to merge into the background at the Landguard. Tonight was no place for the olds.

He could feel a buzz of anticipation and excitement in the air. It was a carnival-like atmosphere. Some had brought torches and were waving them about, making patterns of light in front of them. Once the caravan park had been passed, they shone into the dark desolation that stretched between the sandhills and the road – startling the rabbits. Those sandhills formed a high, humpy spine all the way to the fort and Conor could see figures silhouetted against the sky on the ridge path, making their way along them. They were approaching the Landguard from the other side, to loop around it and join the rest of them in front of the gatehouse.

Everyone was hoping for something special that night, a new experience – a new thrill. There was a tremendous feeling of not knowing what was going to happen. It was almost quarter to nine and around the last bend in the road, the squat, solid bulk of the pentagonal fortress appeared in the distance. Conor half expected to see searchlights fanning the sky and sweeping dazzling discs over the fort's brickwork, but there was nothing, just the steady march of the people river heading towards it and the glittering expanse of the port next door.

The present fortress on Landguard Point is a hybrid spanning the centuries. The five-sided structure, with its bastions at every corner, was built in 1744, but heavily modified and refurbished in 1871. Yet there had been some type of fortification there since the days of Henry VIII, for the harbour is the deepest water between the Thames and the Humber and of strategic significance. If an enemy could land troops there, they would be dangerously close to London. In 1667 the last opposed invasion of England took place when the Dutch attacked the fort. Their aim was to burn the ships in the harbour. But the garrison stationed in the Landguard defended it brilliantly, despite being vastly outnumbered, and the Dutch forces were successfully repelled.

That night a new invasion looked to be taking place. As Conor drew closer to the fort, he was amazed at the numbers. There were thousands of people gathering there. They filled the small car park, stood on the mounded verges and pressed against the railings of the empty moat. Conor had only seen such crowds at football matches or gigs before and he clapped his hands appreciatively. It was going to be an unforgettable night.

Martin Baxter and Paul were also making their way down to the fort. They too were astonished at the volume of human traffic and Martin began to grow concerned. There didn't appear to be any safety measures in place, no crowd-control stewards anywhere. People were drifting across the road. There was no pavement, just a narrow strip of scrappy grass on one side. When cars beeped to get through, the pedestrians shouted and banged on the car bonnets before getting out of the way.

What Conor had found so exhilarating, Martin felt intimidated – even threatened – by.

"You know," he said to Paul. "I'm not sure this was such a good idea."

The boy couldn't disagree more. "It's brilliant!" he said. "We're almost there now – almost at the fort. We'll be able to see who it is!"

But Martin wasn't certain there was anything or anyone to see. There were no vans, no swanky cars and certainly no cameras. The Landguard looked the same as it always did at night – blank and brooding and more than a little sinister.

Martin pulled out his mobile and made a worried call to the police.

It was five to nine and the crowds who had got there early were getting shunted against the fences and railings by the relentless influx of people pouring down the road and up from the beach. Many of them were drinking.

Somewhere in there, Ashleigh and Keeley were bitching about Emma and peering up at the fort doubtfully.

"Why's it so dark though?" Ashleigh asked. "Where's the lights and stuff? Where's the music?"

"Must be inside," Keeley answered. "There'll probably be a big blast of sound and them big doors'll open and it'll all start."

"Hey – who you pushing!" Ashleigh yelled as someone stumbled into her.

"This is literally crammed and I mean it," Keeley grumbled.

At two minutes to nine, Martin pulled Paul to the very edge of the

road and refused to go any further. People jostled and shoved by them. It was getting alarming now.

"But Martin!" the boy cried. "We're so close!"

"No," he said firmly. "This is madness. We're going back."

Paul stared at him beseechingly, but Martin would not be persuaded. The eleven-year-old caught himself about to whine and stopped it immediately. Carol had raised him not to be one of those people who pestered and sulked to get their own way. He didn't like Martin's decision, but he had to accept it.

Trying to walk against the oncoming flow was almost impossible though. The best they could do was stand by the edge and let people pass until the numbers began to thin.

Conor checked the time on his phone. It was dead on nine.

The assembled multitude halted and every face was trained on the Landguard Fort's stout walls. It felt like the countdown to New Year. They held their breath and expected a fanfare, fireworks, an explosion of light and sound and colour. Flashes sparkled from phone cameras and they waited.

Nothing.

Murmurs of discontent began to ripple through the massive crowd. Someone began a slow handclap and others joined in. Voices chanted, "Why are we waiting…?"

Still nothing.

"This is so wrong!" Ashleigh moaned.

"Where's the celeb and paps?" Keeley griped. "I am sincerely freezing my legs off here."

There was a rumble of thunder overhead.

The people still on the beach who could not see that nothing was happening around the front of the fort were getting restless and resentful. They started pushing and trying to get on to the path. Others played their own music from their phones. Tempers began to flare. The expectation and excitement had completely gone, replaced by a sense of being cheated, and people were now feeling angry.

Conor turned around and thrust himself back through the crush. This was a washout, a hoax – someone's lame idea of a joke. He wasn't going to waste another minute of his precious Friday night squashed here. He barged through, none too gently, standing on heels and kicking ankles. Someone roared in his ear and he felt a thump in his back. The fighting began.

It spread through the vast crowd in a violent wave and panic took over.

Ashleigh was slammed against Keeley as a lad blundered into her, felled by a headbutt. The girl kicked him then swung her elbow into his stunned face and broke his nose.

"I'm leavin'!" Keeley cried above the riot. She took her perfume from her handbag and held it in front of her, like a vampire hunter with a bottle of holy water, and sprayed it in the eyes of anyone who came too close or whoever she didn't like the look of.

Fists and bottles were flung in every direction.

Walking back along the road, Martin and Paul heard the fierce shouts and screams behind and they turned to see the furious mob that the crowd had become.

"Hell!" Martin said as it spilled back on to the road and a bottle came sailing through the air to explode into white dust on the tarmac. "We've got to get out of here, fast." Taking Paul's hand, the two ran into the nature reserve and across to the sandhills.

Chaos and aggression raged behind them. He could hear children crying in that seething rabble, but the parents and older siblings who came with them managed to get them out of the brawl and they too came fleeing on to the dark sands.

Conor Westlake dodged the punches aimed at his head, but when he felt a kick to the back of his thigh, he whirled round and retaliated. The gangs were here tonight. He had seen them with their hoods pulled up and saw the bottles of golden liquid in their hands. He battled his way through the thickest heart of that thronging sea, wrenching at coats and smacking hands away from his face.

Ashleigh and Keeley were locked in the very middle of it. Ashleigh had lost a shoe. The perfume bottle had been dashed from Keeley's grasp and her bag had been ripped from her shoulder. It was impossible to move unless it was by the current of the crowd. Then Ashleigh felt something wet and heavy on her head. At first she thought the storm had broken, but then she heard the braying laughter and another bottle was tipped over her. The two girls suddenly saw they were hemmed in by one of the gangs and litres of vegetable oil were being chucked and squirted at them.

Ashleigh screeched and the stuff splashed into her open mouth. She choked then lashed out and clawed the lad in front of her. Seeing a gap, she ploughed through it, retching and dragging Keeley after her.

A dozen plastic bottles went spinning after them, spilling their contents as they flew through the air. People began to slither on the oily road and when other idiots saw that, they lobbed their bottles as well.

Danny Marlow's foot was down on the accelerator and the Fiesta left curves of rubber behind as they turned the corner into View Point Road.

"Slow down," Emma told him. "I want to get there in one piece."

"I'm built for speed, baby!" Danny bragged, turning the radio on and switching to fourth gear.

"So I've heard," she said witheringly.

Queen's 'Bohemian Rhapsody' came on and Kevin reached through sharply to turn it right up.

"Do the Wayne's World thing! Do the Wayne's World thing!" he shouted, wagging his head up and down far too early in the song.

Brian and B.O. joined in. Emma mouthed a string of expletives as she pressed her forehead against the passenger window and took a cigarette from her bag. She lit it and blew a stream of smoke from the side of her mouth.

"I'm stuck in a car with the Muppets," she muttered.

"I like a woman who smokes," Danny said. "It's dead sophis."

He's just a poor boy, from a poor family…

He took his left hand off the wheel and clumsily placed his clammy palm on Emma's thigh.

"OFF!" she demanded instantly.

"Don't be like that," he said.

"If you don't move your sweaty mitt, right now, I swear…!"

Danny didn't hear her. He was staring ahead. There were countless people swarming around the Landguard. He had never imagined it would be so engulfed with them. But something wasn't right. It didn't look like the fantastic happening the email had promised.

"What's going…?"

Emma didn't let him finish the question. With a vindictive smile, she touched the back of his hand with the glowing cigarette.

"OWWW!!!" he yelled, snatching the hand away.

The cigarette was knocked from her fingers. It disappeared between the seats. The car lurched across the road.

"Watch where you're going!" she shouted.

The boys in the back had stopped headbanging and Kevin was peering forward. "That's a fight!" he hooted. "There's thousands of them!"

Suddenly a siren began to blare and blue lights were bouncing in the rear-view mirror.

"It's the fuzz!" Kevin laughed. "Are they coming for you, Danny, or to stop the barney? Ha ha ha ha!"

Emma wondered if they were coming for her.

And then it happened. The turpentine-soaked rags under the seat burst into flames and the boys in the back yelled in fear. Emma thrashed her legs wildly and scrabbled with her seat belt.

"Let me out!" she screamed.

99

"Stop the car!" the boys bawled.

…No! We will not let you go!

Danny was flustered, confused and petrified. He didn't know what to do. The police lights panicked him. The flames terrified him and the voices of his passengers were deafening. The blaring song seemed to be mocking him. Instead of pressing the brake, he reached for the gear stick, but a ribbon of flame scorched his fingers and he threw his weight against the wheel. His foot slammed the accelerator to the floor.

The Fiesta's headlights came bleaching along the peninsula.

Martin Baxter and Paul were standing on the high path of the sandhills. It commanded an excellent view. The port at night looked like a gritty space dock from one of Martin's sci-fi movies and he had always thought those cranes resembled Martian war machines from War of the Worlds. On the road below them, they saw the car go streaking by, its occupants screaming, smoke flooding from the open windows, and that too seemed part of a film – with a rock soundtrack by Queen. It was so unreal.

Dripping and sodden with vegetable oil, Keeley and Ashleigh came staggering and slipping from the thuggish riot as the headlights raced toward them. Caught in the glare, the crowd turned and saw the car hurtling straight on. Anger turned to fear and they fell back like a tide down the shingle, but not all were quick enough.

"Stop the car!" Kevin was shouting, shaking Danny's shoulder.

Danny saw the blanched faces of the horror-stricken people ahead and he finally found the brake. He stamped on it hard.

But the car did not stop. Its tyres had crunched over half empty plastic bottles and they were skating over the spilled oil.

The Fiesta spun in the road. Danny heaved the steering wheel to the right, but it was no good. The vehicle went careering into the people-skittles.

Stark faces flashed by the windows. There were thuds and other, more dreadful noises. Freddie Mercury was raging out the lyrics and the headbanging truly began.

From his vantage point up on the ridge, Martin saw it all. He drew Paul to him and wouldn't let him watch.

Finally the Fiesta crunched into a parked car and stopped dead. The night was filled with screaming. The maths teacher wondered what he should do. If he went back there, would he be of any use? The two police cars were already on the scene, the officers leaping out to give assistance.

Conor Westlake had dragged a woman out of the way as the Fiesta went crashing into the other car. To him it seemed as if the world had slowed right down and he was viewing the whole horrendous scene in slow motion and silence. Then he saw Emma Taylor's face at the smoky window and the noise and clamour came rushing back in. The boy dashed forward.

He yanked the door open and hauled the girl out. She collapsed on the ground and there was Kevin Stipe, crawling out of the back, trying to help his friends out after him.

Emma was shrieking.

"You see to them, yeah!" Conor shouted at a group of staring hoodies. "Get the driver out!" He put his arm round Emma, hoisted her to her feet and led her away from the burning Fiesta.

Suddenly there was a flash behind them and the car exploded. The fireball climbed high into the dark sky. People were running away blindly, and so were Conor and the girl stumbling along beside him.

"Dear God," Martin breathed. How could this be real? Surely it should only be a gruesome special-effect sequence in an action movie? It should have chromed Terminator skeletons stalking through those flames, shooting laser bolts from their guns, or alien saucers hovering overhead.

No, this was genuinely happening. This was real life; it wasn't just fantasy.

A second larger explosion shook the peninsula. The other car's petrol tank had been full.

"Flash... and mob..." Martin observed in a sickened, cracked whisper.

The email had not lied. That night had been a blast and would indeed be on the news. If Martin had allowed himself to believe in such things at that point, he would have realised who the mystery celebrity had been, walking unseen among those young people that hour, choreographing the entire show.

Yet this was just the diversion; the main event of the night was about to take place in the container port.

Lightning jagged across the black heavens.

And the Holy Enchanter had to prove himself worthy to rule whilst his Lord was in exile and so he suffered the Great Ordeal that no other had ever endured, save for the Dawn Prince himself. And thus was their contract made, writ large upon a page that could never be cast away, or misplaced, or stolen by the Jockey, for he could work much mischief with such a deed. And so the Holy Enchanter declared himself the Ismus and his reign in his Lord's stead commenced, with neither challenge nor question, and the new order began.

8

INSIDE THE METAL container on the back of Tesco Charlie's lorry, Jezza`s eyes roved round his disciples. The spectral light in there was courtesy of three cheap LED caravan lamps stuck to the cold, corrugated sides. Everyone had dutifully obeyed his summons.

Queenie and Manda, "the floating girlfriends", as he termed them, were having a whale of a time. Queenie loved hanging with the group: it made her feel younger than her forty something years, but then so did the jet-black hair dye she anointed herself with – and the biker-chick outfits she wore. Pushing her hands up through her unnaturally raven hair, she gyrated when the container shook and made a stuttering dance of her attempts to keep from falling over. Manda was her plumper friend who had abandoned trying to keep up with Queenie's skimpy dress sense and just as skimpy waistline long ago. Manda was currently spending much of her time with Miller and it was him she held on to when the container juddered. Richard Miller didn't seem too happy about that because he wanted to look at his copy of Dancing Jacks, but she kept getting in the way.

Jezza looked from them to Dave. He was an unlikely member of their varied little band. He was an impressionable nineteen and looked up to Jezza in most things. Jezza in turn enjoyed the gradual kneading of his receptive, doughy mind, feeding it the yeast of new ideas that Dave had never dreamed of and couldn't quite comprehend.

Howie and Tommo were sitting on some of the charcoal bags stacked at the end of the container. The tattooist was trying to read more of the strange children's book by the ghostly light of one of the LED lamps. His head was nodding, partly from the motion of the container, but mainly from the rhythm of the words on the pages. He was lost in the world of Austerly Fellows.

At his side, the shaking and lurching about made Tommo feel nauseous. One of the bags had split and the disgorged briquettes were rolling up and down in front of him, making the sensation even

worse. Close by were three large water carriers that Jezza had put on board and the sloshing noises they made didn't help steady Tommo's stomach either. At least he wasn't anywhere near Miller's backside though. He raised his eyes and stared at the other thing the others had brought back from the house.

Shiela was staring at it too. It dominated the centre of the container and it frightened her.

She had spent the better part of an hour waiting at the tattoo parlour alone and hated every minute. She wasn't sure why, but those crates of books unsettled her so she took herself to the rear of the shop and reclined on the tattooist's chair. Yet the thought of the books on the other side of the partition began to gnaw away at her mind and she couldn't stop thinking about them. For reasons she was unable to explain to herself, Shiela began to wonder what they were doing. Were they still in the crates, or had they got out somehow? It was a ridiculous notion, but she couldn't stop herself from glancing over her shoulder more than once.

Eventually she could bear it no longer and had to return to the front of the shop to make sure they were still present in their big wooden boxes. What was it about these strange old books? Why did they fill her thoughts so much? Why did they make her so uneasy? What had happened earlier when Jezza had read from them? Why were the men behaving so weirdly?

Looking at the sofa on which she had flung her copy, Shiela's eyelids drooped. The next thing she knew she was sitting there, the green and cream book in her hand, and she was turning to the first page. She experienced a rush of excitement and felt safe and content. The tatty sofa became a stone bench beneath a castle window, strewn with sumptuous velvet cushions. Golden wire was twisted in her braided hair, a tear-shaped piece of amethyst dangled at her brow and a heavy jewelled brooch was fastened to her bodice. Somewhere in the castle the minstrels were playing; she could hear strains of their music drifting through the galleries. She gazed out of the window that looked down on to the courtyard. The silver fountain was tinkling sweetly, the cascading crystal waters sparkling in the shafts of evening sunlight.

And there was the Queen of Spades, dressed richly in silks and velvets of the deepest midnight blue and studded with sapphire gemstones. Hurrying after was her dull-witted ally and confidante, the Queen of Hearts. As usual, the Queen of Spades was casting around, making sure no one was within earshot, and whispered something to her. The Under Queens were always full of intrigue, Shiela found herself thinking, and that wily one was the worst. What new conspiracies or gossip was she disseminating now? Shiela should speak to the Ismus about her, or maybe the Harlequin Priests could point to a sombre colour on their robes when they...

A car pulled up outside the window and Shiela jolted back on the sofa. Breathing hard, she looked down at the book in her hands and dropped it as if it had burned her. Then she jumped up and hurried to the door.

"All right, She-luv!" Queenie had greeted, carefully negotiating herself out of the car in her ultra skinny jeans. "You OK?

You're white as Manda's bingo wings."

"Where's Miller?" Manda had asked, slamming the other door and looking round. "His bike's here."

Shiela had stared at them, speechless, trying to understand what had just happened.

Then there came the sound of a motorbike and Dave came roaring up on his Honda.

"Here's Babyface!" Queenie had cried, throwing her arms wide in welcome and clattering her acrylic nails over his crash helmet before he had a chance to remove it.

The VW was not far behind. But... there was something tied to the roof rack. Something large and unfamiliar, Shiela could not make out what it was. A Gothic sledge? Before they could ask, Tesco Charlie's lorry came lumbering along the road.

"Well met!" Jezza had greeted everyone with a flamboyant bow. "Now let's get this into Charlie's lovely truck."

By the time Tommo had arrived in a borrowed estate car with everything he had been instructed to fetch, the 'thing' had been manoeuvred off the camper's roof rack and into the huge metal container.

Now, in the phantom light of the white LEDs, Shiela stared at its skeletal frame and feared it.

They had been ordered to remain silent. Tesco Charlie was uncharacteristically forceful about that point. If he was going to smuggle them into the port undetected, they had to be quieter than mice doing a sponsored silence.

Queenie found this rule particularly hard to adhere to. She deplored the quiet and had to plug any silence with noise and even left her television on when she left her flat because she loathed coming back to a mausoleum.

Dancing to tunes in her head, she had wriggled and swayed all the way from the tattoo parlour towards the port entrance and had to be warned by Jezza when she got carried away and started drumming on the metal side. This was a great adventure for her and she was going to live it to the max.

"We must be nearly there," Jezza said softly as they felt the lorry slow down and eventually stop.

They could not hear the bantering exchange between Charlie and the security guard at the gate, but it was soon over and the lorry was off again. It drove into the container port and continued going for what seemed an interminably long time before finally coming to rest. The engine stopped with a shudder and all eyes turned to Jezza.

"Now we wait for the signal," he told them.

Dave looked at his watch. It was a few minutes past nine. They didn't have long to wait. Even inside the container they heard the Fiesta exploding. Tesco Charlie left his cab and began unlocking the doors at the end of the container.

The cool night air blew in.

"How did you manage that?" the long-haired driver asked, peering in at them through his thick spectacles. "It was enormous – it…"

The second explosion drowned whatever he was about to say

next. He ran around the side of the lorry and saw the fireball boiling up to the night clouds. Jezza sprang down and joined him. The fire danced in his eyes.

Charlie had driven his great lorry deep into the massive port. Huge containers just like the one that had smuggled them in were all around, stacked five high. Tommo clambered out next, glad to be back on solid ground, and he recovered rapidly.

"Like ants in a Lego set," he chirped, gazing about him.

A streak of lightning ripped through the darkness and the thunder rolled. Then sirens started – lots of them. The port police were responding to the emergency outside the Landguard Fort. So too were the fire engines and the ambulances. In a matter of moments, they were all speeding through the gates.

"What's going on out there?" Shiela asked as she drew alongside the others. "Is that screaming?"

Howie was holding the book to his chest. "The flock is bleating," he muttered. "They are lost and abandoned and searching for the way. I shall paint this night, I shall paint…"

A savage crack of lightning directly overhead caused everyone to look up. There were sparks spitting from the lamp towers.

"They're going to have to buy new cameras tomorrow," Jezza said simply. "Let's get on with what we came here for."

Miller, Dave and Charlie heaved the great Gothic-looking object out of the container and set it down the right way up. A reverberating clang went echoing between the container canyons.

Shiela approached it warily. It was a great metal chair, no – it was more like a throne. She wandered around it, careful not to get too close. There was something unpleasant, almost malevolent, about it, not just because it was heavy and ugly or because it was too large for a normal-sized person to sit on comfortably. Crafted from fancy cast-iron work, with curling fronds and interlocking patterns, it seemed more than what it appeared to be, as though it had another purpose. Each arm was formed to be like a cage, so was the seat and the high back.

"It's horrible," she said.

Queenie had no such misgivings. She was already using it as a prop to dance suggestively around. Manda had found the beers and was necking her first while Tommo brandished a plastic bag and brought out a packet of burgers and some baps.

"Let's get this party cooking!" he said.

"Don't be a cretin all your life," Jezza told him severely. "Chuck that crap away and get the coals."

The lightning continued to crackle overhead.

"I've never seen an electrical storm like this," Charlie declared. He lifted his hand and viewed it through his thick lenses. The hairs were standing on end. "The air is charged with static!"

"Gather around the Waiting Throne," Jezza told everyone. "Not too close, and keep away from the containers. It might get a bit … frisky up there."

"Ow!" Manda cried as a whisker of blue light leaped from the can to her lip. She dropped it and the beer went foaming over the floor.

110

"What's going on?" Miller called.

"We're just charging up," Jezza answered. "This is the best place for it – all this wonderful metal, like a massive aerial."

"Tuning into what?" Shiela asked.

The man smiled at her. "Whom," he said.

"I love it!" Queenie shouted, tingling as she stroked the arm of the iron chair.

"Ow!" Manda cried again. This time her necklace was throwing out millipede legs of energy and she removed it hastily. It jumped and twitched on the ground.

"I advise you all to get rid of any jewellery now," Jezza told them.

Bracelets and rings were hurriedly taken off and Charlie had to lose his glasses. Shiela could feel her hair lifting and there was an unpleasant tang in her mouth.

"Like licking a battery," Tommo said, voicing her own thoughts.

He had been bringing out the bags of charcoal. Now Jezza ripped them open and, taking one to the chair, twisted one of the designs in the ironwork. The top of an arm hinged open. It took three bags to fill the space beneath. Then he went to the other arm and did the same there.

The lightning continued to flash and split the sky.

Shiela had been staring up at the giant cranes. The electricity was leaping between them, arcing across the port in a spectacular display.

She could not understand what was happening. Why were they really here? When she lowered her eyes, Jezza had filled the seat and the back of the chair, with only one bag to spare. The throne was now packed with charcoal.

"Get the water carriers," he ordered Tommo. "I want them close." Then he gestured for everyone to stand clear.

"I don't like this," Manda said. "I thought we were going to have a laugh. This isn't a laugh. It's mad."

Miller reached to hold her hand. A spark flew across and they jumped apart.

"I want to go home!" she cried.

"Muzzle her," Jezza snapped. "You should be grovelling on your faces to be here, to witness the contract."

Shiela agreed with Manda, but Queenie's eyes were sparkling. She felt more alive than she had in years; she didn't want this to end. She lifted her hands in the air and dared the lightning to strike her, laughing hysterically.

Dave stared at her. Filaments of energy were branching off her body as she danced. He didn't know whether to be terrified or surrender himself to the experience and see what happened. Tommo could feel his hair crackling with the static. It tickled him and he hopped about manically. Spiders of light came leaping from his arms and legs.

Tesco Charlie could barely make out what was happening. It was a blur of brilliant blue zigzags and shapes, but he thought it was amazing and threw back his head to yell out his delight.

"Begin," Jezza said to Howie.

The tattooist had been very quiet and now, when they looked at him, they saw that his piercings were spitting with strands of flickering blue flame and yet he seemed oblivious to it.

"And so the Holy Enchanter dared what only the Dawn Prince before had done," he said, reading out loud from the book. "For there was no other way to bring order to the warring Court. With great courage, he stepped up to the Waiting Throne and proved that only he was worthy of becoming the Ismus. Only he could rule in his Lord's absence and so the pact was made and sealed with fire!"

On that last word there was a deafening clap of thunder and a bolt of lightning came shooting down. It slammed into the iron chair. There was a shrill, razoring chime and the coals within exploded in flames.

Everyone cried out and covered their faces. Shiela turned to run, but the alley between the containers was alive with electricity. The forking streaks were rebounding from wall to wall, forming an impassable and lethal fence.

Manda was sobbing into her hands, but Howie's voice was louder.

"From that day the Holy Enchanter's word was law," he declaimed. The studs in his bottom lip were wreathed with cold fire that snaked throughout his gingery beard. "And none who beheld that contract dared conspire against him! His authority was absolute."

The coals within the iron chair were blazing and beginning to glow a cherry red. Then Shiela realised what was about to happen.

"No," she breathed in horror. But she couldn't stop it. Though her mind told her it was insane, she knew this was meant to be. This was how it must be. Howie's voice was fogging her judgement. She thought she was back in that castle, looking up at the throne, and the entire Court was gathered around them, holding their breath with fear and wonder.

Jezza removed his leather jacket and slipped off his boots. Howie continued reading from the book and still Queenie danced.

Then the rain began. The iron chair hissed and the flames died within the charcoal. The electric forces around them dimmed and were extinguished. Jezza was naked now. With his head bowed, he approached the Waiting Throne.

"Don't!" Shiela begged, her reason struggling to the fore. "You'll die!"

Her boyfriend did not respond, but Howie turned to her and in a solemn, commanding voice said, "Have faith, Labella."

And then, as the rain teemed down, Miller stepped forward, all expression gone from his face. The burly man lifted Jezza by the waist and lowered him on to the scorching metal of the chair and Jezza pressed his bare back against it.

Shiela covered her ears. His shrieks were louder than the thunder that boomed across the harbour. She saw him clench his teeth so tightly that every vein stood out across his neck and chest and he placed his arms on those of the chair. Another howl of thunder – or was it merely him?

Miller bowed and walked backwards.

"Enough!" Shiela screamed, breaking through the enchantment that had smothered her. "That's enough!"

Darting forward, she seized Jezza's hands and pulled him clear.

He went rolling on the ground, curled up in a ball, choking with his pain-filled cries.

When she saw the state of his back, she grabbed one of the water carriers and emptied it over him.

"Call an ambulance!" she shouted. "Hurry!"

"No!" Howie answered.

"He'll die!" she yelled. "Look at him – look at that!"

"It's beautiful," the tattooist said admiringly. "Such exquisite work."

The girl stared at him for an instant. Had everyone gone crazy? Howie was normally so level-headed and sensible. She reached for her phone and was about to dial 999 when a trembling hand knocked it from her grip.

"No hospitals!" Jezza struggled to say. "No doctors! I must… endure it alone."

"Jezza!" she protested. "You need help."

"There is no Jezza!" he screamed back at her. Then he collapsed and lay sprawled face down on the floor, the rain lashing across his body.

Shiela looked round at the others. They were staring at the man at her feet. The throne had seared strange symbols and ancient writing into his flesh.

"The contract is made," Howie announced. "Lift the Ismus. We must bear him from this place."

With the utmost reverence, Miller, Tommo and Dave approached the unconscious man. Tesco Charlie had put his glasses back on and brought a blanket from his cab. They covered the Ismus with it and gently carried him inside the container on the back of the lorry.

Shiela watched in disbelief. Even Manda and Queenie were playing along with it now, walking behind them like overawed worshippers.

Howie emptied the other two water carriers over the Waiting Throne and clouds of steam billowed upwards.

"Come, Labella," he said, emerging from the white vapour with a beatific smile widening in his beard. "Rejoice. We have a Lord to rule over us and govern the Dancing Jacks. When the Ismus recovers from the Great Ordeal and arises, order shall be restored."

Shiela could not comprehend what had happened that night. But she knew they had all taken a step towards something sinister and final and there was no going back.

9

"IT'S ALL QUIET here today, but on Friday night, right behind me, outside the historic Landguard Fort here in Felixstowe, tragedy occurred – a tragedy that claimed the lives of many local young people. At nine o'clock last night several thousand were gathered here to take part in a supposed flash mob. Each of them had been invited via an anonymous email that the police are currently trying to trace. Details are not completely clear yet, but something sparked a riot and, while that was going on, a car came hurtling down this approach road, seemingly out of control. It skidded then crashed into another car, parked over there in that car park, and exploded. The second car followed moments after. You can only imagine the terror, the panic."

A cool female voice interrupted.

"Have the police made any further statement as to how the car came to be out of control?"

The man on the screen shook his head. "Not as yet," he said. "The forensic teams are still combing the wreckage and the area, as you can see behind me. But eyewitnesses we've spoken to say there was smoke coming out of the car even before the crash. Others claim to have seen flames."

"Thank you, Justin, now we can head over to Lyndsay Draymore outside Felixstowe General where the injured and the dying were taken last night."

The image of the suited man standing upon the sandhill, with the road behind him, was replaced by a smart young woman, in front of a red-brick, arched entrance.

"Lyndsay, what more can you tell us about this tragic incident?"

"Well, Tara, medical staff have been working round the clock, through the night here. I understand there was something in the region of a hundred and twenty casualties, impact injuries and burns being the majority of cases that had to be dealt with."

"And I gather the death toll has now risen again?"

"Yes, within the last hour, it has been announced that two more have died as a result of their injuries, bringing the total now up to thirty-eight – with five more still in intensive care and fighting for their lives. An unbelievable loss of life in this usually quiet seaside town, here in Suffolk."

Behind her a nurse emerged from the entrance; she looked tired and drained. Someone behind the camera must have alerted Lyndsay because she turned and almost ran over to her, eager for a word from the front line.

"Can you tell me what it's been like in there?" she asked, shoving a microphone forward.

A startled Carol Thornbury looked quizzically down the lens that came after.

"How is the mood of the medical staff?" the reporter asked. "What can you tell us? How are the families of the injured feeling at this time?"

"Are you bloody stupid or something?" Carol snapped. "How do you think they're feeling? Get that ruddy camera out of my face or I'll give you a colonoscopy with it! And keep this area clear!"

Carol barged impatiently past the camera crew, leaving a thick-skinned Lyndsay smiling benignly. "As you can see," she continued without a blink, "the atmosphere here is tense and tempers are running high. This is Lyndsay Draymore, Felixstowe General, for BBC News."

The picture switched back to the anchorperson, perched informally against the news desk, casually displaying the shapely legs that had served her so well in Strictly Come Dancing the year before.

"And we'll have more of that terrible incident in Suffolk on our main bulletin at six," she purred. "You can tweet us your thoughts and condolences at the address at the bottom of the screen. Now over to our showbiz correspondent to see which pop diva has lost a size, shredding twenty pounds thanks to a new diet from…"

Martin turned off the TV. "Good on you, Carol," he said proudly.

"She looked shattered," Paul commented.

"Must have been a horrible night there," Martin answered. "I'll run a bath for her and do some toast. She'll want something before she crashes…"

He flinched, not believing his unthinking choice of word, and the horror of the previous night rushed in again. He and Paul had returned home in a kind of dream state. The night had been alive with sirens and whirling lights and they had both fallen asleep in front of the rolling news.

The phone rang. It was Carol's mother.

"Hello, Jean. Yes, I saw her on the news just now too. No, television always makes you look fatter than you are. Yes, it's been awful. No, I don't know how many were from the school, they haven't released that information yet. Paul is fine. I'll tell her you rang, soon as she gets back. OK, you too, Jean. Bye now."

It was the second time she had rung. The first was at half six that morning when she had first heard about it on the radio. Other people had called: Barry Milligan had sounded irritable and hungover and his mood wasn't helped by the fact that the rugby game had been cancelled out of respect. Gerald Benning, Paul's piano teacher, had checked to make sure he was safe, and so had members of the family who hadn't been in touch for years. It was positively ghoulish.

When Carol came through the door, she gave her son the biggest,

120

chest-crushing hug he'd ever had. She had worked an extra four hours over her shift. Her face looked grey and drawn and her hollow eyes seemed to attest to the things she had seen in the casualty department.

Martin passed her a cup of tea, which she took gratefully, but refused the toast.

"I couldn't," she stated.

Neither Martin nor her son uttered a word while she drank it. Then, cradling the cup in her hands, she said, "I never want to go through another night like that as long as I live."

"You were just on telly," Paul ventured. "You were fierce!"

"That stupid, stupid woman. Why do they ask such inane, crass questions?"

"It's what they do," Martin said.

"I almost punched her, but you know what stopped me? I knew it'd help her flaming career and I'd end up on some cheap blooper programme that'd be repeated for the rest of my life."

She closed her eyes and seemed to sag.

"There's a bath waiting," Martin told her. He had never seen her like this before. Carol always left the grimness of the job at the hospital and was able to detach herself from it. Not this time. She was too limp to manage the bath. She just wanted to flop into bed.

Halfway up the stairs, she stopped and said, in a small, defeated voice, "I recognised lots of them. Some had been your pupils, Martin. A few of them still are... or were."

Across town, Emma Taylor sat on her bed, staring blankly at the wallpaper. Conor had gone with her in the ambulance. Both had been too stunned to say anything. In casualty Emma had been checked over: superficial burns to the back of her legs, which had been appropriately dressed and, due to the volume of more serious cases coming in, she had been discharged. Conor had been treated for the cuts and bruises he had sustained in the fight, but the sights that wheeled by while he waited never left him.

Emma's usually disinterested parents had been loud and vocal in their sympathy, but of zero use and were more keen to find out if any compensation could be claimed. For the first time, the girl had not milked a situation to her utmost advantage. Instead she went quietly to her room, plugged her earphones in and replayed those moments over and over in her head. She hadn't slept all night.

When her mobile rang, she didn't hear it, but saw the flashing of the screen. She stared at it like it was something new and unrecognisable. The number was certainly unfamiliar. She picked it up and pulled out one earphone.

"Who's that?"

"Conor."

"How'd you get my number?"

"Nicky Dobbs gave it me. I knew you two used to go out…"

"Nicky Dobbs is a waste of space."

"So I thought I'd…"

"What do you want?"

"About, you know. I can't talk to anyone here about it. They won't be able to understand."

"Well, I don't want to talk about it."

"But you were in that car – you know what happened. The police are going to start asking…"

Emma bristled. "Are you going to grass me up?" she said.

"Others will have seen you in it."

"They was too busy running for their lives. Only you and me know I was in that car. Danny, Kevin, B.O. and Brian won't be telling no one now, will they? They're burned and gone. We both saw Kevin flapping about on fire. So you just keep your trap shut, yeah?"

There was a silence.

"You hear me?"

"I'm not sure," Conor said at length. "I can't get my head straight."

"Then try harder!" she told him. "Don't you think I've been through enough?"

"Yeah, course."

"But you want to set the law on me as well? I wasn't even driving!"

"No. I dunno. I can't think."

Emma ground her teeth. "Look," she said, "there's no way I'll be let out of this house today. They're useless, but think I need to stop in so they can claim extra for the trauma. I'll work on them tomorrow and meet you then, yeah? We'll talk it through, yeah?"

"Tomorrow? I'm not sure I can wait…"

"Just sit on it for one more bloody day, will you!"

"OK, OK."

"Down by the boot fair then, about three."

"The boot fair?"

"Where else is busy on a Sunday here? I'm not going to traipse up a lonely beach with you. It's not a date."

"I wasn't asking for one!"

"See you then, then."

"Umm… and Emma…?"

"What?"

"I'm sorry about Keeley and Ashleigh."

The girl's mouth dried. "Yeah," she said. "Thanks." She ended the call and closed her eyes. Images of her two friends caught in the Fiesta's headlights reared in her memory.

Emma snapped her eyes open and continued to stare at the wallpaper.

The rest of that day passed quietly for the shocked town.

On Sunday the papers were full of it. There were sensationalised eyewitness accounts from whoever they could get to talk about the incident locally. Half of those interviewed hadn't even been there. There was a two-page spread with a dynamic graphic of View Point Road and the progress of the car along it, with arrows indicating where the vehicle was going to crash and explode. There were photographs of the deceased, each taken at some point the previous

124

year – all young, all smiling. Danny Marlow had been singled out as the cause of the disaster, but none of his family, especially his brother, would give an interview so the papers had to make do with the gossip they had wheedled out of neighbours and unnamed "close family friends".

As well as all that, there were the usual scaremongering articles on the dangers of the Internet. Sporadic, starred panels voiced the opinions of waning celebrities whose publicity agents had eagerly volunteered their clients' condoling sound bites about the tragedy, even though most of them had no idea where Felixstowe actually was. A photo shoot had been hastily arranged for a teen pop sensation, coyly wearing a firefighter's helmet and little else, to show her support for those brave heroes who battled the flames, while also plugging her latest single, the release of which had been specially brought forward and was available on iTunes that very day.

Barry Milligan read through every paper and cradled his head in his hands. The death toll had now risen to forty-one. Eight of them attended his school. A further twenty-three had been former pupils and twenty-seven were still in hospital. Special services were being held in churches across town that morning and he had sat and prayed with everyone else, to whatever might be listening.

Then he drove to the school. There was an emergency meeting of governors and department heads at 2 p.m. and he wanted to be the first one there. He needed to be in his office to sort out the details for tomorrow. As he approached, he saw that floral tributes and messages were already being laid outside the gate. There was another reporter hanging about, ambushing groups of sobbing girls. News editors loved intrusive images of raw grief. Snot and tears are real attention-grabbers. Barry slipped by them and entered the building.

A school after hours and during the weekend is a strange, lonely place. It needs children to bring it to life and give it purpose. Standing in the corridor, which echoed and smelled of floor polish, Barry wondered how he was going to get through Monday's assembly tomorrow morning.

The meeting only lasted an hour; no one was in the mood to argue and everything was settled. There would be counselling available for any child who needed it throughout the week. It was going to be a rough time and like nothing Barry had ever experienced in his professional life. Downing Street had even been in touch. The Prime Minister would like to come and deliver his condolences in person and give a sympathetic yet inspirational speech to the students. Only one discreet camera crew need be present, the press office assured him. Barry had vetoed that immediately in very colourful language. The week was going to be difficult enough without an unctuous Prime Minister and his entourage having to be considered. The Headmaster's sole duty was to the children. Publicity-hungry politicians seeking to boost their ratings in the opinion polls by exploiting such a tragedy didn't even figure. It made Barry furious.

After the meeting and making the necessary phone calls and doing everything he possibly could, Barry returned home. He donned his favourite rugby shirt and spent the rest of the day with a bottle of twelve-year-old malt. The pubs were infested with reporters, sniffing for grime.

The rest of Felixstowe could not remain indoors any longer. The grieving town needed company: they needed to see familiar faces, to stop and talk, to share their sorrows and disbelief and give thanks if their immediate circle had not suffered a loss.

So that Sunday afternoon saw unusually high numbers wandering down to the seafront. They chatted in hushed, respectful tones while they walked past the cheerfully painted beach huts and deserted amusements, and found their steps gravitated towards the peninsula. But they demurred at completing that solemn journey just yet. Instead they stopped at the Martello tower along the way and browsed through the boot fair that was held there every Sunday, floods permitting, on the surrounding wasteland.

Conor Westlake was sitting on the low sea wall in front of the boot fair. His face still bore the discoloured marks of Friday's fight, but they looked worse than they felt.

The gulls were floating above, shrieking mournfully and swooping down on any scraps that the chip-eaters flung their way. The sea was grey and featureless, except for the movement of the enormous container ships that sailed from the dock around the infamous headland. They were so immense they looked like drifting cubist islands. Conor checked his phone for messages, but there were none. He swivelled about on the wall and looked across the car roofs and bustling boot fair.

The tall, solid, round shape of the Martello tower dominated everything. It was one of many built during the Napoleonic Wars for an invasion that never happened and was now a Coastwatch Station. Others had been turned into eccentric homes, while the rest were crumbling. Suffolk was peppered with old defences along its sea-ravaged coast: pillboxes from the Second World War, or concrete bunkers from the First.

Conor's grey eyes scanned the crowds. The boot fair was busier than usual. More people than ever were inspecting the unwanted junk arrayed behind the cars. He recognised several faces in there. He checked his phone again. Emma was late.

Cursing under his breath, he looked back at the sea. Yesterday had been a blank fog for him. No one at home knew what to say and the more they fussed the more he resented them. Now he felt like a can that had been violently shaken and was ready to explode at anyone who said the wrong thing. The sight of the sea was calming though; he could watch it for hours.

"I don't have no money or nothing," Emma said flatly. "So you can forget that right way."

Conor looked around. The girl was standing beside the wall. He had been so wrapped up in himself he hadn't heard her approach. She was chewing loudly.

"I'm not stopping long," she told him, flicking her ponytail behind her with a toss of the head. "What do you want?"

"Money?" he repeated in confusion. "What are you on about?"

"You tell me, Goldilocks. Aren't you after something to keep you

128

quiet? That's blackmail, you vile sicko. If it's not money you're after then it can only be the other and you have got to be kidding, you filthy perv."

Conor held up his hands defensively. "Oi!" he cried. "I only wanted to talk about it, nothing else. You got it so wrong."

Emma folded her arms and eyed him sharply. She couldn't understand any motive that wasn't selfish.

"So talk," she said at length.

The boy wasn't sure how to begin. He glanced down at the tracksuit bottoms she was wearing and guessed she was deliberately hiding her bandaged legs.

"How are they?" he asked.

Emma shrugged. "I'm not about to marry Paul McCartney," she said.

Conor watched as three gulls fought over a generous piece of battered fish skin.

"It keeps going round and round in my head like a bit in Grand Theft Auto I can't get past," he said. "Nobody who wasn't there can understand."

"Are you confusing me for an agony aunt? I'm not Denise bleeding Robertson. You got problems with it? Go to a head doctor or chuck some Prozac down your neck."

"Don't you keep seeing it in here?" he asked, tapping his forehead. "Those faces – the screams and the panic…"

Emma turned away. "That's my business," she replied.

"But Ashleigh and Keeley…?"

"What do you want me to do, shave my hair off or something? They're in the morgue, dead and blue, but I'm still here. There's no amount of talk or blowing my nose going to bring them back or make it go away. No sense in banging on about stuff like that. It'll do your brains in."

Conor shook his head. "God, you're hard," he said. "They were your best mates."

"I'm my best mate! Have you finished, pretty boy?"

"Not yet. I saw the papers today. No one knows why the car was out of control. What happened?"

Emma chewed and clicked the gum in her mouth. "Danny Marlow was driving, that's what happened. He was a useless pillock. It was his fault – all of it."

"Why don't you tell someone? You should."

"Who? The fuzz? Are you from Norfolk or what? I had a visit from them last night about that Sandra cowing Dixon. I'm not going to give them an excuse to come back and ask me a load more questions. I had nothing to do with that crash. I was just lucky to get out of it alive. The other poor pieces of toast didn't."

"Danny's family would want to know. So would Kev's and the others."

"So what? Not my problem and it's not yours neither."

Conor couldn't think what else to say. He should have known better than to try and speak to flint-hearted Emma Taylor about this. The fact that he had probably saved her life that night didn't even occur to her, or if it did, she wasn't going to acknowledge it, let alone thank him.

He changed the subject.

"I saw Sandra Dixon back there before," he said, nodding towards the boot fair.

"She was lucky we thumped her," Emma declared proudly. "She might be lying on a slab right now with the rest if we hadn't. I told the police that last night. Not that they took any notice. She should be bloody grateful."

"She isn't the sort to go to a flash mob," he answered.

"Don't go sticking up for her! She's so far up herself you don't have to. And she deserved what we done. You know she said you was thick and couldn't read a book without colouring it in. Snobby cow."

Conor managed a grim smile. "She's right there," he agreed.

An elderly couple had been admiring the sea as they walked along the promenade. Drawing close, they paused when they saw the two young people and let out sympathetic groans.

"Oh, you poor lad," the woman cried. "Your bruised face. Were you caught up in that terrible disaster?"

"Awful business," the man added consolingly.

Conor didn't know how to answer them, but Emma said, "Bog off, you nosy coffin-dodgers! Go find someone else to patronise or I'll squeeze your colostomy bags so hard your false teeth will shoot out!"

The couple backed hastily away from the hostile, hard-bitten girl and walked off as quickly as they could. Conor exploded with shocked laughter. She really was relentlessly foul.

Emma watched them leave with a snarl on her lip. Then she

reflected it might have been a mistake wearing tracksuit bottoms. Conor bore signs of battle; perhaps it was time she displayed her wounds too. She had a feeling she would need all the sympathy she could get, especially if that Sandra was going to make a stink. She had been looking forward to at least a week off school, but now she thought it would be smarter to make an appearance tomorrow, with her poor bandaged legs on show.

"Have we done here?" she asked the boy.

Conor didn't think there was anything more to be said.

"So you'll not tell anyone, yeah?"

He felt conflicted. "Not today," was all he could promise.

"Just keep that gob buttoned," she warned. With that, she strode away.

Conor chewed his bottom lip. He didn't know what to do. A brazen seagull alighted on the wall and took a stalking step towards him, hoping for something to eat. Another landed beside it and came bullying forward.

"I haven't got nothing!" the lad said, showing his empty hands. One of the gulls pecked greedily at his fingers and he pulled his hand back.

"Vicious little beggar!" he cried. "Bet your name's Emma as well."

He swung his legs around and jumped off the wall, into the boot fair.

The laden tables sported the usual tat: old toasters, garish souvenirs brought back from abroad, boxes of broken jewellery, rusty

tools, redundant VHS tapes, typewriters, ugly clocks, unfashionable shoes, chipped vases, bent candlesticks, incomplete jigsaws, cracked crockery, vinyl recordings of cover-version compilations, empty picture frames. There was nothing here the red or blue teams of Bargain Hunt could take to an auction and make a profit on.

Conor moved through the crowd, only vaguely noticing what was on sale – until he came to a beaten-up camper van where a young woman was standing behind a wallpaper table covered in a display of old books. The same old book, with a green and cream cover.

With Emma's spiteful account of what Sandra Dixon had said about him still in his mind, the boy stopped and picked one up.

"Dancing Jacks," he read.

The woman behind the table regarded him oddly, shooting him warning looks. Almost as if she was telling him not to look at it, never mind buy it.

Ignoring her, he flicked through some of the pages. The black and white illustrations looked archaic to him and the thought that they really did need colouring in suddenly popped into his head.

"Ha!" he blurted.

"You don't want that," the woman muttered.

"What's it about?"

"You won't like it."

"How much?"

"You'd be wasting your…"

Her voice was cut off as a movement sounded from within the van and a lean-faced man emerged from the sliding door.

"Peasant coins are all we seek!" he said with a crooked grin. "Just thirty of your shiny new pennies."

"Thirty pence? Is that all?"

The man bowed. "For this day only," he said. "Next week they shall be ten pounds each and after that... who knows, a hundred – a thousand, maybe more?"

Conor almost laughed at him, but something about the man's manner commanded more respect than that. Then he noticed that the scuffed leather jacket he was wearing had been added to and was now sporting two long tails, like an old-fashioned fancy dinner jacket. There was an illustration of a character wearing something like that in the book. In fact, it even looked a bit like that weaselly man.

Conor handed the money over and walked away with the book under his arm.

The man's eyes gleamed. Then he turned to the woman and took her hand to kiss it.

"You must endeavour to be more persuasive in your vending, my fair Labella," he told her.

Shiela nodded slowly. "Yes, Ismus," she said in a fearful voice.

Protecting the Ismus, night and day, keeping vigilant watch upon his Holy person are his devoted bodyguards: the three Black Face Dames. No dainty damsels they, but brawny bruisers in black skirts and iron-studded boots, with midnight ribbons tied about their knees and arms. Soot bedaubs their cheeks and brows, for they have renounced their true names and their stomping dance is the deadliest of all. Seek not to gambol with them, only the Jockey has e'er frolicked and jigged in their midst and lived to laugh. Beware their Morris, beware Old Oss's poisoned bite and Scorch's fiery tongue.

10

EARLIER THAT MORNING, Howie's tattoo parlour had been the scene of something inexplicable, perhaps even miraculous.

Tesco Charlie had left his lorry parked outside all weekend, at Howie's insistence. Also on his strict order, they had left Jezza inside the container, with only a bottle of water, no food and no light once the batteries died in those LED lamps. Only Shiela had argued against this insane idea. He needed medical treatment. The others seemed far too ready to agree to Howie's instructions. She couldn't understand why they were suddenly so docile and compliant.

She had slept in the VW that night, listening out for her boyfriend's agonised cries as he drifted in and out of consciousness. She had felt utterly helpless, but when she turned the radio on and discovered what had occurred outside the Landguard Fort, her blood ran cold. What the hell were they involved in? Jezza had spoken of a diversion, but that carnage was horrendous. Shiela knew she was caught up in something she could not begin to understand and that it was totally evil. She was more frightened than she had ever been. She did not know what to do or where to go.

Saturday passed without any more sounds coming from inside the container and she almost wished Jezza had died from his horrific burns. Perhaps then everything might go back to how it was.

Throughout the day Howie and the others would come out of INK-XS to stand along the near side of the container, thereby screened from the road. Sometimes they joined hands and sang a song they had read in that creepy book; other times they would simply stroke the cold metal, rest their heads against it and hum. Shiela had already grown to despise that book and she refused to have one in the van with her, no matter how much Howie tried to persuade her.

"It will bring you comfort," he had told her. "Your questions will be answered within its pages."

"Really?" she had snapped back. "Does it say what to do when everyone you know has turned into a brainwashed zombie and your boyfriend's back looks like a rasher of bacon?"

Howie had merely smiled and returned to the others.

When they were not attending to the lorry and its strange cargo, they sat in the shop where Howie would read to them. It was like a surreal prayer meeting. They had asked her to join them, but Shiela refused and stood in the rear yard, smoking and trying to understand what was going on.

The next time she went back inside the tattoo parlour, Howie and the others were rocking backwards and forwards as they read, and Shiela had hurriedly fled back to the van. This was getting crazier by the hour.

After a while, Manda and Queenie left in Queenie's car. They had curtseyed in her direction before they climbed in.

Shiela desperately wanted to talk to someone. Who would believe her? Her mother certainly wouldn't and none of her old friends spoke to her any more. Since taking up with Jezza, she had dropped each of them, or rather his influence had caused her to regard them and their ideals differently. Shiela wouldn't even know what to say to any of them anyway – she didn't believe this herself.

When she next peered in through the glazed door of the shop, she saw that the guys were still deep in concentration, the books gripped tightly in their hands.

Shiela felt isolated and afraid. She contemplated getting back in the van and driving as far away as possible. But something inside her knew she wouldn't be permitted to escape this. Somehow they would find her and bring her back and it would be worse than ever for her. Besides, all this was her fault. It was she who had suggested going to that old house.

Saturday night passed slowly.

Shiela was awoken from a fitful sleep, just before first light. Queenie and Manda had returned. Manda was carrying something. Was that Jezza's biker jacket? Queenie had a fan in one hand and was holding it in front of her face as she whispered to her plump friend. Both of them had changed their hairstyles. Their hair was now curled and pinned on top of their heads. Queenie had ringlets bouncing down beside her ears and Manda had fastened a diamanté brooch above her fringe. They looked like little girls who had been playing at princesses in front of their mother's dressing-table mirror.

The men had spent a wakeful night in the tattoo parlour. When they came out, Shiela hardly recognised them. Tommo and Miller were usually so full of stupid, infantile energy, but now they were treading in single file with slow, solemn, almost ceremonial steps, their faces grave and their normally playful voices silent. Dave and Tesco Charlie came next. Shiela stared at them in astonishment. They had blackened their faces and rolled up their trouser legs.

Howie came after and he walked over to the camper van.

"Blessed be your day, Lady Labella," he said, bowing outside the passenger window. "It is time."

"Jim," she began. "What's going on?"

He looked at her in surprise. "'Tis the third day!" he exclaimed.

"The Ismus shall arise."

"No, stop that. What are you all playing at?"

"We must welcome him and give him praise," he answered.

"Jim!" she called as he wandered away to join the rest at the back of the container.

"I am the Limner," he corrected with an indulgent smile.

Shiela stepped warily from the van.

Queenie murmured something to Manda behind her fan, but the pair of them curtseyed to her as she drew close. Shiela saw that they had been playing with their make-up too. There was an exaggerated, almost pantomime-like quality to them now.

Dave and Charlie inclined their heads.

"Lady," they greeted.

Shiela looked at their soot-smeared faces. "What are you two doing?" she asked.

"We are the bodyguards to the Ismus, Lady," Dave answered respectfully.

"They are but two at the moment," Howie apologised, "but the third of the Black Face Dames shall be found and soon."

Shiela turned to Miller, hoping to wring some sense from him. Then she noticed that both he and Tommo also had marks on their faces. They were not soot smears. They were patches of colour. On each of the men's cheeks there was now a large diamond shape; one cheek was green – the other was red. But they were not the results of Queenie's make-up bag. These patterns were not removable. They were still scabby and inflamed. Howie had tattooed them.

"God's sake!" she gasped. "On your faces? Richard? Talk to me."

He and Tommo were standing side by side. They put their fingers to their lips and shook their heads.

"The Harlequins do not speak, Lady," Howie reminded her. There was a noise within the container and the Limner clapped his hands with joy. "He has arisen!" he cried. "Let him return unto us!"

The dawn was glimmering in the sky when Tesco Charlie clambered up to pull on the great doors. The container opened with a squeal and creak of metal.

Ruddy beams of the new morning light went dancing within. They fell across the figure of Jezza, standing before the iron throne. The blanket was tied about his waist and his head was drooped over his bare chest, concealing his face.

The others bowed and curtseyed to him.

"You must also, Lady," the Limner prompted Shiela.

The girl looked anxiously up at the man in the huge container. Very slowly, Jezza lifted his arms until they were stretched out horizontally. Then he raised his face. It was rapt in a spiritual, almost ecstatic, expression of contentment.

"Jezza?" Shiela asked.

"Hush, Lady," the Limner admonished. "You must be mindful not to speak of that now. The Holy Enchanter has suffered the Great Ordeal that we may have order restored unto us. All praise the Ismus."

"Praise him!" the others, except for Miller and Tommo, chanted. "Blessed be this day."

Jezza gazed down on them like a kindly parent.

"The contract is complete," he announced and he turned around, displaying his back.

Shiela drew a sharp breath. It wasn't possible.

Bathed in that early light, they saw that the appalling burns had healed completely. Now across his skin pearly scars formed an elaborate, mystical design. The flickering dawn grew brighter and the lustrous shapes and ancient writing appeared to glow and pulse with their own fire.

"The contract is complete," the Limner repeated in a marvelling whisper.

And so Shiela witnessed the arising of the Ismus, and her mind reeled.

The Holy Enchanter stepped down to walk among them. Manda returned his modified biker jacket to him, gabbling how she had cut up one of her own coats to add the tails so it resembled the drawings of the Ismus in the book. The man received it gladly and touched her forehead in blessing.

"I give thanks to you, faithful followers," he said. "You have kept vigil whilst the covenant was made. Your Lord shall not forget it. Now we may truly begin. The Court of the Dancing Jacks must increase and thrive – and the way has been shown."

That was why the van was present in the boot fair later that day. The Ismus had decreed the first seeding of the books was to commence from there. He knew most of the town would be milling around beneath the Martello tower that afternoon.

Dismissing Howie, Queenie, Manda, Tommo and Miller for the moment, he had packed half a crateload of books into the van and driven to the site with Shiela and his black-faced bodyguards.

"You are quiet and deep in thought, my fair Labella," he said to her. "Can there still be doubts?"

Shiela had stared at him with frightened eyes. "I don't know who you are," she answered in a fractured voice.

"I am the Holy Enchanter, your consort," he told her patiently. "You will remember and it will be as it was between us. I will read from the book to you tonight. I shall regale you with tales of our magickal life at Court and the doings of our Prince's subjects. You shall see."

Shiela was quite certain she didn't want to see – ever. But she held her tongue and when they arrived at the book fair she dutifully set out the books as he instructed.

"And if not," he murmured to himself as he watched her, "there is always the minchet."

At first the customers were non-existent. Nobody was interested in the old-fashioned-looking books. The people dawdled by, hardly glancing at them. They really just wanted an excuse to remain outside, away from their stuffy homes, where shock and grief had harboured them since Friday night. The Ismus knew that would change and he waited. His bodyguards remained inside the curtained van throughout, keeping a close and silent watch on him. As the day wore on, and the rest of the boot fair's unremarkable, sundry wares had been thoroughly inspected and rejected, attentions gradually turned to the Dancing Jacks.

"Children's book?" a dumpy, middle-aged woman in yellow flip-flops asked in a bored, fat voice.

"The only one they'll ever need," the Ismus answered.

"Looks very dated," she observed with a disagreeable face. "Children don't want to read old stuff like this nowadays."

"The word is classic. Quality only improves with age. Think how many great stories withstand the passage of time and are beloved by new readers every generation. They are timeless because they contain fundamental truths and are captivating pleasures."

"Well, I've never heard of Austerly Fellows. He can't have been much good."

The Ismus's jaw tightened and his lips drew back, revealing his gums.

"You will," he said through a fixed grin. "And he was far, far greater than good."

The woman blundered on. "So what's the reading age?" she asked.

The Holy Enchanter peered at her as if not understanding the question. His head oscillated slowly on his neck like a snake considering a cornered mouse and he prowled around the table to stand beside her.

"Can there be such narrow limits on fresh thoughts and new ideas and the escape into wild adventure?" he asked.

The woman leafed lazily through the pages.

"I've got a twelve-year-old god-daughter and she's very particular," she said, not bothering to look at him. "She won't read anything beneath her level. She doesn't like stories about children younger than her. This one looks too babyish to me. It's got pictures in it – she's too old for pictures."

The Ismus placed a firm hand on the book and took it from her. The woman's dismissive, trivialising attitude irritated him. Shiela looked across, sensing the mounting tension, and when he next spoke, she recognised the familiar nettled tone of Jezza in his voice.

"How can narratives that enthral and quicken the blood be spurned, merely because their protagonists are younger than the reader?" he demanded. "The darkest, most gruesome fates can befall the smallest infant. I could tell your god-daughter a story set in a Victorian baby farm where the little mites were doped with laudanum to keep them quiet all day. If some of them died as a result, well – not many of the absent mothers objected. And when there wasn't enough money to feed them, because it had been squandered on the matron's gin, the surplus babies were tightly tied in flour sacks and thrown into the river. Would that be too babyish for her – even with pictures? Would she really think a drawing of a drowned, garrotted baby too childish for her grown-up sensibilities? What a screwed-up little psychopath your god-daughter sounds. She should be seen by a doctor and sedated before she harms someone."

The woman blinked at him, speechless, and began backing away.

"Or how about…" he continued, "the tale of the six-year-old boy who drove his governess to suicide by the relentless and artful erosion of her sanity with his diabolic whispering? I could sit your particular god-daughter down and tell her stories of certain children, far younger than her, that would make her scream her twelve-year-old head off and make her drench the bed in urine for the rest of her life."

"You… you can't speak to me like that!" the woman spluttered.

"I'll speak to you any way I want, you sow-brained fleck of crud. Don't come here, boasting about your ignorance, and parade your prejudices about books with pictures in them to me, not to ME! And definitely not while you have this sacred text in your uncouth, porcine trotters. Tell me, do you always smell of sweaty ham or is it a special day today?"

The woman was so outraged by his verbal assault that she raised her hand to strike him. Suddenly two tall men with sooty faces were in his place and towered over her threateningly.

"You want to make some new friends in hospital?" Dave growled.

"Get gone," Charlie spat. "No one touches the Ismus. The next time I see your fat pig face – it'll have my fist in it."

The woman shrank back. "I'll have the law on you!" she cried. "You're raving mad!"

"Oink away, Madam," the Ismus laughed, reclining on the sill of the van and stretching his long legs. "You'll learn."

With an unhappy, frightened glance at Shiela, the woman escaped into the crowd.

"She'll be back," he predicted. "And by then she'll be desperate to pay whatever I ask. Remember her, and her yellow flip-flops. If she's back next week, don't let her have a copy for less than seventy."

"Seventy pounds?" Shiela asked in disbelief.

"And two grand the week after. Oh, she'll pay it," he assured her. "These works will be going for a lot more by the time we're down to the last crate – a whole lot more."

As the afternoon wore on, more people were drawn to the table. None of them were as objectionable as the first woman and so the amount of books finally began to dwindle.

Sandra Dixon had come to the boot fair to escape the suffocating attention of her mother. Since the attack on her, Mrs Dixon hadn't let the girl out of her sight. Sandra had phoned her friend, Debbie Gaskill, about it and they had been messaging one another all weekend, but Mrs Dixon had always been hovering close by.

Sandra had felt strangely numb when she learned that two of her attackers had been killed in what was becoming known as the Felixstowe Disaster. Her mother had sniffed in marked disappointment and, behind tightly folded arms, stated, "Shame it wasn't all three of them!"

Sandra wasn't so malicious. She explained to Debbie how weird she felt, still bearing the bruises those dead girls had inflicted on her. It creeped her out completely. Her living skin displayed, in ugly purples and yellows, the last vivid impressions Ashleigh and Keeley had made in this world and, when those marks faded, what would be left to show for their brief lives?

It was a wonder Mrs Dixon had allowed Sandra out that Sunday afternoon, but the girl's younger brothers needed attention too so she relented, with the proviso that Sandra return after three hours.

It was good for Sandra to feel the salt breeze on her face as she

walked on the shingled beach, even though it made the cut on her lip zing and tingle. She had gazed out at the broad horizon for a full twenty minutes without moving. Then she continued on her lonely way down the shore until she saw the Martello tower in the distance and remembered the boot fair would be on today.

When she found the camper van with its stall of old books, she paused and examined them curiously.

"Lovely!" she exclaimed to the woman standing by the van. "I really like old books like this. Is it a story or a medieval history? Nice illustrations – very clean lines. They remind me of the ones in early Rupert Bear annuals. I've got four of those from before World War Two. My gran gave them to me. I love them."

Shiela looked at the willowy girl with the swollen lip and bruised cheekbone and pitied her. She was too fragile to enter the world of the Dancing Jacks. It would overwhelm and crush her immediately.

"Move on," Shiela said in an urgent whisper. "This isn't for you."

Sandra wasn't certain she had heard her correctly. "Pardon?"

Shiela cast an anxious eye into the van where the Ismus and his bodyguards were reading intently.

"Go, now," she told the girl. "For God's sake, go!"

"I only want to buy it!" Sandra replied, bewildered. "What's the matter with you?"

Shiela was scared the men would hear, so she shook her head and quickly took the girl's money.

"Don't read it," she hissed at her as the girl walked off. "Throw it away!"

Sandra thought the woman must be a bit disturbed. Perhaps the van was from a day centre or a clinic. Then she glimpsed the blackened faces of two of its occupants and was certain of it. They were rocking backwards and forwards.

Turning discreetly away, she saw something that drove the strange woman and the VW van from her mind. It was quarter to three and Conor Westlake was still waiting for Emma to turn up. He was sitting on the sea wall and looking in Sandra's direction. She hoped the lout had not seen her. Ducking behind a group of people, she dodged out of sight and pushed through the crowds to return home, clutching the book.

The afternoon wore on, Conor met with Emma and then he too bought a copy and the pile of books continued to diminish. The Ismus was pleased.

When four o'clock came and the vendors began packing their unwanted goods back into their cars, there were only three copies of Dancing Jacks left on the table.

Martin Baxter and Paul wound their way through the drifting people. Carol had done another night shift at the hospital and was now fast asleep at home. Martin greatly enjoyed coming to the boot fair. Sometimes he found treasures to add to his collection, or an annual he had owned as a child. The nostalgia of seeing those well-remembered pages after all those years made him both sad and happy at the same time. Carol told him he was in love with his own childhood and said he would never truly grow up. Martin couldn't argue with her there.

To him the past was a safer, friendlier place than the world he inhabited as an adult. Life just seemed so much better back then, even though it was less luxurious and the best gadget ever was a pair of shoes with a built-in compass and animal paw prints on the soles to confuse your enemies. People knew who they were and where they fitted into the workings of society. Now nobody knew and everyone was dissatisfied, always scrabbling after more stuff, because that was the only way they could measure their success. No one understood the value of anything any more and things were chucked away simply because the latest version had come out, not because they were broken.

Before Carol and Paul had entered his life, Martin had felt pretty much obsolete himself. Perhaps that was why he had retreated so much into his fantasy world. Now it was such a major part of his life he could never break out of it, not that he wanted to.

That Sunday afternoon he was very pleased with himself at the boot fair. He had found in a box of odds and ends a Dinky Eagle Transporter from Space: 1999 and it was in almost mint condition. That evening it too would be suspended from the ceiling of his inner sanctum. He might even watch an episode. He had them all.

A momentary twinge of guilt troubled him. None of this was really appropriate on the day he had learned just how many of his pupils had perished in the disaster. Another pang of guilt twisted inside his conscience as he remembered the relief he had felt when he saw that none of his favourite students had died. It had mortified him that he could be so callous. And yet he wasn't enough of a hypocrite to pretend he would miss Ashleigh or Keeley. Did that make him a wicked, heartless person – or merely an honest one? He had no idea, but he had kept those shameful thoughts to himself and didn't mention them to Carol because he knew they would shock her.

Driving that confusion from his mind, he patted the spaceship in his coat pocket and went back to wondering which season to pick tonight's episode from: po-faced series one – or the dafter series two? Then Paul nipped in front of him and picked up the very last copy of Dancing Jacks on sale that day.

"Cool," the boy said, appreciating the quaint, period cover.

A strange-looking man in a funny leather jacket bowed to him. "You like the look of it, do you?" he asked.

"It looks like a magic book," the boy said.

The Ismus laughed out loud. Then he leaned forward and whispered, "What if I were to tell you that it is – the most magickal book of wonders and secrets in the whole wide world?"

"Are there wizards in it?"

"No wizards, but there is a Holy Enchanter and Old Ramptana, the Court Magician. Between you and me – he is a bit useless. In fact, everyone knows it except him. Then there's Malinda, the retired Fairy Godmother, who had her wings clipped off by the Bad Shepherd and now lives in a tumbledown cottage in the haunted forest."

"Wicked!"

"No, she's a good old sort is Malinda, not like Haxxentrot, the crabby witch in the Forbidden Tower. You wouldn't want to have

150

anything to do with her: she's an evil old hag and always trying to spoil the happy life of the Court. Malinda is much nicer. She gives away charms and enchanted trinkets to those brave enough to seek her out in that perilous place. Once she gave a pair of silent shoes to the Jack of Diamonds; no matter how heavy his tread, no matter what he stepped upon, he made no sound whatsoever. That is how he stole away the Lockpick's keys when he lay sleeping in his chamber strewn with eggshells."

Paul listened, entranced. The man spoke as if the place was real and he actually knew the characters that lived there. He really was convincing.

Martin stood a little distance away. He had decided to plump for a season two episode. He had always liked the shape-changer in it – with the lumpy eyebrows and iffy blusher sideburns.

He smiled at the spellbound boy. He was a great kid. Carol had done an amazing job raising him on her own.

"Mr Baxter?" a small, nervous voice asked close by.

Martin looked around and saw that a young, ashen-faced woman was addressing him. He was about to nod at her politely, when there was a flicker of recognition. That face…

"Shiela?" he said uncertainly. "Shiela Doyle?"

The woman smiled in confirmation. "You remember," she said and realised she had not been so pleased to see anyone for such a long time.

"Course I do," he told her. "You were one of my stars. Went to university, didn't you? Physics, wasn't it?"

She knew he was eyeing her shabby clothes and unwashed hair.

"I dropped out in the second year," she explained.

"Oh, sorry to hear that. You were one of the smart ones, Shiela."

"It wasn't what I wanted," she said. "Or so I thought at the time…"

"You all right? You look a bit on edge."

The woman seemed wrung with indecision and concern. "Mr Baxter," she began falteringly. "I wonder… do you think I could…?"

Her attention was suddenly diverted by the Ismus talking intently to the young boy.

"Is that kid with you?" she asked in surprise.

Martin chuckled. "He is indeed."

"You didn't have any kids when I was at school, did you?"

"He's my partner's lad," he informed her. "Might just as well be mine though, the way we get along."

"I see…"

"What were you going to say?"

"Never mind that," she said quickly. "Don't let him buy that book. It's not… healthy."

Martin followed her glance. He observed the unshaven, pale features of the Ismus and thought he looked like a dealer.

"Shiela," he whispered. "You sure you're OK? Are you in trouble? Is it drugs?"

She shook her head in exasperation. "Please listen to me!" she said.

"Hey, Martin!" Paul cried out triumphantly, clasping the Dancing

152

Jacks in both hands. "Look what I've got! This man's just let me have it for nothing!"

"Oh, no," Shiela breathed.

Here dances Hearts' fair daughter, see what the curse has brought her. Who can resist her rosebud lips? The bitterest soul they slaughter.

11

SANDRA'S BROTHERS WERE rampaging around the house and yelling at one another as usual. She closed the door of her tidy, apple-white room and sat at her homework table with a fresh mug of tea. Switching on the lamp, she tried to read the poetry book she was currently enjoying, but the din of her brothers kept intruding on her concentration. She leafed through some schoolwork, but their shouts and screams made any study impossible.

The girl took her MP3 player from the drawer and tried to blot out their riot, but she could still hear them crashing around.

Sandra's eyes fell on the old children's book she had bought that afternoon. Taking it in her hands, she examined the illustrations again. Gradually the commotion in the house grew fainter until a deep silence filled her room. Outside the window the light of the afternoon grew dim. Only the lamp was shining,

making the printed pages glow in her fingers.

Sandra could feel a buzzing in her head. As she began to read, she felt as though something was ebbing away, something vital was trickling out of her, but she could not tear her eyes from the words of Austerly Fellows. A shadow rose up behind and fell across her neck. Sandra Dixon began to sway backwards and forwards in the chair.

The Jill of Hearts pulled the plum-coloured velvet cloak around her shoulders and covered her head with the ermine-trimmed hood. She urged her horse forward. Wisps of vapour escaped her lips as she spoke.

It was a crisp winter's night. The moon was high and a covering of deep, frost-glittering snow lay across the realm. Glancing back, the pale girl surveyed the high, solid towers of Mooncaster. The white stonework glimmered like frozen milk and only a handful of windows burned with lantern light. How beautiful the castle appeared against the dark, star-bejewelled sky. She hoped she would return there soon, before she was missed, and before the effects of the sleeping potion that she had fed to Mauger wore off. She hoped her mother, the Queen of Hearts, had brewed it good and strong. Shuddering, she drove all thoughts of that dread monster to the back of her mind. That night she must ride.

Spurring her horse on, she rode through the small village of Mooncot. The peasantry were abed, but threads of pleasant-smelling woodsmoke still climbed from the chimneys of their pretty cottages. The pond in the village green was a clouded ice mirror and the disc of the moon burned like white fire over its surface. The coal eyes of a jolly snowman were the only witness to her passing. Soon the village was left behind and the wintry countryside rolled by, past linen-like meadows and ice-locked streams, past frost-painted hedgerows sparkling with winter diamonds.

The Jill of Hearts' face felt just as cold as that of the snowman, but when she saw the sprawling woodland of Hunter's Chase in the distance, her cheeks burned with excitement.

The lane dwindled to a track and that into a footpath across a field that eventually pierced the outlying thickets of Hunter's Chase. The desolate voice of a wolf cried out in the distance. The horse stamped and tossed its head, blowing steam from its nostrils.

"Peace," the girl calmed it. "Hungry Mister Wolf is atop the hills, crying at the empty moon dish. He will not come down to trouble us. Be of stout heart."

The beast shook its head once more.

"We must enter the woodland," she commanded.

With hesitant steps, the horse passed into the trees.

Hunter's Chase was a wild, perilous corner of the Kingdom. There were many dangers beneath its branches. In high summer the smothering leaves and tangled undergrowth kept the paths dark and secret, but in this stark chill, all was laid bare. The Jill of Hearts marvelled at the icicle curtains that spiked down from the branches and the crystal pillars the longer ones had formed when they reached

the ground. *The surrounding trees were silver and white, their naked nooks and crooks draped with hammocks and bolsters of snow. The cold, sharp air tingled with enchantment.*

A wolf howled again. This time it was closer. Then another lonely howl joined it. The horse trembled.

"Fear not," Jill said in a whisper. "They are still far off. We shall be safe and protected ere they reach us."

"Your steed has better wits than you, my Lady," a deep voice said suddenly. "You should heed it. This is no place for the likes of one so young and fair and brimming with blood."

The Jill of Hearts started and looked around her in fear and astonishment.

A tall, wild-looking man stepped out from behind one of the frozen cascades ahead. The girl pulled on the reins and reached for the dagger at her side.

"Declare yourself!" she commanded.

The man was clad from head to toe in skins and furs. A large axe was strapped to his brawny back beneath a cloak made from many hides and a beaver-skin hat covered his bearded head.

"I am the Woodman," he explained. "May I ask where you are bound on this bitter night when all folk should be huddled before their fires?"

Jill tried to remember what her governess had told her about the Woodman of Hunter's Chase, but she could not. Only one personage had ever interested her in this dangerous place. She had not paid attention to the other stories.

"I do not see why it is any of your concern, Master Woodman," she answered loftily.

The man chortled and stepped nearer. *"Know you the terrors of this wood?"* he asked. *"Know you of the cave up that trail yonder, where the cinnamon bear dwells? Have you not heard of the gnomes who bide beneath ancient roots and reach up with twiggy hands to trip and catch the lost traveller then slit his throat and feed the blood and ground-up bones to the tree? Or the sounder of savage boars with tusks like scimitars that could cut the legs clean off your horse in a twinkling? Perhaps you've heard of the Bad Shepherd who roams here betimes? Or of the Mistletoe King who calls down curses to punish the rash and foolhardy? This wood stretches close to the border and many dark creatures steal in over that unguarded boundary. And what of the wolves, my Lady? Surely you have heard them a-howling?"*

Even as he said it, the mournful howls began again. They were even closer now and there were more than two of them.

"I am not afraid," Jill said defiantly. *"I know where my path takes me. I shall be safe there."*

The Woodman chuckled with understanding. *"Then it is Malinda's cottage you seek!"* he declared. *"On such a frost-biting night as this, no other bolt-hole would offer protection. What can that old Fairy Godmother do for you, I'm wondering?"*

"Again that is my business," she told him.

He bowed in apology. *"My manners are as rough and rude as my garments,"* he said. *"Let me atone by leading you to the one*

secure shelter in this wild edge of the Kingdom – the cottage of Malinda. No evil thing may enter her fences, though they prowl and skulk all around, throughout the hungry night – testing and trying."

The girl wanted to refuse his offer, but the howling of the wolves frightened her. The man came closer. The horse shuddered and the girl could smell the animal skins he wore, mingled with his own grease and musk.

"Lead me then," she instructed.

The Woodman bowed again and smiled. His teeth were white as the surrounding snow and sharp as the hanging ice.

"Love philtres are what most maidens go knocking on Malinda's door for," he said. "Or charms to enhance or restore their beauty. You have no need of either. Ha – you blush, my Lady!"

"You must not say such things," she chided him.

"Surely you are used to praise and tributes? Do youths and princelings not line up to court you? Is there no wooing done within the white walls of Mooncaster? Are the contents of their britches frozen also?"

"Enough, Sir!" she scolded. "Your talk is not seemly."

"And yet I see it has kindled a rosy April in your cheeks!" he laughed. "We know naught of 'seemly' in my wood. The stags rut, the doves bill and coo, the rabbits… well, they do what rabbits do best."

He flashed his smile again. It was wider than before.

"Then I am glad I do not live in this wood," Jill replied. "Now tell me, Sir. What errand lures you from hearth and home this night?"

"I go to meet my brothers," he told her. "When the moon is as white and round as this, we gather and go hunting."

"What quarry can there be in the hollows of a winter night?"

The howling was nearer. The girl gripped the reins tightly to keep from shaking.

"There is always something to hunt down," he said, his colourless eyes shining at her.

"And your brothers," she continued. "Are they woodmen also?"

"They live in the woods," he answered, stroking the horse's neck with his hairy hands.

"Is it much further? Are you certain we follow the correct path? Should we not have turned left when it divided back there?"

"No, indeed," he said. "We are almost at the end."

"Listen to those horrors!" she gasped. "Let us hasten; they sound almost upon us."

"They are famished," he said, hearkening to the chilling wolf calls. "Your steed's sweat has laced the air. Their snouts are tracking it. They want to feast on its steaming flesh. They smell it as strongly as I can scent the fear that flows from you, my Lady."

"Take up your axe!" she urged. "We will have need. Look – over there! Through the trees! A shape. A wolf. There – another!"

The wolves were fast. They loped through the woodland swiftly, their pale eyes glaring at her with steady malevolence.

"Your axe, Sir!" she said again. "They are running us round and closing!"

The Woodman turned about, watching the circling wolves

drawing nearer. The Jill of Hearts drew her dagger and brandished it in warning.

"Begone!" she shouted in as fierce a voice as she could manage.

Then, to her surprise, the man began to laugh. It was a warm, friendly sound and she stared at him incredulously. Had he gone mad?

"Welcome!" he called. "Well met, my brothers. See what I have trapped us. Fill your wagging bellies on the beast, but let the girl feed my appetite before her blood is drunk."

The wolves came prowling from the trees. Loud, threatening growls rumbled deep within their throats. The Woodman shook his head and cast off the cloak of hides. With it went his clothes – and the very skin he stood in. A monstrous figure of fur, claw and muscle remained.

"Werewolf!" the girl shrieked.

The wolves pounced. The nightmare leaped at her. She threw her dagger at his throat and spurred the horse away. The steed galloped down the icy path. The wolves went rushing after.

A fiercer, much louder gargling howl shook the snow-laden trees. The werewolf tore the blade from his neck and licked it. Then, with a snarl, he bounded in pursuit.

Horse and rider fled deeper into the wood. The pack and its fearsome leader were close behind. The hunt was on.

The Jill of Hearts could hear the werewolf bellowing. The horse raced as fast as the winding path permitted. Low branches and fallen trees checked the pace. It leaped and veered, but the hunters were closing. *Sharp teeth clamped about the horse's tail. It kicked back with its hooves. The wolf went flying against a tree and broke its neck. Another wolf sprang into its place. Through their ranks the horrific werewolf came charging. One of his claws lashed out and ripped a gash through the velvet cloak.*

The girl screamed and ducked as the other claw came swiping for her head.

Upon both sides of the galloping horse a wolf drew level. Jill knew they were preparing to jump up and bite. She saw another race on ahead then spin around and tense, ready to leap.

She pulled to the left. The ground rose steeply there and she could see no trees beyond a line of great oaks. Her only hope was to reach open ground. Then her mount could make a desperate dash and the wolves would never catch them.

Her horse whinnied as it swerved aside. It tore up the slope, trampling one of the wolves into the snow with a shrill yelp and a crunching of bones. The other fiends came darting up and the werewolf let out a blood-curdling roar.

"Almost there!" Jill cried. "Almost at the top, then you run – run like you never have before. Fly through the darkness, my love."

A jaw came leaping at her arm. She smacked it away. Another bit at the hem of her cloak and almost dragged her from the saddle.

Then they reached the top. But the Jill of Heart's hopes were shattered. It was only a ridge, encircling a wide, basin-shaped glade. They were doomed. The werewolf came storming up to her and threw back its hideous head to howl. But the chase was not over yet. The

162

ridge was narrow and the horse slithered and slipped. Neighing wildly, it went tumbling down the other side. Jill screamed and was flung clear. She rolled and somersaulted, falling helplessly down into the snow-filled glade below, and plunged head first into a deep drift.

An instant later she exploded out of it, stumbling free and whirling around, ready to fight to her last breath.

Her horse was already staggering upright and shaking its mane. But where were their pursuers?

The girl looked upwards. The wolves were still on the ridge. They and the horror that stood amongst them were questing the air. She saw their eyes gleaming, but they were not staring at her. With her heart pounding, she realised that something was behind her – something that even they were wary of. Trembling, she turned.

The glade was empty and the snow untouched. No trees grew there, except one. A fine pomegranate was growing in the centre. Not a flake of snow had touched its bushy green foliage and bright red blossom shared the boughs with ripe, shining fruits. Yet it was not the tree that filled the wolves and that monster with doubt, but the creature that nibbled at its lowest branches.

"It cannot be," the girl said.

In size and shape, it resembled a roe deer, but there the similarity ended. Its hide was white as the snow its cloven hooves stood upon and a tail, like that of a lion, swished behind its long back. A golden collar gleamed around its neck, from which dangled three links of a glittering, broken chain.

The vapour of a disbelieving breath exhaled from Jill's lips.

A fine, creamy beard sprouted from the animal's chin, but it was what grew from the centre of its forehead that made the girl gasp. It was a long, straight, tapering horn.

"It is a dream…" she murmured. "It must be."

The animal made no sign it was aware of them. It paced around the tree then thrust its ivory horn up into the branches and scraped it along the boughs. Two fruits fell into the snow at its feet. It stamped on one then lowered its head to delicately lick up the spilled ruby-like seeds.

The Jill of Hearts had never seen anything so perfectly magickal before. Even in the Realm of the Dawn Prince she had never believed in the existence of these creatures. But there it was.

"You are beautiful," she said.

The unicorn gazed shyly at her for a moment then stamped on the second pomegranate and began lapping the burst contents. Jill heard an impatient snort close by. Her horse was eyeing the ridge fearfully. The wolves were crouching, shifting their weight from side to side, tensing and making ready to resume the hunt. They obviously did not consider the fabulous beast to be any threat to them. The werewolf was licking his fangs. First the girl, his vicious mind had decided. Then he lusted to rip out the throat of that dainty-footed curiosity.

With a savage yell, he came bounding down, his wolf brothers flanking him.

The girl rushed to her steed. It reared in alarm at the sound of the ravening wolves and bolted out of reach. Jill stood alone

and helpless. The marauding pack came bursting through the snowdrift.

Three wolves raced immediately around the back of her, cutting off any escape. Two more came stalking in from the sides, whilst the harrowing form of the werewolf lumbered straight for her.

She could not look at his unclean eyes. Nor could she stare into his red throat as he rushed to tear her to pieces. She covered her face and waited.

Suddenly a strange, unearthly sound blasted across the glade. It was a strident, bleating scream. The wolves that surrounded her flinched and cowered as they jerked their heads around. A second scream made the werewolf spin about and he bellowed back at it.

Jill lowered her hands to look. The unicorn was shaking its elegant head and pawing at the snow. It opened its mouth again and another eerie scream trumpeted in the night.

Then it lowered its head and charged.

The werewolf gave a snarling laugh. One slash of his powerful claws, one lunging bite, and it would be over. He stretched out his mighty arms. The sinews tensed in his hairy shoulders. His sharp ears flattened against his skull. Saliva dripped from his jaws.

The brutal contest did not last long. Hunter's Chase resounded with fearsome screeches. The Jill of Hearts fell back at the sight of such merciless savagery. The pure white snow exploded with crimson. Flesh and limbs were hurled wantonly into the air, then shredded and spat out. The gory carcass was leaped upon and the tail torn out by the roots.

Straddling the mutilated body of the werewolf, the unicorn reared its head and the dead fiend's blood trickled down the twining groove of its long, lethal horn. It gave a bleat of victory. Then its goat-like eyes stared balefully at the petrified wolves. They could not believe what they had just witnessed. It was as if the most ferocious, mighty lion was hidden within a lamb.

The unicorn sprang at them.

Yowling and whining, the wolves turned tail and ran for their lives. The unicorn raced after. A yelp signalled the end of one. A triumphant bleat heralded the impaling of another. Two wolves scrambled up the ridge and escaped; the remaining one was not so lucky. The unicorn rammed its horn through the beast's brains and tore the head clean off.

Jill looked around her, aghast. Everywhere was stained red. She stared up at the ridge and saw that the unicorn was already returning. Kneeling in the deep snow, the plum-coloured cloak ripped and tattered about her shoulders, she waited breathlessly. The animal was staring fixedly at her and she too was petrified.

"Are you my protector – my saviour?" she asked in a quavering voice. "Or do you mean to slay me also?"

Stepping through the blood-drenched snow, its own hide splashed and smeared scarlet, the unicorn advanced. There was nothing Jill could do. Tears dropped from her eyes.

"Death has so many guises," she said. "But surely none so beautiful. If it must be thus, then bring it and be swift!"

The unicorn lowered its head and came running. Jill squeezed

her eyes shut. Her heart thumped. She breathed hard. Let the ending be quick!

Then, to her amazement, she heard a faint purring noise and felt a weight press against her lap.

Opening her eyes, she found the unicorn was lying before her, resting its head on the white folds of her gown. The animal's eyes were gentle now. They blinked contentedly and a pink tongue licked the tears that had fallen on to her hand.

The Jill of Hearts stroked the unicorn's head, cleansing it of blood, washing it with snow and combing her fingers through the fine, silken beard.

A movement stirred the oak trees that towered around the glade. From the dense growths of mistletoe that clogged the high branches, a small shape dropped on to the encircling ridge.

"You've done it now," said the hearty but warning voice of the Mistletoe King as he looked down on the girl and the unicorn.

"What have I done?" she asked.

"Fettered him in new chains," the little man-shape said. "But those are stronger bonds than the last. He will never be free. Even now they strangle and he shall die before the morning."

"No!" she cried. "Why?"

"You have stolen his heart and pierced it with your beauty. How can he live without it? A unicorn can never survive once a maiden has tamed him. Your tenderness has brought this upon him. It was unwise of you to venture hither to this wood. See what ruin your selfish folly has caused? As he is cursed, so too must you be. You

cannot rob the world of so rare a miracle and expect no punishment."

"Am I to die also?"

The Mistletoe King rustled his glossy leaves and the pearly berries jiggled. "Not so quick and not so easy," he told her. "Hear me now. This then is your portion of the curse. No one who strays across your path shall want to tread another. A daughter of the Royal House of Hearts you are, and hearts you shall collect – as freely as children gather daisies. None whom you wish for shall escape, save one, and that heart shall be the only one you truly desire. It is a bitter cup you have put to your lips."

"I did not want it so!"

"Yet the first sip has already been taken. The curse is placed and I am its witness."

With that, the Mistletoe King jumped back, up into the tree, and rolled along the branches until he merged with another evergreen cloud.

The girl gazed up at the oak unhappily. Then she patted the unicorn's head and bowed her own over it, gathering her ragged cloak about them. She remained there until the first rays of the winter dawn touched the rim of the eastern hills and the unicorn lay dead and withered on her blood-stained lap.

With a cry, Sandra Dixon slumped forward on to the table. Her face was pinched and blue with cold, and frozen tears clung to her cheeks. Her brothers were still bawling at one another elsewhere in the house.

"I am the Jill of Hearts," she sobbed. "I am the Jill of Hearts."

Let the peasants sing, hear their cheery ring, hear them sing out loud and long. Flowers and gifts they bring, and any other thing, to see their betters in the throng. But someone has a knife, to stab and take a life, someone will do bad that day. See the Jockey run, flee from everyone, do not let him get away. What a merry sight, to see him taking flight, soon he will be made to pay.

12

Barry Milligan arrived at school nice and early on Monday morning. The gates were smothered in cellophane-wrapped bouquets and laminated messages. But it wasn't them that caused his stomach to flip and make his hangover even worse. He immediately saw that he had forgotten to cancel the knife arch. The police unit had already set it up alongside the flowers. The clash of imagery was far too good for the early-bird reporters. Photographers were already snapping away and someone was doing a live piece to breakfast television, trying to interview one of the officers.

Barry wished he was a million miles away, but the reporters saw him and came stampeding forward.

"Mr Milligan!" they called, taking pictures and pushing microphones in his face. "Eight of your pupils died last Friday and another twenty-three of the deceased were former pupils here."

"A terrible tragedy," he said. "Let me through."

"It was one of your students, Daniel Marlow, who was responsible for the crash. The three passengers in that car also attended your school. What do you have to say to that?"

"No comment."

"People are calling this a 'Yob School', and the 'School of Death'. What is your reaction to that?"

Barry tried to control himself, but it wasn't easy. "Nobody as far as I am aware has ever called this school those names," he growled.

"Then what is the meaning of this knife arch? Surely, by its very presence, you're admitting that the children here are out of control?"

"Not at all."

"Are you anticipating trouble here today?"

"We just want to get through this difficult time as smoothly as possible."

"So you were expecting some kind of violence! That's a sad indictment of your school, Mr Milligan. Do you think you will be able to keep your job after this?"

Barry really wanted to punch someone. He hadn't experienced a scrum as hostile as this even in his rugby-playing days, but he managed to push his way through and sought the sanctuary of his office.

"What a balls-up!" he said to himself.

The rest of the morning went as expected. After a delayed registration, due to the slow ingress of the children filing through the knife arch, the whole school assembled in the sports hall. Barry read out the speech he had spent most of the previous night writing and rewriting. There were tears, from staff and pupils alike. When it was all over, Barry summoned Emma Taylor to his office.

The girl slouched in. She was wearing her shortest uniform skirt and ankle socks, the better to show off the fresh dressings. She had already received murmurs of sympathy from some of the younger members of staff, but she knew the Head wouldn't be so easily deluded or appeased.

"You know why you're here, Emma," he said, in full television detective superintendent mode.

The girl nodded, but there was a belligerent glint in her eye.

"You're about as low as it gets, aren't you?" he told her. "I'd say you should be thoroughly ashamed of yourself, but that's beyond you, isn't it? The only person you ever think about or feel sorry for is yourself. You disgust me, you know that? You haven't changed from the first day you came through those gates. There are pit bulls, bred and trained to savage other dogs, with more humanity and compassion in them than you've got. Normally I'd exclude you from school for what you and the others did to Sandra Dixon last Friday, but I know you'd view that as a result. I expect the police have already spoken to you about it?"

"Yes, Sir."

"Then it's up to them, and the Dixons, how they proceed. Don't smirk, girl, it's a very serious offence. If they were to press charges and if you were a couple of years older, you'd be banged up in a young offenders' institution. Don't think you've got away with this here, because you haven't. This is going to drag on for you, Miss, and your life is going to get very difficult."

"Already is, Sir," she interrupted. "I was at the fort on Friday when I saw my best mates…"

"Oh, don't even go there!" he shouted. "I know exactly why you've turned up today, flashing your burnt legs. Poor you, poor you. It doesn't work on me. I know you too well, Emma. I've got no sympathy and don't think you can try to skive off lessons by seeing the counsellor this week."

"I had to go hospital!" she protested.

"So did Sandra after you kicked the hell out of her!" he roared back, slamming his hand on the desk. "If you were half as smart as you think you are, you'd be more worried. Without Ashleigh and Keeley, you're going to get the full blame for the attack. Do you understand?"

Emma chewed the inside of her cheek, her eyes fixed on the carpet. "Yes, Sir," she mumbled.

"Now Sandra is in school today," he warned. "If I hear you so much as look at her the wrong way, you'll be out of those gates for good and you won't be coming back – ever. It's my duty to find somewhere else to take you, but wherever it is, God help them, it won't be within walking distance like this place so that's an almighty

172

headache your parents would have to solve, and frankly, I really don't give a monkey's. I'm not making idle threats here. I won't tolerate that kind of viciousness from any of my students. This isn't a bloody zoo. Are you listening? Have I got through that thick head of yours?"

"Yes, Sir."

"Then get out of my sight!"

Emma closed his door behind her. It had gone better than she had hoped. Swinging her bag over her shoulder, she sauntered off to her first lesson.

Martin Baxter's Year 10 class filed in, unusually quietly, and found their desks. Three of them would be empty that day – and every day after. The youngsters' eyes could not help but stare at the vacant places. Owen Williams had always sat next to Kevin Stipe. Today the ginger-haired lad gazed down at the blank space where his friend should be and felt sick. Conor sat in front and he could hardly bear knowing that void was directly behind him. He bowed his head and pressed his fingers against his temples. The knowledge that there had been a fourth passenger in that car was eating away at him. He should have told someone.

At the back, three unfilled places made a large hole in the class. The three witches would normally be making the most noise by now. Martin's conscience had won out. Yes, he would miss Keeley and Ashleigh. In their own mouthy and raucous way, they were entertaining and at the very least always kept him on his toes. "Had been entertaining," he corrected himself.

"OK," he began. "Let's get through these first days as best we can. The sooner we can get back into a routine, the better it'll be."

"I don't think I can sit here!" Owen blurted.

Martin had expected this. The obvious solution was an extra desk, but there simply wasn't room for another. They were squeezed in as it was.

"Does anyone want to swap with Owen?" he asked.

Silence and a shaking of heads.

"I can't sit here – next to where he was!" Owen insisted, scraping his chair back.

A hand slowly went up in front. "I'll swap," Conor said.

"Good lad," the maths teacher told him, quite impressed. "Owen, would it bother you to sit in front of… of Kevin?"

Owen nodded vigorously.

"All right, will anyone swap so Owen can have their seat and they can sit in Conor's?"

A few minutes later the exchange had been made and they were looking up at Martin once more, their faces expectant and respectful. Suddenly it struck him, for the first time, just how cynical and case-hardened he had become over the years. He had come to view most of these youngsters as thuggish gang members or just pointless scum who would never contribute anything to society and would always leech off it. But at that moment, he saw them afresh and clearly. They were still only children.

The disaster had done more than rob them of friends and classmates. It had told them, ferociously, they were not invincible

and immortal. It had demonstrated, in lurid sounds and colours, absolute chaos, and they had been terrified. Now they were searching for sense and order again and there was no better place for that, in their adolescent universes, than in Mr Baxter's lessons. He was a reassuring symbol of constancy and structure.

The maths teacher realised all of this in a sudden instant and, for a few seconds, he struggled with his own sense of shame. But the expectant faces were still waiting.

"Open your books," he said eventually. "We'll start with…"

"What do you think of the number, Sir?" Owen asked.

"Number?"

"Of smiley faces."

"I'm not with you."

Some of the others joined in. The coincidence had been spotted by many of them yesterday and they were keen to discuss it.

"On the invite email that went out," they told the teacher.

"There were forty-one smilies."

"And forty-one people died…"

There was a profound silence. They looked at their teacher, hoping he could make sense of it for them. Martin felt a chill spread down one side of him. Then he realised the door had opened and a cold draught was blowing in.

Emma Taylor entered. Martin's eyes flicked across to where Sandra was sitting. The Dixon girl looked different today. The hair she normally hid behind was pinned up behind her ears in a strange sort of old-fashioned style. She seemed distant and didn't even look up when her attacker came into the room.

"I'm not gonna cause any trouble," Emma promised, also glancing in Sandra's direction. "I've just been with Mr Milligan, Sir."

Martin nodded. "I know," he said. "Look, Emma… if you want to find somewhere else to sit, we've been doing some musical chairs already. I'm sure we could do another round."

"Why would I want to do that?" she asked. "My desk's over there."

Feeling Conor's eyes upon her, she strode to the far left corner of the classroom and threw her bag on Keeley's seat as she sat next to it.

"So what we doing?" she said stonily.

The rest of the lesson progressed as normally as it could, given the circumstances. Emma, of course, had neglected to bring any of her books. When it was over, Martin called Sandra over as the rest of them shuffled out.

"Are you sure you should have come in today?" he asked, concerned. Even for her, she had been unusually quiet throughout the lesson.

The maths teacher studied her pale, bruised face. There was something remote, almost even serene, about her expression. She looked back at him impassively.

"I am most well, Sir," she said when he prompted her again. "Why should I not be?"

"The staff will be keeping a lookout," Martin promised. "We won't let it happen again. I really don't think Emma will try anything though – even she isn't that stupid."

Sandra smiled at him, a strangely playful smile. He noticed that the pupils of her eyes were peculiarly large.

"That was another life ago," she said, as if she were the teacher, patiently explaining the most rudimentary fact to a slow learner. "Now I am reborn, in new and cleaner clothes – to a better, bolder world. Nothing that happens in this grey life matters any longer."

The smile gave way to a soft chuckle and her forehead crinkled. "Blessed be your day," she said, heading for the door.

Martin watched her leave the classroom and he scratched his chin with a pen. He hadn't realised the Dixons were so religious.

Grabbing his briefcase, he headed to the staffroom to grab a coffee and eat his lunch.

It was busier than usual in there. The members of staff who normally popped home or to the shops during the lunch break had remained on site. In the old days, this would have meant walking into a blanket of smog, because most of them smoked like chimneys. Staffrooms had always been bad places for the lungs. Martin was so glad those times were gone; he could munch on his sandwiches without them being poisoned by that nicotine miasma. He always smiled at the irony that nowadays it was the teachers who were compelled to smoke behind the bike sheds.

The customary cliques were already grouped together, but of course there was only one topic of conversation. The disaster and how it had affected the children and their own lessons was on everyone's lips. Martin tuned in to each separate discussion as he peeled the lid from his Tupperware box and took out a ham sandwich.

"Apparently the Prime Minister's just made a flying visit to the hospital," Mr Jones, the head of biology, announced, reading a text on his phone. "Had his picture taken in the children's ward. So he got his warm and fuzzy publicity after all."

"Hyena," muttered Mr Roy of geography.

"And those news vans are still parked outside the gates," Mr Jones grumbled.

"I couldn't get little Molly Barnes in Year 7 to stop crying," said Yvonne Yates, the French teacher. "We had to call her mother to come and collect her and then those swine out there ambushed both of them. It's disgusting."

"They'll vanish as soon as the next actor or pop star is caught with their pants down," Mr Roy foretold. "Which should be any time now – must be a week since the last feeding frenzy."

Martin waved his half-eaten sandwich and joined in. "Can anyone explain what all that is about?" he asked in bewilderment. "Half of those so-called celebrities who keep these magazines in print aren't famous for actually doing anything; they're just famous for being papped falling out of nightclubs and shooting their mouths off. There's no talent or achievement there. Why are people so interested in them?"

Mrs Early, the English teacher, laid her knitting on her lap. "Because they can afford better clothes and go to far more glamorous parties than the readers ever could," she said in her languid,

poetry-reading voice. "And everyone loves to see the overpaid privileged punctured. I know I do. Seeing some silicone-bagged horror gagging on kangaroo testicles in the jungle is just the modern equivalent of watching the guillotined heads of the aristocracy roll into baskets. Nothing has changed. We all lap it up."

I don't, Martin thought to himself.

"Is there a new game or movie out?" Mrs Yates interrupted. "Some of the kids today were behaving a bit... weird."

"We're all behaving weird today," Mr Jones reminded her.

"No, I didn't mean that. It's something else. Like they were role playing or pretending to be different. I couldn't work it out."

"Now you mention it," Mr Roy agreed, "there was one in my class who was acting funny and talking odd."

At that moment the door opened and Mrs Hughes, the school secretary, popped her head round.

"Martin," she said brightly. "Can you come to reception? There's someone to see you. They've been waiting for almost half an hour."

Mr Baxter groaned, resealed his sandwiches and followed her down the corridor.

"I told her today isn't exactly the best time," Mrs Hughes explained apologetically. "But she refused to leave and I suppose, after all, she is a former pupil."

"Is she?" Martin asked in surprise. He didn't have long to discover just who it was. They pushed through a pair of fire doors and entered the school reception area. There, sitting on one of the low comfy chairs that weren't comfy at all, was Shiela Doyle.

The young woman looked agitated and more dishevelled than ever. When she saw Martin, she leaped up and took a step towards him. Then she halted and looked hesitantly around. There was a hunted, jumpy air about her.

Mrs Hughes smiled benignly and disappeared discreetly into her office, but kept the sliding glass partition partly open and busied herself with some papers.

"Hello, Shiela," Martin began, wondering what in the world she was doing here while noting the dark circles around her eyes and jumping to the wrong conclusions. "Twice in two days. What can I do for you?"

Shiela rubbed her arm nervously, which made him think her situation was even worse. He hoped she wasn't going to ask him for money.

"I shouldn't be here," she said quickly. "If the Ismus finds out…"

"The what?"

"The man I was with at the boot fair," she hissed at him. "He used to be called Jezza, but now we have to call him the Ismus."

"And what's one of those?"

"Sort of High Priest, I think."

"Shiela, what have you got yourself into?"

"I don't know," she said. "I really don't understand what's happening. It's just… I don't even know how to explain."

"You seem scared stiff. Get away from him if he's that bad and making you do stuff you don't want to do."

"If only it was that easy," she answered with a pathetic laugh. "If

only I could escape it. I'm only here today because he's gone to Ipswich with his bodyguards and I won't be missed."

"His what?"

"He has bodyguards. They go everywhere with him now. If they knew I was here, talking to you, to anyone…"

Martin gestured to the chairs and they both sat down.

"Has he threatened you?" he asked in a whisper that even Mrs Hughes wouldn't be able to overhear.

The young woman stared back at him with her ravaged eyes. "He's a threat to everyone," she replied starkly. "Mr Baxter, have you ever heard of Austerly Fellows?"

"I don't think… was he a student here?"

Shiela shook her head. "He wrote that book your partner's kid was given yesterday. He… he hasn't read any of it yet, has he?"

"That old book?" Martin asked in surprise. "Shiela. Why are you here? I think you should go to the police if you're…"

"The book!" she insisted. "Has the kid read any of it?"

Martin was taken aback by the urgency in her voice. "No," he answered. "I don't think so. We watched DVDs last night."

Shiela let out a huge breath of relief. "Then you've got to make sure he doesn't," she warned. "Don't let him even look at it. Burn it, bin it, do whatever you have to, but don't let him near the bloody thing!"

"Shiela, you're scaring me now. Have you taken something? I think you need to see a doctor."

"I'm not mad!" she shouted. "I know what this sounds like – I know it sounds crazy, but it isn't. Oh, God – it isn't. Find out about Austerly Fellows! Then see if I'm mad. We went to the house. That's where it started and that's my fault. I thought if I could… it doesn't matter what I thought, not now. Whatever you do, get rid of that book. Please! That's why I've come here."

Her face had turned white and she was shaking with emotion. Martin didn't know what to do. His eyes flicked to the partition and saw that Mrs Hughes was gawping at them. Then Shiela was on her feet again.

"I've got to go," she said with a shiver. "I shouldn't be here. Just remember what I said, yeah?"

"Don't go yet," Martin asked her. "We can go to the Head's office and have a cup of tea or coffee. I'm sure we could even stretch to some biscuits. Let's talk this through."

The young woman's eyes moved off him. There was nothing he could do to help. He had always been her favourite teacher and she had tried her best to warn him of the danger. But he wouldn't listen or believe what she had to say and she didn't blame him for that. She looked over the artworks and announcements that decorated the reception area and inhaled the building's familiar smells one last time. A faint smile pulled at the corners of her mouth.

"I was happy here," she said softly. Then she opened the main door and left.

Martin Baxter watched her walk through the school gates, then glanced at Mrs Hughes.

"Just like Amy Winehouse," she lamented with a sorry shake of the head.

The maths teacher wondered exactly what she meant by that. Speaking to Shiela, he had decided that she wasn't on drugs at that precise moment, but surely her paranoia and nonsensical rambling were the result of them.

"All that talent wasted," the secretary clarified. "Shiela Doyle was such a bright, clever girl. So sad to see what's happened to her."

"Yes, very," Martin agreed.

"What was that about a book?"

Martin shrugged. "No idea," he said, but the girl's forceful pleas had unnerved him. He resolved to check out Paul's boot fair acquisition later that evening and see for himself.

As Shiela made her way from the school and headed back towards the Port of Felixstowe Road and INK-XS, she was not aware that someone had been waiting for her. A person in black slipped out from behind one of the news vans and kept their steady eyes upon her receding figure.

Queenie closed the fan in her hands and tapped it against her palm.

"What have you been up to, my Lady Labella?" she murmured.

The Lockpick holds the keys to every door in the White Castle and carries them on nine hoops that rattle and clink about his belt. That is why he is also known as Jangler. Neither room nor strongbox can deny him. He is so skilled in the art of making and opening locks that the Ismus made him Warder of the Crown Jewels. He sleeps within that very vault, upon a comfortless wooden mattress, surrounded by the strewn shells of eggs and walnuts so that he may hear any who try to steal in during the night.

13

HANKINSON AND WEBB was an old-established family firm of solicitors in Ipswich, dating back to 1911. Situated off the Old Foundry Road, it was respectable and reliable and traditional. They didn't chase injury claims for careless people who slipped on wet floors at work or used the wrong ladders. They didn't even deal in divorces, merely wills and probate and conveyancing. There were no more Webbs in the firm, the last one had retired back in 1954, but plain old Hankinsons sounded like something you blew your nose on and Hankinson and Sons was just silly.

That Monday morning, Arnold Hankinson was with a new client, a Mr Rackley, a first-time buyer, and Arnold was talking him through the process. It was something he had done over a thousand times in his dry career. In his early forties, he had become part of the furniture there and was almost as thin as the hatstand by the door of his office, which wore his hat and coat with more panache than he ever could.

The drone of his funereal voice was causing the client's eyelids to droop and his attention to wander. The office was a library of files and overstuffed drawers. Stacks of buff envelopes and papers were on every surface. A primitive computer with a bulky monitor dominated the large desk and Mr Rackley wondered if he should have taken his business somewhere a little more up to date.

When a commotion began outside the door and the secretary's unhappy voice was raised in alarm, Mr Rackley was almost pleased and he sat upright in his chair, alert once more.

"No, you can't go in there!" Miss Linton called out. "Mr Hankinson's in a meeting."

"He'll want to see me," another voice told her as a shadow fell across the door's frosted glass panel.

"I'll call the police if you don't leave this building right now."

"Not a good idea," growled a third voice.

"Trust me, darling – your boss really will want to see me."

The handle turned and the door flew open.

Mr Hankinson had already picked up the receiver of his phone and had dialled two 9s when the intruder came leaping across the room and tore the cord from the wall socket.

"Don't be rude, Arnold!" the stranger told him. "Don't give my boys an excuse to get noisy with you."

Through the thick lenses of his spectacles, Mr Hankinson stared incredulously at the man. He had never seen him before in his life. He was a peculiar sight, in his leather jacket with tails and grimy, clever features. Then, craning his head around him, the thin solicitor saw the two large companions looming over his secretary. Their faces were blackened. What was going on?

"We don't keep any money here," he said quickly. "Just some petty cash and not much of that."

The Ismus paced in front of the desk.

"I don't want your money," he said. "Or yours either!" he told Mr Rackley.

"I've just got a mortgage," the client burbled. "I haven't got any."

"What do you want then?" asked Mr Hankinson nervously.

The Ismus pushed a sheaf of papers off the desk and perched on the corner. "I want the Lockpick," he demanded. "I want to see Jangler and I don't have all day."

"You've got the wrong place," Mr Hankinson said timidly.

"No, I haven't, Arnold," the Ismus replied, crouching forward across the desk and bringing his face close to the thin solicitor's. "Now bring him to me."

"I don't know who you mean! There's no one here called that."

186

"Get me the Lockpick!" the Ismus demanded, lashing out and toppling a stack of files. The papers within spilled over the floor.

"You can't do this!" Mr Hankinson protested.

"Get me the Lockpick!"

Mr Rackley shrank back in his chair, but the lunatic was not interested in him.

"You'll be on camera!" Arnold shouted. "There's CCTV pointed right at the entrance here."

"I hope they got my good side."

"The police will catch you!"

The Ismus swung his long legs off the desk and strode to the shelves where he began to fling the files across the room.

"Stop it!" the solicitor pleaded. "That's decades of work!"

The Ismus paused.

"You think this crap is important?" he said, clutching a yellow form.

"It is," Arnold insisted.

The Ismus chuckled and wafted the form in front of Arnold's nose. "No, it isn't," he whispered. "Your precious papers can curl up and fade for all I, or the world, care."

As he spoke, Mr Hankinson saw the yellow paper discolour in his fingers. Dark spots of mould freckled their way forward until the whole form was furred and black. He removed his spectacles and shook his head in horror.

The Ismus sneered at him and dropped the blackened form on to the slew of papers that now covered the carpet. Within moments, the mould had spread. It flowed thickly over every sheet, every envelope, until every scrap was caked in stinking mildew. Then it began to creep up the walls, engulfing the patterned wallpaper, invading the framed certificates and qualifications, eating the family photographs. Three generations of Hankinsons were greedily obliterated.

The solicitor and Mr Rackley could not believe what they were seeing. The stench of damp was unbearable, but they could not drag their eyes away from the rapacious, consuming mould as it marched across the ceiling, which bulged and sagged as the plaster crumbled. It was impossible and terrifying.

"That's enough," a new voice said sternly.

Everyone turned to the doorway where a short, balding man in his sixties was standing.

"Father," Mr Hankinson exclaimed. "Get out quick!"

"Don't be an ass, Arnold," the old man said, closing the door behind him and regarding the Ismus with a steady, unflappable gaze. A patch of mould dropped from the ceiling on to the shoulder of his suit and he brushed it off casually.

"What's all this racket?" he asked. "I could hear you clear down the hall."

His son's eyes widened and he gestured frenetically at the Ismus and the room that was now completely covered in thick black mildew.

"Is this your doing?" Hankinson Senior asked the stranger.

A crafty smile spread over the Ismus's face. "Jangler," he greeted.

Old Mr Hankinson held his eye for an instant, but nothing

betrayed his thoughts. Then he turned to Mr Rackley.

"I'm so sorry your appointment has been hijacked in this manner," he apologised in a forced, jovial tone. "Some of our clients are… a trifle boisterous and unorthodox."

"Father!" Arnold spluttered.

"This gentleman is an illusionist from a contemporary and rather radical theatrical troupe," the old man explained. "He's a hypnotist. The two fellows outside are postmodern clowns. They get very good reviews at the Edinburgh Festival, I believe."

The Ismus let out a loud laugh at this spontaneous invention. He approved wholeheartedly. Then the uncanny, voracious mould started to shrivel and fade from the ceiling. It dwindled down the walls and retreated over the floor. The white and pale colours of the papers were revealed, unblemished, once more and the mould seemed to be sucked under the Ismus's shoes until there was nothing left of it, except a faint must of decay that hung on the air.

"You should be on telly, mate!" Mr Rackley marvelled, clapping his hands. "You're miles better than Derren Brown! That was so real! Wow!"

Arnold Hankinson pushed back in his chair and tried to understand what was going on. His father was making conciliatory noises to the client and hoping the interruption wasn't too unpleasant.

"There will, of course, be no charge for our services," he was telling him.

"But, Father!" Arnold broke in. "The police…"

"Oh, do get a hold of yourself," the old man shushed him, "and stop making a drama out of a little artistic temperament. Now if I can take this illusionist gentleman into my office, we'll leave you in peace. This place is an appalling mess, Arnold. What's the matter with you, boy?"

He nodded once more to Mr Rackley then led the Ismus from the room. In a daze, Arnold Hankinson stared at the closed door for several minutes. Then he cast his eyes around the scattered papers and files. "What just happened?" he murmured.

Mr Rackley burst out laughing. "And I thought solicitors were boring and stuffy!" he said. "You're madder than Harry Hill!"

In the outer office, Maynard Rumbold Hankinson was assuring Miss Linton there was no need to panic. He knew these people very well and their theatrics weren't to be taken seriously.

The secretary looked doubtfully at the two large men with soot on their faces and wasn't so certain.

"They're not your usual type of clients," she said suspiciously. "I'm sure I've never seen them before."

"They weren't in make-up before," old Mr Hankinson told her. "Now do calm down and carry on with what you were doing."

He beckoned to the Ismus and his bodyguards. "This way, if you please."

At the end of a dimly-lit hallway, he ushered them into his own office. It was slightly larger than the one his son inhabited, but was lined with identical-looking files and towers of paper. He closed the door firmly and walked over to lean against his desk. Every trace of that phoney joviality had vanished from his face. He smoothed his

neat little moustache with his fingers while he considered the three bizarre strangers.

"Now then," he began testily.

"Jangler." The Ismus addressed him as if he was meeting an old friend. "'Tis I!"

"Don't give me that," the peppery old man snapped.

"I am the Ismus. If you are the Lockpick, you know why I am here."

Old Mr Hankinson's face might as well have been made from granite. "If you truly are who you claim to be," he said, "prove it."

"That's the solicitor speaking," the Ismus tutted. "You have heard me use my rightful name which no other would even know. You have also seen what we can do – and yet you demand a third testament. Doing things in triplicate is such a monotonous obsession."

"Show me," the old man demanded firmly.

The Ismus snapped his fingers and held out his hand. Tesco Charlie took a copy of Dancing Jacks from the large pocket of his black cargo trousers and gave it to him.

"There," the Ismus declared. "This is the moment you and your family have waited for, for almost eighty years."

"It's a book certainly," Mr Hankinson replied, hardly glancing at it. "That isn't the proof I'm asking for. Anyone could have broken into that house and removed the crates. Anyone could have… encountered Mr Fellows."

The Ismus laughed again. "Hardly 'anyone'!" he cried. "What a stout and dogged guardian you are. How well you deserve the title of

191

Lockpick, faithful custodian of the Dawn Prince's keys and secret treasures. You are as solid and steadfast as your grandfather before you."

"We have waited a long time," the old man replied tersely. "That is why I won't surrender what was entrusted to my family without the necessary verification and my patience with you is wearing thin. So, if you refuse to show me, I really will call the police. You not only barge in here and cause a disturbance, you have also, by your own admission, broken into a listed property, which our firm holds in trust, and removed from there…"

His voice trailed off. The Ismus had taken off his jacket and T-shirt and turned his back to him.

The burn scars shimmered in the gloomy room.

"There's your proof," the Ismus said. "The contract upon the living page of my flesh."

"Ismus!" the old man exclaimed. "Forgive an old fool for not recognising the true person of the Holy Enchanter."

The man once known as Jezza grinned and pulled his T-shirt back on.

"You were doing your duty. That is why you are the Jangler. No one slips by you."

Mr Hankinson slid down to one knee and bowed his balding head. "The wait has been so long," he uttered, close to tears. "I feared there would be no one to pass the sacred knowledge on to. My son turned out to be a sore disappointment to me. There is only grey lawyer's ink in his veins. He would never have embraced the candle

faith of his forebears. I thought the sacred trust would end with me."

"The time was not ripe; it took longer than we anticipated."

"Yes, I realise that. I did begin to hope it might be soon. The signs were clear. The children of Cain are more lost and empty than ever. The Hebrew hypocrisies have finally been ousted and the Nazarene's reign is over. The worship of straw idols is in full flood, as was prophesied. The way is prepared and the empty throne is waiting."

"Get up, old man," the Ismus instructed. "All has been set in motion. The Dancing Jacks are already at work. There must be no delay. You know what I have come for, what I must have."

Mr Hankinson rose and hurried to a corner where an imposing green safe stood among the files.

"It is all in here," he said, excitedly dialling the combination and heaving the thick metal door open. "Everything Mr Fellows gave to my grandfather – papers, deeds, account details – everything that will be needed in the glory days to come. There is, as you may know, a considerable amount in various accounts. That sort of money lying idle for almost eighty years can accrue a lot of interest."

"I haven't come for the money. That isn't what I need right now."

"Of course, of course – I know just what it is you'll be needing first of all."

He took out an iron ring, to which large keys were attached, and handed them over.

"Jangler indeed," the Ismus observed with pleasure.

The old man bowed again. "That is the secret name each of us has borne since Mr Fellows ordered it to be so," he said. "My grandfather

passed it down to my father and he to me. We were only told certain things – who we waited for and how to identify him. We were never given one of the bound holy texts; we never knew the revelations and truths they contained. Even in our role as trustees of the house, we never dared venture into the cellar, nor strayed beyond the bounds of our instructions. I hope we did well. We tended to the conservatory and kept it flowering."

"Better than well," the Ismus said gratefully. "You shall sit with me in the Court, in a place of high honour." He gave him the book and the old man received it as though it was the rarest and most precious artefact in the world.

"Thank you, my Lord," he whispered, clasping it to his chest.

"Now, most dedicated Pharisee," the Ismus said with his crooked smile. "Follow me and come with us. We have a very special door to unlock."

Rattling the keys in his hand, he strode from the office. The bodyguards marched after him. Giving the dust jacket of Dancing Jacks a solemn kiss, the Jangler reached into the safe once more to take out a large black Gladstone bag and followed them.

Magick and enchantery are as natural in the Kingdom of the Dawn Prince as the perfumed summer winds or the music of the streams. Yet there are some, who dwell within the circling hills, over whom the Old Ways have no power. These aberrants must be rooted out. They are a danger to his lovely land. Find them, report them, they are a sickness that must be cured. Yea, though they be your bosom friend or even your brother, you must inform upon them. Such is the decree of the Ismus.

14

MARTIN BAXTER DROVE out of the school gates and noticed that one of the broadcast vans had gone and others were preparing to leave. Obviously the Disaster was no longer headline news. It hadn't taken long to shunt the deaths of forty-one young people off the front page; perhaps something even worse had happened elsewhere. He discovered later that an ex-member of a boy band had announced his engagement to a soap actress and the news crews had scrambled to capture footage of them together, with the ring. That's what people were really interested in nowadays.

Paul was in Martin's passenger seat, twiddling his fingers, practising for his imminent piano lesson.

"So how was your day?" Martin asked. "Get through it OK?"

The boy nodded. "Seemed just normal by the afternoon," he said. "It's like the fort was ages ago now, like a dream somehow."

"I thought it was unreal at the time," Martin agreed. "Things like that just don't happen here, except that it did."

"Did you hear about the smilies?"

"Yes. There's another one for the cranks and conspiracy theorists."

"Pretty amazing though."

"Coincidences are, but they're just random patterns that occur in probable outcomes. If there had been one less smiley, no one would have noticed anything."

"And if anyone else dies, it'll blow it out of the water too."

"Let's hope that doesn't happen! You're a bit gruesome today."

The boy laughed. "It's because of Anthony Maskel and Graeme Parker at break this afternoon," he said. "They were being dead wet and drippy and saying stuff that so isn't like them. I couldn't make out what they were playing at."

"Your pals weren't excluding you, were they?"

"Yes, but not the way you mean. They weren't being horrible, just the opposite. It was loopy. As if they'd had their brains rewired – or been bodysnatched by those pods from outer space."

196

"Fantastic movie!" Martin enthused. "In fact, both the first two versions are excellent. That dog with the man's head gave me nightmares for weeks after."

"Ha ha – I thought it was funny! I wanted one."

"You thought The Thing was funny too! That head spider was the worst scare ever when I first saw it. There was no CGI back then. We weren't used to creatures like that."

"It was cute!"

"I despair, I really do."

They had driven along Undercliff Road East, which ran along the coast. The expanse of sky over the North Sea was muddied with cloud and the waves that dragged at the shingle were white and foaming. In an effort to stem the erosion of the shore, hundreds upon hundreds of great angular concrete shapes, like alien sculptures, had been embedded in the beach, to confound the power of the sea. If you looked at Felixstowe via Google Maps, even on the highest resolution, the satellite photographs showed those concrete tetrahedra as ugly dark splodges. It was as if the images had been censored – or spores of black mould were gathering to invade the town.

Martin pulled up outside a large house. The hedges were impeccably clipped and the lawn was like a bowling green, framed by a beautifully maintained flower border. It was a quietly grand place, with no outward sign betraying what it was – one of the most select places to stay in Felixstowe – and it was where Paul had his free piano lessons.

The boy ran up the drive and rang the bell. Martin followed him.

A spry, lean gentleman, there really was no other word but gentleman, answered. There was a welcoming smile on his fresh, pink face, which crinkled the skin around his pale blue eyes in the most genial and friendly way.

"Hello, hello!" he greeted them with genuine warmth. "Wasn't it an absolutely terrible weekend?"

"Hi, Gerald!" Paul yelled.

"Go get yourself a juice," the man suggested. "You know where it is."

Paul grinned and hurried past, heading towards the gleaming designer kitchen.

"Time for a tea, Martin?" Gerald asked.

The maths teacher was tempted, but had to decline. "Shouldn't really," he said. "I've got a lot of marking to get through this evening."

"You teachers work too hard."

"Oh, please, tell the government that."

"And so does Carol. A nurse and a teacher, what a combination. You two hardly ever get any decent time together."

"We don't even manage any indecent time together," Martin joked.

Gerald Benning laughed. He was approaching seventy, but could easily be mistaken to be in his fifties. He was a picture of health and was always immaculately dressed, with no creases ever marring his clothes except the crisp lines he had ironed into them himself. His fine white hair was perfectly groomed and resembled a piped swirl of Dream Topping.

He ran the Duntinkling guesthouse more as a hobby than a business. He enjoyed cooking and meeting new people, but was very selective about who came to stay. If he really wanted, he could be fully booked throughout the seasons, but he could afford to take a more laid-back approach and didn't want the pleasure of being a convivial host to ever become a chore, so he only took sporadic bookings.

Hardly any clues in that tastefully furnished guesthouse betrayed that he had once been famous. There were a few photographs on his piano, but that was in the private part of the house where paying guests weren't permitted, unless he really warmed to them and they somehow recognised him.

"I spent most of my weekend refusing requests from journalists," he said. "I wanted to get on with digging a pond out the back, but the number of calls I had from them, trying to book rooms, I hardly got anything done. I'd forgotten just how pushy and unpleasant those people can be. Well, they got short shrift! I'm not having that sleazy riff-raff in my Egyptian cotton."

"They were outside the school today," Martin told him.

"I saw on the news. Some poor little girl and her mother were as good as attacked by them. It's worse than it ever was in my day."

"That was Molly!" Paul said, returning with a half drunk glass of juice and a matching orange smile. "She was in my class. What a racket she made!"

"God love her," Gerald said. "Now, if we can't persuade Martin to have a cup of tea, we'd best begin. I'll drop Paul round later once we're done. You go attend to your marking."

He waved goodbye to Martin and was about to follow Paul into the house when he paused and called out, "Next Saturday, are you all free for supper?"

"Yes, I think so," Martin answered readily. Gerald was an excellent cook and always tried new recipes out on them before serving the dishes to his guests. A night at Gerald's table was a treat the three guinea pigs greatly looked forward to. "Carol's on earlies so she'll be all right for the evening, thanks!"

Gerald rubbed his hands together and looked apologetic. "I won't be here though," he said with mock regret. "Evelyn is coming for the day and you know we can't be under the same roof."

Martin's eyes lit up. "Really?" he asked. "Oh, amazing! I'm honoured – I can't wait!"

A playful smile flickered over Gerald's face. "It's about time you met her," he said with a wink. "Just don't let her drone on too much. She never knows when to shut up." And with that, he closed the door.

Martin chuckled as he returned to the car and drove off.

Before his retirement thirteen years ago, Gerald Benning had been one half of an extremely popular comedy musical duo. It was stunningly original for the time and was hailed as one of the best acts of its type ever. For thirty years, Hole and Corner, as they were known professionally, packed the theatres, entertained royalty, and had a long-running series on Radio 2. Then, after the untimely death of his partner, Gerald decided the act was finished and did not want to continue as a solo performer. So he left the showbiz world

completely and retired to the seaside town he grew up in, shunning interviews and living a quiet life.

Martin was now greatly looking forward to the weekend. He had first been introduced to Gerald by Carol. She had nursed Gerald's partner in his final months some years ago and had become firm friends with both of them. The rest of the world appeared to have forgotten Hole and Corner, or confused them with later, inferior imitations who didn't possess a hundredth of their talent. Saturday was going to be excellent.

When Martin arrived home, Carol was upstairs, soaking in the bath. He went up to tell her the news and she too was delighted.

"You're so privileged!" she told him. "It took me four years to be allowed to meet Evelyn. Now don't you forget the rules and spoil it!"

"I won't!" he promised. "I've been hoping for this for ages."

"I knew you had an ulterior motive for getting involved with me," she teased, flicking a berg of bubbles at him. "Fetch me a glass of wine, my good slave. I want to be decadent in my suds."

With a mischievous grin, Martin quickly scooped up a handful of foam, pushed it in her face then ran from the bathroom as she spluttered and splashed.

Downstairs he removed the books he had to mark from his briefcase and put them on the dining table. His attention was immediately drawn to the copy of Dancing Jacks that Paul had left there yesterday. Shiela Doyle's bizarre and unsettling visit that lunchtime flashed into his mind.

Martin drew the book towards him and had a close look at the period green and cream cover. "What was she so panicked about?" he murmured to himself.

Sitting down, he opened it curiously.

The room around him became dim.

The end papers were a map: 'The Magickal Kingdom of the Dancing Jacks' – a beautifully detailed drawing of a rural landscape with a moated, medieval castle called Mooncaster in the centre, surrounded by the huddled cottages of the small, picturesque village of Mooncot. A set of stocks was on the green by a pond that was labelled 'cursed', there were streams and woods, enchanted paths marked out by dotted lines, woodland huts and haunted caves, entrances to underground tunnels, the edge of a dark forest, a witch's tower, meadows and pastures and tracks leading to seven of the thirteen encircling hills which were off the edge of the map.

"Is that a gibbet?" Martin asked, peering closer at one part of it. "There's even a skeleton in it – charming…"

He turned the page. The frontispiece was a delicate picture, by the same hand, of an elaborate, wrought-iron chair. Underneath, upon a curling scroll, were the words, "Until the Dawn Prince returns unto us, his throne awaits."

The blood began to pulse in his temples. Martin rubbed his forehead. A low humming echoed faintly in his ears.

Martin found the publishing information.

"Cloven Press, 1936," he said. "Must have been a very small publisher. I've never heard of them."

202

Then he raised his eyebrows at the strange preface from the author. "OK… 'so mote it be'? Is Austerly Fellows an alias for Dennis Wheatley? Did he ever write for kids? That would be so very wrong."

He frowned when he remembered what Shiela had said about the ferrety-looking man she was with at the boot fair. Didn't she claim him to be some sort of High Priest?

Martin continued, and began reading.

The world of the Dancing Jacks was set firmly in a distant kingdom in the mythical time of chivalry, courtly romance, intrigue and magic. Martin's mouth twitched to one side. The prose was occasionally difficult to follow, there were odd repetitions, and sometimes it broke into rhyme for no apparent reason and then became so dense and obscure he had no idea what it was describing, while at other times it was almost babyish. How could children be expected to wade through this? There didn't appear to be a single continuous narrative running through it either.

The book was divided into sections. The first described the White Castle and the idyllic landscape around it, exploring the varied features – almost as though it was a holiday brochure. Then each character was introduced in their own devoted chapter, describing who they were and telling simple stories about them and their adventures. There were clear illustrations of what they looked like, with great care taken over their costume.

They seemed to have been inspired from a jumble of sources: suits of playing cards was the most obvious one, early pantomime another, as well as traditional folklore and the English morris. There were also archetypal figures, such as the witch, the werewolf woodsman, the constable, the fairy godmother, the cunning fox with the gift of human speech, the minstrel, the mistletoe king, the beggar maid, the roaming soldier, the crafty blacksmith and the gallant knight. There was something for every taste. Some of the characters even had their own tunes and catchphrases.

Other personages made brief appearances in each of these introductory chapters, but only one was a constant presence in them all – the Holy Enchanter, the Ismus. Everyone revered him and his word was law. Only the Jockey seemed to have any right, or was audacious enough, to taunt or trick him…

Martin looked up. So that man with Shiela is parading about as this Ismus? Was that really so unnatural? He thought about the science-fiction conventions he had attended where fans thought nothing of spending the day – and the evening – dressed in lovingly crafted recreations of their favourite characters' outfits. He had once enjoyed a hilarious night in the hotel bar of one such event, having a whale of a time with two brilliantly attired and very convincing Klingons and an Asian Superman.

His concentration faltered. He looked about the room. Were the lights flickering? It suddenly seemed brighter and his ears felt as though they'd popped. For some inexplicable reason he experienced the strange sensation that something, somewhere, had failed.

Martin clicked his jaw from side to side and started thinking about his DVD collection and what he would watch that night.

Something he had seen dozens of times before, something familiar to have on in the background as he marked his students' work – perhaps a few Deep Space Nines.

He flicked through the rest of the book. It laid out the customs of the Court and how everyone slotted into its daily life. There were rituals and manners. There were songs and even the dance steps to accompany them. It was a portrait of the complete world; a world where the Ismus was its absolute ruler and in which the infatuated females would fly to him after dusk by rubbing minchet over their bodies. Minchet was the flying ointment they obtained from the Queen of Hearts, who in turn had bribed the Jack of Diamonds to steal the spell of its making from Malinda the reclusive Fairy Godmother…

"Hmm…" Martin grunted. There was no gripping story here, no desperate chase leading to a thrilling conclusion. It was stodgy, repetitive and obvious and in places quite impenetrable. He couldn't understand how anyone would want to waste their time reading it, but there certainly wasn't anything harmful in it as far as he could tell.

Poor Shiela. Whatever substances she had been taking had definitely done terrible damage. He hoped she would seek help and that it wasn't already too late.

"I've had to drink the bath water!" Carol announced, standing in the doorway in her bathrobe.

"Oh – your wine!" he cried. "Sorry!"

"I saw the back of the Prime Minister's head at work today," she told him, towelling her hair vigorously. "He's going bald and sprays it with black webby stuff."

"Image is everything," Martin said. "Never mind the policies, so long as he looks good on camera. Do you remember when that Labour leader, Michael Foot, was ripped to pieces one Remembrance Day for looking like he'd been dressed by Worzel Gummidge? What nobody mentioned was that he was the only politician at the Cenotaph who'd paid for the wreath he laid out of his own pocket. Isn't that the important thing? The eighties was the time when all this image garbage began and the rot really set in."

"Martin, that was decades ago. I was too bloody young to know or care."

"Nothing's changed. Now you get politicians cycling to Parliament because it makes them appear 'green', but it's only for appearances; their ministerial cars are right behind them, carrying their suits and laptops. It's all surface and show: they're the only things that are important these days. There's no substance to any of it. As long as it looks good and it's hyped enough, the masses will buy into it. Until the next shiny novelty comes along."

Carol wound the towel around her head. She'd heard this rant too many times before and had no intention of letting it progress that evening. "What's that you've got?" she asked, changing the subject.

"Paul's book he was given at the boot fair," Martin said, realising he was beaten. He rose from the table and went into the kitchen to pour Carol's wine. "Thought I'd have a look at it."

"You nosy article!"

Martin handed her the glass. "I know, but someone warned me about it today. Turns out they were just out of their tree."

Carol took a sip. "Mmmm... Dutch courage tastes so nice," she said.

"What do you want Dutch courage for?" he asked, before having a sudden panic. "No! You haven't been in my sanctum and broken anything, have you?"

The woman ignored that. She took a deep breath and closed her eyes. "I've been thinking, up there in my teetotal bath," she began. "Look, Mr Arithmetic. You go on far too much about stuff that doesn't matter to anyone else but you and drive me round the bend with your spacey, hobbity obsessions. If you had your way, you'd change the name of this street to Warp Drive and I know you only fancied me at first because you thought I looked like a young Sarah Jane Smith. But my mother likes you – heaven knows how you managed that not-so-minor miracle. Paul gets on with you so well I sometimes feel like a spare part. You've turned him into a mini-Martin! And now the lovely Gerald – he of the faultless taste and character judgement – has invited you to meet Evelyn... that really puts the tin lid on everything, doesn't it?"

"Erm... my Universal Translator is on the blink. I've no idea what you're on about."

Carol started to laugh. "I'm saying that I'd better put a ring on your finger and make an honest man of you. I want us to get married, you big daft geek!"

For several moments Martin could only stare back at her. Then he let out a whoop and hugged her tightly. The wine spilled everywhere, but they didn't care.

"I'm thirty-six, Martin," she continued. "Time, and my lady bits, aren't marching by – they're whizzing past on rocket-fuelled mopeds."

"Like the ones in Return of the Jedi – or Thunderbirds?"

"Shut up and listen!"

"OK."

"Paul and you are the most important people in my life. But, and I've thought about this a lot, I really want there to be another – before it's too late for me. I want to have a child with you."

Putting her glass down, she took hold of his hand before he could say anything else and led him up the stairs.

It was the last time they would be so happy. The book that Martin had dismissed so casually would ensure their joy was short-lived. Their lives were about to explode and a bitter, heartbreaking end was fast approaching.

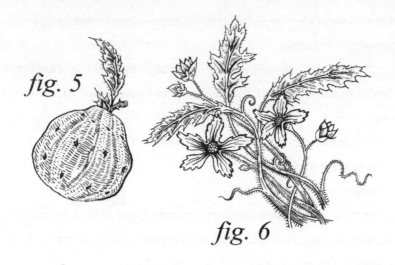

fig. 5

fig. 6

15

FIVE MOTORBIKES ESCORTED the camper van along the coast road that afternoon. The two outriders had tattooed diamonds on their faces, the next had coloured streamers flying from the sides of his helmet and the last two had blackened faces. Manda's car brought up the rear. It looked like the cortège of a rough and down-at-heel head of state.

The Ismus was driving the van and Shiela was next to him. She kept turning round to stare at the passenger sitting in the back. In his neat, charcoal-grey suit, with the Gladstone bag on his knees,

Mr Hankinson was a singular sight surrounded by the faded décor and bric-a-brac of the VW. He looked entirely out of place, but there was a dreamy expression on his face as he read the book in his hands. The illustration of the Jangler might have been a drawing of himself, apart from the medieval clothes, with the hanging sleeves, pointed shoes and the thick belt that bore many hoops of keys. He stroked his smooth chin and decided he would have to grow a little beard to match the one in the drawing.

No one had told Shiela where they were headed and she could not guess, but she could sense the barely suppressed excitement in the Ismus.

The Suffolk coast is cluttered with defences. Most of them, like the groynes that reach down into the water and the concrete tetrahedra, are to protect it from the hungry sea. Others, like the Martello towers and the Landguard Fort, were built to repel human enemies. The ghostly remains of more recent military bases also scar the land. RAF Bawdsey clearly shows where twelve Bloodhound Mark II, surface-to-air missiles were stationed, ready to launch against Soviet jet bombers. The immense Cobra Mist radar array at Orford Ness is like the imprint of a colossal fan on the ground. From Saxons to the Cold War, the fear of attack was always the foundation of those structures, but, in the end, it is the sea that will win.

Only one concrete bunker was ever built for a different purpose entirely. Close to the Felixstowe Ferry Golf Club, at the edge of a remote stretch of the road, was something that the Ministry of Defence had nothing to do with.

The motorbikes kicked up the gravel of a lay-by and the van pulled in behind. A concrete pillbox, half hidden in the gorse and surrounded by wire fencing, was before them.

The Ismus got out of the van and twirled the keys that Jangler had given him. His bodyguards dismounted and came over to walk at his side.

The Harlequin Priests strode to the van, slid open the side to let out a beaming Jangler and removed two pairs of wire-cutters from their toolbox. Shiela lit a cigarette and dug her hands into the pockets of her denim jacket as she watched them advance purposefully towards the fence. The doors of Manda's car slammed behind her.

"Mr Fellows designed this himself and had it built at his own expense, in 1935," Jangler was telling anyone who would listen.

"There were other contributors," the Ismus corrected. "Members of many different 'societies' donated funds towards the project."

"Ah, yes, Mr Fellows was the head and founder of many circles – and so very persuasive."

"He still is."

"Of course," Jangler said reverently. "And our firm has maintained the security around this place since then." He pointed across the road to a larger fenced area near the shore. "National Heritage has contacted me twice in the past eight years, but I told them the land and the structures upon it were held in trust and they weren't to interfere."

"You did well."

"I did only what my father and grandfather had done before me. It was a sacred duty and honour."

Leaning against the van, Shiela looked on as the men she had known as Tommo and Miller snipped away at a section of the wire fence.

"And how are you this blessed day, my Lady?" Queenie's voice broke into her thoughts.

She looked around, startled. Manda had apparently been very busy with her sewing machine. The pair of them now sported new long gowns. Queenie was dressed in black with silver lace and Manda was in red and gold. They must have been up all night to work on those outfits. They were still unfinished, but the temptation to wear them had been irresistible.

"I'm fine," she answered, not really wanting to engage with either of them. They were both far too immersed in this lunacy.

"'Fine', is it?" Queenie asked with an edge to her voice that made Shiela wonder what she was driving at.

"Yeah, just fine," she repeated flatly.

Queenie clasped her hands to her exposed, and pushed up, cleavage.

"Is it not a most joyful hour?" she asked, her eyes flashing at Shiela reproachfully. "To be here, at the unlocking of the hidden way."

"Cut that stuff out. I'm not interested."

"So many things are hidden, are they not?" the other woman said archly.

"What is your problem?" Shiela asked.

Queenie laughed and fluttered her fan in mock innocence. "I have no problem, my Lady," she cooed. "Nay, none at all…"

Crooking her finger at Manda, the two of them sashayed towards the Limner, who was sketching the pillbox.

"She'll be saying 'mayhap' and 'gadzooks' next," Shiela muttered.

The Harlequins finished cutting through the fencing and began pushing the gorse back, revealing more of the low concrete building behind.

"There are so many of these along the coast," Jangler informed everyone, "that one more really didn't attract any attention when it was built. It's as commonplace as a beach hut. How clever of Mr Fellows."

Shiela stared at it without interest. Mr Hankinson was right. She had seen dozens of them before. This pillbox looked just the same as the others. It had an ugly, squat and brutal shape, with a letterbox-like slit facing the sea and a rusted metal door in one of its five sides. It was this door that the Harlequins were busily clearing a path to. When they were done, they stood on either side of it and bowed.

"Labella," the Ismus called.

Shiela stirred herself, realising he meant her. Throwing her cigarette away, she walked over and took his outstretched hand.

"We enter together," he whispered.

The pair of them passed through the gap in the fence and stepped between the parted gorse. The others fell into place behind. Then the

213

Ismus selected the largest key on the iron ring and slotted it into the lock.

It was stiff, but the ring gave him extra leverage and after a brief effort, it turned. The metal door swung inward.

A waft of cold, damp air flowed out. Unimpressed, Shiela peered inside, expecting to see a miserable and poky room. The narrow window allowed only a sliver of grey light into the claustrophobic interior, but what she saw surprised her. In the centre of the pillbox, a flight of concrete steps descended into the ground.

She turned to the Ismus at her side. "I'm not going down there," she refused point-blank.

"We're all going down," he insisted. "You have nothing to fear, my love – 'tis only the ritual entrance way to the larger area yonder." He nodded to the other fenced area across the road.

"This is a subway?" Shiela asked. "What on earth for?"

The Ismus gave her that infuriating indulgent smile. "It symbolises the departure from this world, to the realm of our master, the Exiled Prince," he explained. "There must be a physical journey, as well as a spiritual one, for you and the rest of the Court."

She shook her head and tried to pull her hand from his. "I'm still not going down there," she swore. "I can't keep playing along with this! I've had enough."

Behind them, the Lockpick glanced at the Harlequins in confusion. The Queen of Spades and the Queen of Hearts looked at one another knowingly.

"What is wrong with my Lady?" Jangler murmured. "Why does she protest?"

The Ismus clenched Shiela's hand so tightly that her fingers turned white. "Naught is wrong," he declared. "The Lady Labella has an aversion to rats and dark places, that is all."

"But surely there are no rats down there!" Jangler exclaimed. "Mr Fellows would have seen to that, as he saw to the cellars of his house."

"See," the Ismus told Shiela. "The Lockpick knows. You won't find any vermin down there."

Staring at the Holy Enchanter, the woman wasn't so sure. Besides, it wasn't just rats and the dark that frightened her. Here was another, literal, step into the madness that had possessed them. Then the Ismus entered and pulled Shiela with him.

At once the black-faced bodyguards followed and produced torches from their pockets, which they shone down the steps to light their Lord's way.

"To the Realm of the Dancing Jacks," the Ismus declared. Leading a fearful Shiela, he descended the stairs.

There may have been no rats down there, but the concrete-lined subway was pitch-black and the torch beams did not reach the far end of it. Stagnant seawater sloshed over Shiela's trainers and she recoiled as it soaked through her socks.

"'Tis but water," the Ismus said calmly, his voice distorted and echoing eerily in that dank space.

"Freezing water," she said. "Freezing water in a black hellhole

215

that stinks of damp and I'm a bigger nutcase than I ever realised for being down here in it."

Cursing herself, she followed him along the subway, the seawater slopping around them. Suddenly the torchlight fell upon a hideous, grinning face in front and Shiela screamed.

It was only a painted statue. But the fright had been genuine. The statue was repulsive. The thing had a misshapen body with monkey's arms and an oversized head with glaring yellow eyes and a wide, downturned mouth full of jagged teeth. In the centre of its forehead were two curling ram's horns.

"What is that?" Shiela asked.

The Ismus reached out and patted the deformed stone head.

"Mauger," he said with a grin. "Growly Guardian of the Mooncaster Gate. Everyone must pass this fierce warden if they are to come unto the presence."

"He'll never get on the cover of *GQ*," Shiela commented.

The Holy Enchanter's eyes glittered in the torchlight.

"Soon he will be amongst us," he said. "The first of those I shall bring through." With a grim smile, he led Shiela further in.

Behind them, the bodyguards and the rest of the entourage bowed in turn as they passed in front of Mauger.

Shiela found herself clinging tighter to the Ismus's hand. She hated it down there, as much as she had hated being in the cellar of that horrible house. With huge relief, she saw the torchlight finally strike another set of steps that climbed upwards into the same grey light as before. She had almost expected night to have fallen outside

216

while they had been down there.

She hurried up the slippery stairs as quickly as she dared and found herself inside another pillbox, identical to the one across the road. The Ismus rattled his keys again and yanked and pulled on this door. A few minutes later it squealed open.

The young woman hurried outside, her trainers squelching. But she was grateful for the fresh air and the soft evening light. She lit herself another cigarette and looked around her.

"What is this?" she asked.

They had emerged into a wide courtyard, surrounded by high concrete walls. It was overgrown with sea campion, biting stonecrop and sea holly, which had all taken root in the sand and shingle blown over those lofty walls during the winter storms. At the far end of this strange place there was yet another pillbox, except this one was much taller and wider, and the door that faced them was larger than the one Shiela had just stepped out of. Two sets of steps wound around the outside of it, up to the flat roof, where she imagined there must be a marvellous view of the sea.

"I do not wish you to smoke those things any more," the Ismus commanded, pulling the cigarette from her mouth and casting it away. "'Tis not seemly."

Shiela glared at him, but bit her tongue. She suddenly realised that she had not seen him touch a single cigarette since that first visit to the empty house. He hadn't drunk any alcohol either.

"Not too wild and overrun," Jangler observed, gazing about as he emerged behind them. The legs of his trousers were rolled up to

spare them from the stagnant tunnel water, revealing his sock garters. "Considering how long it's been since anyone set foot here, that's not too bad at all. A good day's labour will clear this lot away handsomely."

"Oh, do you have to?" Shiela asked sadly. "It's like a garden – a secret garden for the sea."

The Ismus snorted in disgust. "It's not a garden," he spat. "You are standing in my Court, Labella! I want these weeds ripped out by tomorrow night." He glared at the Harlequins as they joined them and they nodded in silent reply.

Striding through the plants, he headed for the door at the opposite end and called for her to follow. She did so reluctantly.

Queenie and Manda stepped into the sunken courtyard, the hems of their gowns still in their hands to save them from getting wet. With admiring gasps, they twirled about and cavorted through the greenery.

"Mr Fellows oversaw every stage of the construction," Jangler addressed the two bodyguards. "He even drew the plans himself. He had so many skills – has so many skills."

The Ismus was running his hands over the rusted surface of the large door when Shiela joined him. It was almost twice the height of them.

"What's in there?" she asked. "Aren't you going to open it?"

He shook his head and scoffed at her ignorance. "This is the Dark Door," he told her. "It can only be unlocked from within."

"How is that possible?" she asked, but he was already ascending

the steps that twined up the side of this larger pillbox.

Shiela went after him.

The view from the top was splendid. The beach dipped down before them and the North Sea spread into the horizon. Shiela glanced backwards. They were screened from the road by a jungle of gorse that grew all around the courtyard's walls. Encircling that wild tangle was an even higher wire fence than the one Tommo and Miller had cut through. They really were secluded and hidden away here. From the beach and the road, nobody would even know this place existed. She had never suspected it was here. Taking a step forward, she almost tripped.

Something was jutting from the flat roof. Looking down, she saw the threaded ends of four steel bolts set into the concrete.

The Ismus was watching her.

"For the Empty Throne," he explained. "This is where it shall be affixed, upon this raised dais – towering over the Court below."

"Waiting until the Exiled Prince returns to sit in it?" she asked slowly.

The Ismus's crooked smile grew broader.

"And it's him who'll be opening that Dark Door from the inside, right?" she said in a fearful voice.

"My dear Labella," he congratulated her. "How clever you are."

"My name is Shiela!" she told him. "I'm not your Labella. God's sake! Look at you, look at all of you – you're locked in a shared psychosis!"

She spun around. That was it. She wasn't going to take any more.

219

She had to try and get away, at least attempt to escape their madness. But her way down the steps was barred by Tommo. He stood there, feet planted squarely apart and arms folded.

Shiela turned from him to flee down the other set of steps, only to find Miller was standing at the top of them, forbidding her escape.

The faces of the Harlequin Priests were devoid of expression. Then, staring at her with blank eyes, they pointed to the red diamond tattooed on their cheeks, to indicate their displeasure, and she stepped away from them – afraid.

"Just let me go," she pleaded. "I won't make any trouble. I won't tell anyone anything."

"Oh, but you have already," the Ismus said, stationing himself in the centre of the four bolts, where soon the throne would be secured. "This very day, whilst I was in Ipswich, you sneaked off to speak to someone. Who was it, my Lady? What did you tell?"

Shiela heard Queenie's gloating laugh coming up the steps behind Miller and realised who had followed and betrayed her.

"It was just one of my old teachers," she said hurriedly. "I never said anything to him. I swear!"

"I don't believe you," he answered with a disappointed shake of the head. "Was it the man you spoke to yesterday at the boot fair?"

"No!" she lied vehemently.

"I see that it was. I'm deeply saddened at your rebellion, Labella. I have been chosen to rule in the absence of our great Lord and yet you complain and dodge and baulk at everything I do. You even refuse to read the sacred text. This cannot be tolerated. You are my

consort. The lesser monarchs must look up to you, as they look up to me. Your lack of belief will not be winked at any longer."

"What are you going to do?" Shiela demanded. "Even you're not mad enough to hurt me!"

The Ismus signalled to the Harlequins and they stepped forward to seize her by the arms.

The woman cried out, but it was no use struggling; they were far too strong.

"Miller!" she begged. "It's me, Shiela! Stop it. Tommo – stop it! Please!"

"They cannot speak," the Ismus reminded her. "And those names are meaningless to them now."

"If you kill me, the police will know who did it. You can't play this stupid game with them."

The Ismus looked offended. "Kill you?" he asked. "Whatever gave you that melodramatic idea? If I want anyone killed, I get the Court Assassin to do it for me. No, dearest Labella, I am merely going to open your pretty eyes to the world of the Dancing Jacks, so that you may stand at my side and these misguided mutinies of yours will be forgotten."

He clicked his fingers and Miller pulled Shiela's head back. The woman yelled and tried to fight once more, but it was hopeless.

"Where is the Queen of Hearts?" the Ismus asked.

Manda came huffing up the steps. "I am here, my Lord," she said.

"You have what I instructed you to fetch for me?"

"I have it here, my Lord," Manda answered obediently.

221

Shiela tried to twist her head around, but Miller held her firm and she couldn't see what the woman handed over. Then the Ismus's face moved into her line of sight.

"The Queen of Hearts has visited my conservatory, my fair Labella," he told her. "And behold what she has harvested from the Garden Apart."

He lifted the thing so she could see and Shiela screamed at the top of her voice. Then clamped her mouth shut as she realised what he intended.

The Holy Enchanter held in his fingers an ugly, almost translucent vegetable. It resembled a small gourd, but the waxy skin was a sickly yellowish-grey colour. It was soft and overripe and bruised easily in his grasp. Beads of juice already speckled the surface.

Shiela shook her head as much as she could and her eyes implored the man to spare her.

"You must taste the juice of the minchet fruit," he instructed with calm intent. "It is the only way."

He crushed the repulsive vegetable in his fist and a drizzle of sickly-smelling yellow fluid splashed on to her firmly sealed lips. He glanced at the other Harlequin and the man who had been Tommo pinched Shiela's nose.

For the better part of two minutes she held her breath and prayed for someone to save her.

By then everyone was standing on that roof. The Queen of Spades viewed the proceedings from behind her fan, so that she might

conceal her spiteful delight at Labella's torment.

The Limner put his head on one side and considered what a powerful painting this scene would make. He made mental notes so that he might convey it on to a canvas later.

Jangler knocked his knuckles together with excitement as he looked on. Mr Fellows had foreseen there would be some who would resist the pull of the sacred text. He had foretold there would also be 'aberrants' over whom the blessed scripture would have no power and so the remedy to this had been devised long ago.

Spent air was escaping from Shiela's lips as her lungs felt close to exploding. Bubbles percolated in the puddle of juice that had filled the crease of her tightly clenched mouth. Then, finally, it was over and she gasped and shrieked for breath. In that exact instant, as she gulped the new air down, the squashed, fibrous pulp of the unclean vegetable was thrust between her teeth. Shiela gagged and spat it out. She stared, horrified, accusing and wounded, at the Ismus – at that face she had once loved.

The juice was bitter and it stung her tongue. It was as if a fistful of nettles had been stuffed into her mouth. No matter how hard she tried, she could not rid herself of that rank, prickling taste. Then the bitterness burned down her throat and scorched through her veins.

The Ismus gestured for the Harlequins to release her.

Shiela staggered free of them and dragged her crinkling lips over her sleeve. And then it happened. The others watched in fascination as her face drained of anger and was replaced with something else.

The Queen of Hearts chortled with amusement when she saw the young woman grab hold of the Ismus's hand. The hand that had crushed the minchet fruit, the hand that was still wet and dripping. And then Shiela was licking it, sucking the juice from his fingers. When it was gone, she dropped to the floor like an animal and feverishly snatched up the fragments she had spat out. She crammed them against her thirsty lips.

The Holy Enchanter wiped his hands on his T-shirt.

"Now, Labella," he addressed her. "You have an appointment with the blessed text."

Leeching the last drops from the stringy residue, the Lady Labella kissed her own fingers dry and looked up at him with round, glassy eyes.

"Yes, my Lord Ismus!" she declared fervently. "Let me take my place at thy side in the magickal Kingdom. I beg thee!"

"You're already there," he answered. "And tonight we raise Mauger and bring him through. The Guardian of the Mooncaster Gate must come amongst us. The way must be opened."

"The way must be opened…" Mr Hankinson repeated in a thrilled whisper.

"The way must be opened," the others chanted with excitement.

The Lady Labella threw back her head. "The way must be opened!" she exulted.

Kennelled in a dungeon during the daylight hours, the Guardian of the Mooncaster Gate is let loose on a long lead after dark. Mauger is the beast's name; a monster from beyond, caught by the Dawn Prince himself, and never was there a more terrifying warden of the White Castle's main gate. The slender cord that tethers him is enchanted and was woven from the hair of the four Under Queens. As long as they live, Mauger will be safely bound. But should one or more perish, then the monster will be freed and maraud through the Kingdom. Only Haxxentrot the witch knows this and she plots endlessly to bring about the deaths of the Under Queens.

16

IT WAS PAST midnight and the Paediatric Unit was as quiet as any hospital ward could ever be. A trolley rattled in the distance, a respirator hissed with soft white noise and morphine pumps, and monitoring machines bleeped gently, giving a steady, digital rhythm to the not-quite dark. Light leaked in from the end nearest the corridor, where the anglepoise lamp of the nurse's station shone on the desk.

Joan Olivant, the night sister, was talking quietly to Shaun Preston, the charge nurse.

"Be a love, Shaun," she said. "I'm desperate for a cup of tea. Just nip out and get a pint of milk."

The young man groaned. He didn't want to budge.

Sister Olivant leaned over to him and quivered her bottom lip pleadingly. "Aww, pretty please," she implored. "I'm gagging for one."

Shaun pulled away from her. For some time now he had suspected she had some sort of a crush on him and he didn't feel comfortable when she acted all girlish like this. She was in her fifties, more than old enough to be his mother, with grizzling hair – and built like a wrestler. "Olivant the elephant", some of the unkind and less respectful staff called her behind her back.

Shaun shifted to the edge of his chair and ignored her doe-eyed gaze. Eventually Joan gave up and sat back. She took a deep, resigned breath, which inflated her formidable bosom like an emergency dinghy. Then she started grumbling about the Prime Minister.

It was his impromptu visit that afternoon that had robbed the small staff fridge of all the semi-skimmed. She was glad her shift hadn't coincided with that media circus. Apparently the ward had been crammed with the PM, his entourage of suits and the accompanying press.

"Bed Seven got all the attention," she told the charge nurse.

"Fiona Ellis," Shaun corrected. He didn't like the way Joan dehumanised the patients by referring to their bed numbers instead of using their names. "Not surprised," he added. "She's the most photogenic of them. Burns and fractures can't compete with a twelve-year-old blonde girl with a bandage over one eye. What could be better for his warm and fuzzy publicity? Fiona's like a human Pudsey Bear."

"She wasn't even in the Disaster," Sister Olivant commented dryly. "She was already in here when it happened."

Shaun glanced down the ward. There were twelve beds in total. Eleven of them were occupied by children who had been at the Landguard last Friday. The rest of those injured in the Disaster had been shunted round the hospital – to wherever there were vacant beds.

All was still. Foil balloons, tethered to bedside cupboards, gleamed in the dim light. The whites of the eyes of the Disney characters painted on the walls seemed to glow in the gloom. From one of the beds a sleepy voice murmured unhappily and another responded across the way.

"We can take their pain away," Shaun muttered sadly, "but we can't do anything about their nightmares. The horrors of that night will torment them for a long time yet – poor beggars."

"Some biscuits would be nice too," Joan said, harking back to the subject of tea.

"I don't want any tea," Shaun replied. "I'll get a can from the machine if I want anything."

"Some knight in shining armour you are," the sister huffed. "I'll nip along to Maternity and see if they've got half a pint I can scrounge. If there isn't, I'll pinch a baby's bottle. They always have a big tin of biscuits on the go there as well."

She rose and marched to the security door. Pausing before pressing the large button to unlock it, she looked back. With a wink, she said, "If you're very lucky, Shauny boy, I'll let you dunk a biccy in my brew."

Shaun couldn't think of any response to that, but the nervous, gulping sound effect that was always in old Tom and Jerry cartoons played in his mind. He looked away hastily. One of these days she was going to lunge at him or grope his bottom – or worse. He wondered if he should speak to Human Resources. But it would be his word against hers. Joan would simply laugh it off and everyone would think he was being paranoid or stirring up trouble. She'd been here so long, nobody would believe him over her.

He let out a dismal sigh then remembered where he was. His problems were nothing compared to what these youngsters had been through. He almost felt ashamed to even think about his own petty worries.

Leaving the nurse's station, he paced down the ward, checking the patients. Peter Starkey: thirteen years old, multiple leg fractures; Thomas Goulden: eleven years old, broken ribs and burns; Janet Harding: fourteen years old, multiple fractures; Jonathan Spencer:

thirteen years old, third-degree burns across his back...

Shaun paused when he came to the bed of Harvey Temple. This twelve-year-old had both legs in plaster and dressings on his arms where his fleece had melted to his skin last Friday.

The charge nurse smiled. The boy had fallen asleep with his earphones in. Shaun removed them gently and put the attached iPod on the cupboard, among the get-well cards.

Harvey stirred slightly and whimpered. He too was having nightmares, reliving those awful moments over and over again: the fight, the speeding car skidding out of control, the screams as it ploughed into the crowd, the panic, the explosions, the fire that rained down...

"It'll be OK," Shaun whispered. "Don't dream of all that. Just sleep, Harvey."

Then he heard the sound of Joan's strong fingers jabbing away at the entry keys outside the door.

"No milk to be had then?" he observed, nodding at her empty hands when she came back into the ward.

The night sister walked slowly to the desk and leaned against it. Even though her features were in semi-darkness, he could see there was a strange expression on her face.

"You feeling OK?" he asked.

Sister Olivant smiled. It was a weird, blank smile.

Shaun stared at her and wondered what new flirting tactic she was trying this time. He stepped forward warily. Then he saw the fresh yellow stains around her mouth and the livid juice running

229

down her chin. "What've you been eating?" he asked.

The woman's smile stretched wider and she glanced back at the security door. Only then did Shaun see the thin, scruffy man in the leather biker jacket holding it open and leering in. The first thought that entered the charge nurse's head was that it must be a relative of one of the patients, but at this hour? He didn't like the look of him at all. Before Shaun could say anything, two more men, with blackened faces, rushed in, past the stranger, and grabbed Shaun by the arms. One slapped a large hand over his mouth.

"There now," the Ismus said, sauntering over and casting his eyes around the ward. "They look so cosy, don't they, these little invalids? A trifle too cosy. Are you certain their sleep is troubled?"

"Dreadful nightmares," Joan assured him. "Sometimes we have to change the sheets."

The Ismus looked delighted and he rubbed his hands together.

Shaun could not take in what was happening. Locked in the fierce grip of the two men, he could do nothing. His eyes flicked back to stare at Joan. The night sister was beaming indulgently as the thin intruder strolled down the ward as if he owned the place. What the hell was going on? What did these mad people want? Had Joan gone insane? He tried to yell, but the hand that covered his mouth pressed all the more tightly and his lips bruised painfully against his teeth.

When he heard more footsteps approaching, Shaun's eyes darted back to the doorway and he prayed it was Security, come to deal with this unhinged trio. But no, he saw two others enter and his hopes

were crushed. One was a young, unkempt-looking woman. The other was a small, stout man in his sixties, dressed smartly in a charcoal-grey three-piece suit.

"Quiet," the Ismus commanded in a low voice. "We must not wake our Tiny Tims. That would spoil everything."

He raised a hand and beckoned to the elderly man.

The bald solicitor came forward and Shaun saw he was carrying a large Gladstone bag. He placed it on the floor, flipped back the catches and reached inside.

"Here it is, my Lord," Mr Hankinson whispered excitedly. "Just as you left it, all those years ago."

He was holding up something like a shoebox. The cardboard was dented and speckled with age.

"My grandfather kept it safe for you, that night you disappeared," he continued. "Then my father after him and then myself."

The Ismus grinned. He removed the lid and pushed aside the mottled scrunches of newspaper within.

Shaun could not begin to imagine what it contained. His mind burned with the most horrible suspicions. What were these lunatics doing here? What did they want? What were they going to do with the children? It was then he realised the young woman was regarding him curiously. He saw the same repulsive yellowish stains around her mouth that still glistened down Joan's chin.

"Do not resist," Shiela told him. "This is a night of glory – a momentous hour is upon us. Pathways are to be unblocked. The way is to be cleared. A bridge will be built. You should marvel at your good fortune to witness such wonders… and you shall."

She took her hand from the pocket of her denim jacket and held up a squashy, rank-smelling fruit.

"One soft bite and you will see," she said. "Everything will be clear to you, as it was to me. The trumpets of Mooncaster will call and this grey dream will fade."

She stretched out her hand towards him and putrid drips dribbled through her fingers.

"No, Labella," the Ismus instructed, seeing the fear in Shaun's face. "Not yet. Let Lawrence Nightingale remain afraid a while longer. It is useful."

Helpless, Shaun could only watch as the Ismus lifted an object from the cardboard box. What was that – an old radio? How much crazier could this get?

The Ismus ran his hand over the smooth, brown, Bakelite surface. It did look like an art deco radio from the 1930s, with its large central dial, tuning knobs, brass grill and sleek, walnut-effect finish, but it was far more than that.

"A masterly work of genius, my Lord," the solicitor declared admiringly. "An astounding invention."

"It is merely another key, Jangler," the Ismus told him, "albeit a rather more complex one, and we will need more of them – much larger versions."

His fingers closed about one of the three tuning knobs and clicked it to the left.

"This is the fun part," he uttered, breathless with expectation.

The Ismus turned the next knob, teasing it around delicately – like a safecracker at work.

Harvey Temple mumbled in his sleep again. The Ismus turned to him and carried the strange device over to the bed. A low hum began inside it. Harvey's head twitched.

In the next bed, lying on his front, Jonathan Spencer coughed in his sleep. His forehead creased and he ground his teeth as his nightmares intensified.

Within the Bakelite device a small light bulb flickered on and the outer ring of the dial shone dimly. The hum buzzed a little louder.

The Ismus continued to adjust and tune. A fizzle of static issued from the brass grill of the speaker, followed by electronic whoops and squeals. Another child wept in his slumber.

"It's charging up nicely," the Ismus announced. "Let's see what residue was left behind from that night, before I was interrupted – almost eighty years ago…"

To Shaun's astonishment, music suddenly came drifting out of the strange device. It was an old, crackly song from the thirties, and the singer had a desolate, haunting voice.

"Close your eyes," the disembodied crooner insisted. "Rest your head on my shoulder and sleep, close your eyes… and I will close mine."

In this madness, the song sounded sinister and menacing.

"Close your eyes. Let's pretend that we're both counting sheep, close your eyes."

Mr Hankinson laced his fingers across his chest and nodded to himself. "Ah," he grunted, identifying the mournful singer, "…Al Bowlly."

"No," Janet Harding cried suddenly above the music. "The lights – a car – it's coming this way – it's not stopping!"

Shaun saw her dig her head deeper into her pillows. Pain and the terror of Friday night were flooding her mind.

"Too many people!" the girl continued. "I can't get out of the way – it's here – it's here!"

Like a contagion, the nightmares spread throughout the ward and soon eleven children were trembling and crying in their sleep, as the saxophones and clarinets of the big band continued to fill the air.

"Music play, something dreamy for dancing…"

Peter Starkey yelled out and his body arched beneath the covers. Only Fiona Ellis remained still and silent.

The Ismus laughed quietly. The needle in the centre of the device's dial began to quiver.

Shaun could not understand how the children were sleeping through this. The severity of the nightmares should have jolted them awake by now and the din they were making should have woken Fiona. Even as that thought entered his head, he saw the girl's face contort and tears began to fall from her good eye. She too was suffering in her dreams. Shaun could not guess what grim memory fuelled hers.

Now the ward resounded with the wails and cries of every child. The Bakelite device whistled and squawked sharply, but still the old,

melancholy music played. A cymbal crashed and the Ismus tapped his foot with amusement.

"Time to ramp it up a little," he said, making a further adjustment. The electric squeals and warbles multiplied.

Then Shaun felt the skin on his arms tingle and gooseflesh pricked out across his body. He could feel the hairs rising on his scalp and saw the young woman's shaggy hair lift from her shoulders. The scant white wisps that were combed over the solicitor's shiny pate streamed upwards. A sheet of A4 paper started to flutter across the desk. Then a pen went skittering after it. Paperclips shot upwards. The computer monitor cracked and went dark.

At the end of the beds the patients' charts began to swing and clatter against the metal frames. The lid on a plastic squash bottle popped off and the bright orange contents spurted out. A bag of saline jerked like a pendulum on its hook. Then the whole stand rose off the ground. A morphine pump juddered and rocked backwards.

Shaun's eyes grew wider and wider.

One by one the foil balloons swelled and burst. Get-well cards flew up and flattened against the wall like pinned butterflies. The pale turquoise curtains that separated each bed started to flap and their rings rang on the rails as they billowed towards the ceiling. And then the bed covers lifted, floating up like rafts of thistledown.

Just like the balloons, the saline bags puffed up. In rapid succession they exploded.

Another cymbal crashed. The trumpets blasted and the trombones thundered.

Still asleep, Janet Harding screamed.

The device in the Ismus's hands squawked in answer and its needle whirred around the dial.

The children's limbs lifted into the air and the legs of each bed left the floor.

Peter Starkey was screaming now. Then Jonathan Spencer joined him. The Ismus danced down the ward and soon every child was shrieking.

Shaun saw Fiona Ellis levitate off the mattress. The girl drifted higher and higher until the invisible force suddenly threw her against the wall and pinned her there, upside-down.

Thomas Goulden flew up next. The drip feed pulled from his arm and he was sent spinning into a mural of Dumbo and Shrek. His bedside table came sliding up next to him. The water jug spilled its contents over his face. But still he remained locked in that nightmare sleep.

Leaning against the desk, Sister Olivant watched in quiet admiration. How light and giddy she felt now that she knew this world was not the true one.

Comics and magazines thrashed their pages as they swept by. Battering against the ceiling, they formed a noisy, twisting whirlpool of glossy paper. Then the remaining ten children were plucked from their beds. Harvey Temple was snatched up, legs first, and his plaster casts smashed heavily against the wall when he was hurled against it.

The Ismus revelled in the horror and despair of the sleeping

youngsters. He spun about, delighted, then stared down at the dial on the Bakelite device. The needle had progressed all the way around. It was time. The electronic bedlam that crackled from the grill had drowned out the music. It was almost deafening and the pitch was rising all the time. It quickly became unbearable. Shaun clenched his teeth and squeezed his eyes shut as the noise cut right through him. Mr Hankinson covered his ears and Labella did the same. Joan shuddered and winced and even the black-faced bodyguards were trembling. The noise seemed to drill through their heads until, finally, it soared so high they couldn't hear it any more. There was only the music again and the shrieks of the children.

The Ismus tweaked the tuning. The music stopped at once and a new sound replaced it. Shaun's heart thumped violently. He heard a bestial roar. But it was unlike anything he had ever heard in his life. It was an unearthly, ravening bellow – a noise consumed with terrifying rage.

"Listen," the Ismus declared, stroking the grill fondly. "Mauger is impatient to cross over."

Striding to the centre of the ward, he placed the device on the floor and clicked the third tuning knob. Then he stepped away smartly.

The device began to shake. Suddenly a freak wind came howling from the speaker grill. It punched into the ceiling and the magazines that surged and swirled there were instantly torn to shreds.

The Ismus opened his arms in welcome and laughed his loudest.

Then the gale fell upon the ward. It went racing over the empty beds, tearing through the floating sheets, ripping chunks out of the foam pillows. And then...

Shaun's mind recoiled with terror.

The unseen power had rushed at one of the bed curtains. For the briefest moment the turquoise fabric moulded around its monstrous shape. It was large as a bull, with an enormous head supporting two curling horns. A deep, rib-rattling roar bawled from the awful face that the curtain revealed.

Whether the glimpse of that dreadful thing had so shocked the bodyguards that they loosened their grip, or whether his own intense fear had pumped new strength around his body, Shaun did not know, but a desperate kick and a smash of elbow in a soot-covered face and he was free.

There was nothing he could do to save the children here. They were stuck around the walls, writhing like human fridge magnets. He had to raise the alarm and get help. He seized the broken monitor from the desk, leaped forward and flung it at the Bakelite device on the floor.

There was a flash and both of them smashed and splintered. A cloud of yellow, sulphurous smoke belched out. Then all was chaos. The force keeping children, beds, drips, morphine pumps, ripped magazines, chairs and cabinets up in the air was gone. Everything came crashing down. Shaun glanced around him in despair. It was like the aftermath of a terrorist attack. What else could he do but run? Shouting for help, he charged to the security door, slapped his hand against the release button and pelted down the corridor.

The black-faced bodyguards leaped after him.

"Wait!" the Ismus commanded them. "Don't rob Mauger of his sport."

Another ghastly roar shook the ward. A large, harrowing shape jumped through the yellow smoke and the two bodyguards were thrown off their feet as the thing that had crossed over barged past.

Surrounded by the wreck of the Paediatric Unit, as glossy confetti fluttered down around him, the Ismus called out, "Hunt him down! Bring him back to me."

Mauger's hideous bellow went echoing down the corridor.

"When he does," the Ismus said, turning to the Lady Labella, "feed him the minchet fruit."

"Yes, my Lord," Shiela answered, holding it up and licking the river of putrid juice that ran down her wrist.

And then there was silence, broken only by the agonised weeping and whimpers of the young patients, strewn carelessly about the floor. They were still trapped inside their nightmares.

"What a nasty mess!" Sister Olivant exclaimed with a chuckle as she gazed about the devastated ward. Beds were upturned, curtains yanked from their rails, machines bleeped erratically and red lights were flashing. A mingling flood of squash and saline was spreading across the floor.

"I'm confident you can cope," the Ismus told her. "And the busier you are here, the richer your time in Mooncaster will be."

The night sister nodded eagerly. "And when they ask what happened?" she asked.

"Tell them the male nurse flipped and went berserk," he suggested. "There was nothing you could do to stop him. He won't dispute it."

"Naughty, sexy Shauny," she giggled. "It'll serve him right for being so coy with me."

Shaun Preston ran for his life and, for all he knew, his soul. Around the corner was the door to Maternity. He'd call Security from there. Flinging himself against the locked door, he pounded his fists upon it, demanding to be let in.

"Come on! Come on!" he bawled. "Open up!"

There was no answering buzz from the lock. No curious face appeared behind the glass panel to see who was hammering on it at that time of night. Shaun pressed against the glass and saw that the nurse's station was empty. He couldn't see the nurse on duty. The ward stretched off to the right, out of his vision. She must be at the far end. He yelled even louder and began kicking the door.

An exhausted new mother sat up in the nearest bed and stared over at him, confused at first then angry.

"You'll wake the babies!" she mouthed.

Right on cue, one of the infants started to cry.

"Let me in!" Shaun demanded.

The woman gestured down the ward, waving the night sister over frantically. Shaun saw her lips form the word "nutcase".

"Hurry up! Hurry up!" he yelled.

He heard footsteps running closer. The night sister rushed into view, her face startled and questioning.

240

"Open the door!" Shaun shouted. "Hurry!"

The sister did not hesitate. She ran towards him and pressed the entry button. Shaun wrenched the door open. Then he froze.

Mauger's roar came booming down the corridor. Shaun looked past the astonished night sister to where the mothers and their babies were now awake and either crying or looking anxious and frightened. If he ran in there, the invisible terror would smash its way in after him. He thought of the destruction in the Paediatric Ward and imagined the carnage that monster would wreak in Maternity.

For the second time that night, he heard the old Tom and Jerry gulping sound, only this time it was real. He knew what he had to do.

Shaking his head, he backed out of the doorway. "Don't open this for anyone," he told the sister before he slammed it shut between them. "Not for anyone." Then he fled, further along the corridor. Behind him the terrible force came raging around the corner.

"This way – you ugly Mary!" he goaded. "Come get me!"

Mauger roared again. The noticeboard outside Maternity rattled on the wall. Notes and announcements went flying as the beast stampeded by.

Shaun ran to the lifts and thumped the call button.

"Dammit!"

Both lifts were down on the ground floor. There wasn't time to wait. The air shook as Mauger rushed upon him. Shaun leaped away, ducked behind a vending machine, then kicked open the double doors of an empty, budget-closed ward.

It was dark in there. Mattresses were rolled up on skeletal bed frames. There was nowhere to hide and no other exit.

Shaun swore under his breath. He heard the vending machine buckle and smash outside as Mauger's fury fell upon it. Packets of crisps, chocolate bars and cans of pop gushed over the floor.

The man ran to the far wall, hoping the darkness between two windows would conceal him long enough so he could dodge past and escape. The lifts would be here by now, if he could just reach them…

The double doors flew open. Shaun stared directly ahead and tried to silence his panting breaths.

A solitary can of Tango came rolling into the deserted ward. It trundled under one of the beds and bumped gently against the metal leg. Shaun could feel the blood pulsing in his neck. In the doorway a crisp packet burst as a heavy, invisible foot stamped on it. Another popped and the disgorged contents crunched as the beast prowled forward, into the empty ward.

Even though Shaun could not see the monster's eyes, he could feel them burning into him. It knew exactly where he was. It was a demon of the darkness. Night shadows were no hiding place.

A bed juddered as it lumbered past. Shaun's terror grew.

No! his thoughts screamed. *You won't get me. You won't!*

There was a vicious snarl and, for an instant, the darkness shivered. A faint, horned outline appeared. It was even more horrific than Shaun had glimpsed through the curtain. This time he could see the huge fangs in the downturned mouth.

Any hope of escape vanished. He knew there was only one way

out now. Taking a deep, steadying breath, he went for it.

"Dear God, save me!" he yelled aloud.

Mauger roared as it pounced. Shaun Preston darted sideways. He vaulted on to the windowsill and hurled himself against the glass. The windowpane splintered around him. He dived out into the night. Knives of glass lacerated his hands and face and sliced through his uniform. Howling, he flailed his limbs as he fell the three storeys. The shattered window sparkled around him all the way down.

The awful noise as he hit the ground, followed by Mauger's bellow of frustration, was heard back in the Paediatric Unit.

The Ismus raised his eyebrows in mild surprise. "Put the fruit away," he sighed to Shiela. "We won't need it now. Shauny isn't coming back."

"Such a pity about your wonderful invention," Mr Hankinson lamented, looking down at the fragments of the Bakelite device.

"As I said," the Ismus told him, "we will need more. Now let's bring Mauger to heel before the fuss kicks off."

He ushered his followers from the wrecked ward and bestowed a final smile upon Sister Olivant.

"First thing in the morning I'll send Jangler round with a copy of Dancing Jacks for each of your patients," he promised. "They've earned them. They really have."

"Blessed be," Joan thanked him, beaming.

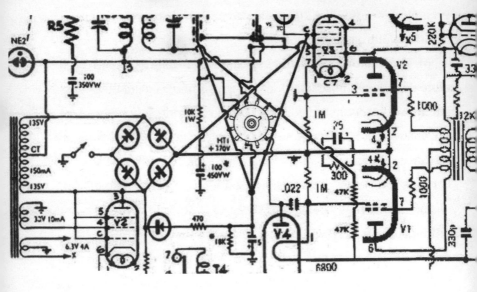

17

PAUL STARTED THE next day in a thoroughly excellent and elated mood. Nothing was going to spoil it for him. When Gerald had driven him home after the piano lesson the previous evening, Martin and his mother sat him down and told him their intentions. Yelling with joy, he had leaped off the settee and punched the air. He could not have been happier. He had been wishing for them to get married for well over a year now. He also longed to have a baby brother or sister and so nothing whatsoever could ruin his day – or even his week. At least that was what he thought.

Martin drove them to school that morning in a similar frame of

mind. Not even the disturbing phone call Carol received from the hospital could dampen his spirits. Apparently a male nurse had snapped and gone on a violent rampage through the children's ward, before throwing himself out of a window. Luckily none of the young patients suffered anything worse than cuts and bruises and one broken arm, but it was a shock to everyone who knew and worked with Shaun Preston.

It was the last thing anyone expected him to be capable of, but you could never really be sure about anyone. Sister Joan Olivant was already telling the press how she had always been uncomfortable in his presence; how he used to stare at her inappropriately and make lewd suggestions. She was certain that her rejection of his attentions and threat to make an official complaint were what had driven him over the edge. It was another media frenzy over there today.

As Martin drove through the school gates, he saw that even more floral tributes had been placed in front of the railings overnight. He wondered how long they were expected to remain there. What was the respectful thing to do with such things afterwards? Barry Milligan would be sure to know; he was good at stuff like that. For all his scary TV cop persona, he could be very tactful when required.

Humming a tune to himself, that sounded more than a little like the wedding march, Martin waved goodbye to Paul and made his way to the staffroom. His good humour evaporated when he saw his colleagues poring over the morning papers.

"Doesn't bode well," he observed. "What's going on here then?" They couldn't have printed the story about the male nurse already, could they?

Mrs Early held up a tabloid in her thumb and forefinger as though it was a soiled nappy. The front page was full of the engagement of the month, but pages 6 and 7 were devoted to 'Dead Drunk Head – Boozy Headmaster of Yob School drinks himself under the desk while kids lie dead'. Sneaky photographs of Barry Milligan, taken over the past few evenings, were plastered across the pages. There he was: drinking in two different pubs, coming out of off-licences and even through the window of his front room where he was sprawled 'dead drunk' on his sofa, nursing an empty glass with the remnants of that night's binge all around him.

"Hell!" Martin swore.

"The man's a liability and a dinosaur," Mr Wynn said. "He's not fit to do the job. What sort of example is that?"

Martin threw the paper down in disgust and stared at the games teacher angrily. "What any of us do in our time away from here isn't anyone's business," he told him.

"The only people who ever say that are those with something to hide," Mr Wynn muttered to himself.

"What was that?" Martin demanded. "If you've got something to say, let's all hear it."

Mr Wynn looked him up and down. He snorted and flexed his broad shoulders then smiled falsely. Zipping up his tracksuit, he swaggered from the room. Martin wanted to run out after him and

punch his stupid orange face, but Mr Wynn would have flattened him with one retaliating swipe.

"Brainless muscle-head," he seethed through grated teeth. "Go squeeze the steroid spots on your back."

"Happiest days of our lives," Mrs Early said wearily.

"So where is Barry?" Martin asked.

"In his office," Mr Roy answered. "Wouldn't be surprised if his phone line melts today. I wouldn't go anywhere near. Cornered beasts are liable to lash out at anyone."

"It's not fair," Martin said. "He's damn good at the job."

Mrs Early shook her head. "Doesn't mean a thing now," she declared. "He's suddenly infamous across the country. No one cares how good a Head he is. He's been tried and judged already. His identity is fixed. He'll never be rid of it. He'll be the Dead Drunk Head forever. It's on his file now and will be dredged up and thrown at him wherever he goes."

"His position is untenable," Mr Roy added.

Martin knew they were right, but it sickened him. The bell sounded for registration.

Mrs Early looked down at the discarded newspaper. "Such is the power of words," the English teacher mused to herself. "They inflict pain, ruin lives and start wars. All it takes is one." With a shake of her head, she left the staffroom, reflecting that there were some words which she too could lose her job over if she uttered just one of them in class. The might of language must never be underestimated.

Elsewhere in the school, Paul Thornbury's happy mood took longer to dissipate.

His friends had been strange with him the previous day and last night they hadn't responded to his pokes on Facebook, where their profile photographs had been replaced by pictures of playing cards. He had wondered how Anthony Maskel and Graeme Parker would react to him today and how he should behave towards them. Should he be off with them and treat them coldly if they spoke to him, or would that make it worse? Were they even worth keeping as friends if they could be this way?

When he saw them that morning at registration, they could not have been more pleasant – too pleasant.

"Blessed be!" they both greeted, grinning like cats that had inherited a combined dairy and salmon farm business.

"Hello," Paul answered cautiously. "You guys OK?"

The two boys smiled back at him. They were not normally like this. Anthony was usually moaning about some imagined ailment and Graeme was naturally a bit morose, but it was those very traits that Paul enjoyed about them. He couldn't make out what had happened to change that.

"We are most well," Anthony answered. "We have been sharing our thoughts on the Court."

"We'd like you to share them as well," Graeme told him.

Paul looked puzzled. "You're not on about tennis, are you?" he asked.

His friends laughed, but shook their heads. "There is only one

Court," Anthony said, reaching into his bag and bringing out a book. "This one."

"Hey, I've got that as well!" Paul exclaimed. "The bloke gave it to me."

"The Ismus gave it you?" they asked, impressed. "You are highly honoured."

"The what?"

The boys blinked at him. "You have not read it?" they asked. "Or are you an aberrant?"

"Am I a what? No, I've not had a chance to start it yet. Is it any good?"

The boys exchanged significant glances and looked as if they knew secrets that he did not. Paul didn't like that.

"Good isn't the right word," Anthony informed him. "Paul, it is the only thing that matters. It is the most…" His voice trailed off, unable to find the correct words to express his feelings for Dancing Jacks.

Paul wriggled on his chair uncomfortably. They were beyond weird now.

"Do you have yours here?" Graeme asked. "We could read it together. It's good reading it together, out loud as one voice." He began rocking slowly backwards and forwards.

"No," Paul replied, feeling extremely uneasy. "I left it at home."

"Then let us read to you," Anthony urged.

"Yes, we will read it to you, together," added Graeme. "And you can share the joy of it with us."

249

Paul looked around to see if anyone in the class was taking any notice, but nobody was looking in their direction.

The two boys held up their books and opened them at the first page to read aloud.

Then the bell rang.

"Saved," Paul breathed, without realising the enormous truth of his words.

Their first lesson was history. Year 7 was learning about medieval realms and the castles of the Normans. There wasn't one child who disliked that topic and just about everyone found it fascinating. That morning two found it even more absorbing than the rest. The usually quiet Anthony and Graeme were asking lots of peculiar and irrelevant questions about the colour of the stonework, the layout of the rooms and how many tapestries they would have. It was as if they were trying to compare a Norman castle to somewhere they had been and found the wooden motte-and-baileys and stone keeps and towers of the Normans lacking in every aspect.

Miss Smyth, the cool, blonde teacher, who always wore crisp, white blouses with a small red or black bow at her throat and whom practically every boy in the school had a crush on, was beginning to get irritated.

"Do you know how many horses they kept in the stables, Miss?" Graeme asked. "And how many hounds and hawks?"

The other children didn't dare titter at his newfound nerve. Miss Smyth was not someone to wind up. She may have been as beautiful

and well groomed as a Hitchcock leading lady, but she was no pushover and only the foolish ever tried to bait her. They watched and listened, baffled at the boys' behaviour, but curious to see how much she would tolerate and just how she would react when pushed too far.

"That would depend on the castle in question," she replied sternly. "Each was different, depending on the wealth and status of who lived there. Only the very rich would keep a large number of any of those animals."

"My Lord Ismus keeps forty fine horses in the stables of Mooncaster," Graeme said proudly. "Each a splendid thoroughbred, with a richly embroidered cloth to wear when the knight goes riding – and the White Castle has three concentric walls and the Keep is five storeys high…"

"Enough!" Miss Smyth told him, pointing her pen at the boy. "If you keep on disrupting the lesson with your stupid remarks, you'll be kept behind after school."

"It's true!" Anthony cried in Graeme's defence. "It is the best castle in the world!"

"With the finest steeds! And in a separate building of its own is the Jack of Club's stallion – the one he saved while it was still only a foal! There's no better or stronger or nobler beast than that one!"

"That's right!" Anthony chimed in again. "It's the envy of every knight and…"

"Be quiet!" Miss Smyth roared, slamming a textbook on the desk, which made everyone jump in their seats. She had no idea what stupid game the pair of them were playing, but she was not putting up with any more of it.

"I'm surprised at you two!" she continued severely. "But one more word, just one, and you're in detention."

The boys looked affronted as though she was being unjust, but they hung their heads and said nothing else for the remainder of the lesson.

Nobody in the rest of the class dared utter a word either. Miss Smyth's face had turned a deep pink colour and her nostrils were flaring. Graeme and Anthony's insolence had made her lose her temper and she barked at everyone to copy out passages from their textbooks.

Paul and the other children stared at the two boys. What were they thinking? Now they were all suffering her displeasure and they sat there, meekly doing their work. When the bell rang, no one attempted to move until she gave her permission and then they filed out quietly.

"You two," she addressed Graeme and Anthony as they passed her desk. "Come here."

The boys stood before her, eyes cast down.

"I don't understand what that was about today," she told them sharply. "But I never want to see the same stupid behaviour from you again, do you hear?"

Anthony raised his face and looked her squarely in the eyes. "We hear you, Miss," he said in a fearless, almost haughty tone. "We hear you and we forgive you."

"You what?" she asked in disbelief.

"We forgive you."

Miss Smyth's mouth fell open slightly. She had never been spoken to like this, and certainly not by someone in Year 7. Anthony continued to stare at her. This was more than disrespect. It was disturbing. She noticed with a shock that his eyes appeared glazed, almost lifeless – like the eyes of a doll.

"You had better be careful, young man," she finally managed to say. "I'll be on to your parents about this."

"They will forgive you too," he answered. "For now."

Then it was Graeme's turn. His face was impassive and calm and his eyes were the same.

"You can't help it," he said in a flat, matter-of-fact voice. "You're just ignorant, Miss."

"Yes, you're ignorant... for now."

"But that will change."

The teacher drew back in her chair. The boys were not normal. "Get out," she murmured in as level a voice as she could manage. "Get out of here."

They waited a few moments more, smiling at her, then left the room.

"Blessed be," they called out.

The pen was shaking in Miss Smyth's hand as she watched the door close behind them. It was broad daylight, she was sitting in a school classroom, one of the safest places imaginable, and yet she had never felt so threatened and intimidated in her life. It took her a full five minutes to recover and rise from her desk, but she was still trembling.

Paul was waiting for the two boys in the playground, wondering what Miss Smyth had said. Looking around him, he noticed that other children in different years were behaving strangely out there. Small groups were huddled together and some of them were rocking backwards and forwards, like Graeme had done that morning in registration.

"Another day in Loonyland," he muttered. To occupy himself while he waited, he took out his phone and sent a text to his mother, just to say 'hi' and ask if she could wash his gym kit for tomorrow.

He had just pressed Send when he saw Graeme and Anthony leave the school building. Paul ran over to them.

"What were you playing at in there?" he asked. "She almost went ballistic!"

"We were not playing," Anthony countered. "We were trying to instruct her."

"She knows nothing of life within a real castle," Graeme agreed. "She needs tutoring."

Paul waggled his head. "Okaaay…" he said, humouring them, but not understanding where they were going with this. "And was she grateful?"

"She isn't ready yet," Graeme answered. "But it won't be long before she is."

"Not long," Anthony echoed, nodding like a plastic dog in the back of a car.

"You two have flipped, you really have," Paul declared. "Is this all because of that old book?"

The boys shot severe looks at him. "Watch what you say!" Anthony warned. "Speak no ill of Dancing Jacks. The penalties are swift and harsh. The Ismus will see to that."

Paul almost laughed. "He doesn't sound like a very merry Ismus then!" he quipped.

Graeme and Anthony's faces looked sterner than ever.

Paul backed away from them. "You know what, Anthony," he said. "You can stick that daft book and your potty Ismus up where the sun don't shine. I'm sick of this stupid game – it's boring and so…"

Before he could finish, Anthony lashed out. He grabbed the unsuspecting boy by the throat, pushed him to the ground and knelt on his chest.

"There is no Anthony!" he snarled in Paul's astonished face. "I am Aethelheard, groom of the stables."

"Get off!" Paul cried in a strangulated voice as he thrashed underneath. Graeme stood over him and trod on his arms, pinning him down even more.

"And I am Bertolf!" he shouted. "I tend to my Lord's hounds. I know a mangy dog when I see one."

"Yield!" Anthony demanded. "Yield and retract your blasphemy!"

"Get off – you mental cases!"

255

"Recant, caitiff!"

"Up yours!"

Anthony's hands squeezed tighter round his throat and Paul choked. He held out for as long as he could. Then he nodded frantically.

Anthony loosened his grip. "You recant?"

"Yes," Paul coughed.

"Say the Ismus is the most noble ruler under the sun."

"Say it!" Graeme commanded, putting more weight on the balls of his feet and making Paul gasp from the pain in his arms.

"The… Ismus… is…"

"The most noble ruler…" Anthony prompted.

"The most… noble ruler…"

"Under the sun."

"Under the… sun. Ow – my arms!"

The boys released him. "Be about your day," Graeme growled. "And make no more vile calumnies against our Lord."

Rubbing his neck and then his arms, Paul staggered to his feet. His face was almost purple. A torrent of emotions gushed through him: rage, shock, shame and humiliation, but the worst, and the one that hurt the most, was the terrible sense of betrayal. He had believed they were his friends. That was the last time he would have anything to do with them.

The boys gave him one last warning glance then moved off and joined a group who were reading solemnly.

In the staffroom Miss Smyth was relating her encounter to Mrs Early.

"They stood there like… like the devil spawn of Ant and Dec," she said. "It wasn't just insolence – there was something abnormal and nasty behind it. I couldn't bear looking at them. Actually, no – I couldn't bear them looking at me."

Mrs Early was so interested she hadn't touched her knitting.

"Those two are usually so quiet," she commented in her languorous voice. "It's like getting blood from a stone asking them to contribute to lessons – they never volunteer to read aloud. It's painful to watch them struggling."

"Well, I'm going to ask the Head to write to their parents," Miss Smyth announced. "They're not getting away with that. Has Barry made an appearance yet?"

Mrs Early shook her head. "Still in his office, still on the phone. I don't think we'll be seeing much of him today."

"I wonder if he had a hearty meal?" the history teacher said sadly.

Mrs Early agreed. His days as Head were numbered and his career in education was finished.

"Oh!" she said with sudden realisation. "I've got those boys this afternoon."

"Watch them," Miss Smyth cautioned. "There's something not right there. Not right at all."

"I'm almost looking forward to it. Might take my mind off who Barry's replacement will be."

"Now that really is something to worry about," Miss Smyth sighed.

Paul's next lesson was art. He normally sat at the same table as Graeme and Anthony, but found an empty seat at the back of the art room and avoided any eye contact with them.

He usually enjoyed this lesson, but just then he wanted the day to be over so he could go home and lose himself on the computer or in a DVD. One thing was certain, the first thing he'd do would be delete those two from his Friends list.

The art room smelled pleasantly of poster paints and drying papier-mâché. Gazing at the walls, Paul saw that several new pictures had been Blu-tacked up since last week. They were fresh, lively paintings of castles. Studying them more closely, he saw that they were all supposed to be the same castle – a white one.

During lunch he took himself to the library to prevent another incident like the one that morning at break. He just wanted to sit quietly and be left alone. Pushing through the library doors, he was surprised to find it crowded. There were at least forty pupils from different years in there. There wasn't a spare seat to be had, except for the ones at the computers. That in itself was extremely odd.

The astonishment must have registered on his face because Miss Hopwood, the librarian, came across to him.

"There's plenty of computers free if you want," she said brightly. "Or you can choose a book from the shelves... unless you've brought one of your own, like everyone else?"

Paul hardly heard her. He was staring at the children hunched over the tables, their eyes glued to the books in their hands, oblivious

to everything else around them. Some of them were swaying backwards and forwards in their chairs.

Without answering the librarian, he turned around and left.

Miss Hopwood didn't blame him. She couldn't understand what was going on. Some of the pupils present never visited the library and she found their intense concentration on the books they had brought in with them to be unnatural. Looking over their shoulders, she saw that they appeared to be reading the same book.

"What's all this then?" she tried to ask Sandra Dixon, in a forced, chirpy manner. "The latest fad?"

The Year 10 girl lifted her bruised face from Dancing Jacks and seemed to look right through her. "I am the Jill of Hearts," she said in a far-off voice. "I am the Jill of Hearts, I am the Jill of Hearts…"

Miss Hopwood stepped away nervously. Then every child began rocking in their chair and chanting under their breath as they read.

The librarian crept out of sight. For the rest of the lunchtime she stayed hidden behind the shelves.

That afternoon during English, Paul was forced to sit in his usual place in front of Graeme and Anthony. Nowhere else was free.

He need not have worried though. The boys did not even glance up at him as he sat down. Anthony had his eyes closed and was moving his head from side to side as if lost in an enchanting dream. Graeme's face was hidden behind his bag on the desk.

When Mrs Early came in, she turned to the boys immediately. She was ready for them – or so she thought.

259

"Bag off desk," she instructed right away.

Graeme peered sullenly over the top of it.

"Bag!" she repeated.

Very slowly he dragged it from the desk, revealing the book in front of him.

"Put that away," she told him. "We're not doing a reading comprehension today, we're having a spelling test – lots of lovely, tough words."

An audible groan could be heard in the room. Mrs Early gave everyone a mildly scolding look. Then she noticed that Graeme had not done as he had been told.

"I said put that book away," she repeated.

He ignored her and continued reading.

"Graeme Parker – are you listening to me?"

He read to the end of the page before lifting his face and staring at her.

"What's the point of spelling tests?" he said flatly. "Every computer has a spellchecker. You're wasting our time. This is an English lesson. We should be reading. I am reading."

Mrs Early was taken aback. She had been expecting some sort of trouble, but nothing quite so rude or said with such flagrant disregard for her authority.

"Don't you speak to me like that!" she told him. "You will do as you are told, young man. Put that book away at once and I will tell you just why being able to spell correctly is important, if only to stop you looking like a village idiot in chat rooms."

"A Master of Hounds doesn't need to spell," Graeme answered belligerently. "That's what I hope to be one day."

"And a groom doesn't need to spell either," Anthony chipped in at his side.

The rest of the class held their breath. The boys were going further than they had in history that morning. Paul shifted around slowly to watch what would happen.

Mrs Early came towards them, arms folded.

"Both of you are stopping behind tonight," she said quietly.

"I'm not and you can't make me," Graeme told her with an indifferent shrug before giving his attention back to the book. "The hounds need me. My Lord is going to hunt the talking fox."

"And I'll need to get the horses ready," Anthony added.

Mrs Early came closer. She was wonderfully composed. They weren't going to unnerve her.

"Give me that book," she said, holding out her hand.

"Get your own!" Graeme answered back.

"Give it to me."

The boy grunted unpleasantly and turned the page to continue reading. Mrs Early's hand reached out and pulled the book from his hands.

His reaction was startling.

"Give it back!" he screamed as though scalded. "Give it back, give it back!"

Mrs Early was already returning to her desk, to deposit the book there before dealing with them properly. Then pandemonium broke out.

Graeme leaped from his chair, clambered on to his desk and launched himself at her. He sprang through the air, landed on her back and bit her shoulder.

"Give it me!" he yelled. "Give it me!"

Mrs Early twisted about and managed to throw him off. The boy hit her desk then crashed to the floor. In an instant he was back on his feet and Anthony was at his side.

"Give it him back!" the other boy screeched. "Give it him back!"

The other children could only stare in horror and disbelief as the two of them attacked her. They tore at her hair and slapped her face. Then they hit her with their young fists. Molly Barnes began to cry and the rest looked on in stricken silence.

Paul didn't know what to do. He was frozen in his seat. The boys were as ferocious and savage as rabid dogs. Then he heard Mrs Early crying for help and he jumped up to drag them off. Three other lads and a girl hurried to join him, but Graeme and Anthony were wild and stronger than anyone could have guessed. The noise and chaos was deafening. It was a fierce, desperate fight that ended only when a terrified girl fled the classroom to fetch another teacher and ran smack into the Head who was striding down the corridor.

Barry Milligan came tearing in. Not wasting a second, he barged into the unholy scrum and wrenched the children clear. Not knowing what had happened, he treated each of them with the same contempt. Seizing them by the collars, he dragged all the boys away from Mrs

Early and pushed them against the wall. The girl he merely glowered at and she tearfully joined the rest of the line-up.

"You!" he thundered in a voice that frightened everyone in the room. "Have made the biggest mistake of your lives. I have had the day from hell today and might just forget myself and knock your bloody heads off!"

The children were breathing hard, unable to answer. They looked into his furious, beetroot face and even the innocent ones were scared. Anthony and Graeme stared at him and the madness was quelled within them. They began to shiver.

"Are you all right?" Barry asked the woman.

Mrs Early leaned against her desk. Her face and arms were scored with red scratches and angry purple slap marks. She put her hand out to steady herself then nodded.

"Dear God!" he said, looking at the state of her. "What the…"

He glared at the children against the wall then turned away from them in disgust. "I've seen some things," he said, clenching and unclenching his fists and struggling to resist the urge to smack each of them into next week. "But this is… you're worse than animals. Let's see what the police have to say about it, but understand one thing – you're all going to be expelled. If it's the last thing I do as Head of this school, I promise you that. As for you, Paul – I'm sickened and appalled at you."

"Mr Milligan," Mrs Early interrupted as she caught her breath and collected herself. "It wasn't all of them. It was only Graeme Parker and Anthony Maskel. The others… they were helping me."

Barry's eyes narrowed. "Right," he said. "The rest of you, back to your seats. You two – in my office – NOW!"

Graeme and Anthony hurried from the classroom in cowed silence.

The Headteacher put a caring hand on Mrs Early's shoulder, but she shrugged it off, angry at herself and bewildered. How had that situation spiralled out of control?

"I'm fine," she said.

Barry thought otherwise. "I'll get someone to cover for you here," he told her. "I need you to come tell me what happened."

The English teacher stared down at the copy of Dancing Jacks on her desk. How could she tell him that when she didn't comprehend it herself?

The forbidden library of Mooncaster is locked – and rightly so! Even Jangler is denied the key to that iron door. The secret knowledge contained therein is far too deadly and dangerous for the Court and Kingdom. It is perilous to pry. Ancient powers slumber within those vellum and parchment pages. Let them sleep, sound and undisturbed. Doors and books are sealed for the best of purposes. Let dust lie deep inside, let spiders spin - do not go poking through the webs.

18

"SO THEY ATTACKED her simply because she'd taken a book away?"

Paul was trying to explain to Martin what had happened in the English lesson as they drove home that afternoon.

"It was like she'd taken a piece of meat from a mad, starving dog," he said. "No, it was even worse than that – like they were junkies and the book was their drug. None of the rest of us could believe what was going on. They'd lost it, totally – absolutely nuts, the pair of them. I didn't recognise them at all – they've never been like that."

"They were both quiet by the time the police came," Martin told him. "I had a word with Barry afterwards. He couldn't get any sense out of them and nor could they. Mind you, when their parents turned up, they were a bit weird as well. What's this 'Blessed be' thing people are saying now?"

"It's to do with that book," Paul muttered. "There's something really wrong about it."

"Funny," Martin said. "You're the second person who's told me that in two days."

Paul stared moodily out of the window. There wasn't anything 'funny' about it from his perspective. He believed it was something to be very, very scared of. Martin hadn't seen the intensity of rage on the boys' faces or witnessed the weird scene in the library.

"This is the last thing Barry needed on top of everything else," Martin continued.

"Is he getting the sack because of what the papers did to him?"

"Don't tell anyone this, but the governors and the local authority have been ripping into him all day. He's been told to resign, quietly."

"Oh."

"No doubt we'll get some clueless drone as a replacement, someone whose tongue is the same colour as the government's posterior. The school will go downhill so fast – just you watch."

"Mr Milligan was great today, just like Gene Hunt – but louder."

"A man out of his time," Martin said sadly. "Someone called him

a dinosaur today, and they were right. Barry Milligan is a T-rex among rabbits and ostriches."

"What does that make you then?"

"David Attenborough!"

They pulled into the drive and Paul hurried upstairs to his room. Sitting at the computer, his cursor hovered over the delete button to eradicate Graeme and Anthony from his contacts, but he couldn't bring himself to do it. Even after everything they had done that day, he pitied them more than he hated them. He sensed that none of it was really their fault.

Instead he typed "Dancing Jacks" into Google to see what it came up with. Most of the results were links to references made by children at his school. One of them was a page created by Anthony about falconry. Paul made a quizzical face. What did Anthony know about that? Checking the page, it seemed he knew quite a lot. The detail there was quite astonishing and it didn't appear to be cut and pasted from elsewhere.

The rest of the results were by other people who had bought the book that Sunday. One of them had started a blog about making a costume for the character she was obsessed with. Through Martin's fanaticisms, Paul had seen similar blogs before. Dressing up as favourite characters was called cosplay and was more prevalent in America than here. The devotion to other worlds could consume a true fan's life. Martin always said that was because the most successful fantasy realms had clearly defined rules whereas the real world didn't any more. It was more comforting to inhabit the clothes and invest in the ideals and merchandise of those invented places when the everyday world was such a confusing mess full of disappointments and contradictions. Everyone escaped somehow.

This woman had certainly done a lot of work since Sunday. She had chosen a character called Columbine, or had the character chosen her? Apparently in the book she was a pretty kitchen maid who wore patched clothes and carried a tambourine with which she warded off the unwelcome advances of the Jockey. A scan of the illustration was on the blog and her replica outfit was almost complete. It was clear she had taken a lot of pains over it.

Paul skimmed through the other links. Then he stopped as the realisation sank in. There was another, even more important, search he should be doing…

Curiosity, laced with a sense of dread, percolated inside him as he typed the name.

"Austerly Fellows."

He pressed Return and waited nervously.

First on the list of results was a Wikipedia entry. He clicked on it. The page flashed up. Paul took a breath, but before reading the text, he stared at the accompanying black and white photograph. It was a man wearing some kind of monk's robe.

"More cosplay," he murmured.

It was an unpleasant face. It looked cruel and arrogant. The thin lips were fixed in a sneer and the sharp nose jutted from scowling brows. As for the eyes…

Paul did not like to look at them. They seemed to stab out of the

monitor at him. When he was very young, he used to think the newsreaders could see him through the television. This photograph of Austerly Fellows, author of Dancing Jacks, induced that same unsettling feeling. The boy told himself he was being silly and turned his attention to the biographical text alongside.

Austerly Fellows (1879–1936) The self-styled 'Abbot of the Angles' and 'Grand Duke of the Inner Circle'. Though now largely forgotten and succeeded by other, less influential and inferior imitators, he was an English occultist, artist, writer and composer.

Paul pulled the neck of his jumper up to his mouth and began chewing it absently. He read on.

Early life The middle child of a successful Suffolk doctor, he also studied medicine in his youth until the untimely death of his elder stepbrother, after which he abandoned his studies.[1] There were rumours circulating at the time that he would have been expelled from the college anyway. He was not a popular student. His eccentricities were becoming too extreme and it was said, even then, that he dabbled in the occult. [citation needed]

Travels At the turn of the century he journeyed to Europe. On the continent he pursued a life of hedonism and debauchery, leaving a trail of scandals wherever he went.[2] Such was his notoriety, Switzerland refused to allow him across its borders. [citation needed]

In Italy he resumed his researches into esoteric knowledge and joined several cults, rising swiftly to the highest levels within their orders. [citation needed] He was ruthless and ambitious and once again he created a new reputation for himself, this time a sinister one.[3] In 1903 there were nine ritual murders in the catacombs of Rome. Suspicion fell on the macabre cult of il Portello Scuro, of which he was, by then, a leading member. But no proof could be found and the only witness was decapitated before she could give evidence.[4] In 1905 Austerly Fellows was a suspect in the theft of an ancient and forbidden manuscript from the Vatican. Again nothing could be proven, but the King of Italy, Victor Emmanuel III, ordered him to leave the country and never return.[5]

From there he journeyed to the Far East and reportedly learned much from the mystics of India and secret priesthoods in Egypt. While living in Cairo, he became known as the English Devil.[6] Rumours circulated that he robbed tombs and was initiated into the cult of the demon Shezmu, whom he later boasted to have communed with in the desert. Eventually the authorities forced him to leave.[7]

Paul paused and looked round his room. The hairs on the back of his neck were prickling, as if someone was watching him.

There was nobody there. He shivered slightly. This bloke sounded like a right murdering fruitcake. How had he ever come to write a kids' book? And what on earth for?

Still nibbling the neck of his jumper, he returned to the screen.

Life back in England When Austerly finally returned to England in 1907, he founded many secret organisations, some of which still operate today.[8] Unlike other occultists of the period, he shunned publicity and there are few details to document his subsequent life. Many of the files held in the public records office were destroyed by a freak occurrence of damp and are now unreadable.[9] However, from 1927 it is thought he was engaged in some major undertaking, which occupied him for the next nine years, but what that work was, and if it was ever completed, remains unknown.

Death Confusion even surrounds the manner of his death. During a Beltane gathering of the Inner Circle at his home in Suffolk, he disappeared in mysterious circumstances and was never heard of again. Local police assumed he had been murdered by one or more of the other occultists, but his body was never discovered and their testimonies no longer exist.[10][11] His estate is maintained by a solicitor in Ipswich. His only beneficiary, his younger sister, died in 1954 in the insane asylum that had been her home since his disappearance.[12]

"Sick," Paul breathed. "So he was some sort of devil worshipper? What took him nine years? Writing that book?"

He clicked off the entry and returned to the results page. It took a few minutes to digest what he had read. Could it really be the same person?

"It's just mad," he told himself.

His eyes wandered down the results list. One link looked promising. He opened it.

It was a website called 'The Saxon Spookers'.

Hi!!!

We are a group of friends who absolutely LOVE TV's Most Haunted. (Come back, Derek Acorah! And let me run my fingers through your bouffant hair!) We meet every third Thursday of the month in the White Horse, Felixstowe and discuss the programme. We are very interested in ghosts and legends and all things spooky so we decided to form our own little paranormal investigation group and that's how the Saxon Spookers was born. We aim to visit local sites that are reputed to be haunted and conduct our own amateur, but enthusiastic, investigations — and have a good time along the way.

Paul grinned. There followed a series of photographs of these four adult friends, taken with an infrared camera in the dark, with mock frightened expressions on their faces. They seemed great fun and Paul liked the look of them. Each one had a potted biography next to their photo, together with a list of likes and dislikes. The main Chronicler of their exploits was a divorcee called Trudy Bishop. She and the others had chosen four places in Suffolk to intrepidly hunt down ghosts over the forthcoming months. Paul checked the date. This website had been started the previous year.

The first place scheduled to be 'investigated' by the Saxon

Spookers was the Landguard Fort, followed by the ruins of Greyfriars at Dunwich, the Hare and Hounds Inn at East Bergholt and finally – the house of Austerly Fellows…

Paul sat upright in his chair. Each account was on a fresh page and he clicked through them. The reports of these experiences were illustrated with photos. There was the Landguard: they hadn't had permission to spend the night inside so they conducted an inept investigation around the perimeter and happily scared one another in the dark. The boy quickly realised that these vigils and experiments were hardly serious or scientific and were more of an excuse to do something unusual of an evening and drink a few cans in different surroundings. Trudy and her friends were more like teenagers than people in their forties. *Were grown-ups often like this?* he wondered, thinking about Martin.

He flicked his eyes down the photos of the ruined friary up the coast at Dunwich, where the ever-hungry sea had gobbled up the town and its eight churches. The Spookers had hoped to catch a glimpse of the ghostly Franciscan monks who supposedly roam the grounds there, but had caught nothing on film and Trudy had stepped in something decidedly unholy.

Then there was the Hare and Hounds Inn, to hunt down a ghost with the totally non-supernatural-sounding name of Fred. Lots of pictures of raised, clinking glasses and this time they were joined by someone's auntie, who claimed to have mediumistic gifts. Apparently it was a successful night: the auntie had sensed a presence in the bar of a very sociable spirit who enjoyed mingling

273

with the customers and pulling the fruit machine's plug out of its socket. The Saxon Spookers considered this to be an absolute triumph and prepared for their next investigation eagerly.

Paul opened the fourth and last page. There was only one photograph of a sombre, large grey house surrounded by trees. A few lines of text accompanied it.

This is the house of Austerly Fellows. I wish we'd never gone. I wish we'd never started any of this. We should have listened to Reg's auntie. It's dangerous to mess about with this kind of thing. We treated it as a game, but dear God, it wasn't. There are things out there none of us can understand. If you poke into dark corners, eventually something is going to be disturbed and jump out at you. I can't believe how stupid we were.

I'm so sorry, Geoff. We miss you.

Trudy x

The page was dated five months ago. Paul stared back at the photograph of the ugly house. What had happened the night they went there? There was only one way to find out.

Paul quickly did a search for her on Facebook and there she was, Trudy Bishop. She worked in an estate agent's in the High Street. Without hesitation, he sent her a message.

Hi,

you don't know me, but I saw your site about
the Saxon Spookers. Could I ask you a few
questions? I need to know about Austerly Fellows.

Thanx

Paul Thornbury

He hoped she would reply soon. With that done, he got up and was about to go downstairs to see how another over-salted lasagne was coming along, when he noticed the copy of Dancing Jacks lying on the end of his bed. He hadn't seen it when he came in. It certainly wasn't there that morning when he left for school. Maybe his mother had put it there. Or maybe she hadn't.

Paul stared at it suspiciously, half expecting it to move. He was ready to believe anything about that book now. The faded green and cream cover that had seemed so charming when he first saw it on Sunday now repulsed him. Knowing what the contents had done to people, he saw it as threatening and deceitful. It was a cheerfully painted mask to disguise the evil within.

His eyelids closed.

The next thing he knew, he was sitting on the bed and the book was in his hands.

The boy did not know how he had got there. He gazed at the bound work of Austerly Fellows and the flesh on his neck crawled once again. He could almost feel a cold breath brush softly across the back of his head.

He uttered a helpless gasp and tried to pull his eyes away from the cover. He wanted to look at the door and run towards it. But the book wouldn't let him.

Then, very slowly, he was forced to open it.

He saw the map. Elements of the drawing seemed to be moving. The banners were fluttering on the castle's battlements; the gibbet was swinging; a breeze was ruffling the treetops of the forest that grew around the witch's tower.

Paul's young, shaking fingers turned the first page and he saw the picture of the empty throne, then the introduction by the infernal Mr Fellows.

He turned again – to the first chapter.

"Come and get it!" his mother's voice yelled up from the kitchen.

The spell was broken. The boy shrieked and flung the book away from him as if he had been bitten. He breathed hard. It had almost got him. He had almost read the first line and then he would have been lost – like Graeme and Anthony and the rest.

Dancing Jacks was lying open but face down by the skirting board. Paul could not bear to look at it. What had that evil man done? What foul inspiration had Austerly Fellows poured into its pages? What diabolic hands had guided his pen?

Paul shivered then cried out again. The book had moved. It had turned over while he was not looking. The open pages were now visible and displayed a drawing of the Jack of Diamonds. The character bore a resemblance to Paul.

The boy snatched his feet off the floor and tucked them under him.

"Martin!" he shouted. "Martin!"

There was no response. If the maths teacher had his headphones on in his sanctum, he wouldn't be able to hear anything.

Paul glanced at the door and was about to call for his mother when he realised the book had moved again. This time it was halfway across the carpet. It was trying to get back to the bed. It was going to make him read.

"No!" the boy whispered.

Ten minutes later, Carol called up to both of them again. Their tea was getting cold on the table. There was no answer. It had been hell at the hospital that day. The press were all over the place again, trying to interview anyone who had known Shaun Preston, desperate to dig up any dirt on him. Carol was exhausted and in no mood to be taken for granted by the men in her life. She stomped upstairs, ready to drag the pair of them down by their ears.

She found her son's room empty. Thinking he was in the sanctum, she looked in.

Martin was standing at the window staring out at the garden below. The headphones were still in his ears.

"What the hell is he doing?" he asked. Carol stood beside him and looked down.

There was Paul. He had dragged the rusted barbecue, which they never used, on to the patio and had started a fire in it with old newspapers.

Curious, they both went downstairs.

"What's going on?" Carol called as she stepped on to the patio.

Her son poked the flames with a long barbecue fork. Thick smoke and glowing ashes were streaming upward.

"Paul?" Martin said as they approached him. "What's this about?"

The boy held up his other hand. In it was his copy of Dancing Jacks. He had wrapped layers and layers of Sellotape around it, binding it tightly shut. He wasn't taking any chances.

"It has to be burned," he told them. "It's not safe."

Carol and Martin stared at him, shocked and concerned.

"You're going to burn a book?" his mother asked, perplexed.

"It's too dangerous to have in the house," he answered. "It's bad, Mum. It does things to people."

Martin took a wary step closer. "Paul," he began. "I know you had a frightening experience today. Why don't we go inside and talk about it? You don't need to do this."

"Yes, I do," the boy replied gravely. "Before this thing gets at us as well. It has to be burned! It's evil!" He prepared to throw the book into the flames.

"But I've read it, Paul," Martin said. "There's nothing harmful in it, nothing that would cause your friends to snap like they did. It's just an old-fashioned, and pretty dull, kids' book."

The boy wavered. "You've read it?" he asked uncertainly.

"Enough to be bored by it."

"You mean that?"

"Jedi's honour."

"Did you rock backwards and forwards?"

"Eh? It didn't play Status Quo at me."

Paul moved around the barbecue, placing it between him and the adults.

"And your name's still Martin?" he asked.

Carol was annoyed. "Stop," she said sternly. "What's got into you? You don't mess about with fires. Come in, right now."

"Is your name still Martin?" the boy repeated, taking no notice of her.

Martin nodded slowly. "You know it is," he said, really getting worried for him.

"Then tell me the Ismus is a stupid freak."

"What?"

"The Ismus is a stupid freak – say it!"

Martin thought it would be best to humour him. "OK, the Ismus is a stupid freak."

Paul let out a breath of relief. That was proof enough. He looked at the sealed book in his hand and, with contempt and revulsion, cast it into the blazing barbecue.

"You didn't have to burn it!" his mother shouted. "You could have given it to a charity shop."

The boy shook his head, watching as the edges of the hardbacked cover blackened and smoked. The Sellotape withered and melted and Paul averted his eyes before it could flap open. "It's the only way to be sure," he said, quoting Sigourney Weaver in Aliens.

Carol and Martin didn't know what to say. Paul had never behaved like this.

279

Suddenly there was a splutter and crackle in the flames as the pages caught light. The fire burned emerald and crimson and a pillar of fierce colour went shooting skyward.

Everyone jumped back. There was a roar and a burst of purple sparks. The garden was lit by a brilliant glare that dazzled them. Paul covered his face with his hands, but as he snapped his eyes shut, he thought he had glimpsed something, something travelling up that column of flame. It was so bright it remained for some moments as a ghostly image on his retina and terrified him. He fell to the ground.

And then it went dark. A chill breeze came gusting into the garden. The fire was extinguished and oily black smoke coiled out of the barbecue. Only ash was left behind.

Carol and Martin wiped their faces. Carol crouched over her son and quickly but expertly checked for burns.

"Did you see it?" Paul cried, struggling out of her arms and running to the barbecue. Raking the fork through the ashes, he shuddered then threw it away.

"See it?" Carol asked, her concern changing to anger. "You could have killed us. You're not stupid so what did you do that for?"

Her son looked at her in confusion. "Do what?"

"The fireworks," Martin answered. "Why did you put fireworks in there? Good God, Paul. They could have exploded in our faces."

"You know how many horrific burns we get in the hospital every November because of careless, stupid idiots like you!" Carol shouted. "I just can't believe you did that! I can't believe it! Where did you get them from?"

The boy stared at them, wide-eyed. "I didn't!" he protested. "There weren't any fireworks. It was the book!"

"Paul!" Martin said sharply. "Drop it."

"Why won't you believe me?" he cried. "Since when have I ever messed about with stuff like that? It was the Dancing Jacks – I swear it!"

Their faces told him they would never believe his version, even though it was the truth. It was an impossible thing to accept. He thought so – and he had actually seen it. There was no way he could ever convince them or anyone else.

"Get inside," Martin ordered.

The boy glanced upwards. He knew what he had seen. He knew it was real. In the middle of those flames, streaking into the sky, there had been a figure – a figure with horns.

So in rides he, the best of all. The Jack of Clubs, so strong and tall. Chivalrous and brave is this dashing Knave. Animals and damsels they are in his thrall.

19

THE PIER AT Felixstowe was once the longest in East Anglia. When it first opened in 1905, it stretched 800 metres into the North Sea, with a landing stage for steamers at the very end. It had even sported an electric tram to transport passengers and their luggage to and from the shore. Now only a little over an eighth of the pier remained and that was unsafe and closed to the public. The amusement arcade at the shore end still buzzed and dinged and blinked with lights, but the high planked roadway over the water would never open again and would eventually be demolished, by man or the sea.

The building in which the amusements were housed was raised on concrete pillars over the downward-sloping shore. The waves slopped and swilled around the base of them, patiently nibbling and gnawing away.

That evening, under the green mossy concrete of the arcade's

elevated floor, a lone figure sat brooding in the growing darkness.

Conor Westlake came here when he was troubled. He liked to sit on the damp, smooth sand in the spot where, when he gazed out to sea, the wooden posts of the pier were aligned directly in front of him and receded out to the horizon, forming a pillared corridor. He would sit there, projecting his mind along it, trying to leave his body and its problems behind, to journey out to the doorway of light at the far end and escape everything.

It had been an uncomfortable day. Owen Williams had told him that Kevin Stipe's parents had asked if he would be a pall-bearer at their son's funeral. Many of the young people who had died in the Disaster were being buried next Sunday. There was also going to be a special memorial service for them that morning. Owen wasn't sure what to do. He didn't want to refuse, but he didn't want to carry a coffin with the dead body of his friend in it.

Conor had listened to his concerns with a guilty heart. Kevin's parents really should be told that their son died trying to help the others out of that car. He had died a hero. Conor couldn't hold on to that secret any longer. He had to tell them, and the police, everything he knew. First thing tomorrow, he'd call the incident number and make a statement.

He had been so preoccupied with this heavy burden that he hadn't been aware of the strange happenings at school. At lunchtime the number of lads who enjoyed a kick-about was depleted and when he saw them sitting cross-legged on the edge of the field, reading, he hadn't thought anything of it. He hadn't even heard about the attack on Mrs Early.

Taking out his mobile, he called up Emma Taylor's number. There were grieving people who could be consoled by what he had to tell them. She was as impervious to feelings as the concrete posts around him. Knowing what he had to do to clear his conscience, he decided. His thumb jabbed at the buttons hastily as he texted her. He didn't owe her any consideration, but it wouldn't hurt to warn the selfish cow.

To: Emma
Had enuf. Gonna tell cops wot hapnd.

She could whine or yell or slate him as much as she liked, but he couldn't live with it any longer. The message's envelope icon went flying away on the mobile's screen. He imagined it zooming down the corridor under the pier, trying to find Emma Taylor's phone.

It was almost dark out there now. The lights of container ships twinkled in the remote distance and Conor rested his chin on his knees as he stared at them, wishing he was on board. What sort of life was there for him here? He had always wanted to be a professional footballer. The fame, the money, the cars, the attention, the WAGs – that incredible world was a life he craved so much. He ached to be a part of it. To wear the sharp suits and endorse endless products, be invited to the most exclusive parties and rub shoulders with A-list movie stars, have lads just like him filled with adoration and envy. To

have tens of thousands of fans chant his name at matches and worship his skill. To be someone unique and special, to have what the media tantalised and promised could be his. Yes, he thirsted for that. Ever since he could remember he had wanted that diamond existence. He had built every dream and hope on it.

Conor covered his eyes. At the age of fifteen he had finally realised he simply wasn't good enough to play in the Premiership. He wasn't even talented enough for the lesser clubs. What was left? Nothing. No other dream could ever replace that one and the certainty of that crushed him. Those glittering hopes had washed down the drain and that universe was totally unattainable. He would stay stuck here, in this grey and empty corner of nowhere, forever. What was the point?

He sat hunched over for some time. When the inevitable reply buzzed in, like a furious wasp in his pocket, he glanced at it without a flicker of surprise. Then he switched off the phone.

"She'll wear out that 'F' key," he said to himself.

A movement in the corner of his eye caused him to turn his head. Someone was on the beach nearby.

It was a girl, perhaps about his age, wearing a long and summery dress, printed with delicate pink and yellow flowers. There was a pale pink sash tied around her waist. The cotton was surely far too thin for this brisker, off-season weather. She was tall and willowy and her long, dark hair was pinned up on to her head. She had left her shoes on the beach and was twirling about in the shallow waves, arms raised, with her face upturned to the darkened sky.

Conor stared at her, fascinated. Hidden as he was in the deep shadow beneath the arcade, she was totally unaware she was being watched.

He smiled. She looked like she didn't have a care in the world. Simply being there, capering and splashing in the sea with the wet sand beneath her feet, was enough to make her glad. It was innocent and childlike – she had to be freezing though. The girl was humming and singing snatches of a song he didn't recognise, but, with a start, he realised he did know that voice.

"Sandra Dixon!" he called out in surprise.

The girl faltered in her gambolling and whirled around, unable to see who had spoken. Conor emerged from his hiding place and she moved a little further into the water.

"What are you doing out here?" he asked.

The girl stared at him dumbly. There was something about her eyes that made him wonder if she was sleepwalking.

"Aren't you cold?"

She shook her head and moved deeper into the sea so that the waves rolled over the hem of the bridesmaid's dress she had worn the previous July. It was the only long dress she owned.

Conor looked at her bare arms. They were stippled with gooseflesh and she was shivering.

"You are cold!" he said. "You'll catch your death in there."

"I am dancing for the Lord Ismus!" she said suddenly. "I have no minchet with which to anoint myself. But if I sing and dance prettily enough, he might notice and bear me away through

the starlight – to the Great Revel."

"The only place you'll be going is to the hospital with pneumonia," he warned.

She gazed upwards, her face expectant and yearning. "I must dance," she called out. "The Jill of Hearts must dance the most daintily of all the ladies at Court."

"Come out of there!" Conor told her.

Sandra did not answer, but backed even further into the water until it reached her thighs.

"I'm not going in after you!" the boy said firmly.

She swayed and bent, this way and that, in the water. Then she turned round and round, gesturing with her arms, like an intoxicated ballerina.

"I must hold every man's fluttering heart captive," she called out. "I must catch them like scarlet butterflies in my cupped palms. I must entrance. The courtiers must adore me."

Conor's concern had turned to fear. The sea was now up to the girl's waist. What had got into her? She was supposed to be clever, wasn't she? Perhaps the beating Emma had given her had done more damage than anyone had realised.

"Damn," he swore under his breath. He scrambled out of his coat and kicked off his trainers. "We're both going to get pneumonia."

The boy stepped into the sea, gasping at the icy bitterness of the water. How could she bear it?

When Sandra saw him, she thrust her hands in front of her and retreated even further.

287

"Stop!" he yelled.

"I must dance!" she cried. "I must be noticed by the Ismus!"

"Sod him!" Conor said through chattering teeth.

Sandra shrieked and moved backwards. The waves were breaking over her back now. Soon they would be over her shoulders.

Conor halted. Every step he took drove her deeper into the sea.

"All right!" he called. "I won't come any closer."

In the black expanse of the North Sea, her chalk-white face stood out starkly. Those dreaming, glassy eyes scanned the night sky, searching and hoping.

Conor looked around helplessly. The promenade was empty. The string of coloured lights that festooned the length of it showed that no one else was about. What could he do? How could he reach her? Then his eyes rested on the shoes she had left behind. There was a book beside them.

"Dancing Jacks!" he said. The girl's face turned to him at once.

"You know the holy text?"

"I bought one of those as well."

She gave a joyful cry. "Is it not the most glorious enchantery?" she asked.

"I dunno, I haven't read it."

"You must!"

"Why the hell should I? You won't come out of there."

"But it will save you!"

"I'm not the one who needs saving here!"

"You are in the dark oubliette of ignorance. Read it and enter the

288

Light – be as one with the courtiers of the Dawn Prince. This is only the empty grey place of sleep. You must wake up to your real life."

"You come here and I'll think about it."

"Promise?"

"I promise."

Sandra took a step forward, but her foot slipped on a loose stone and she vanished below the waves.

Conor watched her white face disappear under the water. Could she swim? He had no idea. Some moments later her head came bobbing back up – even further from the shore and her arms were thrashing wildly. She was too far out and could no longer feel the bottom beneath her feet.

"Bloody knew it!" he swore.

With a fierce yell, full of annoyance and irritation, he charged into the waves and leaped into the freezing sea.

When he reached Sandra, she was kicking and crashing about in the water frantically. The back of her hand smacked him wildly across the face as he swam close and he shouted at her to stay calm.

"I am the Jill of Hearts, I am the Jill of Hearts," she cried shrilly.

Conor grabbed her and began towing her back to the shore. Presently they came staggering up the beach, stuttering with the wet, wintry cold, their clothes stuck to their shuddering bodies.

"So… so… fro… frozen…" she said in gulping, shallow breaths as if aware of it for the first time.

Conor threw his coat over her shoulders.

"M… My thanks, Sirrah," she gasped, pulling the garment tightly around.

"Let's get you home," he told her, passing her shoes as he pushed his feet into his trainers. He was the coldest he had ever been, but she was blue with it. "If we run, it might warm us up a bit."

Sandra looked into the sky once more. "My Lord is not there," she observed with disappointment. "He is gone to the revel without me."

"Come on!" Conor urged.

Sandra picked up her book. "Such peace and joy you will find in these blessed pages," she said.

"I never read books," he answered impatiently. "Don't even colour them in nowadays."

Her own words were lost on her.

"You made a promise to read it," she reminded him.

"No, I didn't."

"As the cloak of night is my witness, I heard you."

"I said I'd think about it, you dopey nutcase! Now can we get going before my voice gets any higher? I want to play like Beckham, not sound like him. I'm a bloody brass monkey stood here."

To his annoyance she laughed and pointed at him. "I know you now," she said. "He who braves fire and water to rescue maidens, he whom the beasts and birds adore. You are the Jack of Clubs."

"I'll be SpongeBob SquarePants if it means we can get going!" Conor retorted, jumping from one foot to the other and rubbing his arms.

"You may lead me, Knave," she said with a flirtatious smile.

At that moment Conor was too chilled and angry with her to notice, let alone care. This was the second time he'd saved someone in the past few days. At least barmy Sandra had thanked him. Emma hadn't even mentioned it.

Their paths home ran together for a distance and they hurried as fast as they could to keep the gelid blood moving in their veins. When it was time to split up and go different ways, Sandra returned his coat and curtseyed in her wet dress.

Conor thought she looked ridiculous and he hoped none of his mates would ever hear about this.

"You'll go straight home, yeah?" he asked. "No running back to the beach or anywhere else?"

She looked at him as though shocked by the very idea. "I am daughter to one of the Under Kings," she said in a superior tone. "Do you think I am unaware of the proprieties?"

"Oh, get over yourself," he said, totally fed up of her mad games.

"Good night, gallant Knave. See you on the morrow."

The boy shook his head and jogged away.

When he returned home, he ran past the open living room door, from where the TV was blaring, went straight upstairs and had a hot shower. The horrendous cold had seeped deep into his bones and it took some time before he felt normal again.

Afterwards, cocooned in a fleece and joggers, he flopped on to his bed and stared at the ceiling. That Dixon girl was totally off her head. He would never have thought it of her. She had always seemed so stuck-up and dull. Why did she keep going on about that cheap book?

Sitting up, he wondered where he had thrown his copy when he returned from the boot fair on Sunday. A few minutes' searching revealed it beneath a heap of discarded clothes. He looked at it curiously. Sitting back on the bed, he turned to the first page and began to read…

The warm, climbing sun beat down on his neck. It was a perfect summer's morning. The sky had never been bluer and the sweet, sherbet-like scent of roses was borne on the lazy, shimmering air. All memory of cold melted from his mind and he was glad of the felt hunting hat, pinked with gold lace, that shielded his eyes from the glare. The Dancing Jacks had been out hawking. They had ridden leisurely through the countryside, flying their well-trained birds and catching rabbits and pigeons.

The young nobles and their retinue were a sumptuous sight. They were arrayed in rich, velvet clothes, with the hanging sleeves that were so fashionable in the Court, and the gold of their diadems and neck chains flashed and blazed in the sunshine. Their horses too were decked in colourfully embroidered cloths, displaying the badges of their Royal Houses and their hooves were painted with the same designs. It was a glorious pageant and the peasants who saw them process by were proud to dwell in a land that boasted such lordly folk.

Behind the nobles, the eager grooms took charge of the fresh kills

and hung the limp bodies on the saddle hooks of the burden beasts. The pantries would be fully stocked that evening. Mistress Cook would be very pleased.

A plump rabbit darted across the path and, in an instant, the Jill of Spades lifted her gauntleted hand and removed the plumed hood from her hawk's head. The bird's apricot eyes burned fiercely and its mistress threw it into the air, releasing the jesses.

The hawk raced away and swiftly swooped upon the startled rabbit. The bird sank its talons into the soft fur and flesh and the animal wriggled piteously beneath.

"To me!" the Jill of Spades called, cantering her horse forward and holding out her fist. "To me, Accipiter!"

The bird spread its wings and tried to fly back to her, with the creature in its claws. But the rabbit was so heavy that it barely lifted off the ground and continued to squirm and wriggle. It kicked and struggled and the ensuing scene of it bouncing over the ground with the hawk clamped to its neck was extremely undignified for the outraged bird.

"A new sport!" the Jill of Hearts wept with laughter. "Let us have rabbit races in future tournaments. We can sew mice to their backs and fashion little outfits for them to wear!"

"Accipiter!" the Jill of Spades commanded.

"The prey is too large for it!" the Jack of Clubs told her crossly. "You expect too much of it. Both creatures are distressed."

"My hawk is the best!" she answered. "It will succeed."

The rabbit jerked and dodged, trying to shake the predator free.

But Accipiter held fast. The pair of them rolled into the ditch at the side of the track. Then the rabbit squeezed through a gap in a hawthorn hedge. The bird screeched as thorns ripped through its feathers and its powerful wings became entangled in the twigs. With that, the rabbit was free. It hopped into the adjoining field and disappeared in the ripening barley where, out of sight, it collapsed and bled to death from its wounds.

Accipiter was still caught in the hedge, its wings ragged and torn. Aethelheard the groom ran swiftly to its rescue, but the tormented bird would not let him touch her. The hooked beak lunged at him and there was nothing he could do.

"'Tis hopeless!" he cried. "She will not let me aid her!"

The Jack of Clubs dismounted and came to kneel before the terrified hawk.

"Hush now," he said soothingly. "Hush now. I am here. Fear no more."

The panic-filled cries ceased and Accipiter's bright, apricot eyes stared beseechingly up at him.

The youth pulled off his leather gauntlet and held out his hand.

"Ware, my Lord!" Aethelheard cautioned. "She can rip through your palm as easy as if it were curd."

"She will not harm me," he replied. "Be still, Accipiter, be still."

The hawk ceased its fearful thrashing and allowed the Jack of Clubs to stroke her head with his forefinger.

"There now," he said softly. "Let me liberate you from your thorns."

Aethelheard watched with wide-eyed wonder as the noble gently freed the hawk from the hedge and carried it out on his bare wrist. There was perfect trust between them.

"I never saw the like!" the groom breathed. "'Tis a marvel, my Lord."

The Jack of Clubs stepped up to the Jill of Spades and nudged the bird on to her gauntleted hand.

"Your faithful hunter returned to you, Lady," he said. "Be more careful upon what you set your sights in future. Your ambitions are oft too high."

With a playful grin, he remounted Urlwin, his horse. The Jill of Spades regarded the hawk on her hand. Its primary feathers were straggled and ragged and it would be some time before it would be the best in the stables again. It was a very sorry sight. She lifted the plumed hood to cover its eyes once more. Then she changed her mind and casually wrung the bird's neck instead.

"My Lady!" Aethelheard cried in dismay. "Accipiter would have been good as new in time!"

The girl shot a severe glance at the boy. "You dare raise your voice to me?" she snapped.

Aethelheard hung his head. "Nay, my Lady!" he muttered, abashed.

With a look of disdain, she slung the dead hawk into the ditch. "Come, Jack!" she called, turning her horse away. "I am weary of this sport. Let us return to the White Castle and find diversions more to my liking."

The Jack of Clubs stared at her in anger and disbelief. She rejoined the other nobles and the pitiless girl was presently laughing at the Jill of Hearts' stories once more.

Aethelheard stepped into the ditch and retrieved Accipiter's body. He cradled it in his hands, holding back his tears.

"I am sorry," the Jack of Clubs said to him. "I would not have had that happen."

The young groom nodded and drew the sleeve of his jerkin across his nose.

"Make haste, Jack!" the Jill of Spades called impatiently. "We are eager to be gone!"

The Jack of Clubs glared at her. He was not ready to return to Mooncaster just yet, and most especially not with her. Reining his horse about, he spurred it on and galloped off along the track.

"Jack!" the Jill of Spades called. "Whither are you going?"

He did not hear her. He wanted to put as much distance between her and himself as possible and his horse was racing swiftly. The hat flew from his head, but he did not care. Trees and hedgerows streaked by. Peasant cottages were a blur and the flowing crystal streams were leaped across with ease. Over path and field Urlwin thundered, through the Guarded Gate and then out into the valley between the encircling hills. They were outside the Dawn Prince's Realm.

The land was rougher here and the poor soil was clogged with great stones that notched and dented ploughs. The grass was coarse and the shrubs were disfigured by the gales that raged behind the thirteen hills. The woods here were dangerous, inhabited by footpads

and highwaymen. Wild men and cut-throats dwelt outside the magickal Kingdom and there were other creatures. It was said that the talking fox came from this place and the herd of untameable horses roamed the plains here.

The Jack of Clubs gave no thought to any of that. He was free and when the thickets of overgrown gorse and spindly trees were left behind, the wind tore through his hair and rushed past his ears as he galloped over open country once more. The sound grew to a roar and the earth beneath the horse's hooves grew soft and sandy. With a yell, he realised the danger they were in and pulled sharply on the reins, calling for the beast to halt.

Urlwin obeyed and stumbled to a standstill – just in time.

The Jack of Clubs bent forward and kissed the horse's head between the ears. "My thanks," he said, patting the sweating neck. "Look yonder, my friend." The steed tossed its head and thudded a hoof in the sand.

Dismounting, the noble gazed ahead. They had stopped just short of a cliff edge. Beyond that the ground dropped sharply and then there was only a sparkling vision of the Silvering Sea. He wondered what strange lands might exist beyond the uttermost wave.

The noble took a step closer to the edge. His feet sank deep into the soft, sandy soil and he peered over the sheer brink. It was a fearsome drop to the rocky pools of the shore beneath.

The sea air felt clean and cooling upon his face. Surely there were other sounds carried upon it? He turned and saw in the distance, on the grassy stretch between the cliff and the woods, a herd of the finest horses he had ever seen. They were cantering and playing, neighing happily to one another.

"The untameable steeds," he breathed. "They're beautiful."

It was said that the mares could only be impregnated by the southern wind and he did not doubt it. They were unlike any creature in the stables of the White Castle. They made his own elegant stallion look like a shambling puller of dray carts by comparison. No saddle or bridle would ever break one of those. Amongst the herd he saw four foals, running alongside their mothers. They were relishing every moment under the summer sun, their long legs prancing high and gladly.

Suddenly the ground under his feet crumbled like stale cake and he pulled back fearfully as a chunk of it fell away and went tumbling down – splashing in the saltwater pools below.

The Jack of Clubs leaped clear. The cliff edge was treacherous. With a shudder, he saw the very spot where he had just been standing drop from sight and, some moments later, heard it crashing into the water.

It was time to return to the White Castle and he made his way back to his own horse.

"A glorious noon, is it not, my Lord?" asked a voice abruptly.

The noble started and spun around, wondering who had spoken.

"But what lures a son of the Under Kings from the confines of the thirteen hills to this perilous point?"

The Jack of Clubs gazed at a wind-sculpted tree a little distance away. There, stretched across the lowest branch, was a large dog fox.

The animal was watching him keenly and the grin on its face was not in the noble's imagination.

"The fox with the speech of man!" he exclaimed.

"Oh, well done, Sire," the animal said sarcastically. "However did you guess?"

The noble laughed in spite of himself. "My Lord Ismus has named you an enemy of the Realm!" he said.

"Then it is fortunate we are outside your borders," came the suave reply.

"He says you are in league with Haxxentrot the witch."

"That poisonous old biddy, with her bats and snakes? I think not! Now don't become tiresome and reach for that short sword at your side. I can dart away and be lost in the long grasses yonder before you could unsheathe it."

"I wish no harm to you," the noble replied, holding up his hands in a gesture of peace.

The fox studied him with interest. "So the tales I hear are not false," it said. "You are indeed the friend of beast and bird."

"I try to be."

"Then heed my words of guidance, son of the Royal House of Clubs. The Bad Shepherd is abroad. He was close to this very spot, two nights since, and won't be far. Do not let him approach you. Shun him. Cast stones at him. Hearken not to his speech. For he will infect you with his madness and begin a screaming in your spirit that will never be quelled."

The youth looked alarmed. "I have heard grim stories of the Bad

Shepherd," he said. "'Tis he whom the Ismus should hunt down."

"He will," the fox told him with a crafty smile. "In time, he will. The Bad Shepherd will be driven out completely. But the Jockey deems that I am competition and wishes me removed before all others. I am the only one who can... outfox him. No doubt he has trickled slanders into the Holy Enchanter's ear about my poor self. I am harmless, am I not?"

The noble nodded. "The Jockey weaves words with subtle skill and artifice," he agreed.

"And thus am I stitched up by him," the fox said.

"The Jockey rides us all at Court, that is true. Yet I thank you for the warning, good master fox. I will not linger here. If you ever need my aid, you know where to find me."

The fox's brush swished behind him. "I do indeed," he replied. "I have crept 'neath your windows many times on my way to pay my respects to the buxom beauties within the chicken shed... but wait!"

The ears flicked on its head and the fox jerked around.

"The herd is coming this way," it declared. "Take an extra crumb of advice, my princeling, and depart before they reach here. You may think yon wild horses are lovely to look at, but they harbour no love for man, nor any other beast save themselves. They bite and kick and trample. I shall not stay to..."

The fox left the sentence unfinished. There was a gleam of copper in the sunlight and it had jumped from the branch. The cream-tipped brush vanished into the long grasses and the animal was gone.

The Jack of Clubs smiled. He had always wanted to encounter

the fox with human speech. He hoped their paths would cross again some day.

He clapped a hand against his horse's flank, slipped a foot in the stirrup and was in the saddle once more.

"Let us return home, Urlwin," he said.

The horse nodded and began retracing its path through the grass and the shrubs, away from the cliff edge. The Jack of Clubs could not resist glancing back at the herd. They were such splendid creatures. He was sorely tempted to remain and see if his skill with animals would charm them also. But he could feel that his own horse was not happy. It did not wish to be bitten and kicked by wild, heathen stallions and was anxious to pick up the pace and gallop away.

The noble was about to give in and let Urlwin have its wish when everything changed.

Further along the cliff, where the gorse and twisted trees grew thickly, a cloud of black smoke was rising. The woods and thickets were on fire. The contented, carefree neighing of the herd was replaced by frightened whinnies and the horses charged away from the crackling flames. Then, from the shrubs, still wielding the burning torch he had started the fire with, came a demented, shrieking figure.

The Jack of Clubs gasped fearfully. It was the Bad Shepherd.

He was tall, with shaggy hair, and dressed in dirty grey robes. Bawling vile curses, he whirled the flaming brand over his head and ran, raging, into the midst of the herd – smiting hindquarters with it and setting tails and manes alight.

"Foul villain!" the Jack of Clubs shouted in fierce outrage.

The day was filled with the terror of the horses. They screamed and stampeded. To escape the evil flames, some leaped blindly over the cliff and their high voices continued to scream till they hit the rocks below.

The Jack of Clubs drew his short sword and spurred his own steed about. With a defiant yell, he went galloping towards the herd, to do battle with the Bad Shepherd and cleanse the land of his disgusting presence once and for all.

The panicked herd had left the insane man behind and he was staring with cruel delight at the chaos and damage he had caused. Throwing back his bearded head, he let loose a deranged laugh. Then he saw the Jack of Clubs racing towards him, making his way through the jostling herd, and he laughed all the more insanely.

The fire spread with awful speed through the dry shrubs and grasses. With that on one side and the cliff on the other, the track way was narrow. Urlwin and the Jack of Clubs were surrounded by frightened horses and could not steer a course through them. The untameable beasts were so desperate to flee, their rolling eyes barely noticed the noble on his stallion and they barged and pushed against them. Alarm and horror drove each one and their hooves pounded frantically over the sandy ground.

It was impossible to ride against that whinnying tide and the Jack of Clubs could only watch as the Bad Shepherd raised a

mocking finger and shook his head. Then he tossed the torch aside and strode off, out of sight.

"One day I shall hunt you down!" the noble vowed. But his main concern at that moment was trying to remain in the saddle. Then, to his horror, he felt Urlwin drop beneath him. And a new threat replaced that of the fire.

The stampede had weakened the already soft ground. The entire cliff path was giving way.

The noble heaved on the reins and Urlwin staggered from the pit that juddered and buckled beneath its hooves. The ground began to slip and slide. Holes and trenches gaped open. Horses tripped and stumbled. The screaming increased.

With renewed urgency, Urlwin battled on – to bear its beloved master to safety. It snorted and pushed through the untamed beasts all around. But it was no use.

There was a deep rumble and a long slice of the cliff vanished. The horses that were running there were suddenly gone. Then another stretch of ground fell away and more beasts went toppling down to the rocks far below. The sand under Urlwin's hooves was quaking. With one final, determined effort, the stallion drove its forelegs deep into the shaking ground and bucked. The Jack of Clubs was flung from the saddle. He flew through the air, high over the ears of the herd, and landed in the long grass beyond.

"Urlwin!" he shouted, scrambling to his feet immediately. "Urlwin!"

Braving the wild kicks of the terrified herd, he darted forward, to lead his faithful horse from danger.

The cliff trembled and a huge section broke away. Urlwin's proud head reared for a moment and then it, with the horses nearby, went slithering out of sight.

"No!" the Jack of Clubs cried. "Urlwin! Urlwin!"

There was another ominous rumble and more horses disappeared. Only a small group of them were left and the fire was getting closer, cutting off any escape.

Fear and smoke poured over the diminishing cliff path. The horses that remained pounded around in circles, their thumping hooves accelerating the cliff's collapse.

The Jack of Clubs felt the ground lurch beneath him and he was hurled off balance. The largest chunk of cliff so far went crashing down. The young noble's legs were thrashing in the empty air. There was nothing below him except a precipitous drop to the ruin and carnage that spilled over the shore. Catching hold of the gnarled branch of one of the twisted trees, he hauled himself out of danger, but the sandy earth kept breaking away under him. He flung himself forward, into the choking smoke of the burning thickets, and hoped the roots there would bind the ground more securely. But the heat of the encroaching flames was intense and he knew he could not remain in that place long.

Anxious, he searched for a way out. Then he saw it. A natural tunnel formed between the gorse and tortured trees. It was filled with black smoke, but so far the flames had not reached it. If he could

make his way through there, he would come to safety on the other side.

The hope soared in his heart and he lunged towards it. Then, with his escape in sight, he heard a sound that made him halt and whirl around.

A narrow promontory was jutting out over the broken cliff and there, standing upon it, shivering and tossing its terrified head, was the last survivor of the untameable horses. It was a foal. It could not have been more than two weeks old. Its long, stilt-like legs were splayed and its large ears were flicking wildly. It had just seen its mother break on the merciless rocks below and the ground upon which it stood was already beginning to tip.

The Jack of Clubs could not bear it. If he ran through the smoky tunnel now, he could save himself, but the foal would certainly perish. He could not let that happen.

Tiptoeing along the crumbling edge, he held out his hands and the foal stared at him with round, horror-filled eyes.

"Hush now," the noble called to it. "This way. Steady, don't be scared."

The foal shied and the earth gave way. The foal slipped and only its forelegs remained on the ground.

It whinnied mournfully and fell.

Jack's hands shot out. He seized the foal by the neck, the shoulders, then below the ribs and hauled it back on to the disintegrating spur of ground. They struggled and he pulled it further on to the cliff. The sand dribbled away under them.

For a moment they lay there, both panting and spent. Then the Jack of Clubs sprang to his feet.

"We can't stay here!" he told the petrified foal. "The fire will soon fill our only escape. Come, this way."

The foal's large, brown eyes looked up at him. Tears were streaming down its face. The Jack of Clubs thought it was merely because of the acrid smoke, but then he heard a noise that wrung his heart.

Not all the horses had died in the fall. Some were still alive down there. But they had fallen into deep pools ringed by sharp rocks and could not get out, whilst others had landed in quicksand. Their terrors were still enduring.

"Don't listen," he said to the foal, cupping his hands around its quivering head. In a gentle, broken voice, he began to sing.

"Shush now, don't hear the noises. Shush now, I won't let go. Stay with me – don't look back. Come with me – come with me. Fear no more. Shush now, shush now."

The foal lumbered up and let itself be led away from the treacherous edge. The Jack of Clubs sang to it the whole time, keeping his eyes locked with those of the frightened animal. The fire had now reached the tunnel and was licking into it. The swirling smoke within was even thicker than before.

Still singing, the Jack of Clubs guided the foal into the churning fumes that engulfed them both completely...

Conor Westlake crashed back against the pillows of his bed, coughing and spluttering from the smoke on the pages. He wiped his stinging eyes. Then fell asleep, exhausted – with his copy of Dancing Jacks clutched tightly in his hand.

"I am the Jack of Clubs," he murmured fitfully. "I am the Jack of Clubs."

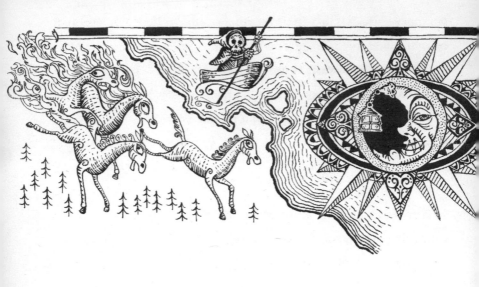

20

Paul
I DO NOT want to answer any questions
about that person. Do not contact me again!
    Trudy Bishop

CHECKING HIS EMAIL was the first thing Paul Thornbury did the next morning. Trudy's reply was so curt it was rude. The boy wondered why insulting messages from total strangers bothered him. They shouldn't, but they did. It just wasn't nice. Some people forgot another human being was going to read their words. A little politeness and civility went a long way in the cold world of cyberspace.

He knew there wasn't any point sending another email to her or trying to explain. Perhaps there was something else he could try. First of all he had to face his mother and Martin.

Last night had been a trial. They were convinced he had put fireworks on the barbecue and sat him down to lecture and scold him. Then they tried to understand what was going through his mind. Did he need to see the counsellor? Was this a symptom of his shock over witnessing the Disaster? They were sure Paul's newfound pyromania was connected to the horrific explosions down at the Landguard.

He had sat there quietly while they went on and on at him. He preferred it when they were shouting than when they attempted to empathise and got it so very wrong. There was absolutely nothing he could say. Any mention of Dancing Jacks was immediately drowned out by their armchair psychoanalysis. Eventually Paul promised never to do anything like that again and then was hugged compassionately before he trudged to bed.

At breakfast it was just as bad. His mother wanted to show him he could tell her anything. Yet the one thing he was desperate to tell her, the only thing that was important, she was not prepared to listen to.

Eating his cereal was an ordeal. Every mouthful seemed to be scrutinised by them. He knew the worst was still to come. Martin would have another go at interrogating him on the way to school.

The journey seemed to drag that morning. He sat there, not

listening to the maths teacher's earnest speeches. Paul was only eleven years old. He had no idea how to make anyone listen and take him seriously. If real life had been like one of Martin's sci-fi DVDs, he would have some outstanding proof to stun them with so they couldn't fail to believe those books were evil. But this wasn't anything like that. Nobody believed him. What could he do? How could he stop what was happening all around him? He couldn't go to the police with this if his own mother refused to listen…

The boy knew it was hopeless. It was only going to get worse. More people would read the book. More people would change. How far would it spread?

It was way too much for him to deal with alone.

They arrived at the school and Paul made the right noises to satisfy Martin that he had taken in what had been said. He was glad to go to registration.

Anthony and Graeme were naturally absent so he found himself sitting alone as the register was taken and announcements made.

Paul was distracted by three of the girls in the class. Little Molly Barnes sat in the middle, showing the other two a book she had started reading last night. All three were rocking slightly on their chairs.

How could he fight this?

In the staffroom Martin learned that Mrs Early would not be in that day and maybe not for the rest of the week. The attack had shaken her more severely than she had been willing to admit.

"I know it's nowhere near the same degree as those two lads," Mr Hitchin, the chemistry teacher, said, "but a lot of pupils are acting out of character. Did anyone else notice that yesterday?"

"I think it's a reaction to the Disaster," somebody answered.

Martin pricked up his ears.

"What does that counsellor the police provided say?" he asked. "I haven't actually seen her about. What's her name?"

"Something Clucas, I think."

"It's Angela, isn't it?"

"I thought it was Ayleen."

"Well, whatever it is, I think Paul could do with paying her a visit and talking last Friday night through."

"That Anthea Clucas is starting to get in my clack!" Barry Milligan's gruff voice barked as he came marching in. "She's swigged enough herbal tea to sink the Bismarck in and handed out Jaffa cakes and sympathy to a grand total of seven kids all week. I could have done that myself."

"It wouldn't be herbal tea you'd be drinking though, would it, Barry?" Mr Wynn said acidly.

"Isn't there a sunbed pining for you someplace?" the Head asked. The games master pretended not to hear.

"You know what she's suggesting?" Barry continued to the others. "Group therapy sessions. She's taken over one of the music rooms and wants half a dozen kids at a time to go in there to share their experiences and draw pictures, blah blah blah. She wants to read poetry to them."

"I think that's a wonderful idea," Mrs Yates said. "Some children might not want to be seen going to her on their own. A few at once isn't anywhere near so bad and they may open up a bit more readily. She's a trained professional – she knows what she's doing."

Barry shrugged. "Well, whatever this 'Blessed be' thing is that's going round," he said, pouring himself a black coffee, "she's caught it as well. God knows what sort of happy-clappy poetry she'll be reading the kids, but I don't think Jesus would want any of our lot for a sunbeam."

"Have a word with her, will you, Barry?" Martin asked. "See if she can fit Paul in sometime."

"Will do, squire. If you think it'll do him any good. She'll be gone by next week though. Once the memorial service is over this Sunday, I think we can start getting back to normal again."

"And when can we look forward to waving goodbye to you?" Mr Wynn asked dryly.

"Oh… long before any of your shoddily coached teams ever win a trophy," Barry answered. "Has anyone ever told you that you've got a truly ironic name?"

The games teacher scowled and left the staffroom, huffing and blowing.

"Something I said?" Barry asked with mock innocence. "How can someone with muscles like that be so thin-skinned? Do you think it's a side-effect of all the tanning he does? He's what's known as a Mangerine."

"So you'll put Paul's name down for the counsellor today?" Martin reminded him.

"Consider it done. He and five of his cohorts can trot off to her this afternoon and she can 'Blessed be' them all she likes."

Martin thanked him, little realising the danger he had just placed the eleven-year-old in.

That morning Anthea Clucas, the counsellor who was supposed to be there to help the children talk through the trauma of the Disaster, saw eighteen pupils. When they emerged from the commandeered music room, none of them were the same.

Sandra Dixon was running a temperature that morning and so her concerned mother kept her off school. She could not understand why her daughter's bridesmaid's dress was on the floor in a sopping wet heap. She couldn't get any sense from the girl. She just wanted to be left alone with a book. Perhaps she should call the doctor?

"No, good mistress," Sandra said when she heard her mother suggest this. "I would be more soothed if you were to stay and read to me."

"You're too old for that!" Mrs Dixon replied. "Have you spoken to Debbie yet? She rang last night wondering why you'd gone so quiet on her. You two used to be so close..."

"Please," the girl insisted. "Read just a page or two. It would give me such comfort – and you too, I believe."

And so her mother sat on the edge of her daughter's bed and began to read to her...

Emma Taylor had spent an anxious night and felt haggard and more irritable than usual from lack of sleep. She had half expected the police to turn up on the doorstep before she left the house. Had that gormless Conor grassed her up or not? She only went into school with the intention of finding out and trying any means she could to deter him if he hadn't already.

At registration she found him hunched over the desk and was surprised to discover he was reading a book, an actual book, not one of the football programmes he usually pored over. She punched him on the shoulder.

"So you snitched on me yet or what?" she demanded bluntly. The boy lifted his gaze and seemed to look right through her.

"What's up with you?" Emma snorted. "Can't read and think at the same time?"

His blank expression changed as he seemed to vaguely recognise her. "You remind me of the Jill of Spades," he said faintly.

"You what?"

"You are the Jill of Spades," he said more definitely.

"Watch your mouth!"

"I have no liking for the House of Spades' cruel daughter."

"I definitely don't dig you if that's what you mean."

"Leave me – I am still angry for what you did to the noble Accipiter."

Emma's forehead scrunched up. "You idiot – it were a knackered Fiesta an' it weren't my fault."

"It was a fine hunting bird. Too good for your murdering hands."

"You been sniffing your trainers, you gonk? All I want to know is, have you called the filth yet? Are they gonna come knockin' or what?"

Conor leaned back in his chair, revealing as he did so the playing card he had pinned to the lapel of his school blazer that morning. It was the Jack of Clubs.

"Your deeds and caprices shall find their own dark rewards," he told her. "One day your plots and schemes will misfire and you will be caught in your own nets."

"Is that a no?"

"It is a caution you should heed." And with that, the boy returned his attention to the book.

Emma stood there, confused and speechless. What was he going on about? Was he threatening her? When the bell rang for the first lesson, she was none the wiser.

At lunchtime she went to the football field to try and speak to him again, but Conor was not there and only three lads were half-heartedly kicking a ball about instead of the usual dozen or so. Moving through the playground, she began to notice that playing cards were pinned to the jackets and jumpers of other pupils. Most were simply number cards, but here and there were picture cards. She could not think what their significance was. Emma was usually on top of all the trends and crazes, and swiftly decided which to adopt and which to ridicule. Had a band brought out an album that had slipped beneath her radar? Perhaps it was sport-related, in which case she didn't care. It would make sense if Conor was showing some kind of allegiance to a team, but playing cards were a weird way of doing it.

Seeing a small boy in Year 8 standing alone in a corner by the defunct drinking fountain, she strode over and jabbed at the five of diamonds secured to his blazer.

"What's this then, you dork?" she interrogated him. "What's it about?"

Instead of being intimidated, as she had expected, the boy looked at her in the same far-off way that Conor had earlier.

"I be a page to the House of Diamonds," he answered proudly.

"You what?"

"There be uproar in the West Tower this day," he said. "My Lord, the Knave, has stole the King of Hearts' great Healing Ruby and will not tell where it be stowed 'less His Majesty's fair daughter buys the information with a kiss. The Court be outraged and the Jill of Hearts swears she won't be bartered with, like a cabbage in the market. I be keeping out the way, for tempers be running hotter than spitting goose fat in every quarter."

"Is this off the telly?" Emma snapped.

"'Tis the honest truth!" the boy swore. "I heard the Constable himself declare it. Oh, what scandal! When the Ismus hears of it, Magpie Jack had best fly."

The boy was so adamant and sure that Emma stepped away from him, unnerved.

"Blessed be," he said, returning to his daydreaming.

Emma looked around the playground. Other children stood apart and alone like him, with the same rapt expression on their faces. But there were also groups gathered in tight circles, reading from books. All of them were wearing playing cards on their uniforms. The girl hadn't seen anything like this before. Whatever was going on, it was unnatural and she didn't like it. She wished Ashleigh and Keeley were here. They would have found something to laugh at in this creepy behaviour. Emma missed them more than she had ever thought possible. She wondered how she would feel on Sunday when they would be buried.

Paul Thornbury had received the message from Martin that he and five of his classmates were to see the counsellor in the last double period that afternoon. Paul rolled his eyes when he heard. Martin was still convinced he needed to discuss the Disaster so that he wouldn't mess about with fireworks again. Why wouldn't anyone listen to him? He thought about the counsellor, Mrs Clucas, and wondered what she was like. If he could get just one adult on his side, he wouldn't feel so isolated and useless.

Standing in the playground, he too saw the playing cards some of the other children were wearing and he realised for the first time just how many pupils that book had affected.

"Or infected," he murmured to himself.

It was like a swiftly spreading disease. Even the teachers on break duty scratched their chins at the new craze of wearing playing cards. When they discussed it among themselves in the staffroom afterwards, Mr Roy thought this fad should be nipped in the bud and the cards banned.

"Remember the Pokémon thing years ago?" the geography teacher said. "Those trading and collecting games just aren't nice. They encourage bullying and cheating and the younger ones get ripped off by the bigger kids."

"But this isn't a swapsy game, is it?" asked Miss Smyth. "As far as I can tell, it's some sort of house identity."

"Then there were those Crazy Bones," Mr Roy continued. "These things get out of control."

"The kids seem a lot quieter if you ask me," Miss Smyth added.

"Wait till this week is over," Barry Milligan told everyone. "Let them do this if they want. It's not offending anyone, is it? No one's fighting, for a change. Like I said this morning, once the funerals and the service are out of the way, we can get back to normal."

And so the playing cards remained pinned to the children's clothes.

Later that afternoon, when the last double period of the day commenced, Anthea Clucas watched the small group of children from Paul's class file into the music room and sit on the chairs that were arranged in a semi-circle before her. None of them were wearing playing cards. She smiled at them, as they looked at her expectantly. Then she raised the book she held in her hands and began to read from Dancing Jacks.

The children fidgeted uncomfortably for several minutes – until the power of the words drew them in and all five of them were lost.

At exactly the same moment, Paul Thornbury was several miles away, walking down Hamilton Road in the middle of town. He had decided to bunk off and avoid seeing the totally unnecessary counsellor. There was someone else he wanted to speak to, far more urgently. His truancy that afternoon saved him.

It did not take him long to reach the estate agent's. He glanced at the photographs of the houses in the window, peering between them to the desks within. There were three of them and at once he spotted the person he was looking for. With a determined look on his face, he pushed the door open and went inside.

Trudy Bishop was tapping placidly at her keyboard. She was surfing the Net while waiting for a call about a property in nearby Trimley St Mary. A shadow fell across her desk and she immediately clicked off the ABBA appreciation forum and glanced up. A young boy stood before her.

"Hello?" she said, looking past him to see if there was an accompanying parent.

The boy took a breath as if summoning up courage to speak. "I'm Paul," he introduced himself.

"Trudy," she replied with a practised, but questioning smile. She was a short, plump woman with spectacles. Her desk was not the tidiest, and there was a half-eaten packet of Monster Munch and a custard doughnut in her drawer.

"How can I help?" she asked.

The boy stared at her intently. "I sent you an email," he said in a

319

low, important whisper like a secret agent as he waggled his eyebrows at her.

Trudy's professional mask slipped for an instant as she thought about the dating site she had joined recently and the odd messages she had received from some of its members. But none of them could possibly be this kid, could they? You just didn't know who was who on the Web.

"Well, you can't be the Capricorn with a four-wheel drive and a boa constrictor," she said dryly.

"Eh?"

"What can I do for you?" she asked.

Paul glanced around cautiously. "Last night," he said. "The one about Austerly Fellows and your ghost hunting. You replied this morning and…"

The woman's face changed immediately. "You sent me that?" she asked in a rush of shock and surprise. That email had come from a child? "I told you not to contact me. How dare you come here! What do you think you're playing at?"

"But I have to talk to you about him! You have to listen to me. No one else will and I'm getting really scared! It's important – really important!"

Trudy could see he was telling the truth. Out of the corner of her eye she saw her colleagues looking over to check what was going on. She waved at them to get on with their work.

"I'll give you five minutes," she told Paul in a hushed voice. "But not in here." She rose and the boy followed her outside.

320

"Bit young for you, Trudy!" one of the other estate agents heckled as they passed. She was too preoccupied to even hear him.

"Five minutes, kid," she repeated when they were standing on the pavement. "And that is more than you deserve for doorstepping me like this. You've got a ruddy nerve."

"I couldn't think what else to do. I had to know what happened when you went to that house."

"Why? What's it to you?"

"Because something is happening right now, something wrong and freaky, and it's all because of Austerly Fellows."

Trudy closed her eyes for a moment. "Anything to do with that man would be," she said. "Whatever it is you're involved in, stop it. If you're thinking of going to that house, don't. What are you, twelve?"

"Eleven."

"Oh, give me strength! I've got underwear older than you. Listen, you stay away from that place, do you hear me?"

"No danger of me going anywhere near it, even if I knew where it was!" Paul assured her. "I just want to find out more about this Fellows bloke. There isn't much on the Net."

"The less you know, the safer you'll be," Trudy said firmly. "He was a dangerous man when he was alive and an even more dangerous one after he died – if he ever did die. You know what he was, don't you?"

"Wikipedia said he was some kind of devil worshipper."

"Do you even understand what that is? It's not like a computer game with red cartoon demons running about with pitchforks. It's not a Hallowe'en fancy-dress party. It's serious and nasty and dangerous."

Paul nodded. "I know," he said. "I've seen that already."

"Then keep away from it," she warned. "Where on earth are your parents? Why are they letting you get mixed up in this?"

"I've tried telling them, but no one will believe me!" he replied impatiently. "No one – not one."

Trudy ran a hand through her bobbed hair. "I wouldn't have either," she said. "Not before that night."

"You think Fellows is still alive?" the boy asked. "Wiki said he'd disappeared. He couldn't still be around, not after all this time."

"Something is," she answered, lowering her voice as a shopper ambled by. "Something is alive and in that house. Guarding whatever's in there."

"Tell me what happened to you, please. It might help."

Trudy rubbed her eyes beneath her glasses. "You've seen the website," she began. "You know we went there looking for... I don't know – a spooky time. We had no idea how stupid we were: me, Geoff with the camera, Reg, Keith and Reg's Auntie Doreen. She's always said she was a bit psychic. She can predict the weather better than John Kettley and is good at finding lost watches and car keys, but nothing big league – just the odd feeling, cold spots and the like. Anyway, soon as we got to the end of that drive, she started to panic. She didn't want to go any further. She said the house was 'full and waiting', her exact words, 'full and waiting'. She said 'he' was in

322

there, 'he had never left'. She was going on and on about blackness, about mould and blackness. Geoff even filmed her and we were laughing. Oh, good God, we laughed at her…"

Trudy's mouth was dry and she tried to moisten her lips with a rasping tongue.

"She made such a fuss that we left the car right there, with her still throwing a wobbly in it. She begged us not to go, but we took no notice. We were so stupid. We had no idea what we were doing, like toddlers putting their hands in a fire to see what it feels like. We walked up that drive, giggling and acting the goat. So bloody clueless."

A bus rumbled by and Trudy waited till it had gone before continuing. "So we get to the front door. It's a big place. You've seen the photo?"

"On your site, yes."

"Then you know it's run-down and boarded up. We take some pics, mess about like teenagers. We have a drink. Geoff films us being daft. We were only having a bit of silly fun – that's all it was ever meant to be. When you get to my age, divorced with two grown-up kids, you'll understand. And then… then I suggest we break in and have a seance. That was my brilliant idea. I egged them on. Well done, Trudy."

She broke off and gazed down the street. It was a quiet afternoon. Only a few cars were moving along the road. The school run was yet to start and the shops were having a sluggish day. Trudy rubbed her eyes again. An orange and cream camper van drove slowly by.

Paul leaned forward. "And did you?" he asked. "Did you have a seance?"

"We couldn't get in. Reg tried the front door, but it wouldn't budge. Geoff hands me the camera and tells me to film him going round the back to find another way in. So Reg, Keith and me are stood there, watching him stride manfully down the path at the side of the property. He disappears around the far corner and we wait, wait for him to find a way in and come open the front door from the inside. And then…"

"Then?"

Trudy's eyes were watering. "There's a scream," she said softly. "We hear Geoff scream. But it doesn't stop. It just goes on and on. He's screaming and screaming and screaming. We run to find him and there he is, staggering down the path, screaming and stinking of damp and decay – as though he's crawled out of a grave."

"What happened?"

"We left that place as fast as we could, that's what happened!"

"But what was it? What frightened him?"

Trudy blinked and shook her head. "We don't know," she answered. "Geoff hasn't stopped screaming long enough to tell anyone. It's been almost six months now. We took him to hospital straight away and they sectioned him. Whatever he saw in that house broke his mind. He's been in a secure ward ever since. The doctors don't understand it and can't help him. All they can do is keep him sedated and feed him through tubes. But, even if he

recovered, he'd never be able to speak again. His screaming shredded his vocal cords. So you see that's why I don't want to talk about Austerly Fellows. Whatever is in his filthy house did that to Geoff."

"What did the police do?"

"I'm an estate agent!" she hissed, nodding at the office behind them. "We don't break into houses. We didn't tell them. Besides, what could I say? They wouldn't believe me. But they might have made me go back there, and there's no way I'd ever do that. That fire burned me and I learned the lesson."

"So nobody went and found out? There wasn't an investigation?"

"You can't fight what's in that place!" Trudy insisted. "Not with the law of the land. There are older, stronger laws than that. The boys in blue wouldn't stand a chance."

"You definitely believe there's something evil in there then?"

"Oh, I know it – absolutely."

Paul breathed a sigh of relief. At last here was someone he could talk to, someone who wouldn't think he was being ridiculous.

"Did you know Austerly Fellows wrote a book?" he said solemnly. "A kids' book?"

Trudy stared at him through the thick lenses of her spectacles. "He did what?"

"A kids' book. Some strange guy was selling them down the boot fair last Sunday."

"A kids' book?" she uttered in disbelief. "That vile man, that satanist, wrote a kids' book? I can't…"

"It's true! Loads at my school have been reading it and it's done something to them, turned them weird or possessed them. It's like – like it takes you over. The one I had tried to make me read it, but I wouldn't. No word of a lie, it tried to make me read it. But I burned it instead and this… thing – it came flying out of the flames. It was a… a shape with horns. It flew up into the sky. I'm the only one who saw it and I can't make anyone listen and more and more kids are being taken over. It's getting worse and worse."

The woman regarded him with a look of frozen horror on her face.

"You do believe me, don't you?" Paul asked. "It's true – every word."

Trudy glanced anxiously left and right. "Yes," she said.

Paul almost hugged her. "Thank you!" he cried gratefully. "Thank you so much!"

"I believe you," she said again. "But I don't know why you came here telling me this. There's nothing I can do."

"You can have a word with my mum and Martin!" the boy told her eagerly. "They'd have to listen then. We could go to the papers and get those books banned and destroyed before it's too late."

The woman backed away from him as if he was a ticking bomb.

"No," she uttered, in a panicky voice. "Go away! You've had more than five minutes. Now go away, little boy. I don't want to get involved. I've been burned, didn't you hear? I'm not going to get mixed up with that again."

"But—"

"Go away!"

"You must help me!"

"And end up in the room next to Geoff, screaming my head off with a tube up my nose, my arms and feet strapped to the bed? Not on your life."

"Please! I can't do anything on my own!"

"You want my help? Not a hope in hell, kid. I won't do anything and never want to see you again. But I will say this – forget what you know, stop asking questions and you might, just might, get away without getting burned yourself. Austerly Fellows didn't die. Somehow he's still in that house. The place is full of him so don't hack him off! Don't do anything to draw attention to yourself. Don't let him become aware of you. You don't want that monster to take an interest in you or your family. But most of all – and I've never been more serious in my life – do not drag me into it. We never had this conversation, do you hear?"

"But the books…?"

"Are none of my business," Trudy said brusquely as she stepped back to the door. "If you don't want to suffer, don't make it any of yours either. You can't fight against that and you'll certainly never, ever win."

She was breathing hard, the fear sapping her round face of colour. What could she say to get rid of him? Why hadn't she deleted that stupid website?

"It'll probably blow over anyway," she said, suddenly trying to sound casual and unconcerned, but failing. "I'm sure it isn't as serious as you make out."

"It is! I'm begging you!"

Trudy shook her head. "Don't come here again," she told him. "Leave me alone!"

She couldn't get away fast enough. She re-entered the office and almost ran to her desk. She turned to her computer screen and refused to look back at the window, where the boy was staring in at her, his forehead pressed against the glass.

After several minutes, Paul tore himself away. He was on his own again; one small lad against forces he couldn't begin to imagine or comprehend.

Leaving the estate agent's behind him, he dragged his feet past the shops, not caring where he was going. What could he do? Perhaps Trudy was right. But could he really sit back and let the rest of the school become zombies to that old book? How could that be safer? The evil influence would spread out from there. No one would escape it. He thought about that old house and wondered just where it was and what awful horrors it might contain. What had really happened to Trudy's friend Geoff? Paul had never seen an adult as coldly terrified in real life as Trudy had been when she was talking about that place.

Staring at the pavement, he was so absorbed in his thoughts that he didn't notice the vehicle crawling along beside him, or hear the doors open and slam when it stopped. Only when he saw a pair of new, pointed, black velvet shoes on the ground in front did he

look up and see the man standing before him.

"Well, if it isn't the boy who wanted a magic book about wizards, and then burned it," the Ismus greeted him with a contemptuous snarl.

The golden bugles sounded clear and loud, the baying hounds tore through the village and the horses galloped after. The Royal Hunt had begun.

21

PAUL LET OUT a yell of surprise. He dodged around sharply to run away, but two men with blackened faces were directly behind him. One of them seized him roughly by the collar and spun him about.

"Almost a century ago," the Ismus began, "…so long ago now… there was a certain shouty little Austrian with a grandiose plan and a stupid moustache. He was a book burner too. But none of the works he burned were as important as the one you destroyed, boy."

His ferret-like features were a grim mask of barely suppressed anger. He squinted at the lad in front of him.

"So much time and effort had been invested in that ridiculous, overblown scheme," the gaunt man continued, stooping to speak close to the boy's face – breathing a foul, dank reek at him. "I suppose you could say we were rivals for our Lord's attention, back in those far-off days. And yet my much subtler, far more potent, plan

was shelved in favour of his tiresomely loud campaign. What a disappointment both he, and it, proved to be for the Dawn Prince. I knew it would fail. Wars don't work – you can't conquer and subdue everyone by force – and where is the long-term fun in that anyway? The pen really is mightier and absolute control so much more satisfying."

"You're mental!" the boy shouted, looking around for help. A knot of fright and alarm was twisting in his stomach. To his dismay he saw he had wandered off the main road and they were in a small side street. There was no one else in sight. Paul struggled, but the black-faced man held him firm.

"Let me go! Who do you think you are?"

"You know who I am," the Ismus chuckled. "You spent the whole of last night and today thinking about me. It's really rather flattering."

"You're not him!" Paul shouted. "You're not Austerly Fellows! You can't be!"

"I am the Holy Enchanter," the man told him, a crooked smile stealing over his face. "And people who play with matches must pay the inevitable penalty. You didn't really think you could burn one of the sacred texts, one of my blessed works, without me being aware of it? The Dancing Jacks are my spores, boy. I put everything I learned, everything I was, into their creation. Nine years I laboured, and those nine years were the culmination of a lifetime's study of the teachings and truths of many ancient faiths, from fallen and forgotten empires. Each book is the kernel for a dormant seed and they are a part of me."

Paul called out again and the Ismus laughed at him.

"No rescue, no salvation," the man taunted. "You live in the wrong times for that. There are no champions left. This modern world has degraded into such wonderful compost. It has become so delightfully low, so ripe and ready to accept anything without question. Awash with cardboard heroes; empty, acquisitive approval-seekers with perfect teeth and Italian suits. There is no substance, no value, just labels. Acclaim and prestige are showered, so liberally, over the undeserving – for so little – whilst anything of true merit and worth is jeered at and derided. What fertile loam for my Dancing Jacks to root in and flourish."

He paused and watched the fear on the boy's face. "Let me tell you what is going to happen," he continued. "Firstly, we're going to go for a little drive. Then, when you're sitting comfortably, I'll read to you. Won't that be nice? Three chapters should do it. And, just to make certain you're fully… captivated, you will taste the minchet. You'll love that, boy – I promise."

"You're crazy – the lot of you!" Paul shouted.

The Ismus grinned at him and tapped a forefinger on the boy's temple. "You don't know the meaning of the word," he chuckled. "I could rot your mind completely if I chose to. If you only knew how shifting is the sand upon which the citadel of your sanity is built."

Paul thought of Trudy's friend Geoff and he shook his head violently.

"This will be so much more amusing though," the man told him. "You see, once you're inside the Realm of the Dawn Prince, you

won't ever want to leave. This life here and now will be grey drudgery and every moment you spend away from the pages of Dancing Jacks will be a torment. Each sacred word will be like oxygen to you. Only there shall you find colour and flavour, so brilliant, so intense that everything else is stale and flat. But because you were so foolish as to consign your own book to the flames, you won't be getting another. Oh, no, I'll make certain you'll be denied that. How will you cope without one? I have no idea, but it will be fascinating to find out."

"You know what I think?" Paul interrupted defiantly.

"What, what do you think?"

"I think – I'm really glad I'm wearing Docs!"

With a defiant yell, he stamped on the Ismus's foot with the heel of his Doc Martens. The Holy Enchanter roared with pain and the bodyguards sprang forward to attend him. Paul elbowed one of them in the ribs. Then he darted between them and ran, as fast as he could, back to the main road.

"Never mind me!" the Ismus bellowed at the men. "Get him – get him!"

Limping to the camper van, he sat on the sill and nursed his throbbing foot. He ground his teeth in anger and speckles of black mould bloomed across his face.

Paul pelted along Hamilton Road. He could hear the clomping boots of the two men chasing him, but he knew he was faster.

Not bad for someone who spends every spare minute on his computer! he thought to himself.

Shops and shoppers raced by. He swerved around shambling pensioners pushing their tartan bags on wheels and jumped over a startled dog tethered to a lamp post. Then, up ahead, he saw a sight that made him call out with joy. A police car was parked at the side of the road and a chubby policeman was giving a woman directions.

Paul punched the air and slowed down. He glanced behind. The black-faced bodyguards were still chasing, but he reckoned that by the time they caught up, he would have had the chance to tell the policeman everything. He wouldn't mention the book, or Austerly Fellows, just that they had tried to drag him into a van. That would be enough to detain them and get the law on to that crazy Ismus character. It couldn't have worked out better.

Holding his sides, because he felt a stitch coming on, he came jogging up behind the policeman.

"…and then take a right into Cobbold Road and you can't miss it, Madam," the uniformed man was saying.

"Thank you, officer," she answered gratefully.

The policeman held up a hand as she set off. "Blessed be," he said.

At the sound of those two words, Paul stood stock-still. The newfound hope and confidence were wrenched from under him. His face fell. The policeman turned around and looked at him with glassy eyes.

"What can I do for you?" he asked.

Paul was too shocked and afraid to speak. He could see the red pattern of a playing card showing faintly through the white cotton of

the officer's shirt pocket. He shook his head and took a step back.

The officer stared at him questioningly. Then he lifted his gaze and looked along the street – at the two bodyguards running towards them.

Without needing to turn, Paul knew exactly what he was looking at and he saw a flicker of realisation cross the policeman's face.

"You'd best come with me," the officer began. "Don't make a scene. Get in the car."

He reached out to take hold of the boy's shoulder, but Paul leaped off the kerb and ran across the road. A horn blared as a car screeched to a halt when he ran in front of it. The driver cursed at him, but the boy was already charging round a corner. The stitch in his side was agony, but Paul did not stop.

He had never been in any sort of trouble. His mother had taught him to respect the law. But now here he was, running from the police like a fugitive. The boy knew he had to get home. But he couldn't risk being seen along any of the roads. He would have to run though gardens and round the backs of houses, jump over fences and hedges. And what then? There was no one he could trust. No one he could talk to. Would Martin or his mother believe any of this or would they think he was simply making up a ludicrous lie to make them forget the previous night's 'fireworks'? Paul was certain they would think the latter.

For almost an hour he dodged and hid, making a gradual, skulking progress through the town, towards their house. When any vehicle came in sight, he vanished behind a wall or ducked around a shrub or postbox.

Once a police car drove by. Peering through the privet, he saw that it was not the same one as earlier. Two different officers were inside. Should he leap out and try to make them listen? Or were they a part of it as well? Paul shrank further back and kept silent.

It was dusk when he finally reached the street where he lived. He peered cautiously round the corner to check it out. Everything appeared normal enough. There was no sign of that Volkswagen – or any police cars. They couldn't possibly know where he lived anyway, could they? But then how did that creepy, skinny man know he had burned the book? Remembering the fiery shape that had shot out of it, Paul wondered if each copy contained such a creature, somehow embedded in the pages – or woven into the words themselves.

Glad to be home, he hurried towards the house. Then he stumbled to a stop as the lean figure of the Ismus stepped out from behind their neighbour's fence and blocked his way. Paul looked nervously around. The camper van was turning into the road.

"You try anything and I'll yell my head off!" the boy warned. "You won't get away with that here."

The man laughed with scorn. "Oh, the terror and tyranny of Neighbourhood Watch," he mocked.

"Just get away from me!"

"I have been thinking," the Ismus said. "And I have had a revelation – an epiphany if you like. I have changed my mind about what to do with you. You see – I know what role has been assigned

to you in my Lord's Kingdom. As yet, it has not been taken up by any other and, although that does not matter, there can be only one prime example of each courtier, one true form to whom all other followers of the part must look. That is going to be you, boy. You have just proven yourself to be most… appropriate. When this petulance and stubbornness are over, and you have finally embraced the sacred work, come find me. Bring what you know you must as payment and perhaps a copy of Dancing Jacks will be yours after all."

"I've no idea what you're on about."

"Not yet, but you will and I shall be waiting."

"There's no way I'm ever going to read that book!" the boy shouted.

The Ismus smirked unpleasantly. The van stopped and he sauntered over to it, with only the slightest of limps betraying the bruised foot in his velvet shoe.

"Just don't try my patience too far," he advised as he got in. "The next time you attempt any violence on my Hallowed Person, you will do worse than die."

He nodded to the black-faced man at the wheel and the van moved off. The Ismus's dark eyes remained fixed on Paul until the Volkswagen disappeared round the corner.

The boy exhaled. He was drenched in cold sweat. Fumbling with his key, he let himself into the house and hurriedly shut the door behind him.

Martin's head appeared from the living room.

"So," he began sternly. "Where did you vanish to this afternoon?"

The boy couldn't think of a convincing lie. "Where's Mum?" he asked instead.

"Already gone to work. She's had to change shifts and don't change the subject. Where were you?"

Paul groaned. "I didn't want to see a stupid counsellor," he said.

"I don't like this new attitude of yours," Martin told him.

Paul was too tired and stressed to offer any argument. "It won't happen again," he said meekly.

"You had us both worried sick!" Martin continued. "You might have phoned or texted where you were. When you weren't around after school, I didn't know what to think. I'm surprised at you. Where did you go?"

"Into town."

"Into town? What for?"

The boy wanted to tell him everything, about Trudy, about the Ismus, about the policeman. But even he, thinking about those things, in these normal surroundings, thought they sounded fanciful and absurd. He couldn't expect Martin to believe him.

"That's the sort of behaviour I expect from the Year 10 deadheads!" Martin was beginning to rant. "You're better than that – or at least I thought you were!"

"I'm sorry, OK."

"No, it's not OK. Don't you ever put your mother through that again! She even rang Gerald and your gran to see if you'd gone to either of theirs. I'd best call and tell both of them you're back, and you – you ring Carol and apologise."

Paul nodded and took his mobile from his bag. He had forgotten all about it that afternoon. He hadn't even switched it on once he had left school. Eight missed calls and five texts from Martin and his mother immediately came beeping in. Paul looked at them guiltily, but there was something massive at stake here. If only they would listen to him, they would understand.

The boy was about to call his mother when he hesitated and smacked his forehead for being so stupid. Of course there was an adult he could trust, someone who had always been a good friend and would listen to him without prejudice, without shouting him down. He could hear Martin speaking to that person right at that very moment, his piano teacher – the wonderful Gerald.

Twenty minutes later, after leaving a grovelling message on his mother's voicemail, Paul sent Gerald a text.

> **To: Gerald**
> Hi! Can I come c u 2moro aftr schl?
> Am in trubl + need 2 talk.

A reply came back almost straight away.

> **From: Gerald**
> Of course! If there's anything I can do…
> Just let your mother know where you'll be!

339

Paul was always impressed at how fast Gerald could text and his messages were always spelled correctly, with no abbreviations and with the correct punctuation. He sent a "Thanx" back and turned to his computer. That evening his Google search for Dancing Jacks turned up twice as many results as yesterday. He prayed Gerald would know what to do.

Later that night, when most of the town had retired to bed, a straggly pilgrimage could be seen moving along the seafront. There were almost thirty figures. All were female: women and girls of varying ages. They had slipped outdoors without the knowledge of their partners or parents and each of them was headed towards the concrete pillbox, close to Felixstowe Ferry Golf Club. Wearing only nightdresses that billowed with the keen wind gusting in from the North Sea, they trod barefoot over sand, shingle, tarmac and gravel. Their eyes were half closed and they walked with slow and dreaming, almost dance-like steps.

Waiting for them at the entrance to the old bunker were the two Harlequin Priests, wearing for the first time their new robes made from diamond patches of different colours. Both of them held an iron poker in one hand and they bowed in silence as the first of the women drew near.

The area around the pillbox had been cleared of gorse and the wire fencing had been completely removed. Hundreds of candles were shining inside and the young woman who had once been Shiela Doyle was standing in the entrance, her arms open in wide welcome.

The High Priestess Labella was dressed in a long white and purple gown. Golden wire was twined in her hair and a tear-shaped piece of amethyst winked on her brow, reflecting the candle flames.

"Greetings, sisters," she announced as the women and girls gathered before her. "The Holy Enchanter awaits you within the Court. Cross the divide and enter in."

The women filed past, to descend the stairs and walk the length of the tunnel beneath. Most were already wearing playing cards pinned to their nightdresses, but some were not and so Labella provided them with one each, according to which Royal House, or which quarter of the White Castle, they now belonged.

"Otherwise Mauger will not let you pass," she told them. "He guards the way and is fiercely vigilant, but show him these and you will be permitted to go by."

The last two figures were a woman in her late thirties and a pale teenage girl swaddled in a dressing gown. Labella attached a card to their nightclothes and bade them enter.

With their glassy eyes sparkling in the candle glow, Sandra Dixon and her mother descended the stairs eagerly.

The High Priestess gazed out across the road – to where the larger concrete walled area was still hidden by gorse. The golden illumination of many lanterns was lighting the thickets and their needle-like leaves. A drum began to beat, a lute played and the sound of merriment commenced.

"The Queen of Hearts has made such a quantity of minchet," the High Priestess murmured with an indulgent smile. "There is enough for all yonder. Take as many jars as you need, ladies. When you return to your hearths and homes, deal it out freely. In the name of the Dawn Prince and his Holy Enchanter, the Ismus Resplendent!"

The Harlequin Priests took her hands reverently. Together, they descended into the tunnel and made their way to the Court. Music and wild laughter drifted up from the spacious, high-walled bunker. It floated out, over the shore, and mingled with the noise of the surf on the shingle.

In dances Magpie Jack, so hide what he may lack. In his palm
there is an itch and the spell he cannot crack. Jools
and trinkets he will thieve, the witch's curse to relieve. Conceal
your rich things from his itchings - for you'll
never get them back.

22

BARRY MILLIGAN STARED out of the staffroom window the following morning, watching the first of the kids arrive through the gates. Martin Baxter was standing beside him. None of the other teachers had turned up yet so they had the room, and the kettle, to themselves. They were discussing Paul's recent bad behaviour.

"And he refuses to go have a chat with happy-clappy Clucas?" the Head was saying.

"He's headstrong as his mother sometimes," Martin replied. "Says it's totally pointless because there's nothing wrong with him."

"Cocky beggar," Barry grunted. "But we can't have him going AWOL every time there's something he doesn't want to do. If every kid did that, there'd only be us staff here, stood about like lemons."

"We can't get through to him. He's going round to see a friend of ours this evening. Maybe Gerald will succeed where we can't. We just don't know what's come over him. He's such a good kid really. You know that."

The Headteacher didn't appear to be listening. He was staring abstractedly though the window.

"You all right?" Martin asked after a long pause.

Barry stirred and looked at him. The familiar steely glint of the hard-nosed TV detective was gone.

"I spoke to the governors again last night," he said. "Or rather they spoke to me."

Martin blinked in surprise. "Oh?" he said.

"I won't be here on Monday," the Head told him in a low voice. "They want me out, soon as."

"They can't do that!"

"They can apparently. I brought the name of the school and the whole teaching profession into disrepute so they can do what they like with me. I just didn't think it'd be this soon. They've already got the replacement lined up and she starts next week so I'm done here."

Martin didn't know what to say. "That's terrible," he mumbled. "What will you do?"

"I won't get another job in education, that's for sure. But you know what, I'm almost relieved. I'm pig sick of it. The government won't let us do the job properly. They've made the exams easier, just

so it looks like their meddling initiatives work when more kids than ever before are passing them. It's a joke, Martin, an absolute joke, and I'm tired of being stuck in the middle of it."

"I'm sorry," Martin said. "Will you manage? Will you be all right?"

"Not thinking beyond this weekend at the moment. I'll see those dead kids buried and pay my last respects before I even think about what to do next."

"That's going to be a tough day."

"A triple hankie job, I reckon."

"Yes," Martin agreed. "Barry, you'll be missed, you know."

The Head coughed and sniffed loudly.

"Just keep my leaving under your bionic lid, old son," he said. "I don't want the likes of Douggy Wynn gloating. No fuss, no cards and no bunny girl jumping out of a cake. Tell no one. Let's give them all a big surprise next Monday morning."

"If you're sure?"

"Oh, I am."

"And you're certain you'll be OK?"

"Saturday afternoon I will be. I'm going to be worshipping at the ground. I've still got my rugby – they can't take that away. I'll have my team's shirt on, paint my face in their colours and be in heaven."

Martin smiled. "And you think my obsession is strange," he said.

"Dressing up as Mr Spock? Yep, that's weird, Martin."

"I've never worn the ears! Ever!"

"Oh, but you would, I bet."

"I'm allergic to the glue," Martin confessed with a laugh. "You should see the lengths some people go to at these conventions. The costumes and make-up are amazing."

"Nah, that's just sad, isn't it?"

"You'd be stunned, they go to so much effort. Must cost them a fortune."

"So where'd they get all the gear from?"

"Some make it themselves. Others get it off the Internet or commission people to make it for them. It's incredible, better than the real thing sometimes."

Barry shrugged and stared back through the window. "We all escape this cruddy world somehow, Martin," he said. "Hello – what did that lot sprinkle on their cornflakes this morning?"

He was looking at a group of children processing through the gates. They seemed to be performing a formal kind of medieval dance. Parading along the path in pairs, they halted, pointed a toe, then turned and bowed to their partner. Then they swapped sides and repeated it.

"Look at those wallies," Barry muttered. "What do they think they look like? You know, Monday can't come quick enough."

Each of those children was wearing a playing card, but the two men observed that they had also done something else to their blazers. The sleeves were hanging empty at their sides and their arms were poking through beneath them.

"What's going on there?" Barry asked.

Martin frowned for a moment. Then he understood.

"They've cut through the stitching under the arms!" he exclaimed. "What the hell?"

"It's that ruddy book," Barry said. "The one Graeme Parker and Anthony Maskel got expelled over. That's what the drawings in it looked like. The sleeves were hanging down just like that. Oh, incidentally, Mrs Early rang me last night to say she's coming back today. She's not going to let what happened keep her off any longer. Good for her."

"Dancing Jacks," Martin said. "What is it about that stupid book? Did you read it, Barry?"

"Didn't make any sense to me," the Head replied with a puzzled frown. "The bit I read was about some character called a Jockey – but he didn't even have a horse. Didn't look like there was any rugby in it either. Not my cup of PG that kind of thing."

"It's strange how it's taken hold here," Martin murmured as he reflected over the past few days. "That's when Paul first started acting nuts. He said the book was dangerous and, before that, Shiela Doyle tried to warn me about it…"

"Phases and crazes," Barry said. "They come and go. I never understand what sparks off the latest daft fad. The only thing I know is that they never last. Their parents aren't going to be happy when they see what the kids have done to their blazers. They'll be bang to rights."

"We can't let them get away with it, can we? We can't let them go about like that with the sleeves flapping and their arms shoved through the armpits."

Barry laughed. "Why not? Like I said yesterday, let the kids do what they want this week. Technically they're still in uniform. They'll be brought down to earth with a bump when the new Head starts if she's any good, which I sincerely doubt. Let the flappy sleeves be her headache. Looks armless enough to me."

"Oww!" Martin groaned. Barry snickered.

"You're a wicked old prop forward," Martin told him.

"Old, clapped-out and on the scrap heap of life," Barry agreed.

Another member of staff came into the room, quickly followed by a couple more. The school day was beginning.

Martin's first lesson was with Year 10. He sat at his desk, experiencing the usual sinking feeling that took hold before every double period with this horrible lot. The children came into the room quietly for a change and sat down and settled faster than usual.

Martin looked at them. Twenty-two out of twenty-seven were sporting a playing card on their uniform and most of those children had modified their blazers so that the sleeves were dangling uselessly from their shoulders. Every one of those pupils wore a remote expression as though they were half asleep in a wonderful dream. Sandra Dixon had come into school that day. She looked paler than ever and could hardly keep her eyes open.

"Morning, rabble." The maths teacher addressed them in his usual bantering tone.

"Good morning, Sir!" the card-wearers answered politely, while their classmates said nothing, but regarded them with suspicion.

Martin noticed with astonishment that Conor Westlake was also

wearing a card, the Jack of Clubs. Surely Conor hadn't read a book? The boy was another of the empty-sleeve brigade. Martin really didn't understand what was going on with the kids in this school any more.

"Does your mum know you've done that to your uniform?" he asked.

"How else should I be attired?" the boy replied. "'Tis the custom at Court."

"The only court you'll ever see the inside of, Westlake, will have a judge in it."

Five children laughed. The others continued staring blankly at the teacher.

"The Ismus is the only judge," Conor answered steadily.

Martin was about to say something further when his attention was diverted by Owen Williams. The ginger-haired boy was chewing noisily, his jaw bouncing up and down.

"In the bin," Martin told him.

"May I not save it for later?" Owen answered politely.

Martin did a double take to make sure it was the right boy. Where had the gangsta rapper disappeared to? Then he realised that the Welsh lad was also wearing a playing card – the three of diamonds. He wondered what the significance was – if there was one.

"No, Owen," he said firmly. "That goes in the bin right now."

Normally the boy would have grizzled and protested and shook his hands with attitude, but not that morning.

"As you wish," he said.

349

He rose calmly, crossed to the waste bin, sucked sharply on whatever was in his mouth then removed it.

Martin caught a glimpse of something grey and yellowish, as a fibrous gobbet dropped heavily into the bottom of the bin, among the pencil shavings and brown apple core that the cleaners hadn't bothered to empty last night.

Owen returned to his seat and Martin saw that his lips were stained the same putrid colour as whatever he had been chewing.

It was a relief when Emma Taylor burst into the room, late and mouthy as usual.

"Poxy alarm didn't go off and my mum was too busy glued to a fat cow talking about cystitis on breakfast telly to notice," she said, sailing to her usual place at the back.

She rummaged in her bag and, for a change, produced her books. Then she sensed the strange atmosphere in the classroom and peered around her.

"Who died in here then?" she asked tactlessly.

The five unaffected children gasped at the girl's insensitivity. How could she say such things when her own friends had perished in the Disaster? Martin glared at her. Emma noted that the other children didn't even blink. On Monday, that ginger minger, Owen, couldn't sit next to Kevin Stipe's empty seat. Today, looking at the vacant expression on his acne-pocked face, Emma wondered if he could even remember Kevin's name.

The lesson proceeded. Without her two friends, Emma's disruptions were limited to moans of how difficult the equations were – or jibes

350

at the "hilarious losers" who had "butchered their blazers". None of the twenty-two card-wearing pupils responded to her insults, no matter how hard she tried to provoke them. They got on with their work in silence. Martin watched them with concern. It simply wasn't normal.

At the end of the double period, when Martin was setting the homework, Emma sat slumped, sullen and scowling, sucking the end of her pen as if it was a thin cigar.

"Can't do this," she declared floppily. "Don't understand it."

"Everyone else is managing," the teacher replied. "Maybe if you'd listened when I was explaining, you'd be able to."

"I was!"

"No, you weren't, you were drawing a beard and glasses on Paris Hilton in your magazine."

"You was droning on, it didn't make no sense. You're a rubbish teacher."

"Do you really have to be so insolent and rude all the time?"

"Just being honest."

"No, you're obnoxious and insulting – there's a massive difference, Emma."

"I'm just being me, ain't I?"

"Why do you think that being you is anything to be proud of? It really isn't. You're thick scum. Try and be something better."

"You can't talk to me like that!"

"I think you'll find I can – I'm the teacher."

"You've never taught me anything."

Martin laughed. "For once we agree," he said. "In all the years you've attended this school, I haven't taught you a single thing. And that's why you're going to fail the exam in the summer and have a totally rubbish life scrounging off the state."

"Tell me how to do it then."

"Have you got thirty quid?"

"Eh?"

"That's how much private tuition costs per hour. I'm not going to waste any more of this lesson repeating myself. If you haven't got the sense or manners to listen the first time, I'm certainly not going to give up my free time for nothing."

One or two of the unaffected sniggered at her, but Emma pulled a disinterested face and shrugged it off.

The bell rang. Five children scrambled to leave. The card-wearers stood, almost in unison, and began filing out.

"So do you think it was Daz or Persil, Sir?" Emma asked the teacher abruptly. It was Martin's turn not to understand. Emma threw her stuff into her bag.

"What they had their brains washed in," she sniped as she barged by everyone. "I might be thick scum, but I'm not a mindless zombie like these sad cabbages. You, and the rest of this grotty town, need to wake up and smell the cappuccino because this… this ain't normal. Out of my way, losers."

Martin knew she had a point. Something was very wrong. He gathered up his books, put them in his briefcase and followed the children out. At the door he paused. Sandra Dixon was still in

the room. He was about to call and hurry her along, but what he saw made him catch his breath.

The girl had walked slowly across the room until she was standing next to the waste bin. For a moment she gazed down into it. Then stooping, she reached inside and fished out the thing that Owen had dropped there. It squelched in her fingers and was still glistening with his saliva. Pencil shavings were stuck to it, but that didn't deter her. Without hesitation, she placed it in her mouth and began to chew, closing her eyes happily.

Martin was too astonished and revolted to say anything. He leaned against the corridor wall and the Dixon girl sauntered past, oblivious to his presence.

"My God," he whispered. "What the hell is going on?"

It was morning break and Paul was sitting alone at the edge of the playground, observing the other children. The number wearing playing cards was almost double that of yesterday. They were either gathered in groups, reading together from that hateful book, or were practising formal dances or exchanging courtly gossip. The lips of some of them were stained a sickly, yellowish-grey. He could not guess what that meant.

The boy longed for the day to be over so he could go and see Gerald and tell him everything he knew. He was sure he would listen.

"Paul?" a voice said nearby. The boy looked up and there was Martin.

353

"What do you want?" Paul asked crossly. "I won't visit that counsellor!"

"Calm down, I know. I've been thinking… what you said about that book."

Paul got to his feet. "What about it?" he asked.

"What were you trying to tell your mum and me the other night when you burned it?"

"Why do you want to know now for? What's changed your mind?"

"Look around you!" Martin hissed, nodding at the huddled groups of children chanting and rocking as they read. "Something weird is going on."

"And you'd really listen to me – without butting in?"

"I'm many things, Paul, but I'm not completely dense. This thing, whatever it is, is starting to scare me."

"Welcome to the club," the boy said grimly. "You've got no idea."

"Then enlighten me."

The bell for the end of break rang across the playground. Paul picked up his rucksack. He wanted to make Martin feel bad for not giving him a chance to explain before.

"You know," he said, "if I'd have told you it was down to an alien invasion, you'd have believed that instead of what's really happening. You spend so much time watching fantasy stuff and collecting the merchandise, but you don't recognise the real thing when it's happening right under your nose."

"How do you mean?"

Paul looked up at the sky. "So many movies about predators coming from outer space," he said. "But that's not where the real dangers are. People in the olden days knew, before science told them it was stupid." He pointed to the ground. "Down there, Martin. Deep down there, that's where it's coming from."

The maths teacher stared at him. "What are you saying?" he asked.

"There's no such thing as aliens. Never was, just a diversion to make us look in the opposite direction and forget. The monsters are already here, Martin – down below. They've always been here and that book, that evil book, is linked to them."

"Paul," the man said firmly. "There's no such thing as devils and demons either, if that's what you're suggesting."

"Yes, there are," the boy countered. "They've been around longer than telescopes and computers and satellites and everything else that says they haven't. I saw one flying up from the barbecue. I did. It wasn't fireworks. Everything you ever thought was superstition and nonsense… is true. Evil is out there. It's in each one of them books. You only have to look at what's going on in this school to see that."

Martin didn't know what to say. The boy was so definite and certain. He was obviously far more disturbed than either he or Carol had realised – and yet…

They were the only ones left in the playground. Everyone else had gone inside for the next lesson. Paul saw that Martin didn't believe a word he had said. No surprise there then.

"I've got English now," he said, moving off.

"Let's carry on with this at lunchtime!" Martin called after him.

"What's the point?" the boy replied. "It's right in front of you and you still refuse to see. If you'd only Google the man who wrote Dancing Jacks then you might start."

"Come find me in the staffroom at lunch?"

Paul turned. It wasn't Martin's fault. He was trying his best. He broke into a grin.

"OK, Obi-Wan," he promised. "But it'll put you right off your sandwiches!"

Martin smiled back at him. "At least you didn't call me Jar Jar," he said. "That's a good sign."

His gaze dropped to the grey tarmac of the ground beneath his feet and he tapped it with his shoe.

"Don't be soft, Baxter," he told himself. "There's got to be a proper, reasonable explanation for all this."

Paul hurried to his next class. The other children were already settled when he came running in. He was happy to see Mrs Early sitting at her desk once more. The English teacher still bore the scratches on her face where Anthony and Graeme had attacked her. The long sleeves of her cardigan concealed the bruises they had inflicted. Every child recognised the garment as the thing she had been knitting over the past few months. The black wool, shot through with glittery purple strands, was unmistakable. Apparently there had been enough of the stuff left over to crochet a snood for her hair as well. It made her look quaintly old-fashioned and matronly.

"Sorry I'm late, Miss!" Paul said.

The woman smiled at him. "Only by a couple of minutes," she said in her languid voice. "Besides, you were one of those who came to my rescue the other day. I haven't rewarded you for that yet."

"Nice to have you back, Miss," a girl piped up.

"Thank you," she said warmly. "So let's make this a fun, enjoyable lesson. No tests, no comprehensions, no written work at all."

A cheer went up from the children – or at least the ones who weren't wearing playing cards. There were twelve of the affected in Paul's class.

He had noticed at registration that morning how many more were possessed by Dancing Jacks. He nodded at how appropriate that word was. The evil book really had 'possessed' them.

There was little Molly Barnes and her two friends, then the five who had gone to see the counsellor the previous day, and four of their mates. The cards they wore were different numbers and suits, but there was nothing above a seven and there were no picture cards. Paul saw that Molly's mouth was that livid, unnatural colour he had seen on the lips of others in the playground. It looked like she had been eating a luminous ice lolly while sucking a pencil – and making a real mess of it.

"What are we going to do then, Miss?" Gillian Gregor asked.

"I thought I'd read to you," Mrs Early told everyone, with a dreamy smile on her face. "Something inspiring and wonderful. Close your eyes and be transported to a magickal place by the power of words written a long time ago by the hand of a genius."

"Ugh… Shakespeare," Terry Farnham uttered grumpily.

"No," the teacher replied. "Not him. We don't need him now."

The hairs on the back of Paul's neck began to prickle. It was the same sensation he had felt in his bedroom, the night he had burned the book.

Mrs Early regarded her students with a benign smile. Her eyes were unusually dark and glassy.

"You will so adore this," she promised.

A book was lying open on her desk. It was the book she had taken home after the attack on her, the book she had read to try and understand what had happened that day. The woman turned to the first page and began.

Fear clutched at Paul's heart.

"Beyond the Silvering Sea, within thirteen green, girdling hills…"

Her unhurried, melodious voice read to them steadily and the children wearing playing cards gasped with rapture. They began to rock backwards and forwards. The others turned to look at them in puzzlement. Mrs Early read on. The daylight dimmed outside the windows and shadows filled the corners of the classroom.

Paul rubbed his eyes and fought to keep awake.

"No," he murmured. "Mustn't…"

Now he was creeping through a stone passageway, wearing a rich velvet tunic of horizontal scarlet and gold stripes. A mask of black silk with two eyeholes snipped out of it disguised his face. It was the

dead of night in Mooncaster. He was making his way to the West Tower, to the apartments of the Royal House of Hearts. Vivid tapestries hung from the walls and flaming torches in iron brackets sent shadows of the deepest violet bouncing along the galleries.

Passing under a vaulted archway, he stepped out on to the battlements. The midnight air was heavy with fragrance: jasmine and night-scented stock. Gold and silver moths were waltzing above the gardens of the Queen of Hearts. Directly ahead, at the corner of the battlements, the West Tower reared up. The lustrous white stonework gleamed in the starlight and the heraldic banners bearing the badge of Hearts fluttered gently in the perfumed breeze.

He held his breath and proceeded cautiously. The Punchinello Guards were at large. The Under King had requested their number be doubled about the West Tower. He had taken the fabulous Healing Ruby from his treasure house in order to sleep with it under his pillow. He had been disturbed by nightmares of late and, for the past five nights, had awakened shaking and weeping with fright. He was sure the ruby would cure him of these terrible dreams.

Such a jewel was too great a temptation for the Jack of Diamonds. In his silk mask and wearing the silent shoes given to him by Malinda, the retired Fairy Godmother, he stole ever closer to the gilded steps that wound up to the tower.

Suddenly a small, ugly creature, whose large head was attached to its chest, without a neck, sprang out in front of him. The hook-nosed Punchinello Guard barked a challenge and jabbed a vicious-looking spear at him.

"Stand and disclose!" it demanded, the beady eyes swivelling in their sockets.

The Knave of Diamonds stifled a yell and thought desperately. The Punchinellos loved to kill, that was the burning passion that drove them. What could he do? Yammering a bloodthirsty shriek, the hideous, hump-backed imp came bounding towards him...

Paul snapped his head up. He was in the classroom again.

"NO!" he shouted.

With a tremendous effort of will, he lurched from his chair. His legs were weak and unsteady and he almost collapsed straight away. Breathing hard, he stared around the class. The other children appeared groggy or asleep, but those wearing playing cards sat bolt upright in their seats – their eyes wide and glittering.

Mrs Early paused in her reading and looked over.

"What are you doing?" he spluttered.

The teacher smiled. "Welcoming you to the blessed Kingdom," she answered softly. "Sit and listen. It is a better world there – a keener world. It pulses with splendour and vigour. There is breathtaking beauty and excitements you will never know here. Come, Jack, your dance is only just beginning."

The boy shook his head. "My name is Paul!" he protested. "Paul Thornbury!"

"You are the Jack of Diamonds," Mrs Early stated. "What a rascally Knave you are. How you set the Court cavorting!"

"I'm Paul!" he shouted back at her.

Molly Barnes and her friends turned to him, their eyes and grins fixed.

⁻"Jack Jack Jack Jack…" they chanted.

The boy stumbled from his desk.

"Wake up!" he yelled, shaking two lads nearby. "Wake up!" They mumbled under their breaths and their heads flopped forward.

"All of you!" Paul shrieked. "Wake up!"

He blundered between the desks, trying to rouse his classmates. He shook and slapped them, but it was no use. They were like rag dolls in his hands. The spell had already gripped and claimed them.

Paul rounded on Mrs Early. "Stop this!" he begged her. "It's evil. Stop it!"

The woman looked away from him and returned her attention to the pages.

"And when the Dawn Prince was in exile, he sent neither message nor sign back to his Kingdom. So, whilst the Ismus and his subjects waited, they filled their days with merrymaking and happy pleasures…"

Paul's limbs grew so heavy, he almost crashed to the floor. There was a buzzing in his head.

The Jack of Diamonds stared at the dagger in his hand. It was dripping with the imp's dark blood. It had been a hideous struggle. Punchinellos fight like no other creature in Mooncaster. They are wild and ferocious and fly into battle with a glee that alarms and dismays their enemies. Jack had been lucky this time. This Guard

was so thrilled and overexcited to have caught an intruder, it had gloated before striking and so Jack lashed out first.

The imp's frilled yellow tunic was soaked with its own blood. But the Guard was not dead. It lay there gasping and croaking like a twitching toad. What a din it made. Others would hear it. They would come running and squawking and then the noble would be captured or killed.

"Tsk... I can't have that now," Jack whispered. "I've got an itch for jools."

Raising the dagger once more, he silenced the Punchinello forever.

Paul Thornbury choked and lumbered through the classroom. He had to get out. He had to escape the words of Austerly Fellows. They were echoing inside his mind, dragging him to that other place.

He threw himself towards the door, but Mrs Early's eyes flicked across to Molly Barnes and her friends. The three girls leaped up and raced past the staggering boy. They slammed themselves against the door and pushed him back when he drew near.

"Let me out!" he demanded, holding his pounding head in his hands. "I won't listen – I won't!"

Mrs Early continued to read.

Jack dragged the imp's lifeless body out of sight. It was only a matter of time before the others caught the scent of spilled blood. Punchinellos didn't have those grotesque noses for nothing. He had

to be quick. He ran up the steps and into the tower.

The court of the Under King was fast asleep. Pages dozed on fur-strewn benches and knights slumbered peacefully next to their empty armour. The royal apartments were at the very top of the tower. Jack hurried up the spiralling steps, pausing only to dare look in on the chamber where the Jill of Hearts slept.

A lantern of blue glass cast a trembling, submarine glamour over the room. Upon a cot, close to the muslin-draped bed, the governess was sound asleep, her hair still netted in her snood. Jack gazed upon Jill's bed. Through the creamy, gossamer-like swathes, he could see the girl's pale face and the contours of her body beneath the silver silk coverlet.

He grinned. The Royal House of Hearts had many jewels he would dearly like to steal. But tonight he would have to make do with just one.

Climbing the final stair, he pushed open the door to the Under King's bedchamber.

"I won't!" Paul screamed.

He drove his fingers into his ears and charged at the classroom door, shouldering the girls out of the way.

Mrs Early gestured at the five children who had seen the counsellor. They pounced on Paul and tore his hands down.

"Come to us, Jack," they said. "Join us at Court!"

"Jack Jack Jack…" little Molly Barnes and her friends sang.

Paul twisted around as they wrenched his arms behind his back and forced him to look at the English teacher. There were too many of them to fight against.

Mrs Early continued.

Paul Thornbury resisted the power of Austerly Fellows for longer than many of the others who came afterwards.

The Jack of Diamonds crept into the King of Hearts' bedchamber. The great four-poster bed was hung with sumptuous crimson curtains. A large wolfhound lay curled up at its foot, but the magick of the silent shoes ensured Jack could creep by without disturbing it. But he was not the only intruder there that night.

Within the draped confines of the royal bed, the Under King and Queen were deep in sleep. The Queen snored like a ferret, with shrill squeaks and snorts, but the King of Hearts was as still as an effigy couched upon a tomb. Yet they were not alone in there…

Creeping down the oak tester, against which their swan-feather-filled pillows rested, a small creature came crawling. It was a Bogey Boy, one of Haxxentrot's servants. He was only two hands high, with a round, shiny face – as white and wobbly as a boiled egg. An adder circled his brow and two more twined about his wrists and up his spindly arms. He wore a rough hessian smock, belted at the waist, and a quiver was strapped to his back.

Stepping gently on to the cloth of gold pillows, the Bogey Boy peered down at the bald King's face. Reaching out, he gave the fat nose a testing prod and chuckled to himself. The King of Hearts was in a deep slumber – so much the better. The Bogey Boy removed

the quiver from his back and sat astride the bald head to begin his night's work.

The quiver did not contain arrows, but was full of Haxxentrot's malignant nightmare needles. They were long wooden splinters, each topped with a different little carving. There was a spider, a claw, a grinning skull, a lightning bolt, a fierce black cat, a serpent and several more with flat paddles, upon which evil marks had been drawn.

The Bogey Boy grinned and selected the one with the spider. He placed its sharp point upon the King's forehead and, with a grunt, pushed it in as deep as he could. Then he unhooked a small mallet from his belt and hammered the magickal splinter even further home.

The Under King groaned in his sleep. The Bogey Boy rubbed his pale hands and took a light from the candle that burned in the bedside lantern and set it to the carved spider. The nightmare needle fizzed and crackled and a brilliant green flame burned steadily for a moment, before sinking down into the King's head, leaving no mark on his skin.

The Bogey Boy snickered. Haxxentrot would be pleased. The old witch had decided to torment the King of Hearts with a month of nightmares and so far the plan was going splendidly.

Suddenly one of the bed curtains moved. The Bogey Boy started. There was someone in the bedchamber! They had crept silently up to the bed! The Bogey Boy snatched up his quiver. In an instant he scrambled up the tester and hid in the corner shadows by the curtain rail. He stared down just as the Jack of Diamonds parted the curtains and peered inside.

Gingerly, expertly, Jack slid his hand under the golden pillow. The King whimpered in his sleep as eight-legged horrors rampaged inside his head. Jack hesitated. Still sleeping, the King put his thumb in his mouth and made a face like an unhappy baby. Jack waited a moment then explored deeper with his fingers. There!

Slowly, carefully, he withdrew. He had it – he had it! He lifted his hand and held it up against the lantern light.

His face – indeed the entire room – was instantly bathed in a rich, red glow – as deep and heady as any goblet of wine. The ruby in his hand was as large as an apple. It flashed and sparked and was the most gorgeous thing Jack had ever beheld.

"Most heavenly jool!" he exclaimed under his breath.

The wolfhound's ears jerked.

Jack kissed the gem in his hand and thrust it into the leather pouch hanging at his belt. The blood-red glow vanished and Jack crept away from the bed.

"Murder!" a croaking voice screeched outside the tower. "Foul murder! Assassins!"

The Punchinello's body had been discovered. The Guards were roused. Jack could hear them running up the steps to check on the Under King. The wolfhound shook itself from sleep. It smelled Jack before it saw him. Then it bared its teeth and began to bark. Jack backed away from it. The Punchinellos were rampaging through the tower; he could hear them storming closer.

No way out! *Jack thought frantically.* I'm cornered! Think, Jack! Think!

Suddenly the King of Hearts let out a yowl. He dreamed he was being eaten alive by thousands of ravenous spiders. His hands slapped and swept at the bedclothes.

"Get them off! Get them off!" he squealed shrilly. "Get them off me!"

He reached under the pillows for the peace the Healing Ruby would bring.

"It's gone!" he yelled. "I've been robbed!"

Startled from sleep, the Queen began to scream. Thundering with outrage, the King flung the bed curtains wide open.

When the bell rang for lunch, all the children in Mrs Early's class were back in their seats. The English teacher stopped reading and viewed them with satisfaction.

"You must return to this drab place now," she instructed. The children uttered gasps of grief.

"This is the shadow life," she told them. "The Realm of the Dawn Prince is the true world. Don't cry. This is only a grey, featureless dream. Your real existence is waiting in Mooncaster. That is where our hearts beat faster, where we are safe and coddled. Go now. Endure this temporary emptiness. You will go back to our proper place very soon. The Ismus will care for us. Blessed be, all of you."

"Blessed be," the class answered as one.

The children rose. Paul Thornbury pulled his rucksack off the desk and followed the others out.

"I am the Jack of Diamonds," he muttered in a far-off voice. "I am the Jack of Diamonds."

23

BEEEEP: "HELLO, MARTIN, Gerald here. I don't want to worry you, but… is Paul with you? He didn't show up here like he said he would."

Martin had supervised a detention that afternoon, so had only been in the house a few minutes, just long enough to remove his tie and reach for the biscuits. He listened to the message Gerald had left on his voicemail and cursed under his breath.

"What's that lad up to?" he muttered.

He hadn't seen the boy since morning break. Paul hadn't come to the staffroom at lunchtime as he had promised and Martin

hadn't been able to find him.

Perhaps there would be a clue in his bedroom. Martin hurried up the stairs. To his astonishment he found Paul sitting on the bed, staring into space.

"What's this?" Martin asked severely. "What are you doing? Why didn't you go round to Gerald's?"

The boy stirred slowly, but did not look at him.

"I don't need to now," he answered.

"Well, why didn't you call or text him? That's damn rude!"

"Is it? I forgot."

"Has something happened?" Martin asked with concern. He crouched down and looked at the boy's face. It was vacant and his pupils were unnaturally large. Only a thin ring of the hazel iris was showing. "Paul? Paul?"

The boy focused on him reluctantly.

"I have no book!" he said in a mournful voice. "I am shut out. I'm in the shadows."

Martin's scalp crawled. "What book, Paul?" he asked, dreading the inevitable answer.

"The blessed word – the Dancing Jacks."

The man sagged. "Oh, no…" he breathed. "Not you, Paul, not you."

"I should not have fought it," the boy said regretfully. "I should have gone there days ago. I was very wrong."

"Gone where?"

"To Mooncaster."

369

Martin didn't understand. "The castle in the story?" he asked.

"It is the most beautiful castle ever built," Paul answered and the longing in his voice was awful to hear. "It shines bright white in the day, then like gold at sunset and milky silver at night. I want to go back."

"But it isn't real. You can't actually go there."

"Yes, I can. The book takes me. The blessed words spiral out and make this emptiness disappear and I am there again. I am my true self. I am the Jack of Diamonds."

"You're Paul Thornbury! You live here. Look – that's your computer where you spend hours playing World of Warcraft – there's your Manga collection – that's your favourite T-shirt, the one you won't let your mum wash!"

The boy shook his head sadly. "This is the dream of nothing," he said. "This poor hovel is not real."

"Of course it's real!"

"No, this is the place in between. The blankness of unhappy sleep."

"Then who am I?"

"You are the man Martin. We live in this emptiness with the woman Carol."

"She's your mother!"

"Only here. The Queen of Diamonds is my real mother. I want my real mother – I want my father – the King! But I cannot go back to see them. I burned my book. I burned it. I cannot go back there without it!"

He began to sob. Martin reached out and hugged him, but the man's mind was reeling.

"What happened today?" he asked. "What happened to you?"

"I was wakened," the boy wept. "I realised who I am. I want the book! I must get back. I don't want to be trapped here. Please help me, Martin Baxter."

Tears streaked down his face. He cried into Martin's shoulder for over half an hour until the uncontrollable weeping subsided and he fell asleep, exhausted.

Martin laid him down and tucked the edges of the duvet over him.

"Jools," the boy mumbled in his impoverished dreams. "Magpie Jack shall steal your jools clean away…"

Martin didn't know what to do. Then he caught sight of the blazer lying on the floor. A Jack of Diamonds was pinned to the lapel.

"Hell!" he whispered.

Leaving the room quickly, he returned downstairs. Carol was at the hospital. Her mobile would be off. He called Gerald.

"Hello, Martin," the sprightly old gentleman answered. "Have you heard anything yet…?"

"Paul's here," the maths teacher told him. He could hear a CD of classical music playing in the background of Duntinkling. "Sorry, Gerald, I don't know what's the matter with him. Right now he's lying spark out on his bed. There's something going on, some strange stuff happening to all the kids. They're catching it like the flu."

The old man listened attentively as Martin struggled to explain.

"And this phenomenon is spreading through the whole school?" Gerald asked.

"Through every year."

"Listen, I don't wish to cause you undue alarm, but it's not illegal substances, is it?"

"That's what I thought at first, but no, Paul wouldn't touch anything like that. He's too sensible."

"Has he been bullied at all? Peer pressure is a common way for those habits to start."

"He says it's an old kids' book."

"A what?"

"A kids' book!"

"I don't understand. Is that modern slang for something else?"

"If only it was. Then I might be able to get my head round it and do something positive. No, it's just an old-fashioned children's book that everyone seems to be hooked on – even the kids who don't normally read. It's like they think the story is real and any time away from it isn't."

"Pardon? Wait a moment. Let me turn Beethoven down – he's about to go into a stormy third movement. There, carry on."

"Did you ever see Avatar – the movie about the blue people in the forest?"

"Smurfs?"

Martin remembered that Gerald's world did not revolve around cinema or sci-fi. "Not quite," he said. "Anyway, when that first came out, many who went to see it suffered from depression afterwards."

"Oh, dear, was it that bad?"

"The opposite – it was too good! They made the alien planet look so beautiful and colourful that people came out of the cinema hating how dull their real surroundings were. I think it's a bit like that with this book. The kids are addicted to it and they don't want to be here with the rest of us."

"It's only a book though, Martin," Gerald commented airily. "It's splendid they're reading something other than emails, isn't it?"

Martin pressed his hand against his temple in frustration. There was no way Gerald could understand how unsettling and disturbing the behaviour of those affected by Dancing Jacks really was. He suddenly realised how Paul must have felt when he had been trying to make him and Carol listen.

"Well, that doesn't sound so serious," Gerald carried on. "It'll blow over and the kids will be into something else before you know it. Now are you three still coming round for dinner this weekend? I had a note from Evelyn, ordering me to remind you."

Martin hesitated then forced a chuckle out. He had totally forgotten about the dinner invitation.

"Yes, we'll be there – looking forward to it."

"That's because you haven't sampled her catering."

Martin's fake laughter came into play again. The conversation ended and he gazed up the stairs. What could he do to help that lad up there?

"Nothing," he said miserably. "I can't do anything." He sent Carol a text and waited.

*

When Paul awoke, it was late and the house was quiet. Martin had gone to bed. The boy's eyes roved about his darkened room. Nothing there held any interest for him now. He closed his eyes again and tried to will himself back into the Kingdom of the Dawn Prince, back to what he believed was the real world, where excitement filled every moment and each day delivered its own new adventure. He concentrated hard, but only blurred rags of memory crowded in. It was no use; without the book, without reading or hearing the words, he was trapped here.

He sat up and looked at the computer. He switched it on and searched through some images on the Web. Then he replaced his main Facebook photo with a picture of the Jack of Diamonds he had found and sent messages to Bertolf and Aethelheard.

"I have to get another copy of the sacred text," he told himself. "I itch for it. The Holy Enchanter said he would give it to me if I brought him something… but what? But what?"

He was still awake trying to figure it out when Carol finished her shift at the hospital. He heard her return home, dump her bag in the hall, then go into the kitchen and clatter a spoon as she made a final cup of tea. Then Martin's slippered tread on the stairs testified that he hadn't slept. The man went down to greet her and discuss what was happening with her son.

Paul heard their voices, indistinct but full of concern. He wondered why they were pretending to care so much. This place didn't matter. They were nice, simple folk, but they were only

ordinary peasants, nothing more. In fact, Martin showed all the signs of being an aberrant and should be reported.

A short while later his door opened a chink and Carol looked in on him. The boy let her believe he was fast asleep. Her worried conversation with Martin continued in their bedroom through most of the night.

In the morning Carol ensured she got up with the others. She looked ill with worry. Paul came downstairs in his school uniform. His mother tried not to stare and behaved normally, but she couldn't help noticing the playing card on his blazer and exchanged glances with Martin.

"Good morning!" she greeted her son. "Proper breakfast today for a special treat. Bacon and scrambled eggs. How about that?"

The boy nodded indifferently.

"Sleep well?"

"I slept empty, how else could it be?"

"I was thinking," Martin began, trying to sound cheerful and enthusiastic. "How about we have a good old family night tonight?"

"Family?" Paul murmured.

"Yes, we can have a laugh on the Wii, order some pizzas and you get to choose what DVD you want to watch."

"Will I still be here?"

"This is your home, Paul," his mother said gently.

"I am not Paul."

Martin shot her a look and she turned away hastily and began griddling the bacon. Presently they were sitting at the table, eating.

The two adults watched him with sadness in their eyes.

"Do you remember my friend Ian?" Carol asked, trying to sound casual. Paul chewed mechanically. The food here had no taste.

"Ian," she repeated. "My friend at the hospital."

"The physician?"

"He's a doctor, yes. I was wondering if you'd like to come and see him this afternoon, after school?"

"But the day is Friday here, isn't it?"

"Yes."

"The boy Paul has musical lessons on Friday."

"You're Paul!" she said with agitation in her voice. "Besides… Gerald wouldn't mind."

Paul's attention faded and a wistful smile drifted across his face.

"It is market day at home," he sighed. "The merchants and tradesfolk will be stood by their carts and stalls, calling out joyous rhymes to tempt and tantalise. The Queen of Hearts will be haggling like any vulgar villager whilst her friend the Queen of Spades hatches schemes and flashes her eyes behind a crow-feathered fan."

Carol didn't know what to say. She raised her eyebrows at Martin. The man leaned forward.

"Tell us about the market," he asked curiously. "What is it like?"

Paul's faint smile broadened and he half closed his eyes. "The colours are dazzling," he said. "From the bolts of finest cloth, to the round, ripe fruits that vie with the treasure vaults for splendour. The bashful gold of apricots, the burnished copper globes of onions and

376

the wide-awake yellow of quinces. The tumble of greengages, plums, goosegogs, redcurrants, raspberries... looking like precious jools winkled from a crown. Then there is the brilliant, flashing silver of the fresh, flapping fish on the cart nearby. So intense, so deep, and dancing a clamour of colour. All under cheery patterned awnings, supported on wooden posts whose gilded, turned tops glisten and flame 'neath the sun."

He paused and stared into the distance. Carol looked at Martin. She had never heard her son speak like this before. But the boy had not finished.

"Then there are the smells," he continued. "A new delight with every forward step. Scents that move the heart to love or make the stomach yap. Heaped spices of rainbow ochres that tickle the nose and set the tongue a-tingling. The hanging herbs to sweeten an airless chamber or infuse in potions. The sharpness of clove-steeped vinegars that pickle and souse and make the mouth squirt. The pinkly marbled meat, swaying from hooks – with warm, tangy blood dripping into cream stone jars below. The nosegays casting their perfume into the morning, underscoring everything with the yearning song of violets and rosebuds. And then there are the magickal wares, the goods that can only be found in the Dawn Prince's land – take care what you buy and barter there..."

Carol pushed her chair back, shocked and dismayed. What was happening to him?

Paul blinked and directed his staring gaze at her.

"So you see," he said. "That is why I must return there. Why I

377

must escape this dingy tomb. If you keep me here, I will wilt and wither."

"I'm calling Ian," she announced, unable to bear it any longer. "We're going to see him right now."

Martin tried to keep calm. "There's nothing he'll be able to do," he told her.

"But Paul's ill!" Carol cried. "Listen to him, look at his eyes!"

What could Martin say? Yes, the boy seemed distant and not normal, but his description of the market was so detailed, so lucid and real. It wasn't merely delusional rambling. It sounded like somewhere he'd really been. The maths teacher didn't know what to suggest.

"OK," he agreed. "Take him to see Ian."

And so, as Martin left for school, Carol drove her son to the hospital where Ian Meadows examined Paul, took blood and urine samples and asked him questions. After an hour he led Carol aside and informed her that there was nothing physically wrong with the boy. He was perfectly healthy.

"Apart from the dilation of the pupils, I can't find anything."

"Well, that isn't right for a start!"

The doctor agreed. "Mydriasis occurs for a variety of reasons," he explained. "Blown pupils like his can be caused by drugs, trauma, disease…"

"He's not on drugs," Carol insisted. "But there was trauma aplenty last Friday at the Landguard. He was there, at the Disaster!"

"Not that sort of trauma. I meant a head injury. It could be

damage to the oculomotor nerve, but I don't think that's likely here. The sample tests will determine if there's anything I've missed. I'll get toxicology to hurry things along there and call you as soon as I get the results."

"But what about this obsession?" she asked desperately. "He won't even acknowledge I'm his mother."

The doctor frowned and was at a loss how to explain it. "And yet everything in that fantasy has its own rationale," he said, rubbing the back of his neck. "It has its own internal logic. In fact, it makes more sense than most orthodox religions."

"That doesn't make it sane!" Carol countered. "What's the matter with him?"

Doctor Meadows scratched his head. "I'm not an expert in child psychology," he admitted. "I can give you the name of someone who is, but you wouldn't get to see them till sometime next week."

"Not till then? What will I do?"

"Just treat him normally. Maybe he'll snap out of it, whatever 'it' is. I'm sorry, but that's the only advice I can give. Paul's in no danger, remember that."

"No danger?" she retorted. "Right at this moment he thinks I'm some peasant and this… this world isn't real life. How can that be safe? What if he thinks he can fly in that other place and jumps off a building? What if he thinks he can breathe underwater? What if…?"

"Carol!" Ian said gently. "Don't get hysterical. The boy isn't stupid. Whatever he thinks he can do in that other place, he knows this one is different. He won't try anything silly."

"I wish I could believe you," she replied. "And if I get hysterical, there's a good reason for it – you know me well enough to understand that."

"Look, see how he fares over the weekend then call me again Monday morning and we'll take it from there. If you like, I could prescribe you some junior sedatives if he starts getting anxious."

The woman shook her head. "I'm not doping him," she refused flatly. "He's not a mad dog. He's my son." She was disappointed and angry. It had been a wasted journey.

"If it's any consolation," Ian told her as she left his office, "this isn't the first case like this I've seen this week. In fact, you're the twenty-seventh person to have come here, worried about a child or family member experiencing the same fixations and hallucinations."

Carol stared at him, incredulous. "And you don't think that's something to get hysterical about?" she cried. "There's an epidemic happening in this town and you're fobbing us off with pats on the head and sleeping pills!"

Taking Paul by the hand, she hurried him from the office.

"You need some leeches in here," the boy advised the doctor as he followed her out.

"Plenty of them in the NHS already," Ian muttered to himself.

Rereading Paul's notes, he tapped the desk irritably. "What the hell is going on in this bloody place?" he blurted, kicking the filing cabinet so hard it hurt his toe and dented the side.

"Can I go to the school now?" Paul asked as they got in the car.

Carol fumbled with the keys in the ignition. "I think you should stay off today," she said.

"I think Paul should go to school," he told her firmly.

"You're going back to the house," she replied.

The boy glowered at her. "Paul should be with his friends," he said forcefully. "Paul should sit with them in the library so they can read together."

"In that case there's no chance," she said. "I'm not going to let you read any more of that rubbish." Carol started the car and drove out of the car park, heading for home.

The boy's face flushed red and he began to judder with rage and frustration. Suddenly he screamed and lashed out at her. He wrenched at the steering wheel and smacked the side of her head.

The car veered across the road. Carol cried out in panic. The front tyre mounted the kerb. She elbowed her son back against his seat and braked hard. Paul tugged at the seatbelt and pulled on the door handle.

"The child lock is on!" she shouted.

"Let me out! Let me out!" he shrieked in her ear. "Let me out – you evil scold!"

The woman stared at him in horror. He was having a fit. It was like being next to a rabid animal.

"Take me to that school!" he demanded, hammering his feet on the floor, slamming the dashboard and banging his head on the passenger window. "Take me there now!"

"We are going home," Carol said, struggling to remain calm and trying to think how to reason with him. "If you do anything stupid like that when I'm driving again, you'll never get back to your other world. Do you hear me?"

"If I had my dagger, I would plunge it in your heart," her son told her as he folded his arms and glared out of the window. "If you possessed one."

The car drove off and Carol held the tears back. She wished she had taken that prescription from Ian.

When they pulled into their drive, and the lock clicked up, Paul tried to make a run for it, but she caught him and pushed him into the house.

"Gaoler!" he screeched in her face as he thumped and tore at her. "You are in the service of Haxxentrot the witch. I hate you! I hate you and your poverty-reeking stink!" Then he spat at her.

Carol's hand flashed out and she slapped him hard. The boy yelped. Carol uttered a cry. She had never hit him before. She stared at the reddening mark on his cheek and despised herself.

"You will suffer for this, peasant," he vowed. "I swear it!"

"Go to your room," she ordered in a cracked voice. "Go now."

Paul looked her up and down disdainfully. Then he turned and stomped up to his bedroom. When the door closed behind him, his mother fell against the banister and broke down.

The game of Hoodman Blind is a great favourite at Court and the Jockey's delight. Watch the victim grope about in his darkness, seeking for something tangible, something to hold and clutch at in his blundering. Prod him, poke him - make him squeak - make him stagger. Keep him guessing, lead him on - keep him spinning.

24

MARTIN BAXTER WALKED through the school gates that morning, yet again amazed at the massed heaps of floral tributes and cuddly toys that had multiplied over the course of the week. Was it really only a week since the Disaster? It seemed far longer.

A pungent, rank perfume of sweetness and decay filled the air. If memories of old love affairs had a smell, it would be just like this. Once more he wondered what Barry was going to do about the rotting bouquets. This was one problem he wouldn't leave for the new Head to deal with. He would want to sort it himself. He had a responsibility to the memory of those dead kids and ex-pupils. Martin shook his head. The school really wouldn't be the same without Barry Milligan. In the space of just seven days, everything had changed so drastically.

He wondered how Carol was getting on at the doctor's with Paul. There just had to be a sound and sensible explanation for this mania. There was no possible alternative.

Before entering the building, he scanned the playground. The children waiting to go inside were abnormally quiet. He noticed that even more of them had cut up their blazers to achieve the hanging sleeves illustrated in Dancing Jacks. Was there anyone without a playing card pinned to their uniform now? If there were, he couldn't spot any. Some of the children turned to him as he pulled the door open. Their blank expressions were disturbing – even chilling.

Martin's thoughts were so taken up with Paul's condition that he didn't notice how quiet some of the teachers were in the staffroom. Mrs Early was sat whispering to Miss Smyth, who was gently rocking backwards and forwards.

Emma Taylor had decided not to go to school that day. The other kids were getting too weird and mental and she was sick of having to check her behaviour and bite her tongue, knowing that the Head had her in his sights. Besides, there was yet another double maths that morning. Whoever composed that timetable needed shooting. So she decided to play the sympathy card with her mother and complained that her burned legs were giving her jip. She spent a cosy, lazy day lounging about the house in her dressing gown, eating as much toast as she liked and cackling during Loose Women. It was a

blissful world away from the bizarre happenings at school.

Martin's first lesson was eerie. The Year 9 class were sitting upright in their seats, their eyes weirdly dark and staring. Their lips were stained and discoloured. Every child wore a playing card and they were like dummies. They listened impassively to everything he said and, when he told them to get on with it, diligently picked up their pens and began working in silence. In all his years of teaching, he had never known anything like it. After twenty minutes he could bear it no longer.

"So what do the cards mean?" he asked a blonde-haired girl wearing the two of clubs.

She looked slowly up from her work and touched the card pinned to her blazer. "It shows to which Royal Household we belong," she said.

"They remind us," a boy added, "when we are here, in the empty dream time, who we really are."

"And the numbers?"

"Our rank and station in the White Castle of course," the girl replied impatiently, as if the question was a stupid one. "I am but a lowly kitchen maid of the South Tower."

"You really have bought into this completely," Martin said. "But why would you choose to be a rubbish servant? Where's the fun in that?"

"It is who I am," the girl answered.

"And yet here you are in school, without a castle in sight, doing sums."

"We cannot order our dreams," the girl said with regret.

"And we need this rest so that our proper lives can be lived with more vigour – more excitement," a second boy chipped in.

"The Ismus says that sunshine is paid for with rain," the girl agreed. "This place is…"

"A wet Friday in Felixstowe?" the maths teacher suggested.

"Dreams are not to be understood," the child said. "They make no sense, they are only necessary."

Reaching into her pencil case, she took out a small glass jar containing a putrid-looking ointment and, with her fingertip, rubbed some on her lips. A slight tremor shuddered through her. She closed her eyes and nodded with pleasure.

"What's that?" Martin demanded.

"Minchet," one of the boys told him.

The girl smiled and opened her eyes. Her lips were more discoloured than ever. "When we are awake, we use it to fly to the Holy Enchanter at the Grand Revels. But here, in the dull dreaming, the taste of it keeps us and nourishes us. It helps us see the banners of Mooncaster more clearly in our minds when we are away from them."

Martin strode over and took the jar from her hands. He sniffed the yellowish-grey contents warily. There was no smell.

"You may keep it if you wish," the girl said. "I have more."

The maths teacher screwed the lid back on. "Who else has got this muck?" he shouted. Every hand went into the air.

"Right – I want all of it on my desk now!"

The children looked at him in puzzlement, but they obediently went to his desk and deposited jar after jar there.

Martin ground his teeth in anger and wanted to throw every one of those filthy pots in the bin. He was furious, not with the children, they can't have realised what was happening – it wasn't their fault. No, he was furious with himself for discounting the obvious and only answer right from the start, even though at the back of his mind he must have known. It was simple and sordid after all – drugs. Why had he even considered it might be otherwise? So this was the cause of the abnormal behaviour. But the scale of this was staggering. Someone, and he had a shrewd idea who, had supplied the entire school with powerful hallucinogens and heaven knows what else. The thought of that enraged him. He could almost feel his blood boiling.

The children returned to their work and he waited impatiently for the end of the lesson.

When the bell rang, Martin ushered the pupils out of the classroom and, with a grimace of disgust, swept the jars of minchet into his briefcase. On the way out, he checked his mobile. There were seven unhappy and urgent texts from Carol. He called her back immediately and she explained what Doctor Meadows had said at the hospital and what had happened afterwards.

"I know this sounds crazy," she hissed down the phone, "but Paul was like a demon. I'm scared, Martin."

"What's he doing now?"

"Just sat quietly on his bed, rocking back and forward. I can't reach him. Can you come home? I don't like being here on my own with him."

"He's your son, Carol!"

"Is he? I'm not so sure."

"Don't talk silly. I've just discovered what's behind all this – and I'm mad as hell. I'm going to speak to Barry right now and call the police in."

"Please come home!"

"I can't!"

"Martin – please!"

"I think he'll be fine once it wears off. Let him rest. I'll see you both later."

"When what wears off?"

"I don't have time to explain, but check his pockets for any small jars of vile-looking stuff. Don't touch it. Just take it off him. I'm going to…"

A boy from Year 8 had charged blindly into him. The mobile flew from Martin's hand and smashed to pieces on the floor.

"Hoy!" the maths teacher yelled. "Look at that! What are you doing running in the corridors, Leo Henderson? Get back here!"

The boy didn't stop to apologise. "They're after me!" he yelled, racing away, trying to find a place to hide.

"Unbelievable!" Martin snarled, picking up the fragments and trying to fit them together again. It was hopeless.

Fuming, he marched down to Barry Milligan's office and banged on the door.

388

The Headteacher's strident voice yelled back, "If you're one of the governors, you can kiss my…"

"It's me – Martin!"

Barry was about to tell him to enter, but the maths teacher had already barged straight in. He dumped a handful of jars on the desk.

"What's them?" Barry asked in surprise.

"That's what's behind all this mad behaviour!" Martin shouted. "Some sort of drug. Every kid in my Year 9 class had a pot of it."

Barry picked up one of the small jars and inspected it carefully. "You sure?" he asked.

"I don't know what's in it, but it's got to be an addictive narcotic. Look how lethargic the kids are, look at their eyes, look at the way their lips are the same colour and the way those two lads attacked Mrs Early the other day."

Barry slid into his chair. "But that's almost every kid in the school," he said in a shocked voice. "Who's been pushing this filth on them?"

"The same man who was selling the Dancing Jacks at the boot fair," Martin answered. "No wonder we thought those books were part of it. But all the time he was dealing this garbage, turning every kid here into a junkie."

Barry's rugby-beaten face set hard and grim. "I'll have him," he seethed. "This might be my last day here, but I'll have that scumbag. Horsewhipping's too good for the likes of that. He'd best hope the police find him before I do because I will personally kick seven shades out of him. If I had my way, sewage like him would be turned

389

over to the families of his victims, and they'd be in a line – with cricket bats at the ready."

"The law is on the criminal's side nowadays," Martin said bitterly. "If someone breaks into your home and you thump them, you're the one that gets done. I could swing for the person who gave Paul that stuff."

"What a bloody screwed-up society this is," Barry uttered in disgust. "Total madness. First there was the oiling. Then the violence and the knife, then the Disaster – now this. What have we done to our kids? They don't deserve any of it. You know, I was going to suggest turning a redundant corner of the playing field into a garden of remembrance for those we lost last Friday, with some sort of memorial stone with all their names on."

"That's a great idea."

"You'll have to suggest it to the new Head yourself. The governors won't listen to any of my ideas any more. I was going to have the floral tributes turned into mulch for it. That'll just end up fertilising the rose beds of a park somewhere now, I suppose."

He picked up the phone and called the police.

Out in the playground, the few remaining unaffected children were looking at their former friends uneasily. What had got into everyone? They were so strange and unfamiliar. The huddled groups were larger now and the chanting had become a chorus of voices reciting the sacred words.

The outnumbered children felt excluded. They were frightened.

390

Some of them, in their innocence, begged to be allowed to play this confusing new game with the rest. So they were drawn into the gatherings and the words of Austerly Fellows wrapped around them.

Several children, sensing the danger, ran to the teachers on break duty for protection. Mrs Early and Miss Smyth took no notice of their tearful pleading and looked away coldly when a mob dragged the hapless boys and girls from them.

Terrified shrieks cried out. A few kids were chased across the playing field or out of sight, behind the sports block. Hordes of the affected pursued them, bringing them down and forcing them to listen and be converted.

Mrs Early took a small jar from her pocket and applied the strangely coloured salve it contained to her lips. She smiled faintly across the playground at Miss Smyth who was doing the same.

When the bell rang for the next lesson, there wasn't one child left in the school who didn't consider the Ismus to be their Lord.

Before the police arrived, Barry gathered the staff for a hasty meeting and showed them the confiscated jars of minchet. He told them to collect as much of it from the students as they could. Many of the teachers were shocked at the revelation that the whole school was hooked on the foul substance, but several of them, the ones who had read Dancing Jacks, had to conceal their smiles because they knew how mistaken Barry and Martin were.

When the police arrived, Barry didn't let the fact that it was two of the officers who had broken up the fight on the football field the previous Friday distract him. The judgemental female officer who had shown him the knife seven days ago listened to everything he had to say without comment, but he knew exactly what she was thinking. Perhaps she and the tabloids were right and he really was a disgrace to his profession. How else could these things have happened in his school?

The officers wrote pages of notes. Then Barry took them to speak to several children of different ages so they could see for themselves. When they were back in Barry's office, they agreed that something was definitely not right about those kids, but they didn't recognise the symptoms. If it was a drug-induced state then it was unlike anything they had come across before. But then new types were being introduced on the street all the time. Perhaps this was yet another new concoction. They would take the jars to be analysed. If it was proven to be an illegal substance then immediate action would be taken and every child would have to undergo a medical to assess what damage, if any, had been done and receive appropriate treatment.

"What a bloody mess," Barry muttered.

"Isn't it just, Sir," the female officer said critically. "And this Mr Ismus is the one you think is doing the dealing?"

Barry nodded. "That's what my head of maths believes," he said. "Some hippy biker bloke, according to him. Operates from a beaten-up Volkswagen camper, so Mr Baxter tells me."

"Shouldn't be too difficult to trace if he's still round here," the policewoman said. "We'll be in touch as soon as there's any news."

"I won't be here after today," Barry told her. "I'm leaving the

school. There'll be a new Headteacher taking over next week."

The woman stared at him, stony-faced. "Good thing too if you ask me," she commented. "You've got a duty of care to these children and you've let them down abysmally. If I had kids, I wouldn't send them to this place. You should be ashamed of yourself, Mr Milligan."

Barry flinched. Her stinging words had hit home. "Is that all?" he asked.

The officers departed. Alone in his office, Barry began removing his photographs from the wall and emptying his desk.

The rest of the day passed uneventfully. Barry patrolled the corridors, like the captain of a ship inspecting the decks and gangways one final time before saying a final farewell to it. An eerie hush lay over the school. Even though the classrooms were full, the children were deathly quiet and absorbed in their work. The teachers who, like Martin, were still unaffected could not understand how any drug could produce this effect and they found the silence sinister and the pupils creepy.

During the final break, Barry sought out Martin and explained what the police had said.

"I've had the secretary type out a letter to the parents," he added, "warning them about the situation and suggesting they search their kids' rooms and take any of that muck off them. Every pupil will take the letter home tonight. But, just to make sure the parents get them, they'll be posted as well."

"Sensible precaution," Martin agreed. "I'll be turning Paul's room upside down this evening if Carol hasn't already."

He looked at Barry closely. The once robust, no-nonsense man seemed a shadow of his former self.

"None of this is your fault, you know," Martin told him.

"Isn't it?" the Head replied. "That police bird was right. These kids were under my protection. I should have spotted what was going on a lot sooner and sorted it right at the beginning. I failed them, Martin, failed them big time."

"Hey, we aren't responsible for them once they're outside those gates. You can't beat yourself up over what they get up to out there."

"Can't I? Why not? No one else gives a monkey's any more. The parents haven't got a clue what they're doing for the most part. We taught most of them when they were kids themselves, Martin, we know how useless they were back then. If my students can't feel or be safe from the outside world in here then, yes, that's totally my fault."

"You're being too hard on yourself."

The Head shrugged. "Look," he said after a moment's contemplation, "it's my last day here. Nobody knows on the staff except you. What say you and me down a few bevvies later?"

Martin had to decline. "I can't tonight," he told him. "I have to get straight home to Carol and Paul. I'm sorry."

"Nothing to be sorry about!" Barry said, hiding his disappointment behind a hasty smile. "Course you have to get back. We'll do it another time."

"Absolutely! And I'll be buying!"

"Hope Paul gets better soon," Barry said. "See you soon, mate." He turned and walked briskly down the corridor, back to his office.

Martin felt wretched and guilty. But Paul had to come first.

At the end of the school day he watched the children leave through the gates in orderly streams. He went to find Barry one last time and wish him well, but the Head was not in his office. Martin left the building knowing he had let his old friend down. He hoped the rugby team would win tomorrow. That would lift Barry's spirits.

Half an hour later Martin opened his front door and steeled himself for the tough evening ahead. What state would Paul be in by now? The house was quiet, but there was a strong smell of fresh paint. What had Carol been doing? He removed his jacket and hung it in the hall.

"Hello?" he called. There was a movement in the living room.

"What?" Carol's voice blurted.

He looked inside and found her on the sofa, rubbing her eyes.

"You been asleep?" he asked.

"Must have nodded off for a minute," she said. "I hardly got any kip last night when I finished work. So glad you came back early."

"I didn't. It's gone four!"

The woman glanced at the clock on the fireplace and swore under her breath. "I must have been out for hours!" she exclaimed, jumping to her feet. "My God – Paul!"

She dashed past Martin and ran to the stairs. They hurried up to the boy's bedroom, but it was empty.

"Damn!" Carol yelled. "Why couldn't I stay awake? Of all the times… Where's he gone? He could be anywhere by now!"

Martin didn't answer. His gaze was drawn to a dribbled trail of blue paint on the landing carpet, leading from his precious sanctum.

"No, no, no…" he whispered.

With a sinking heart, he hurried into his special room, but nothing could prepare him for the horrible spectacle he found there.

His precious inner sanctum had been completely trashed. His expensive collection of fantasy merchandise – the models, the figurines, the replicas – were smashed. The wondrous items he had spent his entire adult life assembling were totally destroyed. Every spaceship had been torn down from the ceiling and stamped on. The life-size dalek had been kicked to pieces and the Star Fleet uniforms had been cut to shreds. The display cabinets were empty and the Lord of the Rings busts had been thrown against the wall and were in countless fragments. Hundreds of DVDs had been bent or scratched or snapped in two and, over everything, splattering the wreckage and dripping from every shelf and poster, was a thick and ruinous layer of blue gloss paint.

"Oh, Martin!" Carol cried in horror as she stumbled in behind him. "Your things. Your collection!"

The man was too stunned to say anything. He felt as if a huge part of him had just died.

"I'm so sorry," Carol said, squeezing his arm. "I'm so sorry. I know how much this meant to you."

"No, you didn't," Martin murmured. "Only Paul did."

"I can't believe he would do something like this. I really can't."

"There was no one else here," he told her. "Paul did this." He turned away from the horrendous destruction and looked at her in shock and confusion.

"How did you sleep through it?" he asked. "How?"

Carol shook her head. "I don't know!" she replied. "I just don't. I don't understand any of it. What's happening to us? None of it makes sense."

She gazed at the fractured chaos and held her head in her hands. "Where did he even get the paint from?" she asked.

"It's Venetian Crystal Blue," Martin whispered. "We were going to paint our police box with it... when we got round to building one." He cast around the devastated room and saw the splintered remains of the fresnel lens Paul had found on eBay. Martin bit the inside of his lip to keep from shouting – or crying. He wasn't sure which.

Carol wanted to hold him, but she was afraid he might push her off. She took a few careful steps into the room to see if she could salvage something – anything. But it was no good. Then she noticed the blank area behind the open door. A message had been scrawled with the paint.

To Martin the Aberrant
I have taken your jools!
LMAO!!!!
J of D

*

"The Jack of Diamonds," Martin interpreted.

"I can't believe it," Carol muttered. "I told you, that wasn't my son today."

"Don't fool yourself!" Martin snapped. "He's just another kid off his face. Well, he's gone too far this time."

He stormed from the room and thudded downstairs.

"What are you doing?" she called after him.

"Calling the police. What do you think?"

"I think I agree with you," she said. "And while you do that…"

She ran to find her mobile and called Paul's number. To her surprise, the boy answered.

"Paul?" she cried. "Where are you? What have you done?"

"Hahahahahahaha!" she heard him shouting. "I stole the jools – I stole the jools!" And then the phone went dead.

"Paul?" she yelled. "Paul!" She tried his number again, but it was unobtainable. He must have switched the phone off.

After Martin finished speaking to the police, he sat on the stairs in stricken silence, waiting for them to turn up. Carol was alone on her son's bed. She didn't know how to comfort Martin and she was beside herself with worry. Her entire world was in chaos.

After a while Martin appeared in the doorway.

"The stuff in there," he said, nodding back at the sanctum. "That's all it is, just stuff."

"Your lovely things," she began.

"That's just it. They were things. But Paul isn't a thing. He's missing and in trouble. He needs us – more than he ever has."

Carol began to cry and she threw her arms about him. "God! I love you, Martin!" she wept.

At that moment the doorbell rang. The police had arrived.

A short while later they left with a full statement, Paul Thornbury's description and a couple of recent photographs. As only a few hours had passed since the boy had left the house, they were sceptical about the seriousness of the situation, even when shown the wreckage upstairs. Carol almost lost her temper with them, but they promised her they would do everything they could to find him and bring him back safely.

"They always say that though," she said as the police car drove away. "What if they never find him? What if he's gone for good?"

"Don't think like that," Martin told her. "You'll drive yourself mad."

Carol's mobile rang. She rushed to it, but it wasn't her son. It was Ian Meadows.

"Just thought I'd tell you the test results," the doctor said brightly. "Hello… Carol?"

The woman had almost forgotten about that morning. "Sorry, yes, I'm here."

"You all right? You sound terrible."

"Paul's gone missing, Ian."

"What? Oh, Carol, I'm sorry. Have you called…?"

"Yes, they've just left."

"If there's anything I can do…"

"Err… thanks. No, I don't think there's anything."

"Well, if it helps in any way, those results… it's good news. There's absolutely nothing wrong with him. We screened for all sorts."

"Drugs?"

"Not a trace of them. Totally clean."

"You sure?"

"Nothing gets past these analysers, I promise you. If there was something nasty in his system, the HPLC would find it."

Carol rang off and looked at Martin. "You were wrong," she said blankly. "It's got nothing to do with that stuff in those jars. Martin – it really is the book. That's what the kids are addicted to. Remember, Paul told us it was evil. He was right. It's… devilish."

"Do you realise how neurotic you sound? Carol, I'm the one who does fantasy here – not you."

"They've done a High Pressure Liquid Chromatography spectroscopy on his samples," she said. "There's nothing there, no hallucinogens – nothing. What Paul told us about the book, what he tried to tell us… it's the only thing that makes any kind of sense."

Martin refused to discuss it. He opened his briefcase. There was a single jar of minchet left in there. "Take this to your friends at the hospital," he told her. "Get them to analyse that. The police are already doing it, but we might get the results a bit quicker this way."

"No, Martin," she said. "It's the book that's dangerous, not this."

"Just go," he urged.

"But they don't analyse this sort of thing in the hospital. They'll need to send it to a university lab."

"You'd better get a move on then. The sooner it goes off the better."

"What if Paul comes back here?"

"Then I'll call you. I'll call you as soon as I hear anything. Just hurry."

And so Carol drove to the hospital and Martin waited.

At exactly the same time, Emma Taylor was applying some mascara in her bedroom and scrutinising herself in the mirror. It would do for a Friday night outside a bar. A message beeped into her mobile.

From: Conor
We need to talk. Meet me in an hour by the Landguard.

The girl cursed. The fort was the last place she wanted to be that night – or indeed any time ever. She sent a filthy refusal back to him and painted her lips her favourite poppy shade with a steady hand. She didn't know what had come over those retarded saps at school, but she wasn't going to have anything to do with them, especially at the weekend. As she pulled on her leopard-print jacket, his reply came in.

From: Conor
Meet me – or else

"Damn!" she snarled.

She knew precisely what that threat was. He was going to tell the police she had been in that Fiesta. How long was he going to hold that over her? This needed to be sorted once and for all and she would go to any lengths to stop it. Emma changed out of her best trainers and pulled on a more practical pair of boots. So much the better for kicking him where it really hurt if that's what was needed. No one was going to have that sort of power over her. Her eyes fell on a pair of nail scissors on the dressing table and, with a cruel curl of her red mouth, she pocketed them. This business was going to end, tonight.

Midnight trysts – 'neath scented bowers or in high towers, in moon-shone fields, o'er candlelit meals, on roseate balcony or down on one knee – how heady is the wine of romance, how giddy doth it make us dance.

25

VIEW POINT ROAD was deserted, a complete contrast to the previous Friday night.

It was dark and quiet. The lights of the container port on the right were fewer than last week. So many had blown during that electrical storm that the maintenance teams hadn't got round to replacing all of them. The security cameras were still out of action too, but that was a secret the port authority hadn't told anyone.

A cold breeze blew in over the high ridge of sandhills to the left. Torn ribbons of police tape fluttered in the branches of ugly trees and gorse bushes. Forensic teams had scoured the length and breadth of this road for a full five days without discovering anything new and the one who could tell them everything was striding down it right now.

Emma's young face was locked in a scowl. With folded arms, she marched the long, lonely route to the Landguard Fort, her boots stomping over the tarmac. Memories of that horrendous night crowded in from every side. The frozen, terrified faces of Ashleigh and Keeley shining in the full glare of the Fiesta's headlights as it spun into them flashed into her mind. She dug her nails into her palms and concentrated on what she would say and do to Conor Westlake.

The final stretch of the road kinked to the left and the great low bulk of the fort appeared ahead. There were no vehicles in the car park in front of it. The burned-out wrecks had been removed and only the scorched grass of the verges showed that anything had happened there. There weren't even any bouquets. The forensic investigation had kept everyone out. That was why so many tributes had been left outside the school.

The place looked abandoned and creepier than she ever remembered it to be. Night shadows filled every corner and hollow. A week ago, almost to the very hour, forty-one young people had died here, or of the injuries they had sustained here. Emma was too sceptical and cynical about everything in life to believe in ghosts or anything like that, but she was unnerved all the same.

"Blessed be," said a voice nearby.

Emma jumped back and yelled a string of obscenities. A figure had been sitting on one of the verges and was now rising, silhouetted against the star-filled sky.

"You flaming idiot!" she ranted. "What you trying to do – give me a heart attack?"

Conor Westlake jumped off the raised verge and pulled the hood from his head.

"Why are you startled?" he asked curiously. "I said I would be here."

"What do you want?" she demanded. "I don't have time for this. I could be getting legless on Breezers and pear cider right now."

"You must forgive me for drawing you hither this night, my Lady," he began. "But…"

"Stop all that crap!" Emma snapped. "You and the rest of the zombies might have found God…"

The boy laughed. "Is that what you think?" he asked. "You are so far from the truth."

"Scientologists, Jehovah's Witnesses, Salvation Army, trainspotters – whatever. I don't actually care. I'm just here to tell you to stop jerking me around. I won't be blackmailed. Don't you think I know people? Some of my old man's mates have been inside and if I have a word with them, they'll come looking for you. Do you like playing football, Goldilocks? You'd find it hard with both legs busted in five places and your knees chiselled off. So keep out of my face, yeah?"

Emma turned to leave. That should do it, a short, sharp warning – although she really wanted to hit him, it was better to let him fret about worse future violence.

She stopped abruptly. The way back along the road was blocked. At least thirty people were now standing there, having stepped silently from the darkness in front of the sandhills. Emma spun around and glared at Conor.

"I know people too," he said, smiling.

"What is this?" she shouted.

"The Court is incomplete," the boy told her. "We need our Jill of Spades to join us. You should have been at school this day. We missed you."

"You can go and do one!" she bawled. "I wasn't joking. My dad's mates will have you. You won't be so pretty when they've finished. The doctors won't know which slit in your face is your mouth! Tell those freaks to back off and let me pass."

To her consternation, Conor began to sing.

The Queen of Spades' dark daughter, is it blood in her veins or water?

What schemes, what vices, what not very nices has her royal mother taught her?

The crowd that blockaded the road joined in, humming the tune – forming a barricade of sound as well as with their bodies. Emma looked at their faces. She recognised a few of them as kids from school, but the rest were adults and all were completely devoid of expression except that their eyes were wide and staring. With a shock, she saw that two teachers were there, Mrs Early and Miss Smyth. How demented was this getting?

The people joined hands to seal any gaps between them and began to move towards her. The defiant girl stood her ground.

"Out of my way!" she shouted at them. "Go on – shift!"

Conor continued to sing.

A plot, a lie, her spit in your eye!

You can bet your life she'll twist the knife, as she artfully gets her own way.

There is no other, not even her mother, who so clouds the sunniest day!

The crowd advanced further.

"You're mental!" Emma cried. "Let me by!"

She charged forward and lunged at the weird mob, trying to break through them. They pushed her back and continued walking forward.

Emma rounded on Conor. This wasn't funny. She wanted to escape this loony lot.

So have a care and don't trust a hair – on the Jill of Spade's treacherous head.

Don't turn your back on this Dancing Jack, she'll make you wish you was dead.

"Tell your goony gits to let me out," Emma warned. "Or someone will get very hurt and it won't be me."

The boy stopped singing, but instead of doing what she wanted, he laughed. "How very like the Jill of Spades!" he said, holding out a playing card to pin on her jacket. "Come join us at Mooncaster. How can there be revels without your perfidious presence?"

Emma glanced around quickly. The crowd were still humming and still moving into the car park, blocking her retreat. She looked past Conor, to where the path that ran beside the fort dipped down to the beach.

"Here's a present for you!" she called out. A well-aimed kick sent the boy crumpling to the ground, howling and clutching his groin. Hooting with glee, she ran to the shore. Served the nutcase right.

The crowd continued to follow her. Emma dashed over the shingle. She would run round the Landguard, then back up the peninsula along the sandhills till she reached the town again. Then she skidded to a halt. Across that wide, unlit beach, just up ahead, an even greater crowd was waiting silently.

"You got to be kidding!" she exclaimed. There had to be over a hundred of them there. "What is this, a special night out from the loony bin?"

A woman dressed in a black ballgown that glittered with glass beads, wearing a sparkling tiara on her head, stepped from the assembly. She came towards Emma, swishing the ample skirt of her gown around her as she walked, and leisurely wafted a feathered fan in front of her face.

"You dolled up like that for a bet or what?" the girl barked aggressively as she came closer. "Isn't it a bit early for panto? Where's the other ugly sister or are you minging enough for two?"

"Come, daughter!" the Queen of Spades chided. "We knew you would be a tricky one to call to Court, but our patience is not immeasurable."

"You ain't my mother! You scrag-end. You look more like Dracula's auntie."

"Don't keep the Ismus waiting any longer," the woman who had once been known as Queenie scolded. "He sent us to fetch you."

"You can forget that right now!" Emma said forcefully. "I'm not

going anywhere with you lot! I don't like rooms with rubber walls."

She looked over her shoulder and saw that the first crowd of people had come on to the shore and were approaching. Conor Westlake was limping along behind them. She was trapped.

"Get out of my face," she growled at the woman. "Or I'll rip your head off and gob down your neck."

The Queen of Spades closed the fan and tapped her palm with it irritably. "Enough now, daughter," she said. "A struggle would be so undignified and just the sort of spectacle the Queen of Diamonds would enjoy. Don't give her that pleasure."

"Raving mad, every single one of you," Emma declared. "Right, I've had enough…" She pulled out her mobile and started to dial. "You're in so much lumber now."

The Queen of Spades laughed dismissively. "If you think to summon the police of this dreary dreaming place then look yonder. She pointed behind her with the fan. A chubby police officer moved to the front of the crowd.

Emma was neither impressed nor intimidated. "So you've got a tame pig," she jeered. "I wasn't calling the law, you rancid dog's dinner. I'm phoning my old man… hello, Dad? I'm down the fort – come get me double quick! Bring your battle gear, there's a load of freaks and nutters here trying to…"

The Queen of Spades smacked the phone out of her hands. It went flying into the dark surf and disappeared with a plop. Emma screamed in anger. She punched the woman in the face, then the stomach and kneed her in the chin as she doubled over.

"You mad old munter!" the girl shrieked. "You are so dead!"

The two groups of people came rushing towards them. Emma tore at the woman's hair, ripping the tiara from it. Then she shoved her on to the shingle and swung her leg back to kick her. Suddenly strong hands seized her arms. The two crowds had converged and surrounded them. They dragged the screeching teenage girl clear and held her firmly.

"Get off me – you mentalists!" she screamed. "Get off! My dad is going to kill you!"

The Queen of Spades was helped to her feet.

"The sacred text," she instructed quickly, gasping and clutching her stomach. "Read it!"

The police officer moved in front of the struggling girl. He switched on a torch and lifted his copy of Dancing Jacks into the beam.

"Beyond the Silvering Sea," he began.

But Emma refused to listen. She let out a deafening shriek that drowned out the policeman's voice. Then she flung her head back and smashed the nose of the man grasping her arms. He yowled and let go. At once she swung her hands round, dashed the book from the policeman's grasp, then pushed him fiercely in the chest. The overweight officer lost his balance and fell backwards. The girl lunged at the next person, hitting them out of the way. Then she elbowed another aside and headbutted a third. Someone came running up with a glob of minchet on their fingers, ready to smear it across her mouth.

410

Emma snatched the nail scissors from her pocket and stabbed the air in front of her. The person retreated and spread the sickly-coloured ointment over their own lips.

"I'll stick anyone who gets in my way!" Emma yelled, and she wasn't bluffing.

"Let her go!" the Queen of Spades commanded. "Let the fool go!"

The people parted and Emma moved through them warily. "Who wants some of this?" she asked. "Go on – keep back."

They obeyed and at last she was clear. The dark desolation of the nature reserve stretched in front. Without a backward glance, the girl ran.

The Queen of Spades watched her racing away into the gloom.

"I knew it would not be easy," the Jack of Clubs said as he hobbled up to her. "Your resourceful daughter is a force to be reckoned with."

"She is magnificent," the woman declared with maternal pride. But such sentiment would have to wait.

"The Ismus has ordered she be gathered amongst us tonight," Jack reminded her.

The Queen of Spades flashed her eyes at him. "Jill shan't get far," she assured him. "Mauger will bring her down."

Emma pelted over the scrubby, rabbit-cropped grass that grew on the barren flats of the nature reserve. Sporadic clumps of gorse were the only features on that empty stretch and in the darkness they appeared as dense and solid as boulders. Beyond them the black, silent sea reached to the horizon where container ships twinkled as they passed one another.

A small shape darted in front of her and Emma gave a startled yell. It was only one of the countless rabbits that infested this place. She reproached herself, but was it any wonder she was so jumpy?

Then she realised she was out in the middle of nowhere. She had run too far – like a panicky rabbit herself. The high mounds of the sandhills were way off to the left. They stood between her and the road, cutting her off from it. When her father came speeding to the rescue, she wouldn't be able to see him. She wished he'd get a move on; she couldn't run much further. Her lungs were busting and her legs ached like anything.

Catching her rasping breath, she realised just how unfit she was. She had never been sporty and always ducked out of games, citing women's troubles even before she had any, so hardly ever got any proper exercise. The cigarettes didn't help either.

Gulping the cool air down, she wondered if those maniacs were still chasing her? What were they even up to? It was too mental to begin to understand. Were they trying to kidnap her or preach at her? Mad stuff like that didn't happen here in crappy Felixstowe.

Veering aside, she ran on to the wide concrete access path that snaked across the reserve, towards the sandhills. Her boots thudded over the hard grey surface. As the hummocky mounds reared closer, the shadows deepened about her. The gorse here grew thick and tall, spilling through the railings that ran alongside the ridge.

When she came to the point where the path ran between two hills,

412

she paused for a moment. Her heart was hammering in her chest and she coughed and felt giddy.

A section of View Point Road was before her, running parallel to the grassy dunes. There was no sign of her dad's car yet and the dark, lonely road looked threatening. More of those nutters could be lurking anywhere in the shrubs that lined it.

Without hesitation, Emma hurried up the steps of the nearest hill. The high ridge path on top of the mounds afforded the best vantage point. She could see into the container port across the road, or in the opposite direction, over the flat expanse of the reserve and to the sea. Then in the distance ahead, there were the gleaming lights of the town. When she reached the topmost step, Emma dared to look behind her for the first time.

That part of the nature reserve, near the Landguard Fort, was empty. There was no movement, no sign of those crazies at all. Nobody was following her. It was a massive relief. The sudden release from fear and anxiety hit her like a cold wave and at once she felt exhilarated and light-headed.

Cackling at her triumph over them, she jumped up and down, thrusting one finger into the air.

"In your faces, losers!" she crowed, almost disappointed that they had given up so easily. "In your stupid faces!"

But she was too exuberant and careless in her boisterous leaping. She missed her footing and slithered part way down the side of the hill.

Spitting sand from her mouth, Emma yelled abuse at the world then started climbing back up. Her right hand squelched in something wet and warm. The girl stared at the patch of coarse dune grass curiously. Even in the dark she could see what was lying there and she gave a shriek of disgust.

It was the torn remains of a rabbit – a very freshly killed and mutilated rabbit.

Emma scrambled to her feet and wiped the blood from her hands as she regained the high path.

"Ugh – gross!" she retched. "That is so puke-making! I'm goin'…"

Her words died as she caught sight of something moving through the gloom, down there – on the reserve. A large shape was darting from one clump of gorse to another, scooting swiftly across the ground, but keeping within the shadows. What was it? It wasn't a dog – it was too large – but what? It moved more like a gorilla than anything else she could think of, but that was impossible.

"What the hell is that?" she breathed and fear crept quickly over her.

A glimpse of two shaggy forearms almost made her believe it really was a great ape, perhaps escaped from a zoo somewhere? But the next time it broke cover and rushed to the next concealing shrub, she saw the squat, muscular body and powerful back legs that weren't part of any monkey. One thing was certain, however – it was coming this way.

"That ain't right," Emma whispered and her skin began to creep and crawl.

414

The mysterious creature leaped across the concrete path and she finally saw the ram's horns curling back from its head. Two hostile points of burning yellow blinked in the darkness.

"It ain't real..." she muttered, shaking her head. "Can't be."

The shape halted as if it heard. It snorted the air. The malevolent eyes glared across the scrubland and shone straight up at her. Emma dropped to her knees in terror, but it was too late. The thing, whatever it was, had seen her.

She wanted to scream and almost stumbled down the hill again in fright. At that moment, the shape threw back its head and gave a ferocious, bestial roar. Then it came tearing over the scrub – towards the dunes.

A silent, strangled cry wheezed from Emma's lips as the horror sprang on to the first step below. Petrified, the girl could only stare at it. She saw a wide, downturned mouth in a repulsive wide head and the jagged points of many sharp teeth. She saw the rolling of powerful shoulders as the ape-like arms swept it up the hill after her and heard the savage panting of its sulphurous breath.

Then, finally, she found her voice.

"Sod you!" she cried.

Spinning around, Emma ran. The demon came pouncing over the topmost step and landed on the high path with a gloating gargle. The dreadful fire of its eyes blazed at her. The brutal head pulled into the wide shoulders. The fangs scraped together. Then it gave chase.

The path ran level for a short distance then dipped again as that hill ended. Emma bolted down the far steps. Then almost flew up the next. The monster came bellowing after, raking up sand and shingle with its claws. It leaped across the gulf between the two hills, closing the gap between it and her.

Emma could hear the thing getting nearer and nearer. She heard its vicious growls and snarls and the crunching of its snapping jaws. What the hell was it? Where had it come from? Frantic, the girl pushed herself harder than she ever had. She thought of that dismembered rabbit and ran even faster.

"Dad!" she cried. "Dad – where are you? You useless waster!"

Up on that high, hummocky sandhill, the terrified girl and the fiend that pursued her were two black shapes silhouetted against the night sky. There was a wild roar and the hunter catapulted itself forward. The shapes tangled into one. A girl's shrill scream blistered over the nature reserve and the creature had her.

*The Queen of Spades' dark daughter, is it blood
in her veins or water?*

26

EMMA TAYLOR BLINKED her eyes open. There was a dull throbbing pain on the side of her head. She sucked cold air through clenched teeth and winced. She was so tired. Her limbs were so heavy. Then she remembered.

With a blast of returning horror, the girl sat up. The pain thumped even louder in her head.

"You should not have run away like that," the Queen of Spades told her. "Mauger is not very gentle. If he hadn't been given the most strict commands, there's no knowing what he would have done to you."

Emma looked around groggily. She was lying at the bottom of the sandhill. The state of her clothes and hair told her she had tumbled all the way down it. She realised, with a sickening sense of hopelessness, it was not the side that faced the road.

That great gang of weirdos was gathered in front of her. Conor

Westlake was among them. She wished she had the strength to kick him again. The girl looked nervously into the shadows on either side of her. Where was it? Where was that… that awful thing?

"Mauger is back yonder," the Queen of Spades reassured her, guessing what was in her mind and waving vaguely at the dark nature reserve. "He likes to catch rabbits. Sometimes he eats them. Sometimes he just pulls them apart for fun. Soon he will progress to larger playmates."

"What is it?" Emma asked, shivering at the memory of the horrendous face that jumped on her. "Some experiment gone wrong? Sew it together from zoo leftovers, did you? It's disgusting."

"He is the Growly Guardian of the Gateway," the woman answered. "He has been awakened, as other things shall waken and they also shall pass through."

"You sad, mad cow! You should get yourself a chihuahua instead, luv. That'd be so much more you."

The Queen of Spades was not listening. She turned aside and the fat policeman took her place, the book and torch in his hands.

"Let it be done," the woman instructed. "If she tries to escape, Mauger may not be so biddable and obedient a second time. If she tries her little scissors on him – he may just bite her arm off."

Emma heard her and tried not to look scared, but inside she was frothing with fear. What were they going to do to her? Would they chop her up and use the bits to make more freaks of nature? What filthy cult was this? Some kind of Frankenstein appreciation society?

The officer shone the torch on the open pages and a thrill of

expectation spread through the waiting crowd. He began to read and then Emma heard the most wonderful sound in the world – a car engine.

Behind the sandhills, her father was speeding down View Point Road. She twisted about and shouted at the top of her voice.

"Dad! Dad! I'm here!"

"Be quick!" the Queen of Spades urged the policeman.

Emma tried to make a break for it. She scrambled up the dune. If she could only reach the road – her old man was bound to see her. But the crowd would not let her. Those at the front were too quick. They surged forward and snatched at her, dragging her back down. Then they stood in a tight circle around her.

"Dad!" she howled. "I'm here! Da—"

A rough hand pushed against her lips. There was something greasy and bitter on the fingers. They pushed into the girl's mouth and slathered the unctuous matter over her tongue. Emma choked and gagged in shock. Her tongue curled up as an acrid stinging burned down her throat. Her eyes watered and she fell back against the legs that hemmed her in.

Spluttering, she looked up at the pitiless faces and the policeman's voice droned on. The words drilled into her mind, becoming one with that overwhelming sharpness. She felt a dark curtain lifting. Something was slipping away from her, but she didn't mind. It didn't matter now. Her head buzzed. The people around her began to nod in unison, caught in the enchantment's rhythm. A cold breath kissed the back of her neck. Her vision swam. The words of

Austerly Fellows embraced her, drew her in, loved her as nothing else ever could, promised to sustain and keep her, to coddle and bless her through all of time. There was only sweetness, warmth and pleasure and a wondrous unfurling. How bright it was!

Cradling her chin in her hands, she gazed down over the balcony. Hundreds of candles were ablaze in the Great Hall. Evergreen garlands had been strung between the arches and golden ribbons were tied round the stone pillars. Beneath the high, jewel-coloured windows, the long oak table had been pushed against the wall. It was groaning with delicious-looking dishes.

The kitchens had been preparing for this night for weeks. Every species of bird and hoofed beast was roasted and glistening on golden platters, decorated with their previous plumage or slices of orange, or piped with patterns of soft cheese studded with cherries and almonds, and stuffed with mushrooms and chestnuts. There were three suckling pigs glazed with honey, a golden apple in each little snout. Loaves had been baked in fancy shapes: hedgepigs, smiling moons, rayed stars, wheat sheaves, round towers and even little coffins with sprigs of rosemary sticking out of them, looking like the feet of dead crows. There were bowls piled high with candied fruits and exquisite little brown cakes topped with yellow cream and crystallised petals of roses and violets. There were kilderkins of strong ale for the knights, rundlets of wine for the Under Kings and Queens and a jorum of spiced punch for the other guests.

It was a sumptuous feast and the delicious smells that rose from the table filled the vast hall – swelling up into the high ceiling. Along the oak beams there, mice crept dreamily, taking deep, delightful breaths of the mouth-watering scents and yearning for the revel to be over so they could sneak down and reap the crumbs.

The Jill of Spades cared nothing for the delectable spread. The minstrels were already playing and the girl tapped her toes to the cheery tune. It promised to be a great night. The guests were arriving early, so as not to miss a moment of this most special festivity. Old Ramptana the Court Magician was fussing with some props as he continued to rehearse for the performance he was to give later. Then his long white beard got tangled up in a trick with a length of rope and he had to go scurrying away to extricate his whiskers.

The Ismus was down there, sitting upon the carved chair that stood before the Waiting Throne, and the Lady Labella was at his side. Both were dressed in their finest, for the autumn revel was one of the grandest nights of the calendar. Jill studied their attire with interest then turned her attention to the gathering guests.

"Let us see, let us see!" an anxious voice cried out behind her.

"We want to look, we want to see the fashions!" called another.

The Jill of Spades turned around and looked down crossly. Two rag dolls were hurrying along the gallery to join her. One of them was limping. They dashed to the edge and thrust their soft heads between the balustrades.

"Ooh!" exclaimed Ashrella, the doll made from grey and black silks, with woollen hair, lacy skirt and glass bead eyes. "The Queen of Hearts is getting fat! If she had an apple in her mouth, she'd

421

look just like those suckling pigs!"

"But not as tasty!" snickered the other doll. This one was made from scraps of different coloured velvet, with gold buttons for eyes. There was a moth bite on one of its legs, which caused it to hobble along. It had been a gift from the Lockpick when Jill was very young. Two cloth keys were sewn about the doll's neck and so the girl had called it Keykey.

"Coo – there's Magpie Jack!" Ashrella declared, pointing her stubby hand at a slight figure moving through the crowd. "He looks pale. Has he been in gaol again? See how he covets the ladies' necklaces! It's jools, jools, jools all the way with him, isn't it?"

"There's his mother!" Keykey observed. "What is she wearing? That wimple so does not match that gown with those scalloped daggings – what a frocktroll!"

"And there is the Jill of Hearts. What a beauty she's grown into, much fairer than our own plain, sulky-faced Jill of Spades. See how every head turns to get their eyeful! Lords and ladies – they're all drooling."

"What a steamy strumpet! She's loving it. Even the pages are tripping up as she glides by. A proper wanton saucepot she's become. Is anyone safe from her?"

"Such a goodly number of knights," Ashrella sighed. "How their armour blazes under the candles."

"I've never seen so many shiny cuirasses in one place!" the other doll tittered.

"And look at the hair on that matron – did she cut it with a blunt sword?"

Keykey hopped up and down in excitement. "There's the Jack of Clubs!" she squealed. "He is well comely!"

"He can unpick my stitching any time he likes!" Ashrella agreed, wagging her head through the balustrades. "Such a shapely leg in that hose and how becoming the hanging sleeves are on his fine shoulders."

"Oh – oh – look – there's Malinda. She's still got that old pink dress with the gold lace and stars! Get something new off the mercers, dearie!"

"Or freshen it up with accessories at least! Some new dangle purses – gold slippers, a jewelled shawl... even one of those two-horned headdresses would lift that tired old look. Does she even wash that frock? Looks musty to me."

"She probably stinks of old lady pee."

"No wonder she lives out in the woods then, away from the dainty noses of the gentry."

"And see the Ismus! Oh, how fine he looks in that black velvet."

"Labella too, she looks well in purple."

"Nay – the Ismus could do better – and he does, frequently!"

The dolls began giggling.

"What are you two doing here?" the Jill of Spades demanded angrily.

The dolls took no notice of her at first until they spotted a man meandering through the guests below. He was dressed in a tight costume of caramel-coloured leather, with a matching cap. The dolls drew back at once and shrank fearfully into the shadows.

"Well?" the Jill of Spades asked impatiently. "How did you get out? Why are you here?"

Ashrella folded its silken arms and tilted its overstuffed head – huffily. "It's horrible in that cupboard!" it said. "You never play with us any more."

"It's not fair!" Keykey agreed. "You used to take us everywhere. Now we never get to see anyone. You wouldn't like being shut away with only a cup and ball and a wooden elephant with a wheel missing for company."

"We wanted to see the party!" Ashrella said defiantly. "We love parties."

"You can't just forget about us, not after all this time."

"I didn't forget," Jill replied. "But I'm too old to play with you now."

"Too old?" Ashrella squawked indignantly.

"You're the one who bullied the Jack of Diamonds into stealing the soul sparks to put into each of us when you were younger!" Keykey remonstrated.

"That's why Haxxentrot set the itch into his palm when she caught him rummaging in her Forbidden Tower!"

"You can't undo what was done. You have to care for us. We're yours for the rest of your days. That was the bargain you made, those were the terms you accepted, to free Jack and get the life spells."

"If I'd known how annoying you two would become, I would have

424

let Jack rot in that dungeon and got myself a goldfinch instead – at least that would sing. You two never could."

"That's just spiteful," Ashrella said, greatly offended. "We were your only friends for years and years. Then you grew up and weren't fun any more."

"And you're a nasty piece of work," Keykey put in. "There's only us knows just how cold and cruel you really are and what dark ambitions you have. We could tell on you, we could."

"Easily."

The girl laughed. "Who'd believe two old mothy dolls, driven mad by being locked in a cupboard for three years?"

"One moth bite!" Keykey cried dismally. "Just one little nibble on my knee. It's not much. It could be so much worse. The neglect we suffer would make the stones of Mooncaster weep."

"You're heartless!" Ashrella moaned to the girl. "We're never going back in the cupboard again."

The Jill of Spades snatched them up in a temper and stormed over to the nearest iron candle stand and held the dolls close to the flames.

"If we burn then so do you!" Ashrella cried, the glass bead eyes flashing fiercely. "That's how the bargain was sealed, with two pinpricks of your own red blood. You can't destroy us without bringing about your own end."

The girl's face quivered with rage. She knew the doll was right. The closer she held the dolls to the flame, the more she felt the fierce heat herself. The soul sparks that gave them life had been bonded to her. Without her, they would revert to being lifeless rags and her own *doom was tied up with their fate.*

"Then it's back to the cupboard for you!" she growled. "And this time I'll drag a heavy chest in front of it so you'll never get out again!"

"No!" the dolls protested. "The ball has just started. We want to see the new dances!"

The Jill of Spades was not listening. She strode from the gallery and out on to the battlements. A fork of lightning ripped through the clouded night sky. A Punchinello guard leaned on his spear and watched her curiously. The girl hurried down the steps, across the lawns – until the North Tower reared into the night before her. The banners of the Royal House of Spades jumped in and out of the lightning flashes. With a backward glance at the Great Hall, whose windows were ablaze with candlelight and from where the sprightly music was playing merrily, she pushed open the stout door and hastened up the spiralling stairs.

Her chamber was on the topmost level. When she reached it, she was out of breath.

"You're mean!" Ashrella told her. "We told her you were mean."

Jill paused before she opened her door. "Told who?" she asked.

"The one who let us out of course," Keykey replied. "How else do you think we escaped that nasty locked cupboard?"

"Who let you out?" the girl demanded. "Who has dared enter my bedchamber?"

"The one who is waiting there still," Ashrella answered with a sly smile.

426

The Jill of Spades glared at her door. She threw the dolls down. They wailed when they hit the floor, but bounced back up again and punched her legs with their soft, mitten-like hands. She did not feel them. Her whole attention was focused on that door. Very quietly, she reached for the secret dagger she always carried, strapped to her arm, under her sleeve. Then she kicked the door wide and leaped into the chamber.

For a moment she stood, poised and ready to strike out. But no attack came. Her eyes darted quickly about the room. The bed, hung with black, beaded lace, was empty and there was no one hiding beneath it. Nor was there anyone behind the chests and cupboards. Another jag of lightning crackled above the tower and then the Jill of Spades saw her.

There she was, an old wizened woman, crouched upon the sill of the arched window. A tall, conical hat was fastened to her head by a wide, brown ribbon, tied beneath her warty chin. She wore a dark green cloak over her ragged clothes and a two-pronged hayfork was clasped in her gnarled hands.

"Haxxentrot!" Jill cried.

The witch cackled and raised the hayfork in greeting. "Well met on this harvest home night, my dark little maid," she greeted.

"Begone!" the girl commanded. "Before I summon the Guards. You have no business here."

"No business?" the hag shrieked. "No business? Have you forgot who supplied thee with playmates when no other child would suffer thee? A brooding, hateful brat thou wert, but a treacherous, *iron-hearted woman thou art becoming. Who else but Haxxentrot would have any business with thee?"*

"Guards!" the girl called. "Come quickly!"

"Very foolish," the witch said, hearing the Punchinello Guards come stomping towards the North Tower. "Now I must be brisk and brutal." With that, she clapped her bony hands and the two rag dolls went scampering over to her and climbed on to her lap.

"Good mother!" they called happily. "Bear us away. We don't like it here. You won't shut us in a cupboard. You won't forget us."

The crone bent her ugly head to kiss them and her eyes gleamed at Jill. "You should have taken better care of your playfellows, my dark missy," she said. "They are mine to bid now. If old Haxxentrot asks them to leap into the fire, they would do so, full willing... and you know what that would mean for thee."

The Jill of Spades gasped. She was totally in the witch's power.

The clamour of the guards had already reached the spiral stairs.

"What do you want of me?" the girl asked desperately.

"Much," the crone sniggered, grinning with her gums. "But this night I will settle for two things only."

"Name them."

"Bring me Malinda's wand," she told her with a greedy chuckle.

Jill's face showed her shock and dismay at this impossible demand. "And the other thing?" she asked.

Haxxentrot held up a small bottle of green glass. The lightning cracked outside and sinister shadows danced around the bedchamber.

"When the revels are ended," she croaked, "when the mummers

428

lead the ladies out on to the battlements and those fine wives and tidy matrons remove their cloaks and gowns to smear the minchet over their hungry flesh and fly to the Ismus up on the highest tower... go with them."

"I was going to anyway."

"Of course thou wert. What damsel could refuse the invitation of the Holy Enchanter to dally with him upon that lofty height – that lonely bare roof 'neath the moon, reached by neither step nor stair? That space which only birds or bees can view..."

"Is that all?" Jill asked, staring doubtfully at the bottle.

The witch's eyes glittered at her. "There will be a jorum of sweet wine waiting up there," she said. "The Ismus likes his ladies to drink of it before they partake of his... affections. Take this bottle and empty the contents into that great bowl. Make sure all the ladies drink it down."

"What will it do?" the girl asked.

The hag let out a foul, wheezing laugh. "Why, poison them of course!" she crowed. "They shall wilt, they shall shrivel. Fire will burst out their bellies and breasts, their hair will stand stark white from their scalps and every tongue will swell and blacken. Grey shall be their flesh and the very life will leak from their ears."

"I can't do that!" Jill exclaimed in horror.

"What carest thou for the dames and slatterns who look on you with distrust and disdain? They have no regard for thee, my dark missy. This is thy chance to purge this castle of each one. Think of them as obstacles in thy way to what thy heart desires the most."

"I already do," the Jill of Spades answered in a calmer, interested voice.

"This tiny bottle will rid you of them forever and clear thy way to so many delights. Imagine a Court devoid of females, always prying, always scolding…"

"And what of my mother? Am I to poison her also?"

"Whatever you wish," the hag replied.

"Poor Mumsy," Jill said with evil relish.

The noise of the Guards had almost reached them. Haxxentrot threw the poison to the girl then straddled the hayfork and leaped from the window. "And don't forget Malinda's wand!" she called over her shoulder as she flew through the electrified sky.

Jill watched her disappear into the distance, the cloak flapping madly around her, the two dolls clinging to her filthy skirts.

"I won't," she muttered.

At that moment seven Punchinello Guards burst into the bedchamber jabbing their spears forward and glaring round with their beady eyes.

"What – what – what?" they barked ferociously.

The Jill of Spades spun around to face them. "You must forgive me," she apologised coolly. "The lightning frightened me. I feared the bouncing shadows and the thunder crash, nothing more."

The Guards sniffed the air with their great noses and glowered at her suspiciously.

Later that night, once the dancing was over and the feasting done,

Ramptana the doddery Court Magician began blundering through his abysmal tricks to entertain the nobles. He did not get far. He was halfway through pulling coloured silk bunting from his mouth when he gave a sharp yelp and twisted violently to one side. The live ermine he had hidden in one of his large sleeves, intended for the big finale where he would make it and other animals 'magickally' appear from his hands, had caught scent of the other secreted creatures. Ramptana had forgotten to feed it before the performance and so the ermine was ravenous. It shot up the sleeve and down his shirtfront, raking its claws over his chest and belly, searching for the prey it knew was here somewhere. The old man shrieked and howled as it tore around his body.

The audience watched in surprise whilst the conjuror's clothes wriggled and writhed as the savage animal went scrabbling beneath them, running round and around him. He wasn't usually so good, they murmured to one another.

The old man hopped around the floor, his long, white beard twining about him as he spun around, trying to catch the creature rampaging under his garments.

Then it happened. The ermine discovered a white rabbit cowering in a concealed inner pocket. It pounced. The Court Magician felt the brief struggle. He ceased his wild dance then stared morosely at the audience. No one except him knew what was happening. Then suddenly a patch of his beard turned bright red. Were they supposed to applaud? What a peculiar trick.

Then the long whiskers shook and the ermine's fierce little face thrust through them, a rabbit's head dangling from its jaws.

One of the ladies fainted. The shock of the others quickly turned to anger and they began booing and jeering. One of the knights threw a pickled walnut at him. It knocked the hat from his head and the white dove that had been hiding there went flying up into the rafters.

"My lords!" the magician beseeched them. "Pray let me finish. I have not shown you the marvel of the magick hoops and how they knit together… please!"

"Get off!" the audience heckled.

At the end of the Great Hall, the Ismus rose from his seat. "Incompetent idiot," he said contemptuously. Bowing to kiss the Lady Labella's hand, he whispered to her, "You know where I shall be, join me there." Then he strode away.

"We want to see real magick!" the audience demanded.

The poor magician was struggling to free his beard of the ermine, but the animal bit his fingers. Then it ran up on to his bare head to chew one of the rabbit's ears.

"You're a hopeless charlatan!" the King of Diamonds announced. "To the stocks with him! Pelt him with filth!"

"I can do magick!" the old man cried pathetically. "Please, your Royal Majesties, lords, ladies…"

Two tall knights came clanking to grab him. Then they halted and backed away. Ramptana was aware that something was happening behind him. Slowly he turned to look.

The one suckling pig that had not been eaten was shaking the parsley garnish from its back then it rose on its hind trotters. Standing

432

upright, it peered curiously around the hall with its shrivelled eyes and spat the golden apple from its mouth.

This time the King of Clubs fainted.

The roasted pig held on to its sides and made grunting sounds as though it were laughing. Then it went skipping along the length of the long table. When it passed an untouched pheasant, the bird hopped up on its drumsticks to join it and every other cooked animal that had not been carved was soon prancing along behind – dancing and capering between the bowls and dishes.

The nobles gawped in shock. And then, in a gurgling, squealy voice, the pig began to speak.

"Gallant lords and ladies all, we hope you enjoyed our harvest ball. If we did please and fill your tums then up do raise your royal thumbs. Now clap your hands and give a cheer – to grand Ramptana, the mighty magician here!"

With that, the pig took a bow and the crackling split all the way up the length of its back. The roast fowl followed suit then flapped their plucked wings to instigate the applause. For several moments there was only stunned silence and then the Great Hall erupted with cheers. The old man was lifted on to the shoulders of the very same knights who had been about to put him in the stocks and paraded around with much admiration.

The Court Magician did not know what to say. He did not understand what had happened and tears filled his eyes. He stared at the pig on the table, but it had lain down and was lifeless and inert once more. Had he really done that? He did not know how. For the rest of that night, and for many months after, he was treated with a new respect.

The minstrels struck up a tune and the nobles carried him triumphantly around the hall whilst their spouses and sweethearts slipped discreetly away. Only one lady lingered for a time. Malinda, the retired Fairy Godmother, brushed her spun, sugar-like hair from her eyes and smiled gently as she saw the happiness on the old magician's face. She lifted the crooked silver wand, which she used mainly as a walking stick nowadays, and gave the amber star at the tip a fond kiss.

Across the hall, the Jockey observed her and he tapped his hands together in silent applause. Then he pointed his toe, bowed and went tittuping out.

Outside, on the battlements, thirty ladies were aflutter with excitement. Usually the mummers would lead them out here, but they could wait no longer. The Queen of Hearts had prepared a fresh batch of minchet that very afternoon and was handing out little pots of it to everyone present. The Jill of Spades was already there, waiting for them.

She took a pot of the flying ointment and gazed up at the central tower where a lone figure was standing, the tails of his velvet jacket fluttering in the autumn wind. A splinter of lightning snapped behind him and he raised his face to laugh at the approaching storm. The girl reached into her sleeve where the small bottle of poison was concealed. Mooncaster would never be the same again after tonight.

The thought of that thrilled her beyond measure. These silly, twittering females would soon be dead. She could hardly keep from laughing.

"Who will our Lord choose tonight?" the Queen of Clubs wondered aloud.

"Let it be me!" one of the noblewomen sighed wistfully.

They all began removing their cloaks and gowns until they were only standing in their shifts and petticoats. Then they dabbled their fingers in the minchet and rubbed it over their shoulders and throats and the backs of their necks.

"Was there ever a more handsome and wise Lord?" the Jill of Hearts cried out. "I am ready! Lift me to yon high tower and his embrace!"

As she spoke, the power of the ointment began to work, her feet left the battlements and she rose into the air.

The Jill of Spades rapidly smeared the salve over herself. She had to get to the tower first. She had to pour the witch's bottle into the wine that was already up there.

All around her the women were cooing and giggling with the marvellous sensation of being carried aloft. Dancing slippers dropped from waggling feet and bare legs dangled in the empty air. What a delight, what a beauteous feeling – with the Ismus waiting at the end. Perfect, absolutely perfect.

And then they realised something was wrong. They were not headed towards the central tower at all. They were drifting away from it.

"What is happening?" the Queen of Hearts shrieked in confusion. "Not this way, go back – go back!"

The floating women thrashed their arms like clumsy birds and kicked their legs like frogs, but nothing would alter their course. They flew high above the castle lawns, high over the curtain wall where a group of Punchinello Guards stared up at them and hooted at the sights they glimpsed soaring over their heads.

"I don't understand!" the Queen of Hearts was howling as she flailed her flabby arms.

"You stupid woman!" her friend, the Queen of Spades, scolded as she went sailing by. "You brewed it wrong this time."

"I didn't, I swear. I followed the recipe to the letter, same as I always do."

They were almost over the outer wall. Beyond the moat lay the sleepy village of Mooncot.

"The peasants will look up my petticoats!" the Queen of Diamonds wept dismally. "Oh, the everlasting shame!"

The Jill of Spades was just as helpless as the rest of them. What was she to do now?

"We might never stop!" one noblewoman cried. "We could fly on and on – over the woods – over the hills! What will become of us?"

"Now I remember!" the Queen of Hearts yelled. "It was him! He came by. He visited me this afternoon after I had brewed it. He must have meddled with it as it was cooling."

"Him?" the Queen of Spades shouted back. "Who him?"

"The Jockey!" her friend answered with a fretful, warbling groan.

As if in answer, they all heard a hearty laugh from below. Staring down, they saw a man in a caramel-coloured suit performing a gloating jig.

"I tricked you, I trumped you!" he sang out. "I rode you, I rid you! The Ismus won't be bestowing his favour upon any of you this night, dear ladies. Haw haw haw!"

"How dare you!" the Queen of Diamonds shrieked, gathering her petticoats closely about her. "Bring us down at once – you tampering trickster!"

The man laughed even louder. "But of course!" he called up. "This is the end of thy journey, my Lady. This is as far as the enchantment takes you."

The women did not have time to think. They each felt the power of the minchet failing. Then they realised where they were and they screamed and shrieked all the more. Too late. One by one they dropped like stones from the sky. Down and down. The castle walls rushed past and then the night was filled with splashes as every single one of them plunged into the moat.

The Jill of Spades came up gasping for air, covered in duckweed and choking with the murky water. Around her the other women were doing the same and yowling wretchedly. They floundered and bobbed and paddled for the water's edge. Jill reached the bank first and realised with a sickening shock that the bottle of poison was gone from inside her sleeve. She had lost it in the moat. What would she

437

say to Haxxentrot? And she hadn't even thought how she might steal Malinda's wand. What terrible retribution would the witch visit upon her?

As the women heaved themselves on to dry land, dripping with mud, sobbing and shivering, the girl glared up at the Jockey. She could not see his face, but she could make out his cap, leaning through the crenellations. He was waving his hands and dancing around, revelling in his latest mischief.

"You have made an enemy of me this night," she whispered. "Watch your back from now on, Jockey. The Jill of Spades has a score to settle with you."

A shrill scream caused her to look around. The others were now standing upon the grass, but staring at their hands and scratching at their necks and shoulders.

"I said the enchantment took you this far!" the Jockey's voice shouted down to them. "I did not say it had ended. Haw haw haw – I tricked you, I trumped you. I rode you, I rid you. I dropped you, I drowned you. I groomed you, I teased you!"

The Jill of Spades was confused. Then she too realised. Where she had rubbed the minchet on to her body, her skin was burning. It was a hot, prickling pain, and then, to her dismay, she saw bristles sprouting everywhere.

"I'm covered in hair!" she cried. "I've got hair on my hands, on my arms and shoulders!"

The rest of the women were screaming along with her. Every one of them was now covered in coarse, dog-like hair – everywhere the

sabotaged flying ointment had touched their skin.

Above them the Jockey's braying laughter was even louder than their panicked screeches. Then the lightning ripped through the heavens, the thunder clashed directly overhead and the rain began to pour from the sky. The women shrieked all the more.

Emma Taylor clutched at her throat and rubbed her hands anxiously. She fell back against the sandhill and tore at her shoulders. Then she opened her eyes. Her palms were smooth. Her neck was not thick with hair. She grunted with relief.

The woman who had been Queenie knelt beside her.

"Daughter," she said gently. "Welcome back."

The girl grinned at her. "Hello, Mumsy," she said, raising one eyebrow archly. "I am the Jill of Spades."

"The Ismus will be well pleased you have joined us at last."

Emma held out her hand and Conor Westlake helped her to her feet.

A man's concerned voice was calling her name in the distance, down by the fort.

"That will be Mr Taylor," Emma said. "He is looking for the girl. I will go to him. I will play-act and dissemble."

"It's what you do best, my child," the Queen of Spades said proudly.

With a last, sly look at everyone gathered there, Emma hurried away towards the Landguard.

"And now the Court is complete," Conor declared happily.

439

The woman tapped her fan on his shoulder. "Not yet, Jack," she said. "There is still one who has not been found. The Jockey is not here amongst us."

"I can wait a goodly while till that happens!"

"As can we all. But who knows, maybe he is already out there, simply biding his time till he stands forward? That would be so like him."

The boy shuddered. "I fear the Jockey," he muttered.

"So do the rest of us in Mooncaster," she told him. "Yea, even perhaps our Lord Ismus himself."

The Malinda Waltz

27

Martin Baxter waited almost two hours for Carol to return. He had done his best to clear the wreckage in what remained of his sanctum, but in the end the blue gloss paint defeated him. He was too tired to cope with that tonight. He did discover, however, that certain pieces of his collection were missing. Paul had taken some of his most valuable items: an original sonic screwdriver, the screen-used phaser from the Next Generation's first season and the Blake's Seven teleport bracelet. The boy really had taken the 'jools' of his collection.

There was still no word about Paul. They rang round everyone they could think of in the vain hope that the boy would have gone there and Carol tried his mobile again, but it was still switched off. She called her mother and spent half an hour trying to explain what had happened. At five to midnight they rang the police again, but they had no news.

"He's only eleven years old!" Carol snapped at them. "Anything could be happening to him. Why aren't you doing more?"

"I assure you, Mrs Thornbury, we're doing all we can to find your son," the sergeant told her.

"Well, obviously that's not enough, is it?" she retorted. "You haven't found him yet!"

"Would you like an officer to come over and be with you there?"

"What? No, I wouldn't! If you've got people to spare, they should be out looking for my son!"

"We're doing our best, Mrs Thornbury."

"I'm sure you are," she said sarcastically. Carol ended the call and bit her lips in frustration.

"What if they can't find him?" she said. "I don't know what I'd do. You hear about these things – kids disappearing. How many do they find safe and well? Not many. We'll have to do one of those press conferences and appeal for help. The families on those always look shifty and guilty…"

"Carol," Martin told her, "stop it. You're torturing yourself. Paul hasn't been abducted. He ran away. Whatever's the matter with him, he isn't stupid. He's a bright kid. He won't do anything silly."

The woman pointed upstairs. "What he did to your collection was

sensible then, was it?" she asked.

"No, but he was rational enough to write that message on the wall. Whatever he's on will wear off eventually. He'll come back then."

"You still think it was that stuff in those jars!" she cried. "It was the book, Martin."

"Rubbish!"

"I'm not going to argue with you. I should be out there looking for him."

"Where? Where do you think you can look that the police haven't?"

"I can't just sit here waiting." Carol grabbed the car keys again and headed for the door. "I have to feel as though I'm doing something."

"So you're just going to drive round Felixstowe all night long, is that it?"

"It has to be better than doing nothing."

"I'll come with you!"

"No, one of us has to stay – in case he comes back."

"Why does that have to be me?"

"Because I'm his mother!" she shouted.

The phone rang and Carol ran to it. "Paul?" she cried desperately. "Oh… no. Hello, Gerald. No – no word. Yes, we're still waiting. Look, I can't talk, I was just on my way out – here's Martin."

She pushed the phone across. Martin scowled at her, but she was out of the house before he could do anything.

"Hello?" Gerald's voice sounded from the phone. "Hello?"

Martin heard the car leave the driveway and he reluctantly lifted the phone to his ear. "Hi," he said wearily. "Sorry about that. She's in a state – as you can imagine."

They had already spoken to Gerald Benning earlier, but he hadn't seen anything of the boy.

"Poor Carol," the old man said. "It's a nightmare."

"Yes, yes, it is."

"I never thought Paul would do something like this."

"No, me neither."

"What was that you were saying yesterday about a book?"

Martin wasn't in the mood to talk to anyone. Gerald was a lovely, sweet old guy, but the maths teacher just wanted to be left alone right now.

"Oh, just a book that's become part of this craze at school," he said. "Listen, I really have to…"

"I still can't understand how you think it's to blame for this."

"I don't, not any more…"

"And it was written by who?"

"Doesn't matter… Austen someone. No, Austerly someone. Like I said, it doesn't matter. I really have to get going…"

There was a long pause and Martin thought Gerald had quietly put the receiver down. Then the old man said, "Austerly Fellows?"

"Yes, that's the one. I'll call you in the morning, Gerald."

"Martin!" the old man's voice was suddenly forceful and urgent. "Martin! Don't hang up!"

444

"What's the matter?"

"Oh, my dear Lord. Martin – I'm so sorry. So very sorry."

"Gerald?"

"I should have listened to you. You were right the other day. You say that book was written by Austerly Fellows?"

"Yes, why?"

"You don't know who he is? What he was?"

Martin held the phone away from his face. What was Gerald gabbling about?

"I do know, Martin!" the old man declared. "I know. And Paul is in far greater danger than you can ever imagine."

"Thanks, Gerald, that's just what I needed to hear."

"Come round. Come round here – you have to be told, you have to know."

"Eh?"

"Martin, I'm serious. Come round right now."

"I'm not going anywhere. Carol's just gone out and someone has to stay here, just in case."

"Tomorrow then!"

"That depends what happens tonight."

"I'm begging you!"

"OK," Martin promised, taken aback by the intensity of the old man's plea. "What's the big deal? Why can't you just tell me now?"

There was another pause. "Because there's something I have to show you," he replied.

"What sort of something?"

"I can't explain over the phone, but I'll tell you this much... the police won't be any use to you – not in this."

Martin frowned. It wasn't like Gerald to be so cryptic and he sounded genuinely afraid. Then he remembered one of the last things Paul had said to him in the playground yesterday morning – when he was still normal. He had told him to Google Austerly Fellows.

"Gerald," he said suddenly. "I have to go. I'll see you tomorrow."

Before the old man could answer, Martin put the phone down and ran upstairs. His own computer was splashed with blue paint so he sat down in front of Paul's.

The PC blinked on. Martin hesitated. What was he doing? Was he admitting there might be some supernatural explanation for these events?

"Ridiculous," he said aloud. "I'm just checking, that's all."

The Google search showed its results. Martin clicked on the Wikipedia article. The page appeared and Martin found himself staring at the black and white photograph of an unpleasant-looking man in monk's robes. He began to read.

Austerly Fellows (1879–1936) The self-styled 'Abbot of the Angles' and 'Grand Duke of the Inner Circle'...

Martin stopped. There was a spot of grime on the screen. He scratched at it, but it was beneath the glass. Then he noticed another – and another. As he stared at them, they increased in size and more began to bloom across the monitor. It was like mould, ugly black

mould. Within moments, it had spread over the whole screen, totally obliterating the Wikipedia page. Martin grabbed the mouse and dragged it round and punched at the keyboard, but the screen remained dark. Then he smelled a horrible reek of damp and decay. It was coming from inside the monitor. A thread of smoke rose from the back, followed by a snap and a spit of sparks. Martin jumped out of the chair and pulled the plugs from the wall.

"What the hell?" he exclaimed as crumbs of black fungus dripped from the monitor on to the desk. The man hurriedly left the room and slammed the door behind him.

"OK," he said. "Now I'm ready to believe!"

Carol drove aimlessly around the town. She had seen nothing for hours. Felixstowe was eerily silent. As she trawled through those empty streets, she became increasingly uneasy. The fear for her missing son was paramount in her mind, but gradually another thought nudged its way forward through that pain.

All of the houses she passed were dark, with drawn curtains, but many times, in the rear-view mirror, she thought she caught a movement in those dead windows. A curtain corner lifted or a blind swayed back into place. At first she told herself it was her imagination and then, when it happened more and more, she reasoned it was only natural for people to wonder who was driving by so slowly at such a late hour. But there was a furtiveness about it that wasn't normal. She never saw any faces. No lights were switched on. It was sly and stealthy, marking her progress through the town.

At half past two, when Carol was certain she had been observed from every house in one street, she stopped the car, slammed the heel of her hand on the horn for a full minute, then got out.

"I'm looking for my son!" she yelled at the top of her voice. "Have you seen him? Do you know where he is? Can anyone help me?"

The houses remained dark. No lights snapped on. No one appeared at the windows to see what the commotion was – and that, in itself, was sinister and threatening. Carol suddenly felt alone and afraid. She hurriedly jumped back into the driving seat, revved the engine and headed home.

Martin was dozing on the settee when she returned. The woman covered him with a coat and slid into the armchair opposite. How could she sleep, knowing Paul was out there somewhere? Only then did she realise that in all the time she had been out, she hadn't seen a single police car.

The hours before dawn crept slowly by.

At six o'clock sharp, she called the station. There was still no news. The policeman on the duty desk assured her that officers had been out searching for her son. Carol didn't believe a word of it and her responses were so angry they woke Martin in the next room.

Scratching his stubble, he came into the hall to find her staring at the phone – a look of disbelief and shock on her face.

"What's happened?" he asked, fearing the worst.

Carol turned to him slowly. "Nothing," she uttered. "Still no word, but…"

"But what?"

"The policeman just then… when he said goodbye, just before he rang off… he said, 'Blessed be'."

"My God," Martin murmured.

"I'm so scared," she said. "What's happening? I got spooked driving out there last night. I'm not paranoid. This thing, this madness, is getting bigger and bigger."

"Dancing Jacks," the man muttered. "Paul was right, you were right."

"What can we do?"

"Come and see Gerald with me. He's got something he wants to show us."

"What is it?"

"I don't know, but he was very insistent."

"I don't like the thought of no one being here in case Paul comes back," Carol said. "Look, I want to go and see my mother, make sure she's OK. Wait till I get home before going to Gerald's, OK?"

Martin agreed. After a shower and breakfast, he spent the rest of the morning clearing his inner sanctum. The debris filled seven bin bags. There was nothing worth keeping. Once he looked into Paul's bedroom. It smelled of damp in there and there was a patch of mould on his desk where the monitor had leaked. The man pulled the door shut and shivered.

Carol didn't return from her mother's until late in the afternoon.

On the way she had stopped off at the police station in the vain hope of finding someone who wasn't under the influence of that book, but she couldn't get past the officer on the desk. He had stared at her with large, dark eyes and assured her everything would be fine.

Her own eyes were sunken with grief and tiredness. In spite of her protests, Martin put her to bed. She would be no use to anyone if she didn't get some rest.

A little while later the maths teacher got in the car and drove through the town. For a Saturday afternoon, Felixstowe was very quiet. Martin only saw a handful of people going in and out of the shops and there was hardly any traffic on the roads. He reached Duntinkling, the guesthouse of Gerald Benning, in next to no time.

The muted sounds of the old man's piano greeted him as he stepped from the car. It was something tuneful by Ivor Novello. Martin recognised it from the movie Gosford Park. It was the only way he ever knew music, through soundtracks. He was a total ignoramus otherwise. He waited for the song to end, then pressed the bell.

Presently there came the sound of clipped footsteps ringing along the hallway and the front door opened.

Martin was halfway through saying hello when the word froze on his tongue. The person who had answered was not Gerald Benning. It was an elderly-looking woman with austerely coiffed steel-grey hair and horn-rimmed spectacles attached to a fine chain that looped around her neck. She wore an old-fashioned but smart

black evening dress and a double string of pearls with matching earrings. She looked at Martin with impatient curiosity.

The man blinked at her. He had seen her many times in his life, on the television and once in the theatre – Professor Evelyn Hole.

Martin's thoughts stumbled clumsily. Here was one half of Hole and Corner, the once famous double act. Gerald Benning and his late partner, Peter Drummond, had created two of the most endearing and fondly remembered characters in British entertainment. Hole and Corner were two genteel but vivacious spinsters. The act was simple and brilliant. They were supposed to be part of a musical quintet. The stage would be set with all five instruments, but the other three musicians never, ever turned up. There was always a different and hilarious reason for this and Hole and Corner would have to amuse the audience as they waited in vain for the others to arrive. They did this by relating funny anecdotes about their errant colleagues and performing songs in their absence, eventually playing each of the forsaken instruments themselves.

They were so successful at portraying these two temperamental but lovable old ladies from a bygone age that some people refused to believe that they were really two men in drag. In fact 'drag' was the wrong term entirely. This was no crude, 'I'm a Lady, I do Lady things' type of sketch that couldn't sustain interest for more than five minutes at a time. The illusion here was absolute. Their skill at weaving this convincing world made their audiences long to believe it was true and their policy of never giving interviews as their real selves helped it along enormously.

Martin continued to stare. He was trying to look through the impeccable, yet simple, make-up of the woman standing before him, to see if he could recognise anything of Gerald in there. But no, it really did stand up to close scrutiny. Carol had always warned him that if he was ever lucky enough to be introduced to 'Evelyn' then he had to obey certain rules. Staring with your mouth open, trying to see the joins in the disguise, was a definite shattering of rule number one.

"Yes, young man?" a female voice, not a bit like that of Gerald Benning, asked.

Martin hastily pulled himself together, but questions were gurgling through his mind. Why was Gerald dressed up like this? They had cancelled tonight's dinner over the phone yesterday, as soon as they told him Paul had run away. Then he recalled what Carol had once explained about 'Evelyn'.

The Hole and Corner act had been in existence for over thirty years and in that time Gerald and Peter had created a detailed and totally believable life and history – not just for those two characters and the always absent musicians, but also their whole world. When Peter had died, taking the querulous Bunty Corner (MBE) with him to the grave, Gerald found he couldn't kill off Evelyn. She had been such a massive part of his life for so long, he felt it would have been disloyal, even disrespectful, to pretend that she never existed. To him – and indeed to the millions who enjoyed their performances – she did. And so, every few months, Professor Evelyn Hole was allowed to breathe again, and enjoy the house she had paid for.

Carol had her own theory as to why Gerald had to keep his alter ego 'alive'. Yes, it was another way of keeping the memory of Peter fresh and close, but it wasn't just that. After imbuing Evelyn with such vivid life and energy for so long, perhaps she really had taken over a part of the old man's psyche and refused to be forgotten. She was bonded to his identity now. Anyone who was honoured enough to be let in to enjoy her company on these occasional reappearances understood that they had to maintain the illusion completely. Those who blundered, or were crass enough to try and catch her out, were never invited back.

"I'm Martin," the maths teacher said, remembering this basic premise, but still wondering why this charade was being played out. "A friend of Gerald's."

"Ah, yes," Professor Hole answered as though meeting him for the first time. "Carol's fiancé, the one who's frightfully clever at sums. I've heard so much about you from Gerald – all good I might add. Do come in."

Martin followed Evelyn into the large, airy house and she led him into the gleaming designer kitchen. She glanced sniffily at the brushed steel surfaces – the decor wasn't to her taste at all.

"I'm so deeply sorry to hear about my friend Paul," she told Martin. "Have you heard anything more?"

Martin shook his head. This was really weird. The walk, the mannerisms, the vocal inflections, the bird-like tilt of the neck, this really could be an old lady.

"Nothing from the police," he replied. "But Carol thinks they've

453

been got at by the book now as well."

Evelyn clasped her hands before her. "This is a deadly business," she said gravely. "You may not realise just how perilous it is. Typical of Gerald not to see the significance of it straight away when you first told him. The man's a perfect imbecile at times. I don't know why you and Carol put up with him."

Martin wasn't sure how to react to that.

"Gerald said he had something to show me," he said, really hoping it wasn't simply this performance. He had always wanted to meet Evelyn, but this wasn't an appropriate moment. There wasn't time for this today.

"I upbraided him for not going straight round to show it to you last night!" Evelyn declared. "But what's done is done. Let us hope it isn't too late."

"What isn't?"

"You must learn and understand what you're dealing with here," she told him. "That man, Austerly Fellows. Anything to do with him… is incalculably dangerous." She paused and pointed at the designer kettle. "Would you like a cup of tea? It may be an ugly thing, but it still boils water. Please don't ask me to make you a coffee. His machine looks like something from Flash Gordon."

"No, thanks."

"Then what are we doing in this hideous kitchen? Come along with me, Martin. Hurry – there's a lot to see."

She left the kitchen and entered the private part of the guesthouse. Martin followed, noticing the subtle changes that took place

454

whenever Evelyn was in residence. There were different photographs on the piano, including a large one of her and Bunty meeting the Queen after a Royal Variety Show, fresh flowers were arranged in porcelain vases that Gerald wouldn't give houseroom to and a Tiffany lamp shone a warm glow over the wall.

A large, black trunk was another foreign element in the room. Evelyn knelt before it and turned to Martin.

"Gerald has his uses," she began. "Before he departed this morning, I made him lug this old chest down from the attic. Before you see what it contains, allow me to explain…"

She waved Martin to a seat – one of Gerald's masculine leather armchairs that had been softened by draping a fringed shawl over it.

"Has Gerald ever told you where his family came from?" Evelyn asked.

"From round here, wasn't it?"

"Just so, and did he tell you what his grandparents did for a living, his grandmother in particular?"

"Don't think that ever came up. I don't see how this is relevant…"

Evelyn held up her hand. "You will," she explained. "Indulge me a little, I beg you." Resting her elbow on the lid of the trunk, she continued.

"Before she was married, Gerald's grandmother was in service. She was the upstairs maid in a grand house, owned by a very well-off country doctor – Bartholomew Fellows."

She let the name sink in before carrying on. "Imagine what this town was like, a hundred years ago," she said. "A thriving little resort with good connections to London, not just by rail but steamer too. Doctor Bartholomew had a very successful practice in the capital before he came to settle here. But his wife died young, leaving him only one heir."

"Austerly!"

"No, a clever little boy called Ezra. And then there was a scandal – the doctor remarried."

"Why was that so scandalous?"

"Because he married one of his servants. No, not Gerald's grandmother – the woman who was employed as nanny to little Ezra. In Victorian London society, such things simply were not done. It still raises eyebrows when that kind of thing happens today, so think how outraged people were back then. Doctor Bartholomew had no choice but to leave London altogether. He took his new bride and Ezra out to the Suffolk countryside, not far from Felixstowe, and that was when he discovered his new bride was not quite what she seemed."

"How do you mean?"

"The new Mrs Fellows, Nettie, was what was known in those days as a fallen woman. She already had a child of her own. She had been seduced by her previous employer and had kept the existence of the poor mite a complete secret by entrusting it to one of those disgusting baby farms – one of the grimmest places imaginable. They were squalid houses where old crones were paid to take in babies because society decreed it impossible for the mothers to keep them. They were terrible times. The shame and stigma of being an

456

unmarried mother was the ruin of many. Women would lose their jobs and their homes if such secrets were discovered and so there was no choice but to pay these greedy hags to mind the baby for them and visit the little mites as often as they could.

"Of course, those baby farmers weren't interested in the welfare of their charges. They could have dozens of infants under their roof at any given time and drugged them with laudanum to keep them quiet. If the children didn't sicken and die from neglect then they were starved to death or perished as a result of the powerful drugs stirred into their milk. It was nothing less than wholesale infanticide. Do you know, there were more laws about the keeping and mistreatment of livestock than there were for children. Anyone could become a baby farmer and advertise their services in the newspaper. Children had no rights at all. There's Victorian values for you."

Her fingers tapped out a tune from HMS Pinafore on the lid of the trunk. Then she sang the words.

A many years ago
When I was young and charming
As some of you may know
I practised baby farming.

She pursed her lips with displeasure and shuddered.

"The infant that Nettie had put into the 'care', for want of a better word, of one of those foul people was called Austerly."

Martin sat up, but Evelyn had not finished; there was still much more to tell him.

"When Doctor Bartholomew found out about Nettie's secret, he was incensed and accused her of marrying him under false pretences, but somehow she managed to calm him. What a character she must have been and how she must have had him wrapped around her finger in those first years. Bartholomew forgave her and even raised the boy as his own, bringing him to Suffolk to grow up alongside Ezra. Then a year later Nettie bore him a daughter, Augusta."

Evelyn gazed at the colours and shapes the Tiffany shade threw across the wall. "That's where Gerald's grandmother came in," she said. "She began working in the great house the doctor had bought near here and hated every moment of it."

"Why? Were they cruel to the servants?"

"Not cruel, but extremely strange, as you'll discover. It was a peculiar house. Bartholomew shelled out a considerable part of his fortune to remodel it in the high Gothic style he admired so much. But he was no architect and so it ended up an ugly, frightful place and the atmosphere within matched it perfectly. Nettie Fellows was never happy there, and her misery mounted with each passing season. She and Bartholomew grew apart and she eventually took to her bed and stayed in it for the rest of her life, never once moving from that room, until they came to carry her out. There were other macabre occurrences in that house and every year the shadows deepened."

"But what about Austerly?"

Evelyn took a deep breath and stared down at the trunk.

"When Gerald's grandmother married his grandfather," she said, "a year before Nettie died, in 1907, she was given this as a wedding present."

Evelyn lifted the heavy lid. It contained musty clothes. "A trunk full of cast-offs," she announced. "Gerald's grandfather was furious, but didn't dare say anything and appear ungrateful. They were so poor you see and had to make their way in the world and couldn't afford to insult the rich doctor in the big house. Anyway, he forbade Gerald's grandmother ever to wear any of these hand-me-downs. It didn't stop her looking at them though and that was how she came across this…"

Evelyn reached into the trunk – delving under the Victorian day dresses and broken corsets – and brought out a large photograph album.

"This may have been left in here by accident," she said. "But I don't think so. I think Nettie wanted someone else to see what her husband was really like."

She handed Martin the album and he glanced at the first page.

"Bartholomew took up the relatively new hobby of photography almost as soon as they moved in," she explained. "He turned one large room on the first floor into a studio and made the adjoining one his darkroom. He fancied himself as something of an artist and roped many of the household in to take part in historical tableaux so he could photograph them. Have you ever seen such wretched expressions? Nobody is enjoying that."

Martin studied the sepia pictures. They showed uncomfortable-looking people decked out in crudely made costumes wielding wooden spears and swords, in ridiculous poses.

"There," Evelyn said when Martin turned the page. The next image was of two young boys.

The eldest could only have been about seven years old. He sat astride a rocking horse, his face in profile, holding a sword out in front as if charging at an enemy. The other boy could have been no more than four. He stood alongside, in a sailor suit, staring straight at the camera. It was a striking face. Martin had seen those penetrating eyes before; last night before Paul's computer had blown up.

"That's Austerly," he said.

"Yes, that's him. There are a few more of him with Ezra or his sister, but always the same intensity of expression – did you ever see such eyes?"

"It's as though he's looking right through the lens, right at me," Martin murmured, shifting uneasily.

"Indeed. He was a horrible child. As he grew, his nature showed itself more and more. He would torture pets for pleasure. Once he took hold of Augusta's canary and squeezed the life out of it because he didn't like its song. He was inhumanly cruel, but fiercely intelligent. Now turn the page and see the other sort of pictures Doctor Bartholomew enjoyed taking."

Martin did so and his eyebrows lifted high into his forehead.

"Quite," Evelyn said, reading his reaction.

These photographs were of scantily-dressed women masquerading

as historical or mythical figures. Some of them weren't wearing any clothes at all.

"Are these the servants as well?" he asked. "What a dirty doctor."

"No, I think they were from the village. Gerald's grandmother certainly didn't recognise them as being part of the household. Imagine how shocking that would have been at the time when even the sight of a bare leg was enough to cause outrage. No wonder Nettie fell out with him."

Martin leafed through several more saucy pages. Then he paused when he saw a much more formal, and clothed, portrait of a severe-looking woman sitting stiffly on a chair with Ezra and Austerly on either side. The boys were a few years older now.

"Is that Nettie?" he asked. "She's younger than I thought – and just look at Austerly's face. It's thunderous."

"Oh, no, that isn't Nettie," Evelyn corrected. "That was the new governess, Grace Staplethorpe. You're right about Austerly though. He detested her. She was very strict and denied him the freedom he had been used to. The other servants didn't like her much either. She was a highly-strung, self-righteous zealot and totally unsuitable for that position. She staunchly believed in the fire and brimstone of the Bible and was determined to put the fear of God into the Fellows children."

"Did she succeed?"

Evelyn regarded him over the rim of her spectacles. "Quite the reverse," she stated sombrely.

"How do you mean?"

"Martin, slide that photograph from its securers and turn it over."

The man obeyed and saw that it had been written on. Brown-black ink flowed across the back of the photograph in confident, copperplate handwriting.

When I was six, Grace Grace of the sour stony face entered my life and the mutual loathing was immediate.

Martin glanced up in astonishment. Evelyn nodded slowly.

"Yes," she said. "That is the handwriting of Austerly Fellows. At some point, I think when he was about ten or eleven, he found this album and wrote on the back of the photographs. Most of his notes are pure filth, but this, and another, are… illuminating."

Martin read on.

I hated her as I had hated no other previously. She punished me far more frequently than she did Ezra. She beat me with fervour and told me stories of hell and damnation. And so, after only two months, I determined to systematically destroy her and commenced a campaign against her sanity. She tried to make me fear the power of heaven so I vowed to terrorise her with the certain might of the Devil and all his works. I whispered and worked at her. I made her believe demons were coming to claim her. I put dead things in her bed, drew uncharms in her shoes, wrote infernal menaces in her ditchwater diary and made a talisman to attract dark elements. I sewed this into her pillow and her nightmares were exquisite. How I loved to hear her screaming in the silent watches of the night. I was so artful that, within one lunar month, victory was mine…

Martin put the photograph down.

"What did he mean by that?" he asked.

Evelyn leaned over and took the album from him. She turned to the next page and removed another photograph, trying not to look at it. Turning it around, she read from the back.

Behold my triumphant face. I can recall, quite distinctly, the sheer elation of that day. This was my first thrill of tangible power – my first murder of a human being.

Evelyn frowned and the photograph fell from her fingers.

"That morning," she explained, "Grace Staplethorpe was found hanging in the stables. Before Doctor Bartholomew called the police, the ghoulish man photographed her and called upon the children to assist him. This despicable picture is of the six-year-old Austerly grinning gleefully into the camera as he holds her legs steady so the image did not blur. I don't think you want to see it."

"No, I don't. What sort of a horror was he?"

"As an adult, he was even worse," Evelyn said. "When he finally inherited the big house, he pronounced himself the Abbot of the Angles and practised all manner of terrible things in there. He founded horrible cults and made that place a byword for evil. You weren't brought up in these parts, Martin. You never heard the bogey stories that were whispered about it. He was one of the Devil's own, there's no doubt about that."

"Devil worshipper?"

"Oh, yes. Gerald's grandmother heard frightful stories from the servants she kept in touch with, before he replaced them with foreigners he brought back with him from the East. He was the fiend of the neighbourhood, a reputation he justly deserved. It was said he had sold his soul to the Devil, but I don't think he'd had one to begin with. One night, in 1936, he held a special gathering of his most infernal group…"

"What happened?"

"No one knows. The nearby villages felt the ground shudder and heard screams coming from the house. Those who were brave enough ran to see what had happened and saw figures in coloured robes fleeing for their lives through the woods. Austerly Fellows disappeared that night. No one who survived the experience ever told what had occurred. A number of them, including Augusta, his sister, had been driven insane. But the rumour spread through the villages that Austerly had called up the Devil that night. At first they thought Old Nick had taken him down to you know where, but as time went by, word got about that Austerly's presence was still very much in the house. He's been there ever since, biding his time, waiting and watching."

There was a silence. Martin leaned back in the armchair.

"No," he said at length. "I can't believe that. That's what Paul

464

was trying to say. Devils and demons? It's not possible."

"And where is Paul now? He believed – and the book of Austerly Fellows got him. Don't underestimate the power of words, Martin. For thousands of years sacred writings have ruled the world. Don't you think Austerly Fellows knew this? Don't you think he would have attempted to write his own powerful book to do the same? A Devil's Testament – an unholy writ."

"But Dancing Jacks is for kids."

"So was the gingerbread house where the witch lived, the witch who wanted to eat Hansel and Gretel. Don't dismiss something simply because it's aimed at children, Martin. It can be just as deadly – if not more so. The earliest fairy tales were extremely gruesome and sadistic. Besides, what do the Catholics say? 'Give me a boy until the age of seven and I'll show you the man.' Indoctrination begins with the young, Martin. Austerly Fellows was merely following a proven pattern with his insidious children's book."

Martin glanced out of the window. They had been speaking so long, it had grown dark outside. "Do you think Paul might be at that house?" he asked.

"You can't go there!" Evelyn cried.

"I certainly can't if you don't tell me where it is."

"I won't do that, Martin."

"Please. For Paul's sake – for Carol's!"

Evelyn wrung her hands and squeezed her eyes shut.

"If you're going then I'm coming with you," she announced.

Martin laughed grimly. "That house is no place for a lady," he said. "Besides, I need you to call Carol and tell her where I've gone. I don't have a mobile any more."

"Martin, don't go there!"

"We both know that I have to. Who else is there? I can't call the police. Can you think where else Paul might be, because I can't. If there are any answers in that house then I've got to find them."

Evelyn placed the photograph album back in the trunk and closed the lid. "Very well," she said. "But remember this: possibly the greatest danger you face is the one you're taking with you. There is still doubt in your eyes, still disbelief that this can be happening. You must understand how real this is and know that there are such forces in the world. Austerly Fellows was no ordinary person, no ordinary man. He may not even have been human – his mother, Nettie, knew. That's why she took to her bed."

"Hang on, I don't understand. What are you saying? Not human?"

"Nettie broke down once and confessed to my… to Gerald's grandmother. The infant she had entrusted to the baby farmer had had a birthmark on his knee. The child she had brought home to Felixstowe from there didn't. No one knows what happened to the real Austerly, but one thing is certain, the creature who grew up in that big ugly house wasn't him. It was a monster."

How deep do the roots of the minchet tree reach? Down to the secret darkness, beyond the glistening paths of grave maggots and further yet. Past old dry bones, past forgotten tombs of ancient chieftains, down into the unlit caverns of the Old World... where the pets are waiting.

28

THE ROADS OUT of Felixstowe were empty that evening. Martin followed the directions Evelyn had reluctantly given him – past Trimley St Mary and turn right before reaching Trimley St Martin. As he drove, the dark emptiness of the open farmland streaking by, he tried to make sense of everything he had been told. He couldn't. It was too big, too frightening to dwell on. What he had to do was concentrate on Paul. The rest of it, Dancing Jacks and the evil of Austerly Fellows, were things he could worry about once the boy had been found. Then he would fetch Carol and they would all drive as far from this crazy mess as possible.

Evelyn had told him to be careful not to miss the final turning. It was in a country lane, hemmed in by thick woods and easy to overlook. The beams of the car's headlights swept over crowded tree trunks, causing black shadows to dart and fly between them. Martin passed the turning three times and wasted almost an hour trying to find it.

Before he began the journey up the long drive to the Fellows' house, he switched off the lights. The car crawled and bumped along the pitted track. It ran for almost half a mile. The trees that lined the drive bent inwards overhead, forming a tangled tunnel. It was so dark and the surface so full of potholes that Martin began to wonder if this was the right way after all. Then the trees began to thin. He saw the night sky once more and up ahead, stark and solid against it, the ominous shape of the ugliest building he had ever seen.

Suddenly a dark figure reared up in front of the windscreen. Martin braked and let out a cry of surprise. Then he leaned upon the steering wheel and laughed at himself. It was only a tree: the drive was so neglected that it was growing right up through the middle of it.

Taking a torch from the glove compartment and slipping it into the pocket of his jacket, Martin got out of the car. He had intended to leave the vehicle a little distance from the house anyway. He didn't want the noise of its approach to alert whoever might be waiting inside that place. "Or whatever," he couldn't resist adding.

Stepping stealthily through the weeds, he drew closer to the house. It seemed to swell in size before him. Martin hadn't realised just how frightened he would be. He wished he was a million miles

away from this awful place. He could feel the fear clenching itself around him. His heart was punching against his chest and cold sweat was trickling down his neck.

"Stupid, stupid, stupid…" he murmured under his breath.

Staring up at those blank, boarded windows, he felt the terror manifest in his stomach and was almost sick with it. The bravest thing he ever did was to continue.

Martin lowered his eyes and looked at the front door; it was half open. Was he expected?

He tried to think of the most inspiring adventure movies he had ever seen. The ones whose heroes would have cracked a bullwhip and gone charging into such a place with a wisecracking one-liner ready on their lips. But he didn't have a whip and he couldn't think of anything remotely pithy to say. He was just a geeky maths teacher, not Indiana Jones.

"Phasers on stun, Baxter," he told himself instead. "Hell! Who are you kidding… Exterminate – exterminate!"

In the end, it was the thought of Carol, suffering without Paul, that propelled him on. He pushed the front door fully open and stepped inside.

It was pitch-dark, but he waited many minutes before reaching for the torch. The house was filled with silence and the awful stink of damp: the same smell of dripping decay that had flowed from the monitor of Paul's PC. It was so quiet. Martin could only hear the thump of the blood in his ears.

He took out the torch and prayed that nothing horrific was going to be revealed when he switched it on. In fact, nothing at all would be great too. Gripping the cold metal cylinder in his hand, it reminded him of a lightsaber pommel. That thought brought him a crumb of comfort. He assumed the correct Jedi stance, said "Zummmmm!" and clicked it on.

An instant later its circle of light was sweeping over a staircase. Humming the sound effects, Martin waved the beam around the large hall. What a place, what a sinister, unwelcoming nightmare of a place.

Taking small, wary steps, he moved further inside. The loose parquet floor rattled and clacked as he trod on it.

"Paul?" he hissed. "Are you in here, Paul?"

The lack of any reply was actually a relief. Martin peered into the first of the reception rooms. The empty armchair and card table were still there. They gave him the horrible feeling that someone was used to sitting there. He withdrew smartly and closed the door behind him. The torchlight fell across the open doorway beneath the stairs. He dared to look down into the darkness that led to the cellar and hoped he wouldn't have to venture down there tonight. How much worse could this expedition become? This was beyond the most nerve-shredding scene in any movie: the suspense of the unknown – the terrors hidden in the darkness…

"I've seen far too many films," he berated himself.

The next door revealed a long room lined with empty shelves. Apparently this had once been the library. He wondered where the books had gone and what kind of diabolical works had someone like

Austerly Fellows read anyway. The torch revealed another door at the far end of the room. Martin approached it cautiously. The torchlight wobbled over the peeling varnish because he couldn't stop his hand trembling. It kindled a dull gleam in the brass knob. He twisted it and shone the light inside.

The reek of cold, rotting decay was suddenly overpowering. It fell on him like a wall. Martin covered his mouth and nose and blinked in surprise and revulsion. Then he stared before him, incredulous and amazed.

Along the entire length of the house at the rear was a grand Victorian conservatory. It was like a slice of the Crystal Palace. Wrought-iron girders towered upwards, curling under, beneath the arched ceiling, like gigantic fern fronds. The white paint was flaking off them, but they remained an impressive spectacle. Martin couldn't begin to count how many panes of glass it took to fill the gaps between. Some of them were smashed and the rest were caked in the grime of many decades, but the lower portion of the structure had been boarded over, preventing too much vandalism. When new, it must have been like a diamond cathedral.

Martin's eyes wandered off the overblown ironwork, and he looked at the workbenches that ran along both sides of the conservatory. He brought the torch beam down to bear on them. Deep trays and troughs crowded the surfaces. He went over for a closer inspection. They were filled with black earth, or was it mould? Whatever it was, this was where the atrocious smell originated. It was like a dank and fetid grave. Martin grimaced. Then he realised that there was something else in those planters. Black stems poked from that reeking soil. Something had been growing there and had very recently been harvested. He checked further along the bench. Yes, every tray contained some form of weird stalk. From a huge pot that dominated one corner, a straggling black vine had been carefully trailed through the ironwork, along the full length of the conservatory. Whatever fruit it had borne had also been removed; only a few unhealthy-looking leaves remained. Martin couldn't imagine anything wholesome could grow in such disgusting soil.

Swinging the light from side to side, he walked down the central aisle. Towards the end he halted and swore. The torch had flashed over a heap of small glass jars. The same type of jars that had contained the minchet he had confiscated from his pupils. Next to them was a large plastic bowl, smeared and greasy inside.

"You should have seen this place yesterday," a voice said abruptly.

The maths teacher spun round. Standing at the door of the library was the man he had seen at the boot fair last Sunday – the one Shiela Doyle had called the Ismus.

Dressed from head to toe in sable velvet, the ferrety-looking man stepped into the centre of the conservatory and three burly bodyguards with blackened faces followed him.

"It was such an incredible sight," he continued. "Everything was ripe and luscious – positively fecund. What a bumper harvest we had, what an abundance of flying ointment the Queen of Hearts made."

Martin gripped the torch more tightly and breathed hard. But, to

472

his surprise, he realised he was no longer frightened. If the worst he had to face in here were four blokes then he had been fretting needlessly. It was the unknown that scared him. In fact, he felt good and angry – and ready.

"What's in that junk?" he demanded.

The Ismus chuckled. "Not what you thought was in it," he replied. "Just old-fashioned unnatural ingredients. A liberal dollop of harmless grease, mixed with the juice of some fruits grown here, that's all. What a fool you made of yourself, Mr Teacher. There's nothing from my garden that can be analysed by your science and there's certainly nothing habit-forming in it. Only the sacred text is addictive, you silly man. The minchet fruit merely opens the way and keeps the link connected. You would find it most agreeable. But there's no, how would you say… nutritional value in its pulpy flesh. Not for humans anyway. No – it is to nourish those things which are yet to come through."

"Things? What things?"

"They're all in my book," the Ismus said with a cold smile. "In one form or other. Soon they'll be walking amongst us and people will be glad. Their presence here will reinforce their belief that the world of Mooncaster really exists and make this place far less… humdrum."

"Look," Martin interrupted, " I don't pretend to understand what the hell is going on with you and the rest of this…"

"Why should it matter if you do? You're of no importance, Mr Baxter."

"I just want to find Paul."

"Paul?"

"You know who I'm talking about – Paul Thornbury. He's only a child."

"A child?" the Ismus scoffed. "There are no children in this world any more. You dress and treat them as mini-adults. You let little girls play with dolls that look like Berlin prostitutes. The morality and hypocrisy I used to find so stomach-turning no longer exist. You foist on to your young people role models whose brains are never as active as their underwear, and whose talents or achievements extend only as far as the bedroom door and the ability to blurt every detail of what happens behind it. You give your precious offspring access to a lightning-fast network of corruption and danger. You immerse them in computer games far more violent than the most savage and dirty war, and target prepubescents with inappropriate music and imagery – giving them a vocabulary that would have revolted sailors back in my day. There are no stigmas, no taboos, no boundaries, no respect and certainly no innocence left. To be pregnant at thirteen is no longer an everlasting shame, merely a career choice.

"If ever there was a need for Dancing Jacks and my rule of law, it is now. This chaotic degradation is on its knees and crying out for order. It was right to delay publication of the sacred text. The world was not ready in 1936. Back then people still knew who they were. They had their own identities and were proud of them. No one likes anything about themselves now: the way they look, their jobs, where

they live. They need to be told what to wear, what to eat, how to decorate their homes, then they painstakingly trace their ancestors in the hope the joys or struggles of the past will give their own defunct lives purpose and meaning... such a conglomeration of moribund, unhappy failures."

"Just tell me!" Martin yelled fiercely. "Paul Thornbury – have you got him?"

The man's crooked smile never wavered. "There is no such person, Mr Baxter," he said. "That boy you knew ceased to be when he assumed the prime role of the Jack of Diamonds. What a resourceful lad he was though. You and his mother should be proud of what he managed to accomplish. He gave me a very royal runaround, resisted the pull of the sacred text and even burned one of them – most impressive for a small lad like him and all on his own too. Shame on you for not listening when he needed your guidance and protection most of all. What a lot of suffering you could have saved yourselves. If you'd paid attention and put two and two together, you might even have escaped the inevitable... for a little while at least. Such a pity you didn't add everything up until it was too late, Mr Teacher."

He held out his hand and one of the bodyguards passed him three objects. Martin recognised them immediately: his phaser, sonic screwdriver and teleport bracelet.

"Magpie Jack brought me your 'jools'," the Ismus said, regarding the items from the inner sanctum with derision. "What a sad case you are, Mr Baxter. How could you set any value on this piffling dross? Infantile rubbish all of it. You really have wasted your life, haven't you?"

Martin ignored the insults. "Where is he?" he demanded. "What have you done with him?"

"Done with him?" The Ismus laughed. "Why, nothing at all. The Jack of Diamonds is where he belongs, with the Court. And I gave him a fresh copy of the book as a reward for his diligence. At this moment he's happier than he ever was before. You should be glad for him. He is now one of my four original Knaves. He will be famous. Children all over the world will look up to him. Boys whose personalities are similar will view him with envy. He is their paragon, the ideal they must emulate. He doesn't need you any longer. He doesn't want to see you ever again. You're nothing to him, just someone in the grey dream away from his real life at Mooncaster."

"You can't do this, you can't take kids away from their families!"

"He came full willing. Besides, you're not his father, Mr Baxter, merely his mother's latest, now what is the current term…? Ah, yes, merely her latest 'squeeze'."

Martin could feel his face burning with rage. "His mother wants him home!" he shouted. "If you don't take me to him right now, I'll go to the police and I don't mean the ones in Felixstowe. Your sacred bloody text won't have spread as far as Ipswich yet."

The Ismus tutted and placed the three objects on the workbench.

"I think not," he said. "You see, you won't be leaving this place without sampling some of the Queen of Hearts' hard work. She's been so industrious – I insist you try some."

476

"Stick it!" Martin told him.

"You aberrants really are monotonously irritating," the Ismus said, slipping a hand into the pocket of his tailed jacket and holding up a full jar. "Still, a small dab of this and you'll be one of us. I wonder what role you're best suited to in the Dawn Prince's Kingdom? I do hope it's Dung-Breathed Billy – the Midden-Man. He was cursed by the witch to receive fifty kicks a day, every day, from the villagers. You'll suit those bruises, Mr Baxter."

He unscrewed the lid of the jar and took a step closer.

Martin tensed. He wondered how long he would last in the imminent fight. Not long against the four of them, but he would do as much damage to that Ismus lunatic as possible before those black-faced minders dragged him off.

The Ismus read his intention and laughed scornfully. "Have you learned nothing yet?" he asked. "Aren't you the one who teaches by repetition? You drill and drill the same things into those poor young heads every week and yet you refuse to be taught in the same way. So pig-headed. After everything you've heard. You're a very stupid creature to even dare think of raising a hand against me. I am the Holy Enchanter of Mooncaster, the Ismus, the owner of this house, the author of Dancing Jacks – I am Austerly Fellows!"

"You're insane!" Martin snapped back. "You're not him!"

The Ismus's grin became wider. "Oh, but I am!" he said. "I am!"

He threw his arms wide and Martin stared in horror as dark spots of mould blotched across the pale skin of the man's face and hands. Thick streams of spores shot out from his sleeves, striking the boarded-up windows on his left and the bricks of the house on his right. Foaming waves of mould gushed upwards, racing high until they streaked across the pitched ceiling and met in the centre where they blossomed into a festering, clotted cloud that throbbed and pulsed above their heads.

The torch fell from Martin's hand. The lingering vestiges of doubt were finally banished from his mind. The three bodyguards cast their eyes downward and bowed, calling out praise to the Holy Enchanter.

"I have been so very patient," the Ismus said, but the voice was not human and seemed to emanate from the heart of that grotesque, swelling growth above.

"Waiting so long for the right time and the right person," it continued. "But my Prince was right to make me wait. There was never a better moment than now. Your world is empty and starving, little man. Dancing Jacks will fill it – all of it. There will be no other Word but mine."

Martin was too horror-stricken to move or say anything. The black mould spread across the windows and clustered over the cast iron, furring the girders, and fine, hair-like filaments formed branching webs across the gaps.

The Ismus turned his mould-bloomed face to Martin and held out the jar of minchet.

"Take it," the cloud commanded. "Lick it."

Martin was too terrified to refuse. His spirit was completely quashed. He could not fight this. Nothing in the world could. He reached out a tremulous hand and took the jar.

The mould frothed and bulged overhead and violent ripples surged over the encrusted wall and windows.

"Do it," the voice instructed.

Martin scooped a large glob on his trembling fingers and lifted them to his mouth.

The cloud quivered and spores rained down. A curtain of mould stretched to each of the Ismus's shoulders, forming huge, bat-like wings. "Join us," the gurgling voice of Austerly Fellows cried.

Martin closed his eyes and took a last breath. He thought of Carol and wished he had been able to save her and Paul. He put the sickly grey-green ointment to his lips.

Then there was a smashing of glass and a roar of heat and flame. The bodyguards cried out and leaped back. Something had been hurled through one of the windows. The Ismus spun round. A pool of liquid fire was spreading over the floor. Another pane exploded inward and a second fiery missile crashed against the wall.

Martin thrust his hand under his armpit and wiped the disgusting minchet from his fingers. Someone was outside. Someone was saving him!

The Ismus yelled. Flames were crackling all about him. The bloated cloud above gave a fearsome rumble, then came streaking down, pouring on to the Holy Enchanter's back. It flowed up over the velvet collar of his jacket and retreated down into his neck.

Outside the conservatory a loud voice let loose a mocking laugh. "Haw haw haw!" it sang into the night.

Hearing that, the Ismus vaulted over the flames and jumped on to

479

the workbench. He stared through the broken panes and searched the darkness outside.

"Jockey!" he shouted. "I know you're there!"

Martin didn't know what to do. The bodyguards had removed their coats and were thrashing the flames with them. He was cornered with no escape. Suddenly, behind him, the boarding was prised clear of the windows. A brick came flying through the glass, followed by a caramel-coloured boot that kicked the remaining shards away.

"Haw haw haw!" the unknown man guffawed again and then, in a falsetto voice, he sang, "I rode you, I rid you. I flamed you, I fled you! Hoo hoo hoo!"

Martin saw a glimpse of someone in a leather costume, the same colour as the boot, skip away from the freshly made hole. The figure darted over the tumbledown wall of the kitchen garden and vanished into the dark.

The maths teacher hesitated only for an instant. Then he seized his chance and squeezed though the empty frame.

"My Lord Ismus!" one of the Black Face Dames shouted. "The aberrant is escaping!"

The Holy Enchanter was still staring at the spot where the Jockey had disappeared. "Why hasn't he come forward?" he raged. "He'll pay for this when he does. I'll make him sing a sorry song. I won't be ridden! I won't! He'll dance to my tune, not his own."

"The aberrant!" the bodyguard repeated. "He's getting away."

The Ismus leaped from the bench. The fire was almost out.

Leaving one of the Dames to finish the job, he took the other two and ran through the house.

"He won't get far!" he promised. "There's no saving the teacher now."

Martin charged around the building, down the side alley and dashed for the driveway. They'd be coming after him. He had to jump in the car and tear out of here. He'd drive to Ipswich and head straight for the police station. He would have to do everything he could to convince them while trying not to sound like a crazy person. They had to be made to believe and understand just how dangerous and real this was. The situation here had grown so big. They might even have to call in the army.

But, haring over the weed-covered drive, he saw a sight that made his heart sink and dashed any hopes of escape. The Ismus's camper van had pulled up right behind his car. Reaching the vehicles, he found the car completely blocked in. With the tree directly in front and the van almost touching the back bumper, there was no way he could get it out of there.

"Dammit!" he cursed, glaring at the Volkswagen and thumping its rusting side.

Suddenly a ferocious, bestial clamour sounded within the van. The camper juddered and rocked wildly from side to side. There was a tremendous crunch and a dent punched up into the roof.

Martin jumped backwards. What the hell was in there? A wild bull? An angry rhinoceros? The van lurched and jolted. Then a curtain was torn from one of the windows. Martin yelled out loud.

A grotesque, oversized face pressed against the glass. Two bright yellow eyes with small, red-rimmed pupils fixed on him. The window clouded over as steaming breath snorted up from the creature's flattened nostrils. The van's side banged and pounded as wide shoulders lowered and the head bent down. Two curling horns battered against the sliding door.

Martin did not see them. He was already stumbling down the drive, running for his life.

The Ismus and the men who had been Tesco Charlie and Dave sprang from the house. The bodyguards were about to set off after the terrified maths teacher, but the Ismus held them back.

"No," he said, observing the van's violent shaking. "Let us be generous and give Mauger something bigger than rabbits to catch this night."

Darting to the camper, he wrenched the buckled door open and the monstrous shape leaped out. It gouged the grass with its claws and bellowed a horrendous roar.

"After him, my pet," the Ismus commanded. "Go, hunt him down. He is yours!"

The horrific beast snapped at the air then bolted down the driveway.

"That's the best way to deal with aberrants," the Holy Enchanter laughed.

In the darkness of the overgrown drive, Martin heard the bestial roar and knew the creature was chasing him. The maths teacher had never been good at sport, his mind and imagination were the most

482

active and agile parts of him, but at that moment he ran faster than he ever had in his life.

He didn't dare look back. He didn't have to. He could hear the nightmare pursuing him. He could tell it was gaining. The snorts and growls and clashing of teeth were quickly growing louder. Martin pushed himself harder than ever, but it was no use. Then, in that tree-enclosed gloom, his foot hooked under the arch of a protruding root. A cry of dismay burst from his lips and he crashed to the ground.

Mauger bounded towards him. The man lay there, winded and panting. The demon sprang and Martin knew it was over.

In that instant a glimmering missile came spinning from the trees. It was another of those fiery bottle bombs. It struck Mauger's powerful back and erupted in flames. The monster shrieked and came thundering through the air. It landed back on the drive, barely missing Martin, then went rolling down the sloping way, writhing and bawling, engulfed in fire.

Martin lifted his face and stared at it, incredulous. The beast was thrashing about wildly, screeching and yowling.

Then, from the trees, a stern voice hissed, "Get up, man! Run – you idiot!"

Martin turned, just in time to see that same caramel-coloured outfit nip back into the shadows.

"Thank you!" he called. But the figure was gone and all he heard was a high "Haw haw haw!" trailing into the distance.

Mauger's frantic struggles were almost over. The thick fur of its

gorilla-like arms was now only smoking and the fires that burned across its back were almost extinguished.

Martin realised he had waited too long. He leaped to his feet and, with his heart in his mouth, he pelted past the smouldering horror. Mauger's unwieldy head swung around and the glowering yellow eyes watched the man race by. Two great claws clamped around the last burning patch of fur and smothered it. A fearsome snarl drew its red lips back over purple gums and a loud, rumbling growl sounded deep in the drum of its chest. The eyes flicked momentarily at the trees. The smell of new leather was strong on the air and the river of that scent wound far into the woods and out again. The Jockey could wait.

Mauger lumbered on to all fours and shook itself. Singed and burned, it was even more horrific a nightmare than before – and now it was enraged beyond control or recall.

Shaking its horns, the demon roared louder than ever and leaped after Martin. Very soon it would be feasting on aberrant flesh.

Martin's trousers were ripped at the knee and a deep cut across his shin was singing as he ran. Blood was running down his leg and he knew the creature behind could smell it. He tore down that forgotten driveway without a thought of what he would do next. Fear alone drove him now. Then he was clear. The drive ended. He flung himself forward, out on to the remote country lane beyond. The smooth surface of the road felt jarring under his feet after the rough slope of the drive. He staggered and slipped, but didn't stop. The demon was closing.

Martin ran blindly, charging down the centre of the deserted lane. It was the middle of nowhere, with nowhere to run – and no shelter. In the far distance, he could see the lights of houses, but he would never reach them in time. Behind him there was an exultant cry and the fiend came rampaging out on to the road. Its claws clattered and skated on the tarmac for a moment then it wheeled around and the fury-filled eyes shone down the lane – on Martin's desperate and hopeless fleeing figure.

The jagged fangs dripped in anticipation and Mauger stampeded after.

Martin heard it, and for no other reason than to drown out that awful approach, he shouted. "Help! Help me someone – help me!"

And then, to his undying relief, there was light and noise. A car horn blared behind them. Headlights dazzled and a car came racing up the lane.

Mauger spun about. The light blinded its eyes and it shrieked in pain. Its claws flew before its face to shield it from the glare and the demon stumbled sideways into the hedge. The car horn continued to sound.

Martin had not dared to stop running, but he looked over his shoulder, squinting into the harsh lights. The car was almost upon him. He jumped to the verge and the vehicle braked sharply. The passenger door was pushed open and the strident tones of Professor Evelyn Hole were telling him to get in.

Moments later Martin was inside, huffing and wheezing and clutching his stinging knee. Evelyn's sensible brogue stamped on the accelerator and the car screeched away.

In the rear-view mirror she saw Mauger jump back into the road and give chase.

"So much for the thirty mile an hour limit," she said as the speedometer nudged up to sixty, then seventy. The demon's monstrous shape receded and was soon lost in the darkness behind. A desolate, bone-numbing howl of frustration echoed across the open fields.

Evelyn waited until Martin was ready to speak.

"Thank you," he said eventually. "If you hadn't turned up just then…"

"Did you really think I'd let you go off to that hellish place alone, dear boy?"

"Then it was you, dressed as the Jockey? You really had them fooled back there – and me!"

"I'm not with you."

"You didn't rescue me from the conservatory? You didn't throw those Molotov cocktails? You weren't dressed in that strange get-up?"

"Strange get-up?" Evelyn asked in surprise. "Martin, what do you take me for? Who is this Jockey you're talking about?"

The maths teacher didn't know whether she was teasing him and wished Gerald hadn't chosen today to let Evelyn take over. He glanced at the back seat, expecting to see the Jockey's discarded leather costume. It was empty. Perhaps the outfit was in the boot.

Martin stared at the dark road ahead, trying to make sense of everything.

"I saw him," he said after a short silence. "I spoke to him. Austerly Fellows. It's all true."

"Did you find out about Paul?"

"He's got him."

"Then there's nothing we can do on our own," Evelyn told him flatly. "We have to get out of Felixstowe tonight. We have to get help from outside. It's our only chance. Everyone's only chance."

Martin was thinking hard. "No," he said. "There might be just one last hope. But it'll have to wait till first thing tomorrow."

"We shouldn't wait, Martin."

"We have to."

"Very well, if you're sure. But you and Carol can't spend another night at your place. It won't be safe. You'd best stay with me – at Gerald's."

Martin agreed. Then for the first time he realised something – the Ismus had gone to that old house expecting to find him there. Why else would he have brought the things Paul had taken from the inner sanctum? But who else except Evelyn had known Martin was going there that night? Who else could have told the Ismus?

Martin stole a quick, suspicious glance at the person behind the wheel. A determined and grave expression was on Evelyn's face. He wondered what else that make-up and wig might be concealing. Martin Baxter suddenly realised he couldn't trust anybody.

29

"...AND WE'LL HAVE more of those scandalous allegations involving the England team later in the programme for you. But first it's over to Felixstowe again where Lyndsay Draymore reports on the special memorial service being held there today – Lyndsay."

"Yes, a very sad day here in Felixstowe this Sunday morning, Tara. Nine days ago, this Suffolk town was torn apart by what has gone down in history as the Felixstowe Disaster, when a car, driven by fifteen-year-old Daniel Marlow, ploughed into a crowd of young people and exploded. Daniel and his three passengers died almost immediately, but there were a total of forty-one fatalities as a result of that night. The police are still no closer to discovering the cause of that terrible crash. Today the first eight funerals will be taking place – all of them pupils who attended the High School here."

"Now that's the school that the press have labelled 'Yob School', isn't it, Lyndsay?" the anchorwoman interrupted, edging forward on her seat behind the news desk and jabbing her pen at the green screen where the reporter was superimposed. Tara's ardent pen-jabbing was one of her trademarks, a mannerism which the impressionist Jan Ravens always mimicked so mercilessly. It was important to have a personable gimmick when reading the news, so the viewers could enjoy a more rounded experience while watching. Tara had practised hers so much that now it looked completely natural and she was sure it would lead to other presenting jobs higher up the ladder within the corporation.

"The tabloids really have had a field day with this during the past week," she continued, stabbing away like a mini-musketeer. "Felixstowe has hardly been out of the news. First the Disaster and then the male nurse who ran amok, before throwing himself out of a hospital window. And, of course, the revelations about the Headteacher at the school. The tabloids really laid into him, didn't they?"

"That's right, Tara. The tabloids showed no restraint there and branded him 'the Dead Drunk Head'. In a special report later tonight, we'll be profiling Barry Milligan and interviewing members of his staff, the board of governors and the Education Minister – who has been one of his harshest critics over this past week. In that programme we also speak to his ex-wife for the inside story of his broken marriage and reveal that Mr Milligan has a history of violence and intimidation towards his staff and students. So it comes as no surprise to discover that he has been persuaded to step down from his job. However, the question on every one's lips must surely be – why did it take the deaths of forty-one young people for that decision to be made and if Barry Milligan had been 'expelled' earlier, could this Disaster have been averted?"

"A sobering thought, Lyndsay – if you'll excuse the pun."

Lyndsay Draymore gave her professional grin then remembered she was standing in a churchyard with mourners milling around behind her. Her face locked down into serious mode and she nodded gravely to camera.

Tara let her flounder a few moments longer than necessary. "But there has been an unexpected and, dare I say it, a positive development in the wake of this tragic event, I hear," she eventually prompted. "What's all this about a children's book I've heard rumours about?"

"Yes, Tara. As strange as it may sound, an old storybook has taken this town by storm and glued this grief-stricken community together during this dreadful week. I spoke to a group of youngsters earlier and they were in no doubt that without this book they simply could not get through the days."

"Astonishing – is it by anyone famous?"

Lyndsay shook her head. "I'm afraid not, Tara," she told her, before consulting her notes. Tara winced at this unprofessional

gesture and hoped the camera was on her when she did it. She would have memorised all relevant information or had it written large on a board just out of shot.

Lyndsay continued.

"The book is called Dancing Jackets – sorry, that's Dancing Jacks – by Austerly Fellows. What sort of dancing they do isn't clear."

"Ballroom maybe?" Tara interjected, reminding the audience she had been on Strictly.

Lyndsay's wooden expression told her what she thought of that. "Who knows, Tara," she said. "What is certain is that these simple fairytales have helped the people of Felixstowe deal with their profound grief and that's the most important thing."

Tara wasn't accustomed to being put in her place by provincial reporters. She turned to Camera One in the studio and cut the item short. "Linda Draymore there," she said, getting the name wrong on purpose. "And there'll be more from Felixstowe in our lunchtime bulletin later. Now what do a Spice Girl, a grumpy celebrity chef and a Weatherfield landlady have in common? Yes, they're gamely taking part in a bid to create the world's longest strand of spaghetti…"

Back in Felixstowe, Lyndsay Draymore prodded her earpiece. "Hello, studio?" she said. "Hello, Tara?"

"The link's down," Gavin the cameraman told her.

"The bitch," Lyndsay hissed through her teeth. She had been planning to end her piece with, "So it's a big thank you to Austerly the author – he really was a jolly good Fellows." Still, there was always the midday news. She could work it in there. "OK," she said.

"Where's that little man with the coffees? I'm parched!"

"Should I carry on taking shots of the mourners?" Gavin asked. "Do you want the usual hearses and pall-bearers stuff?"

"Too damn right I do!" Lyndsay told him. "I want to see wailing kids, teddy bears holding weepy messages, parents breaking down – the full snotfest. If there's a dry eye anywhere to be seen then stick your finger in it. Oh – and if you spot that Headmaster in the crowd before I do then for BAFTA's sake don't keep it to yourself. He's been harder to find than Madonna's natural hair colour, the coward. Make a fantasmic addition to my programme later that would. Contrition, guilt, anger – whatever edits in best. I'll provoke a reaction even if I have to kick him. With any luck, he'll do the old thumping the cameraman routine – that's always documentary gold."

"Oh, geez thanks, Lyndsay," Gavin moaned.

"And no wobbly camerawork or crash zooms," she warned. "We're not doing drama and trying to juice up a shonky script." The reporter stomped over old grassy graves to find out where her skinny latte had disappeared to. She had driven here three hours ago and so far the only caffeine she'd had was before she'd left her house and she was gasping for more.

With the camera on his shoulder, Gavin roamed the churchyard, quietly filming the groups of people arriving for the special service and the first of the funerals. He was the only news cameraman there. There were too many celebrity stories to be covered that weekend and he had drawn the short straw. There were plenty of tabloid photographers present however.

492

To Gavin's irritation he saw that the mourners were unusually calm and reserved. He couldn't see any handkerchief action, not even from the grannies. The photographers weren't pleased about that either. Then Gavin noticed something…

The children were turning up in their school uniforms, but there was something peculiar about them. What had they done to their sleeves? Gavin peered at his small LCD screen and zoomed in. Were those playing cards pinned to the lapels? What was this? Had the funerals been sponsored by an online poker site? And what on earth was going on with their mouths? Why were their lips that putrid colour? What had everyone been eating? Lyndsay wouldn't be happy with this crappy footage. He could see the paps were grumbling among themselves too.

More and more people were arriving. They began to fill the churchyard and then the hearses sailed serenely through the gates. The first funeral was a double one. They were two teenage girls. Because they had been friends, their families had expressed the desire that it be a joint ceremony. Gavin pushed through the crowd to station himself in the best position to capture the stricken faces of the immediate family. Then he was so surprised at what he saw, he forgot about filming altogether.

He had never seen anything like the wreaths on those hearses. On the roof of one was a great big red diamond, made from hundreds of flowers, and on the roof of the other car was a huge black club.

"I've seen it all now," he muttered. But he hadn't.

The coffins were slid from the hearses and the pall-bearers took them on their shoulders. They too had cut up their suit jackets in order to have those strange hanging sleeves.

Gavin focused in on one of the girls' mothers. She was composed and dry-eyed. In fact, her glazed expression looked more bored than sorrowful.

The chief undertaker stepped to the front of the coffins and placed the black top hat on his head. Gavin gasped. Surely not! Yes – there was a playing card tucked into the black ribbon of his hat! Gavin's disappointment at the lack of emotion now flipped into excitement. There was something wrong here, something way off normal. And he was going to film every warped moment of it.

Dodging back through the crowd so he could get a front-on wide shot, standing by the church door, he held the camera as steady as his feverish anticipation allowed.

The undertaker began the slow walk to the church and the pall-bearers followed. The packed churchyard maintained a respectful silence. There wasn't a single sniffle. And then…

"Wait!" a voice called out.

A murmur ran through the crowds and every head turned to look beyond the gates. Someone was coming.

"Are you getting this?" Lyndsay growled at him as she barged her way to his side. "What the flaming Panorama is going on?"

"No idea," he whispered back. "But you wanted gold and this is it."

"This is bloody platinum with diamond knobs on, Gavin," she said eagerly. "This is better than a Christmas EastEnders. Here, let

me get in shot for this. Shoot past me, but I have to be in these images! This might get seen around the world."

"Wait!" the voice called again. It was the voice of a girl. "Stop the funeral!"

The undertaker turned smartly about on one foot. He held up his hand for the pall-bearers to halt. Everyone heard the clip-clip of stiletto heels marching along the road and a buzz of recognition spread through those nearest the gate.

Gavin was one of the last to see who it was. The ruddy coffins were in the way! Then, on the camera's LCD screen, he saw a pair of glossy black ankle boots striding into view. He panned upward. The attached legs were in netted tights and those legs went on and on.

Lyndsay's mouth dropped open. It was one of the shortest dresses she had ever seen outside a raunchy nightclub and it was certainly something she would never wear, nor indeed could wear, with her cellulite and chankles.

But what the audacious black outfit lacked at the front was made up for at the back. It had a train of taffeta that trailed on the ground behind. The bodice of the dress was decorated with countless diamantés that formed the shape of a large sparkling spade over the stomach.

Gavin tried to get a close-up of the face, but the outrageous newcomer was wearing a black silk hat with a matching veil of lace that covered her features. She was certainly young though, that much he could make out.

495

Walking between the coffins, the girl traced her silk-gloved fingers along the sides of them. Then she struck a pose and, with a dramatic flourish, lifted the veil from her face.

"The Jill of Spades!" the crowd exclaimed. Someone began to applaud. Here and there were chortles of laughter. One of the dead girls' fathers smiled indulgently.

Lyndsay stared back at Gavin and mouthed her disbelief to the camera. The photographers were snapping away furiously.

Emma Taylor made a great show of kissing each of the coffins and was certain the photographers caught her from every angle. Then she spied Gavin and turned to face his lens.

"Ashleigh and Keeley," she proclaimed. "Were Emma's... were my best friends. I have come here today to make my confession. I was the one who caused the Disaster. I, Emma Taylor, was in that car next to Danny Marlow. I was the one who made him crash it. I stubbed my cigarette on his hand. I set fire to the car. The blood of forty-one innocent people is on my hands. I am responsible for all of this. I – Emma Taylor! Blessed be!"

She tossed her head triumphantly. The crowd repeated her last two words with a great, jubilant shout and then began to cheer. Hooray for the Jill of Spades! She could always be relied on to liven things up – even in this dull, unreal world. The photographers went wild. They rushed forward and surrounded her. Lyndsay hurriedly joined them, pulling Gavin after. Emerging from the church, the vicar nodded his approval. "Yes, blessed be!" he called out, clasping a green and cream book firmly to his chest.

With her hands on her hips, the Jill of Spades threw back her head and laughed.

This is what the girl Emma had always wanted – to be the centre of attention – to be photographed and be in newspapers and magazines. If she, the Jill of Spades, had to endure this dreary dream life when she was away from Mooncaster then she might as well make it as interesting and entertaining as possible. She would make the girl Emma famous – or infamous, it didn't matter which here. As long as people knew who she was, that was the only important factor in this grey place.

Lyndsay could hardly believe her astounding luck. She was the only television reporter there. What a scoop! Oh, she could already see the awards lining up on her mantelpiece. She could even see Tara's bright green face. All she had to do was get an exclusive with this insane girl before the police waded in to arrest her.

"You on me?" she barked at Gavin as she ducked in front of the lens. "Yes? Great. Hang on – my lips are like sandpaper. Wait a second."

She reached into her pocket. One of the youngsters she had spoken to earlier had generously given her a pot of lip balm. She unscrewed the lid hastily and dipped a finger in.

"Here, give me some of that," Gavin said, moistening his own lips.

And though the moon may sink behind those green, girdling hills,
Mooncaster will ever stand proud and defiant.
None shall shake its foundations - they are stronger than
any mind can guess.

30

As the strange scenes unfolded outside the church, down by the seafront a very different event was taking place.

In the shadow of the Martello tower, where the boot fair was normally held every Sunday, that morning there was only one vehicle. No others were parked there, selling the usual bric-a-brac and bits of junk. Instead the waste ground seethed with a mass of clamouring people.

The vehicle was a new and gleaming black transit van with tinted windows. It was tucked into one corner of that empty lot and the trestle table in front of its open rear doors was stacked with copies of Dancing Jacks and jars of minchet.

Labella the High Priestess was there, supervising the distribution

of the sacred text. She was flanked by the Harlequin Priests. Eager, anxious customers, desperate to obtain their own copies, were handing over huge sums of money to the Lockpick who deposited it in a big, metal strongbox. Even the Ismus had underestimated how successful the Dancing Jacks would be. Thousands of books were now in circulation in Felixstowe. Within a week, they had managed to empty four of the six large crates they had found in the cellar of Austerly Fellows' house. After only twenty minutes of setting up the stall that morning, they were already reaching the bottom of the fifth. There would not be nearly enough for everyone there.

The Lady Labella smiled to herself when she saw a woman in yellow flip-flops elbow her way to the front. She recognised her from last Sunday.

"I need a book!" the woman pleaded, brandishing a wad of twenties and fifties.

"Have you changed your mind?" Labella asked archly. "Isn't your god-daughter as particular as you thought?"

"It's not for her!" the woman spat fiercely. "It's for me! I have to have it! I can't live without it! I'll give you anything – anything! I've got 700 quid here in cash, but I can get more tomorrow when the bank opens."

The High Priestess's smile widened, knowing what the Ismus would have done. Beside her the Harlequins pointed to a dark colour on their patchwork robes with the pokers in their hands. Labella nodded in agreement.

"Maybe next Sunday," she said.

The woman let out a shriek and tried to push the money on her. She made a grab for the books, but the people behind dragged her away roughly. The banknotes fell out of her grasp and went blowing over the low sea wall and down over the beach. She was thrust back into the crowd. Her outraged wails went unheeded.

Jangler chuckled to himself. His strongbox was already overflowing. He had to start shoving the money into his pockets and then, when they were stuffed to bursting, into the empty crates.

Countless hands reached out to buy and beg a book or a jar of minchet. If there had been a lorry containing 10,000 books, they would have sold them all that morning.

Martin Baxter hurried on to the waste ground and viewed the scene in disbelief.

He had spent an anxious night at Gerald's. Carol had been subdued and quiet. The stress of the past days was taking its toll. She had been relieved to learn that her son was 'safe'. Although Martin explained that really was not the right word, she still slept more soundly than she had for a while. Just hearing news of Paul was some comfort.

After everything he had seen, Martin was almost afraid to sleep, but eventually he nodded off in an armchair and was spared any ugly dreams.

At first light Gerald woke him. The kindly old gent was his usual self once more and Martin noticed that Evelyn's little domestic touches had been discreetly removed from the living room. He wondered if and when she would make another appearance. The

doubts and suspicions of the previous night were still troubling him however. He simply couldn't trust Gerald and refused to tell him what his plan was. If the old man was hurt by this, he hid it admirably.

Martin's one hope, which he told to no one, not even Carol, now lay in finding Shiela Doyle, his ex-student. She had been so concerned about Paul's welfare last week. Surely, if the Ismus had the boy hidden away, she would know where and would help. That was why he borrowed Gerald's car and drove down to the Martello tower as early as possible. He had gone alone, leaving Carol to fetch her mother. As soon as they found Paul, they were going to drive out of Felixstowe and try to alert the authorities. They had debated whether to ring the police in Ipswich last night, but what on earth could they say over the phone? It was going to be difficult enough face to face.

Stepping on to the waste ground, Martin grunted with irritation and amazement. He had not expected to see such a vast sea of people already gathered there. There had to be several thousand – each hungry for a copy of Dancing Jacks. Then he told himself he should have expected it. So many were under the spell of Austerly Fellows' words, but not all of them had their own copy to pore over whenever they needed their Mooncaster fix. They were reliant on family members or neighbours or friends. No one would be satisfied until they each possessed their own book.

Climbing on to a wall, Martin stared over the mass of heads and saw Shiela over by the new black van. He would have to push his way to the front. This wasn't going to be easy.

He jumped down and began jostling and negotiating his way through the crowd. All of the people there had enlarged pupils and most had stained lips. Martin felt horribly aware that he wasn't wearing a playing card like the rest of them. He should have thought about that. What would he do if challenged? Progress was slow. Each forward step was an effort and a struggle. His impatience mounted. He felt like punching somebody – anybody. Many people objected to him squeezing by. Trudy Bishop, the estate agent, huffed in indignation and swore at him. Doctor Ian Meadows, his face smeared and dripping, peered at him irritably, but was too busy chewing on a mouthful of fibrous minchet fruit to do much more. Martin went a good way before anyone physically tried to prevent him. Then a strong hand gripped his arm and yanked him back.

"Wait your turn," a familiar voice growled in his ear.

Martin looked up at the man who had stopped him and was astonished to see the tanned, orange face of the games teacher, Mr Wynn.

"Douggy!" he said. "Let go, it's me, Martin Baxter."

A faint spark of recognition glimmered in the man's glassy eyes. Then he turned away and said, "There is no Douggy. I am Sir Darksilver – knight of the Royal House of Clubs."

"You would be," Martin muttered, eyeing the ten of clubs pinned to his tracksuit.

"I must own the holy text," Douggy said, but he was really only speaking to himself. "I must return to Mooncaster this very day

and continue my real life there. I am to ride with my Lord Jack and the other knights this afternoon, to cleanse the caves beneath the ninth hill of the Marshwyrm that has crept in and made its abode there. My Lord Jack will need my sword."

Martin rolled his eyes, but there was no way Douggy would let him pass. Then he had an idea.

"Stand aside, Sir Knight!" he ordered, inwardly thanking all the fantasy films he had ever watched. "I am on an errand for the Lord Ismus. How dare you hinder me? This is treason – you flout the authority of the Holy Enchanter himself!"

Confusion clouded the games teacher's face. His eyes searched Martin's clothes for a playing card to tell him what rank this man held in the White Castle.

Martin thought quickly. He could try to bluff it out and explain that the card was on his other jacket, or that it had merely fallen off. But it would be far better if there was a character who no one would think of questioning; someone who they were even afraid of. They already knew who the Ismus was so who…? Then he had it!

"Haw haw haw!" he laughed. "Out of my way!"

Douggy inhaled sharply and gave a nervous bow. Hastily he made room for Martin to get past. The people around them who had heard Martin impersonate the Jockey's mocking laughter drew back and cleared a path straight to the front.

Martin tried to remember the strange skipping steps he saw the figure in the caramel leather outfit do last night and did his best to copy them as he made his way forward. The stifled gasps of apprehension he heard on the way made him realise just how alarming that character was for everyone.

When he reached the front, he saw the two Harlequin Priests staring at him with sombre expressions on their diamond-tattooed faces. Martin knew it would be dangerous to try and fool that pair. They were dressed in full medieval motley and were far above having to wear playing cards. He averted his face from their intense scrutiny and looked at Shiela Doyle.

The young woman was totally different from when she had come to see him at school last Monday. Gone was the slightly grubby, unkempt appearance with lank hair sporting faded, bleached ends. Now she was elegant and striking, with immaculate, ornate eye make-up, blackcurrant-painted lips and hair that had been dyed raven black. A gown of purple silk hung from her shoulders with silver clasps and an amethyst-studded belt sat loosely around her hips. Martin's hopes and confidence began to waver.

"Shiela?" he said. "Shiela? It's me, Martin Baxter."

The High Priestess Labella turned a curious face to him. "You wish to buy the Hallowed Word of the Holy Enchanter?" she asked.

Martin sidled along the trestle until he was directly in front of her and leaned forward. "It's me," he hissed urgently. "Your old maths teacher – remember? You came to see me – about Paul. My partner's lad?"

Labella's large, dark eyes gave him nothing.

"Some minchet then?" she suggested in a leaden voice.

Martin could feel he was still under the scrutiny of the Harlequins. He knew he didn't have much time and tried not to panic.

"Shiela!" he said.

"Labella," she corrected. "I am the High Priestess, consort of the Ismus. I know you not. I cannot place your face at Court. If you are not here to buy, you should leave."

Martin wanted to shake her, but that would do no good.

"Please," he implored. "You're my only hope, my last chance. Please listen to me, please remember – I'm Mr Baxter…"

The woman's empty eyes stared right through him. "Aberrants will not be tolerated," she stated coldly. "They will be rounded up and compelled to enter the Kingdom of the Dawn Prince, one way or another."

Martin drew back. He was beaten. Without Shiela's help, there was no way they could get Paul away from the Ismus. He and Carol would have to leave Felixstowe without him. How was he going to manage that? Carol would never agree to it. The anxious crowd swarmed past and the books continued to be sold. Martin raked his fingers over his scalp. If only there had been a way to break through that evil book's hold on Shiela. If only he had been able to reach her true self.

The maths teacher uttered a cry and smacked a fist into his palm. It was a stupid, mad idea, but he had to try it. Feverishly he scrabbled in his pockets, searching for a pen and paper. The people nudged against him as they pushed by, but he ignored them and concentrated on the problem he had set himself. It was something he had done many times when Shiela had been one of his best students. It was a game they had both enjoyed.

With shaking fingers, he wrote on the scrap of paper he had found, as clearly as his nerves allowed. Then, turning back, he barged through to the front once more.

"Here!" he yelled, thrusting the paper forward and putting it in Labella's hand. "Read it! Read it!"

The High Priestess hardly glanced at him, but continued serving the crowd. Martin saw the Harlequin Priests bristle and move in his direction. He cried out to Labella to just look at the scrap of paper. Then he withdrew. It was no use. Shuddering with emotion, he stumbled back, heading out of that agitated gathering by the shortest route possible. Wiping his eyes, he blundered through to the edge and found himself by the low sea wall. He lurched on for a few more steps then sat down and buried his head in his hands. The sound of the sea lapped gently over him.

Back at the van, Labella handed over a copy of Dancing Jacks to a feverish woman in uniform. It was the judgemental police officer who had been so scornful of Barry Milligan the Headteacher. She paid out a fistful of money and snatched the book savagely.

"I am the Mistress of the Inn," she told herself. "I am the Mistress of the Inn. I am the Mistress of the Inn…"

Labella passed the cash to Jangler and he threw it merrily into the large crate. The High Priestess looked down at her hand. She was still holding the scrap of paper that the aberrant had given to

her. With a distracted air, she smoothed it out on her palm and stared at what was written there.

If y = 5 then

$$y(y^6 - 8y^3 + 4) + 2(y^5 + y^4 + y^3 - 8) \times 10^{-5} = ?$$

Labella's forehead crinkled. There was a kindling of dim remembrance. She faintly recalled there had been a love of numbers. In this greyness the woman Shiela had found genuine pleasure in solving equations like this. She tilted her head in fascination. The recollection sputtered like a pilot light in her mind. Standing back from the trestle, she wandered to the side of the van – away from the calls of the crowd – and gave the problem her attention. The numbers seemed to pop and ignite her thoughts. The veil began to lift and beams of colour filtered into this world once more. A delicate smile lifted the corners of her mouth as she began to solve the puzzle in her head, multiplying, subtracting and adding and moving the numbers around on her dark internal canvas. It was good to do this. It was real. It stimulated her brain and excited her – more than being in Mooncaster.

She cast about for something to write the answer on. There was nothing and she had neither pen nor pencil. Kneeling, she smoothed the soft, dry sand that had blown over the sea wall and drew the figures into it with her finger.

There was something weirdly familiar about that long number, something special and individual to her. Somehow it was a joke that she had shared with someone, when she was younger. This same number had kept cropping up in problems that were set for her. It was a rapport between teacher and student. But no... the number didn't look quite right. Labella studied it through half closed eyes, trying to remember. Then she giggled softly, re-smoothed the sand and drew it the way it would have looked back then – on the digital display of a pocket calculator.

Labella stared at that. It still wasn't quite right and she grinned as she realised why. The woman rose, walked around the patch of sand and then viewed the number upside down. At once the irises closed in around the black circles of her pupils.

"My number!"

Shiela Doyle gasped with shock. Her limbs went weak and she fell against the van.

"What am I doing?" she cried. "Oh, God – oh, God!"

She stared aghast at her purple gown. Then gazed fearfully over at the mass of people desperate to buy Dancing Jacks. Shiela pressed herself against the van and shrank away. She looked around wildly, until she saw a man sitting on the sea wall, bent over in despair.

Hitching up the hem of her gown, she ran to him.

"Mr Baxter!" she called. "Mr Baxter!"

Martin looked up. "Shiela?" he asked uncertainly.

"Yes!" she said. "Yes – it's me! You brought me back! You got through – you woke me up! Oh, Mr Baxter!" She threw her arms about him and sobbed on to his shoulder.

Martin held her for a few moments. His mind was racing. So it was possible to break the book's hold over people! It would be difficult and time-consuming, each person would respond to different stimuli, but it could be done. It wasn't as hopeless as he had thought. The relief came crashing over him. The strain of the past days had been intolerable and he almost buckled as it finally snapped.

"Tell me," he said, battling to keep it together. "Paul – do you know where he is?"

Shiela lifted a fold of her gown and wiped her nose on it.

"He's with Jezza – the Ismus," she told him. "At the corner of the Golf Club, on the way to the ferry, there's a pillbox. It's the entrance to a hidden courtyard. They're all in there. There's a celebration going on today – and a market."

"More books?"

Shiela shook her head. "There aren't many books left! There were

509

only six crates of them. We've almost finished the fifth one here. The Ismus is keeping the last one back for 'special readers', whatever that means."

"But that's brilliant! This madness can't spread without them!"

"It can with the minchet fruit!" she told him. "That's what's being sold in the market. They're going to plant that disgusting stuff and grow it in gardens and nurseries. It'll be everywhere."

Martin was only half listening. "I've got to get Paul out of there before I can do anything about that," he said. "Help me, Shiela, please."

The woman glanced nervously back at the crowd clamouring in front of the van. "If I leave here now, Jangler and the Harlequin Priests will be on to us straight away," she said. "You'll have to go there on your own. We won't be here much longer – there's hardly any books left. I'll get there as soon as I can. But you won't get in without a playing card – Mauger won't let you past – and today there's no one below a nine permitted inside. Wear a ten and you'll have no problem, they're for knights and nobles. Get your lad out of there, Mr Baxter. You don't have any idea what this is really about."

Martin stared steadily into her eyes. "I do," he said. "Believe me, I do."

"No, you don't!" Shiela insisted. "You don't know what I do. That fruit isn't just to turn people into slaves of that book. It's to feed the creatures that are coming."

"What?"

"The book is only the first part of it. There are things – horrible,

terrifying things – waiting to come through, to crawl and creep among us. The Ismus, Jezza, Austerly Fellows, whoever he is, is wanting to turn this place – not just this town…"

"Into a vision of Hell," the maths teacher murmured.

"Exactly. And when he's done it, when it's ready, the Dawn Prince is going to rise."

Martin stepped away from her. He couldn't think. It was too gigantic, too repulsively immense to comprehend. He forced himself to think of Paul. He had to focus on him.

"I've got to go," he said.

"I'll be there soon," she promised. "For God's sake, get the boy away from here. As far away as possible – and Mr Baxter… thank you."

Martin nodded and sprinted back to Gerald's car.

Shiela watched him leave. Then she turned back to the horde of expectant people and took a deep, calming breath. She had to blag it big time; she had to return and play the part of Labella again.

"Damn!" she cursed under her breath. "I'm gagging for a smoke."

Steeling herself, she assumed an air of cool dignity and walked back to the van. The Harlequin Priests were waiting for her. Their grim, accusing eyes said it all and the tips of their pokers were pointing at the black diamonds on their robes.

"No," Shiela whimpered.

Sing ye for the glory of the Dawn Prince, that his exile might end the sooner. Summon the minstrels and enter into the dance. In the Holy Enchanter's name. So mote it be!

31

MARTIN DROVE like a maniac through the deserted town. He stopped only to dash to a newsagent's. The shop was closed. Martin kicked against the door with fury. He had to get in. He hammered on the glass and shouted at the top of his voice, but there was no answer and there wasn't a soul to be seen along the street. He ran back to the car and popped the boot. There was no caramel-coloured leather outfit in there as he had suspected last night, but there was a spare tyre and a car jack. Martin seized the latter and hurled it at the newsagent's plate-glass window. A cobweb of fractures appeared. He hurled it again and again. The window smashed completely. Martin stepped over the crunching glass crumbs and made a frantic search of the shelves.

When he found a pack of cards, he ripped it open. Then he tore the lid off a box of safety pins. He paused before leaving. He could

hear the sound of voices chanting in the flat above. The newsagent and his family were reading from Dancing Jacks. He visualised them rocking backwards and forwards. With a fierce determination, he hurried back to the car.

Cliff Road was devoid of any other vehicles. Martin's foot was right down and he raced along it faster than he had ever driven in his life. It was still only eleven in the morning. The sweeping view of the sea on his right was glittering beneath a bright winter sun and seemed almost blue for a change. Its clear beauty was lost on Martin. He wished he had thought to bring Carol's mobile. He wanted to call her and assure her everything was going to be all right. In a few hours they would be driving away from this place with Paul. Then their real headaches would start – how could they convince anyone what was going on here?

Suddenly he saw a line of cars blocking the road up ahead. They were police cars and officers were standing on guard nearby. Martin slowed right down and wondered what was going on. As he drew closer, he could see the pillbox just beyond the blockade. The Ismus was apparently taking no chances. He pulled into the side, fumbled with the card pack for a moment then got out.

"Blessed be!" he called to the nearest policeman.

The chubby officer returned the greeting and glanced at the ten of clubs on Martin's jacket.

"I am… Sir Darksilver!" the maths teacher declared hesitantly, struggling to remember what Douggy Wynn had spouted earlier. "This day I am to ride with my Lord Jack and… rid him of the worms." Martin bit his tongue. That was so not right.

The policeman did not appear to notice. He bowed and waved him through. Martin couldn't believe his luck and prayed that it would hold. How he was to get Paul out, past these guys, was something he'd worry about later.

The sound of medieval music was drifting across the road. He looked over at the dense shrubs of gorse that concealed the sunken courtyard and wondered what that metal structure was jutting above them at the far end. But there wasn't time to stand and think. As casually as possible, he walked towards the concrete pillbox.

Once inside, he hastened down the steps that led to the underpass. The stagnant water had been pumped out and lanterns were suspended from iron hooks in the ceiling.

Martin caught his breath. There was a shape up ahead. It was the same shape that had chased him down the drive of Austerly Fellows' house – the demon, Mauger.

He halted. The creature was unnaturally still, but Martin could feel a presence, an awareness beating out of it. He touched the card on his lapel and hoped it would give him protection. Shiela had said it would. Then, to his amazement, he saw that the monster was just a statue carved from stone. He almost laughed until he saw the blackened scorch marks across it. The maths teacher averted his eyes and hurried by.

Moments later he was ascending the second flight of steps, out of the tunnel and up into the Court of the Ismus.

The transformation of that place was complete. The weeds, sand

and shingle had been cleared away and market stalls with colourful awnings crowded the area at the front. Martin stepped between them, staring about him in revulsion.

The stalls were groaning under the weight of produce. The bumper harvest of Austerly Fellows' conservatory was here. They were bulbous growths he had never seen before. Sweaty-looking gourds, trays packed with fat and swollen grass, rows of translucent, waxy vegetables that reminded him of lumpy legume, and small, sloppy-looking fleshy fruit. But all of them were that same sickly greyish-yellow colour, and most of it was speckled with black mould. An unpleasant, rank sweetness hung in the air.

Crowds of people were queuing up to buy those nauseating wares. Most of them wore home-made fancy-dress costumes, but here and there he spotted what seemed to be professionally produced outfits. There was a woman in an elaborate black taffeta gown with a fan in her hands and a glittering tiara on her head. She was utterly absorbed in her role of the Queen of Spades and haggling with the mercers. Little dramas, fresh from the pages of the book, were re-enacted all around him. Everyone was living their character.

Martin moved through the market area searching for a glimpse of Paul. Then he found he could go no further. In the centre of the courtyard a morris dance was being performed. The spectators had formed a wide circle to watch and he couldn't get past. A pipe and tabor were playing and he stared between outlandish hats and headdresses to view what was going on.

The three Black Face Dames were there. They were now in full costume. They wore battered top hats surrounded with feathers and were dressed solely in clothes the same colour as the ebony make-up that covered their features: shirts, waistcoats, boots, trousers that were rolled up and tied around with ribbons. Everything was black, as was the full skirt that covered the trousers. It could have looked ridiculous, but instead it looked strange and menacing. Two further figures were dancing with them. One was a bald man, covered in tattoos and with a ginger beard. He was dressed in an artist's smock and scraps of colourful cloth had been sewn to it, imitating splodges of paint. Martin did not recognise him, but he knew the fifth man only too well. It was the Ismus.

It was unlike any morris dance the maths teacher had ever seen. They each carried a long stave in their hands and they smashed them, one against the other, in violent strokes. It was more like a vicious martial art than anything else. Martin winced at the brutal blows, and splinters of wood went flying into the flinching crowd. One of the Dames received a cut to his cheek and a river of red came pouring through the make-up. The morris men yelled and roared at one another and the moves became wilder and wilder. They leaped over swooping staves; they ducked when they came slicing at their heads, then with deafening shouts they leaped and swapped positions. It was a carefully rehearsed and breathtakingly savage display. One mistake and bones and skulls would have been shattered.

Martin hoped the Ismus would make such a mistake. He lifted his eyes above the crowd and gazed at the far end of the courtyard. The larger pillbox reared up into the clear morning sky. Bolted to its concrete roof was the oversized cast-iron throne. That was the metal structure he had seen jutting above the shrubs from across the road. It was a sinister, ugly object and Martin looked away quickly. He scanned the faces around him. Most were chewing something bought from the market, the putrid stains fresh on their lips. Where was Paul?

Just then the music came to a thudding stop. The morris men stamped and bowed to one another. The onlookers applauded then fell into a hush. They turned to the far end. Something was approaching. The people shuffled aside to make way and into the cleared space a macabre creature came prancing. It was a crude representation of a skeletal horse, with a startlingly carved wooden head and a fringed, rib-striped skirt draped over a wicker frame to conceal the operator within.

"Oss Oss Oss!" the crowd chanted, clapping their hands. "Oss Oss Oss!"

The creature paraded around the perimeter, demonstrating that its jaw was hinged, and it went snapping at squealing victims. After one circuit around, it came to rest near the dancers and bowed its head. The watchers buzzed with expectation. The show was not over yet.

Martin fidgeted with impatience. He couldn't see Paul anywhere. How long would he have to wait until this was over?

A jet of flame drove the question from his mind. The fiery stream shot into the air from the back of the crowd. There were cries of admiration and mock fear and then another bizarre creation came lumbering into the centre.

"Scorch Scorch Scorch!" they called out.

It was a dragon, fashioned in the same way as the horse. This one was slightly more elaborate. The neck was longer and a forked tail swished from the back. It was covered in scales of green cloth and the head was fully articulated. The jaws on this did not move, but there was a flexible metal pipe fixed between them.

The dragon angled its head high and another torrent of flame went shooting in a wide arc over their heads. It did this several times. Once, when it was facing Martin, it paused and the man felt a rush of fear. He half expected the flames to come streaming towards him. But no, the painted eyes of the dragon veered away. Finally it came to a standstill opposite Old Oss. The two acknowledged one another with a little jig. Then another figure came into the circle.

At once every voice was raised in 'Boos' and heckles. Fists were shaken and angry shouts rang out.

Martin's eyes widened as he saw this new creation. It was a tall effigy of a ragged, bearded man with a fierce and ugly face, and required two people to operate it. One carried the torso while the other walked in front, moving the arms via long poles. The head and hands of the unpopular character were made from papier-mâché and the robes it wore were of ripped sacking. It made the tour round the crowd to never-ending jeers before being conveyed out again.

"Drive the Bad Shepherd away!" the Ismus commanded. The 'Boos' increased until the effigy was lowered to the ground. Then the music began again.

The morris men danced around, more ferociously than before. The staves clashed and now daggers were held in the other hand. It was a hideously lethal form of orchestrated combat.

Martin found himself wishing for the Ismus to get battered and then stabbed for good measure. Then he caught sight of a man on the far side, taking photographs of the show with his mobile. In those surroundings, with these people, it was a jarring sight. He wondered who the man was. He appeared to be in his thirties and looked pretty smart in a dark blue suit with an open shirt collar. He fitted in here even less than Martin did.

There was another rush of flames from Scorch. The people cheered and the music ceased. The morris dance was over. There was applause and the horse and dragon followed the dancers out of the clearing. People began wandering across and back to the market. Martin pressed further in. Where was Paul?

The man with the mobile phone congratulated the Ismus as he came towards him.

"That was beeyootiful," he said enthusiastically. "And that's in the book as well, yeah?"

"The dances are all in there," the Ismus answered. "As well as the music. The whole world is contained in those pages."

The man shook his head in bewilderment. "I've never seen anything like this before," he admitted. "I've been in this business over ten years and have never once encountered anything even remotely similar. You can forget everything else. This book beats everything hands down. It's staggering!"

"Wait till you read it," the Ismus said.

The man nodded eagerly and inspected the copy that the Holy Enchanter had given to him just before the dance began.

"And it's been languishing someplace since 1936?" he said, flicking through the pages. "I can't believe it. You sure you have the sole publishing rights, yes? The copyright is definitely yours and yours alone?"

"My solicitor can vouch for that. He has all the legal papers."

"Beeyootiful, effing beeyootiful. Wait till I touch base with head office in the morning. We are going to shift so many units."

"Units?"

"Books, I meant books. We call them units."

"You make them sound like tins of beans."

"Just a term for the accountants, don't you worry about it. You won't have to deal with them. It's the marketing guys who'll be all over you like eczema. They are going to wet themselves when they see all this. A book that is totally immersive. That's got everyone in this town fired up and actually dressing as characters from it – even the police! Oh, wow – something with a bit of quality and substance going for it for a goddam change!"

"Aren't the 'units' you publish quality?"

"Are you kidding? It's the big chains and supermarkets that dictate what we put out there now. What they want is more of the same of anything that sells in bulk. Bookshops want to lure customers off the street so that's why they demand crap by celebrities. Punters who never normally go into bookshops will

520

queue for hours for the chance to gawp down a real live famous pair of hooters. They don't care that the book is trash and that the dim celeb can hardly sign her own name, let alone write a novel. They don't even care that her knockers are just as fake. It's all about slapping a famous face on a cover and Joe Public touching the hem of that glamour. It's the branding that sells it, not the rubbish inside. But this is different. It's lush – and you've got a fully worked out brand of your own already."

The Ismus smiled. "And am I to be famous?" he asked.

"Oh, man, everyone will kill for a piece of you. When you come for your first meeting, they are going to freak. You've got it all going on: the personality, the style, the cult following here. You're doing the PR girls' job for them! They won't have to dream up a gimmick to hang the campaign on. We're not talking foul-mouthed ex-nuns, knee-jerk shockers to get the Daily Mail in a flap or one-hit wonder schoolkid authors here – it's the real deal."

"You think so?"

"Hey, believe me, once the publicity machine revs into action, you can kiss your old life adios. There'll be interview after interview. I've been doing some blue-sky thinking. Screw the trade stuff like The Bookseller, I see you on the covers of trendy lads' mags – you've got that Noel Fielding, Russell Brand thing about you. There'll be radio, television. We're talking Jonathan effing Ross here and Oprah will be kicking your door down to get you in her book club when the US division swings into action. I promise. Those units will rocket off the shelves as if every bookshop was effing NASA!"

"I just want the books out there."

"Sure you do. But it's not just about the books nowadays – they're only the first level. Our media arm will be looking at movie rights and console games and don't forget audio – we can get anyone you like to read them on CD. I'm talking big A-listers here – real stars! The merchandise potential for this property is through the effing roof. You are going to be one mega-rich man!"

"I'm glad I called you," the Ismus said. "Thank you for coming here at such short notice."

"No, no – thank you!" the man said effusively. "You have made Terry Johnson one deliriously happy sales director. I'll go to head office in London tomorrow morning and call an emergency meeting."

"And they'll listen to you?"

"What? You wouldn't believe the power we sales guys have in there now. The editors can't do anything if we turn our noses up at the pretentious stuff they try to show us. They have to publish what we want to sell and if we don't like it, they effing well have to change it till we do. Oh, they'll listen all right. We'll be singing from the same effing hymn sheet by the end of it."

He paused to take a breath and considered the green and cream dust jacket of the unit in his hands.

"We'll have to change this though," he said. "Bring it up to date. Our design department is effing amazing."

"You can't alter the text inside," the Ismus warned. "I cannot allow that."

"No, no!" Terry said hastily. "I wouldn't dream of it. Some

522

stuck-up editor might have a look and think it needs fiddling about with, but I'll put my foot down and they'll leave it alone… no – it's the cover."

"You may change the cover if you wish."

"It really has to sing out on those shelves. It has to scream for attention out there. Shelf space is a battleground. Holographic film, foil type, embossing, feathers, rhinestones, even flashing lights; anything to get it noticed."

"That sounds a trifle crass. It doesn't need any of that. It's a book, not a Christmas tree."

"No, no, you're right… but… hmmm."

"Something else you wish to change?"

"Just shooting from the hip here, but the title, it's a bit… limp and girly. The shops won't like it. There'll be resistance from key accounts."

"Nevertheless, that is what the book is called."

"OK, hear me out. Let me run this up the idea flagpole. What would you say if we put an X in the word Jacks? Huh? Huh? Dancing Jax – same title, just spelled different. It doesn't mean anything, but it gives the thing a more edgy, contemporary vibe. The shops would lap that up."

The Holy Enchanter grinned. "I like you, Mr Johnson," he said. "You will remember to take some jars of minchet with you when you leave, won't you? You can give them to the people at your publishing house. It's only lip balm. Our Queen of Hearts makes it herself."

"See – you're creating your own merchandise already! Effing incredible!"

The pipe and tabor sounded again. This time it was joined by the sound of a lute and richly costumed nobles gathered to take part in a stately dance.

"Hey, time's marching on," Terry said. "I'd better go."

"Will you not stay and watch the burning of the Bad Shepherd? We have the effigy ready and waiting."

"I'd love to, but I've got a lot to do this afternoon, a lot to plan for tomorrow, and I really should sit down and have a read of this tonight."

"Yes, you should."

"I'll be off then."

"The Black Face Dames will escort you to your car, Mr Johnson. I'm giving you twenty copies to take to your meeting."

Terry seized his hand and shook it firmly. "You'll be hearing from me," he promised. "This is going to be effing huge! We're going to sell millions of these babies!"

"I hope so, Mr Johnson. I do hope so."

The sales director made his way through the courtyard, followed by the three bodyguards carrying books and bags containing minchet. The Ismus watched him go. He leaned against the large metal door set into the great pillbox and chuckled to himself.

"My Lord," a voice said. The Holy Enchanter turned and there was the Lockpick and the Harlequin Priests.

"Jangler!" he greeted the small man. "You have just missed

524

the…" His voice trailed off when he saw their expressions. "What is it?"

The Lockpick clasped his hands across his chest and gave a heavy sigh. "We have a problem," he said.

He looked over his shoulder at the Harlequins. They stepped forward and the Ismus saw that, between them, they had firm hold of a frightened Shiela Doyle.

Martin had not seen them pass by. He was on the other side of the courtyard. His attention had been fixed solely on the group of nobles who were pairing up to commence the courtly dance.

There was Sandra Dixon, wearing a gown of crimson velvet. She was trying to catch the eye of everyone present, flirting and smiling coquettishly. Opposite her was Conor Westlake, looking heroic in doublet and hose, and next to them…

Martin jolted upright. There was Paul!

Paul Thornbury was dressed in the horizontal gold and scarlet stripes of the Jack of Diamonds. His face was set and serious. His eyes roamed over the costume jewels of the ladies and the crowns of the Under Kings and Queens and the sight of them made him smirk covetously.

The dance began. It was very sedate and regal. They circled one another, joined hands, then changed direction.

Martin could only watch. He felt completely powerless. If he grabbed Paul and tried to make a run for it, there were at least a hundred people to get through before he reached the underpass. All he could do was wait and hope a better opportunity would present itself.

The dance continued.

At the end of the courtyard the Ismus was glaring at Shiela.

"I'm sorry, Ismus," she said. "I'm sorry!"

He strode over, gripped her face roughly and examined her eyes.

"You are not my consort," he declared. "You are not the Lady Labella!"

"I am!" she cried. "I mean, I can be again. Give me more of that stuff – you'll see."

The Ismus recoiled as though she was contaminated. "You have already had more chances than you are worth," he said in disgust. "You are an aberrant." He turned his back on her.

Shiela implored him to give her another chance, but he would not listen. He folded his arms and surveyed the Court. Shiela looked past him, to where a familiar face was staring intently at the dancers. She almost called out when she saw Martin Baxter, but she checked herself in time. At once she understood his predicament. He was waiting for an opportunity that would never come and any moment now the Ismus would spot him. There was no knowing what he would do then.

The woman thought feverishly. Her old teacher needed help. He needed a diversion. Uttering a convincing, fainting groan, she sagged and collapsed against one of the Harlequins. The Holy Enchanter twisted his head to sneer as she was laid on the steps that wound up to the pillbox's roof. Through half closed lashes, she watched and waited till the Priests looked away. Then, snatching her chance, she raced up the steps.

"Get her!" the Ismus yelled. "Get her!"

The Harlequins went charging after.

Reaching the top, Shiela ran past the huge iron throne and teetered on the very edge of the concrete roof. It was a horrible height to jump from. The beach was far below and thick tangles of gorse hugged the concrete walls directly beneath. If, by some miracle, she managed not to break any bones, she would be ripped to ribbons in those bushes. Shiela uttered a grim laugh. Both options were better than staying here. The young woman leaped forward into the air.

Strong hands grabbed at her. The Harlequins plucked her back and dragged her away from the edge. Shiela began to scream, but the one who had once been called Miller clamped a hand over her mouth and held her so tightly she could hardly breathe.

The Ismus came prowling up the stairs. He regarded his former consort with contempt.

"Gag it," he ordered coldly. "Then go fetch in our uniformed friends from outside. Everyone should be here to witness this."

The crooked smile appeared. "And bring me the head of the Bad Shepherd," he added.

Down in the courtyard the music had stopped and the dancing ceased. Everyone was gazing up to see what the commotion was. Martin didn't dare take his eyes off Paul. If the boy disappeared from sight, he might never find him again. He didn't even realise Shiela was here.

The Harlequin Priest formerly known as Tommo returned up the stairs, carrying the large papier-mâché head of the Bad Shepherd.

When the courtiers saw that garishly painted caricature, they commenced booing once more. Paul's voice was among them. In the corner of his eye, Martin saw the dayglo glare of hi-viz jackets as the police officers emerged from the underpass. The Black Face Dames were with them. For an instant he thought they were coming for him, but they came running to join the throng, adding their jeers to the rest.

Martin's heart leaped. Without the police on duty outside, it would be easier to get Paul away.

Then, he couldn't believe it, he saw Paul glance furtively back at the market. It was empty; even the merchants had come to watch the proceedings on the roof and the revolting fruit was left unattended. Martin saw the boy snigger and take a black eye mask from the pocket of his tunic. He tied it around his head like the illustration of the Jack of Diamonds and tiptoed away from the crowd, stealthily making his way to the stalls.

"Give me your jools!" he sang to himself. "Give me your jools! Magpie Jack has itchy palms."

He ran his thieving fingers over the minchet fruit and wondered which was the best, which should he steal? A shadow fell across the stall. The eleven-year-old started and looked over his shoulder. There was a man. It was the man Martin – Martin the aberrant.

The Jack of Diamonds tried to cry out, but Martin ripped the eye mask from him and stuffed it into his mouth.

"Sorry, mate," he whispered, holding him securely. "Don't struggle."

528

But the boy did struggle. He kicked and arched his back. He grabbed at the minchet fruit and hurled it in the man's face. It splattered against Martin's temple and he wiped it away hurriedly, fearful in case the pernicious juice trickled down into his mouth.

Paul reached out again. Martin gritted his teeth and his temper flared. He didn't have time to mess about – or be gentle. He hoisted the lad off the ground roughly and half carried, half dragged him to the steps leading down to the underpass.

On the great pillbox, the Harlequin Priests were tying Shiela on to the iron throne.

The Ismus faced the crowd. He held the papier-mâché head of the Bad Shepherd up high and shouted. "Shun the Bad Shepherd. Shun all enemies of the Dawn Prince. They must be hunted down. They must be punished. They must suffer. They must die!"

Below him the Court joined in and called for the death of all enemies of the Dawn Prince.

The Ismus revolved slowly on his heel and his eyes glinted at Shiela.

"I must find me a new Labella," he said. "One who is deserving of my holy company."

The woman writhed and strained against the ropes that tied her to the huge metal chair. The gag around her face bit into her mouth and she could not speak. Her one consolation was that she had seen Martin hurry down into the underpass with the boy and she was glad. She blinked her tears away and stared accusingly at the face of the man whom she had once loved. But she knew Jezza the human being had ceased to exist over a week ago.

The Ismus approached her with great solemnity and lowered the hollow, papier-mâché head over her own. Everything went dark.

"Bring the kindling and fuel," she heard his muffled voice tell the others.

Shiela pulled on the ropes more desperately than ever. She wasn't going to give up, not for a second.

Martin hurried through the tunnel. Paul was an impossible burden to carry. He squirmed and wriggled and did everything he could to make the man drop him. When they came to the statue of Mauger, Martin prayed the playing card pinned to his lapel would still allow him by. To his overwhelming relief, it did.

"Keep still!" he growled at Paul. "It's for your own good!"

The sunlight was streaming into the smaller pillbox that covered the top of the steps ahead. The sight of it made Martin's spirits soar. They were almost there. The possessed police were all in the courtyard and no one was going to stop them escaping.

"Thank God, thank God!" he uttered, reaching the concrete steps and hauling the boy up with him. An elated laugh sprang from his lips, but it was too soon.

Paul finally managed to spit the eye mask out of his mouth and he sank his teeth into Martin's shoulder. The man yelled and the boy was free. He raced back down the stairs, but Martin screamed in fury and launched himself after him.

His hands caught him by the collar of the velvet tunic and he wrenched the lad off his feet.

530

"You're coming with me!" he bawled, shaking him with rage. "I'll knock you out cold if that's what it takes and worry about the damage later. You hear me?"

"I hate you, you dirty aberrant!" Paul shrieked back at him.

"Whatever!" Martin shouted in his face.

The maths teacher began heaving him up the steps again. Then he halted.

A shadow had fallen across the top of them, cutting off the sunlight. Martin's heart thumped violently. A pair of trainers came into view as the person began to descend. It made its way down three steps then stopped.

Martin blinked. The daylight was flickering around the figure and dazzled him. Then he recognised it.

"Carol!" he exclaimed.

The woman stared down at him, but said nothing. Martin felt afraid.

"I… I've got Paul," he told her.

The boy's mother remained silent.

"Carol?" Martin said, climbing the steps to stand beside her. "How… how did you know I was here?"

The boy in his grasp began to giggle.

The woman lifted her face and turned to him. Martin choked back a cry. Her eyes… her eyes were dark and glassy.

"Not you," he whispered dismally. "Dear Lord, not you."

"The woman Carol wanted to be with her son," she answered in a cold, unfeeling voice. "So yesterday she sampled the minchet. It

531

was not unpleasant for long, Martin. Try it."

She raised her hand and held out an open jar. Martin tore his horror-stricken gaze away from her emotionless face and looked at the vile ointment.

"You can be with us always, Martin," she told him. "Come to Mooncaster with us, with Magpie Jack and I."

Martin began to tremble. Now he knew who had betrayed him to the Ismus last night. He let go of Paul. His hands were shaking. He reached out to take the jar from her hand.

"The Kingdom of the Dawn Prince is all you ever wanted, Martin," she continued. "You hate this grey world already. Why do you hesitate? There is order under the rule of the Ismus, there is respect, there are standards, there is magick and wonder – everything this nothingness lacks."

"And who are you in that place?" he asked in a shuddering voice. "If I taste this stuff – will we even be together?"

"I am paired with another there," she answered. "This is the emptiness of sleep, Martin. It is not real. It does not matter. You will know that when you join us."

The man looked at her one last time. His vision was bleary with tears. Then an awful sound of abject despair came welling up and screeched out of him. He dashed the jar from her hand and it smashed on the steps below.

Carol regarded him blankly.

"Come away with me!" he begged her anxiously. "From this place – it isn't too late. There is a way back. I know there is."

And then a new voice interrupted them.

"Haw haw haw!" it laughed.

Martin stared around them. Through the open doorway of this smaller pillbox he saw an old man hurrying towards them along the road. It was Gerald Benning. Concern and anguish were written on his face. But the laughter had not come from outside. It had echoed up from beneath – from the underpass.

"Hoo hoo hoo!" the mocking voice sounded again. "I rode you, I rid you. I played you, I puzzled you. I helped you, I hindered you – and now… I've shocked you!"

Martin felt a sickening coldness in the pit of his stomach. He knew that voice now. He turned from the sunlight and peered back down the steps to the mouth of the tunnel.

There came the squeak and creak of new leather. A pair of caramel-coloured trousers danced into sight. The torso above was paunchy and the brand-new, bellboy-style costume was slightly too tight, just as in the illustration. At first the peak of the cap concealed the face, but Martin didn't need to see those florid features.

"Barry," he uttered.

The Headteacher raised his face and let out another "Haw haw haw!" The ex-rugby player, the man who had always looked like a hard-bitten detective superintendent, came skipping forward.

"The Jockey has been up to his usual naughty tricks," he confessed with a mischievous twinkle in his eye and a shrug of his shoulders. "The Ismus is most displeased, but now I shall atone and be spared the gaol. I will deliver unto him something he prizes most highly and earn his gratitude. My pranks shall be forgotten – till the next time I ride those at Court. Hee hee hee!"

He lifted his arm and beckoned. "We must not keep the Holy Enchanter waiting," he said.

Paul smiled and hopped down to join him.

Now Martin understood why Barry had allowed the card-wearing and the hanging sleeves of the uniforms to continue through the week at school. And that was why he had brought up the subject of getting bespoke fantasy outfits made.

Martin struggled for something to say. Then he realised Barry was still beckoning.

"Come!" the Headteacher said again, with a welcoming wink. "Come, Carol… abella."

Without giving Martin another glance, the woman walked down the steps. She took the Jockey's outstretched hand and he capered around her. Then he led her and Paul back along the tunnel and they danced out of sight.

Martin slumped against the wall, stunned and bereft. His world was shattered.

Moments later Gerald Benning found him there, staring at the emptiness of the tunnel entrance.

"Martin!" the old man cried. "Martin. I followed Carol here. I think – I think she's been…"

The maths teacher stirred.

"She's gone with them," he murmured desolately. "She's one of them now. It's over."

534

Gerald's face went pale, but he tightened his jaw and somehow managed to pull Martin to his feet.

"It's not over!" he said angrily. "It'll never be over. Hurry, Martin, back to the car."

Martin stumbled after him – out into the open air. But what was the use? He looked across the deserted road, to where the gorse thickets concealed the sunken courtyard. He could hear the sound of chanting. The Ismus had commenced a reading from Dancing Jacks. Every voice was reciting the infernal words of Austerly Fellows.

"Beyond the Silvering Sea," the many voices of the Court repeated joyously, "within thirteen green, girdling hills…"

A plume of thick smoke was rising into the sky. A fire was blazing upon that iron throne. He could see they were burning the effigy of the Bad Shepherd.

"Quickly, Martin!" Gerald urged.

"Why?" the maths teacher asked, wretched and bitter. "What can we do?"

Gerald stared at him. In a resolute voice, the old man said, "We have to fight, Martin. We have to warn the world."

The dance will go on…

Addicted to *Dancing Jax*?

Then watch out for the sequel in February 2012.

———————————

And if that's too long to wait, get another fix of Robin Jarvis

with his darkly mysterious *Wyrd Museum* trilogy,

coming soon in paperback...

The Wyrd Museum, Book One:

The Woven Path

Out July 2011

Dare to enter the Wyrd Museum, where fantasy meets the seriously sinister...

In a grimy alley in the East End of London stands the Wyrd Museum, cared for by the strange Webster sisters – and scene of even stranger events.

Wandering through the museum, Neil Chapman, son of the new caretaker, discovers it is a sinister place crammed with secrets both dark and deadly. Forced to journey back to the past, he finds himself pitted against an ancient and terrifying evil, something which is growing stronger as it feeds on the destruction around it.

HarperCollins *Children's Books*

The Wyrd Museum, Book Two:

Raven's Knot

Out October 2011

Brought out of the past, elfin-like Edie Dorkins must
now help the Websters to protect their age-old secret.
For outside the museum's enchanted walls, a
nightmarish army is gathering in the mystical town of
Glastonbury, bent on destroying the sisters and their
ancient power once and for all…

**Revisit the chilling, fantastical world of the Wyrd
Museum in this sepell-binding sequel to**
The Woven Path.

HarperCollins *Children's Books*

The Wyrd Museum, Book Three:
The Fatal Strand

Out February 2012

The thrilling conclusion to the chilling trilogy.

But something has come to disturb the slumbering
shadows and watchful walls of the Wyrd Museum.
Miss Ursula Webster is determined to defend her
realm to the last as the spectral unrest mounts. Once
again, Neil Chapman is ensnared in the Web of Fate,
facing an uncertain Destiny. Can he and Edie avert the
approaching darkness, or has the final Doom
descended upon the world at last?

HarperCollins *Children's Books*

BRANCH	DATE
Sp	7/4